RATS! BLOODY RATS!

There weren't supposed to be any in the sewer under Fleet Lane. The guv'nor wouldn't be best pleased, but with the flow as low as this, what could he expect? Now he was nearer, Williams could see a heaving mass of large bedraggled rats, some of them a foot long and more. He gave a thunderous shout which echoed down the tunnel, but none of them so much as lifted its head. As he came up to them he shouted once more and began to rain blows on them with his stave. Reluctantly they gave way and withdrew down the tunnel.

It was certainly flesh that they had been eating and a big chunk at that. At a guess, it looked like the best part of a side of bacon. Williams turned the lump of flesh over with his stave. Yes, there was skin on this side all right, though it looked softer than bacon rind—it was half a side of pork, that's what it was . . . But why was there only one nipple? . . . Oh God! . . . With the bile rising in his throat, he blundered back up the tunnel for help.

COUNTERFEIT
OF
MURDER

RAY HARRISON

*A Sergeant Bragg-
Constable Morton Mystery*

BERKLEY BOOKS, NEW YORK

This Berkley book contains the complete
text of the original hardcover edition.
It has been completely reset in a typeface
designed for easy reading and was printed
from new film.

COUNTERFEIT OF MURDER

A Berkley Book / published by arrangement with
St. Martin's Press

PRINTING HISTORY
St. Martin's edition published 1986
Berkley edition/May 1989

ISBN: 0-425-11645-X

A BERKLEY BOOK ® TM 757,375
Berkley Books are published by The Berkley Publishing Group,
200 Madison Avenue, New York, NY 10016.
The name "Berkley" and the "B" logo
are trademarks belonging to Berkley Publishing Corporation.

PRINTED IN THE UNITED STATES OF AMERICA

10 9 8 7 6 5 4 3 2 1

To Simon and Jane

CHAPTER _____
_____ *ONE*

Matthew Gibson counted out the crisp five-pound notes mechanically, and pushed them across the polished oak counter. He took a step backwards in disengagement, and watched the customer count the money again and stow it in various pockets about his person. He looked like a countryman; an auctioneer perhaps. It would be a vast sum to such a one . . . Had he joined a country bank, instead of the Bank of England, Gibson mused, he might have been the manager of a branch now, with his own office, and receptions for the local notables. Ah well, things would not really have been any different.

The man walked off briskly, casting wary glances around him, and his place was taken by a good-looking woman in her early thirties. She placed a twenty-pound note on the counter, and asked that it be changed into fives. Her smile, as she gathered up the notes, had an indefinable challenge in its warmth, as if to say: 'Our intercourse has to be confined to exchanging bits of paper, but, oh, it could have been much, much more . . . ' Gibson shook off the enticing images. If he were not careful, he would be losing his job, on top of everything else. At least, no one could deny that in his profession he was extremely successful, and that he had excellent prospects. He was the youngest cashier ever appointed in London by the Bank, with the way to Chief Cashier open ahead of him. There were a couple of men around his age in the midlands branches, but the court of directors had never yet transferred anyone in, to fill a senior vacancy.

He accepted a pile of notes from a clerk in a crumpled morning-coat and sweat-stained bowler, sorted them into the various denominations, then counted them. As he raised the edge of each note, with a twist of his thumb and forefinger he tore off the bottom right-hand corner, which contained the Chief Cashier's signature. The notes, thus cancelled, he put into a box for collection by the clerks who would complete the entries in the Bank's ledgers. Then with a grave smile he handed over a single oblong of paper worth a thousand pounds. It always gave him pleasure; the black copper-plate script on the immaculate white paper; England's bank-note of highest denomination and a work of art in itself. The clerk was unimpressed. He stuffed it into the inside pocket of his coat, ducked his head in acknowledgement and scurried off.

Another clerk appeared, with a two-hundred pound note to be changed into small-denomination notes. Gibson glanced up at the clock. Ten minutes to twelve. Another hour and the rest of Saturday was his own . . . Once, he would have relished it—something fresh to do, somewhere new to explore. When they first got married and rented their tiny house, they would be off in a hansom to the markets, for knick-knacks and ornaments; eager to please each other, determined to enjoy every moment of their intoxicating new life. He could hardly doubt that they had been in love then. But now . . . And yet Tom Sutton's wife had had another child—if anything, more easily than the first. Mabel shut her ears to that, of course. 'She must on no account have any more children,' the doctor had said, and that was enough for her. 'How can we prevent it?' he had asked. 'You will have to join Colonel Condom's regiment, won't you?' the doctor had replied, and stomped off angrily, as if Gibson had deliberately wanted his wife to have a bad time . . . It had been three months before he'd dared to approach Mabel again, and she had quickly made it plain that physical relations were in no way essential to her happiness. They had a sweet baby daughter and, so far as she was concerned, the sexual part of their marriage had been fulfilled.

He had remonstrated and pleaded with her, but had suffered another six weeks of unremitting subjection, before she had agreed to try it with a sheath. It had been a near-disaster. She had endured it in worried frigidity, while for him there had been about as much sensation as poking the fire. Afterwards, he lay on top of her gasping, trying to pretend it had been wonderful. They both knew nothing had been solved, that this skirmish had left the battle-lines undisturbed; yet each had wished to prolong the cease-fire, and they had lain together for a long time. By then, of course, his thing had shrunk and when he withdrew, he'd left the condom behind. She'd screamed blue murder, saying that they were not safe, that he didn't care whether she lived or died so long as his bestial appetites were satisfied. She had even embarked on a series of lugubrious visits to her relatives, making it quite clear where the responsibility would lie, if she were taken from them. Even when she knew it was all right, she hadn't told him; she had let him sweat for a couple of months, till he had summoned up the courage to ask. Then she had declared that there were to be no more experiments; the intimate side of their life was over. Yet what did she expect him to do? When he asked her, she merely curled her lip in scorn.

Gibson gloomily checked the piles of notes against the details on the list, putting a precise tick at the end of every line; then he placed the notes and the list inside a stout envelope, and pushed it over the counter.

'Thank you, Mr Gibson,' said the clerk. 'Allow me to wish you a pleasant weekend.'

Gibson smiled to himself. The next customer was a tall, blond man, who returned the smile intimately as if he had been sharing his thoughts.

'Would you change this for hundreds?' he asked, placing a thousand-pound note on the counter.

'Yes, of course,' mumbled Gibson. He counted out the notes hurriedly and passed them over. It was only when he turned to tear the corner off the note he had received, that he noticed it had been issued by the Hull branch . . . Surely none of the branches issued thousands?

'Just a moment, sir!' he called.

The man was walking away and did not hear him. If anything he had quickened his pace.

'Stop, sir!' Gibson shouted.

The man began to run for the doorway to the courtyard, and Gibson, vaulting over his counter, started after him. A porter tried to intercept as the man crashed through the door, but was bowled over. By now there was a growing commotion and it seemed he would easily be detained. The only way out of the courtyard was through the main entrance, which was guarded by the Bank's staff. In addition the City police always had a couple of detectives on the premises, when it was open to the public. Indeed, as the man reached the gateway, a burly figure hurled himself out of the crowd and grasped him round the knees. The impact was not sufficient to down the fugitive, however, it merely threw him against the wall. He beat down with his fist at the head of the detective, who hung on grimly. To Gibson, the tableau held still for a space, then . . . slowly it seemed . . . slowly . . . the man reached into his pocket and brought out a revolver. They were all caught up in a frozen horror of disbelief as he carefully, almost gently, placed the barrel behind the detective's ear and pulled the trigger. The noise of the shot set off a frenzy of movement. The blond man kicked himself free of the detectives's clutch, and launched himself towards the gate, the crowd in the courtyard started forward angrily; there were two more shots, echoing round the courtyard, then suddenly it was quiet, the sounds of pursuit fading in the distance, the dead eyes of the policeman staring up at the clouds.

'I understand that you personally dealt with the murderer, Mr Gibson, and that when he ran off, you pursued him?'

'That is correct, sergeant.'

'So you saw the whole incident?'

'Up to the point where the man escaped through the gate, yes.'

Sergeant Joseph Bragg of the City of London police picked up the thousand-pound note, stared at it briefly, and passed it to Constable James Morton sitting beside him. The hue and cry after the murderer had soon petered out in the narrow alleys north of Threadneedle Street. Bragg has been sent to commence the investigation, while the uniformed branch made a thorough search of the area. He and Morton had been given a desk in the room of Frank May, the Chief Cashier, so that any assistance they needed could be instantly provided.

'Can you give us a description of the man, sir?'

'Well, he was tall . . . ' Gibson pondered for a moment. 'I would say he was six foot three or four inches. His hair was blond—like those Swedish sailors you see around sometimes. I did not catch the colour of his eyes, but he had a mole on the left cheekbone, just below the outer corner of the eye. I suppose that he would have been about thirty years of age.'

'What about whiskers?' asked Bragg.

'He had none. His hair was cut short, in the modern way, and he was clean shaven.'

'Do you recollect what his clothes were like?' asked Morton.

'I cannot say that I noticed,' replied Gibson defensively.

'Which probably means that they were what most other people would be wearing, on a July Saturday morning,' remarked Morton with a smile. 'Did he have a hat of any description?'.

'Why yes, he was carrying a silk top-hat. I remember thinking that he would look like a lamp-post when he put it on.'

'Now, what about the coat?' Morton pressed gently. 'Was it a morning-coat, or a lounging coat, or a frock-coat?'

'I . . . just a moment.' Gibson frowned in concentration. 'Yes. In the gateway . . . The blond man had his shoulders against the wall, and your officer was clutching his knees in a rugby-tackle. Then the man put his hand into his pocket . . . Yes, it was a black frock-coat.' Gibson gave a small smile of gratification.

'Can you remember how the incident began?' asked Bragg.

'Well, we were on the point of closing the counters,' said Gibson, 'so I was under some pressure. The man put down that note and asked—in a pleasant, cultured voice—if I would change it for hundreds. I counted out the new notes and passed them over, then I examined the note I had received.'

'I would like you to understand, gentlemen,' said May interrupting, 'that there is no standard procedure for scrutinizing the notes tendered to us for payment. If we subjected every such note to exhaustive examination, we would rapidly come to a standstill. After all, we receive over fifty thousand notes for payment in the course of an average day. We expect our cashiers to be on the alert for stolen or counterfeit notes, but we do not expect more.'

'So what about this note, then?'

Gibson shifted uncomfortably on his chair. 'When I examined it, I saw that it was dated the twenty-ninth of March eighteen eighty-nine, and had been issued by the Hull branch.'

'Are you saying it was too new-looking, for a note that had been in circulation for three and a quarter years?' asked Bragg.

'That could hardly be it,' May jumped in again. 'We print a hundred thousand notes with the same date, and many of them will not be issued for months—particularly from a branch. Then again, it could have been kept in a strong-box, from the day it was issued to the day it was presented for payment.'

'So it was not the condition of the note?' Bragg prompted.

'No.' Gibson glanced apprehensively at May. 'I am afraid I had forgotten that Hull had issued thousand-pound notes for a period. Normally, notes of a denomination higher than one hundred pounds are issued only from London.'

'We did thousands for Hull from 'eighty-two to 'eighty-nine,' remarked May cheerfully. 'Something to do with the needs of the fish trade.'

'Right, Mr Gibson,' said Bragg. 'So you glanced down, saw the note had been issued by the Hull branch and thought there must be something wrong with it?'

'That is correct.'

'And is there?'

'So far as we can tell, there is not,' said May. 'Naturally, examination of it has so far been confined to the people in this room; but neither Gibson nor I can see anything odd about it. However, I have asked them to send up the ledger, so we should be able to check it ourselves shortly.'

'Very well,' said Bragg. 'At all events, Mr Gibson, you thought for a moment that the note might be a forgery. What happened then?'

'I said, quite involuntarily, "Just a moment, sir." The man kept on walking away. I shouted again and he began to run. He shook off one of the porters and pushed through the people in the courtyard, till your man collared him in the gateway.'

Bragg swung round to Morton. 'Does the description mean anything to you, lad?'

'No, sir. He is pretty distinctive, and I have seen no description like his in either our circulars or those of the Met.'

Bragg began to chew his ragged moustache in thought. 'But why would a half-hearted challenge from a bank-clerk justify murder?' he asked.

An affronted look flitted across Gibson's face.

'Perhaps the Hull police have a warrant out for him?' suggested Morton.

There came a tap on the door and a clerk entered bearing an enormous ledger. He placed it before the Chief Cashier with an obsequious murmur and withdrew.

'Right,' said May. 'Let me see what this has to tell us.' He wrote the number of the bank-note on the top of his scribbling-pad and began to turn the thick pages of the ledger. Then he ran his finger down the margin of a left-hand page and stopped. His head jerked from side to side as he checked the pad with the ledger, then he looked up. 'It has already been paid,' he announced, his lips pursed in concern.

'But how can you be sure?' asked Bragg.

'Very simply, sergeant. Every note issued by the Bank has its particulars entered separately in a ledger—this one contains the record of the printing dated the twenty-ninth of March eighteen eighty-nine. It shows that this note, or should I say a note with this serial number, was issued by Hull Branch on the twelfth of June that year, and was paid at that branch on the twenty-seventh of October in the same year.'

'Is it possible that the register could be wrong?'

'About the payment, you mean?'

'Yes.'

'Every system devised by man is fallible, sergeant; but there should be no greater danger of error by reason only that this was a branch issue. Their cancelled notes are sent to London for the ledgers to be made up . . . It is, of course, possible that the note paid in Hull was counterfeit.'

'Would you like to see if we still have that paid note, sir?' asked Gibson eagerly.

'A good idea. It should not have been destroyed yet. And while you are about it, ask the head printer to pop in, if he has not already gone home.'

Gibson left the room at a run.

'A promising young man,' observed May. 'I hope this business does not prey on his mind . . . I remember when I first started,' he went on. 'That was with the Provincial Bank, and I was on the securities section. One of our customers was a dear old lady of sixty or so. She had most of her savings in a company that became insolvent, and it fell to my lot to explain why her loan-stock certificates were not worth the paper they were printed on. After most of an afternoon I finally got her to accept the fact, even if she did not understand the reason. She thanked me politely, went straight home and took cyanide. It was a long time before I got over that, I can tell you.'

There was a rap at the door, and a cheerful head was poked into the room. 'You just caught me, Frank.'

'Come in, John. I have something here that might interest you.'

The printer was slim and studious-looking, with the hands of a musician. He looked at the two bulky policemen, then back to May. 'Is it something to do with the fracas in the courtyard?'

'Yes. Just before he ran off, the man had changed this note with one of our cashiers. I thought you might like to have a look at it.'

John glanced at the note casually, then began to examine it intently. He took it over to the window, where the sun was beginning to stream in, and held it up to the light; he passed it between his finger-tips, eyes closed, like a doctor feeling for a pulse; then he began to make a series of measurements with a small steel ruler. Finally, he embarked on a prolonged scrutiny of every inch of the surface with a lens. Then he looked up with a cluck of admiration.

'Beautiful, isn't it?' he said. 'It totally deceived me for a moment. We don't know who made it, I suppose? I would like to offer him a job!'

'So it is a forgery?' asked May.

'Oh, yes. And so good a one, that I would not remotely expect a cashier to pick it up in the ordinary course. Just look at that watermark!' He held it up to the light by one corner. 'Absolutely marvellous! And the engraving is perfect. God knows how many hours were spent on that plate. It is only by looking through a powerful magnifying glass that one can see it has been plate-printed rather than surface-printed.'

'Are you saying that England could already be awash with counterfeit notes that only someone of your technical skills could distinguish from the real thing?' asked May aghast.

'I am virtually certain that he has incorporated the serial numbers into the plate, which would mean that all the notes printed would have the same number. If so, they should be easy to identify.'

'That gives no comfort whatever!' exclaimed May, springing up from his chair. 'I must see the Governor directly.

Goodness knows what his reaction will be!' He strode to the door and vanished.

'You are not having him on, by any chance, are you sir?' asked Bragg darkly.

'By no means, officer,' replied the printer, his hands raised in protest. 'Here, I don't mind telling you what led me to it—though I would not want these administrator chaps let into the secret!'

'What is it then?'

'Why, it's the paper. Feel it. That's the way, just let your finger-tips brush lightly across it. Not quite right, is it?'

'I've not handled all that many notes, myself,' said Bragg passing it to Morton. 'Here, lad, it is more in your line.'

Morton took it, and slid it gently through his fingers. 'It seems just as I would expect,' he remarked.

'Then we are in trouble,' said Bragg, 'If the aristocracy can't see it's a wrong-un.'

The printer looked quizzically at Bragg, but received no elucidation. 'Of course,' he said, 'I handle the genuine paper all day, every day, so I should be able to tell the difference. But it was the bottom deckle that clinched it for me.'

'How do you mean?' asked Bragg.

'Well, if you look at any note, you will see that one of the short sides of the oblong is clean cut, and the other three have a rough, ragged border to them. That is the deckle. It is caused by a small amount of the raw material seeping under the wooden frame, when the paper is being made. Now, a Bank of England note is about five and a quarter inches wide, by eight and half long. What we do, is print two notes side by side on a piece of paper seventeen inches long, and then divide it. This gives us two notes, one with the cut edge on the right side, the other with it on the left.'

'This has a cut edge on the right, and deckles on the other three sides,' said Morton.

'Yes, but look at the bottom deckle,' said John. 'Here, use this glass. Look particularly at the direction of the fibres, compared to the other deckles.'

'They look straighter, less matted, than those of the other two sides,' ventured Morton.

'Exactly!' said the printer in satisfaction. 'It is not possible to get quality hand-made paper of the right dimensions to give the three deckles of a bank-note, so the deckle on one of the long sides had to be manufactured.'

'How did they do that?'

'They would have to wet that edge of the paper, put a ruler along to protect the true edge of the note, say a sixteenth of an inch in, and then tease out the projecting bit with a wire brush, or something like that. Very tricky! Then they would dry it, put back the sheen on the treated edge with a warm iron and hey presto! one bank-note blank.'

'The fibres of the other deckles have the same degree of entanglement as the paper itself,' said Morton. 'I suppose that is because they have not been interfered with.'

'That's right. Now, shall we put all my theories to the test?' asked the printer with a broad smile. 'If you are ever in doubt about the authenticity of a note, this is a simple test that ought to be conclusive.' He took a tumbler of water from May's desk and carried it over to the window. Then he drew a five-pound note from his pocket-book and stuck one end into the glass. He waited for half a minute, then removed the note and placed it against the window-pane. 'Now,' he asked, 'have you any observations on the watermark?'

'If anything,' said Morton, 'the half that you have wetted has even more brilliance than the half that is dry.'

'Good! Now let us apply the same procedure to our suspect note.' He dipped one end into the glass and stood back. Morton gazed expectantly, hoping to see the ink begin to run, but nothing happened. It was just as the other had been.

'Now,' said John with a confident smile, 'if I am wrong I shall probably lose my job.' He took the note from the tumbler and spread it against the window.

'Great heavens!' exclaimed Morton. 'There is no watermark at all where the note is wet.'

'That is because the paper at a genuine watermark is thinner than the surrounding paper, so immersing it makes little or no difference. But when you set about to create a watermark on paper, you use a chemical which will make it translucent at that point. So when all the paper is made translucent by wetting it, the spurious watermark disappears.'

'What chemical do they use?' asked Morton.

'It varies,' said the printer. 'If ever I am lucky enough to be introduced to the creator of this note, it would be the first question I would want to ask him.'

The door opened again, and May bustled in. 'I am to take you to see the Governor,' he announced. 'Perhaps you ought to come too, John, in case he wants to ask any technical questions.'

'Then I had better bring the evidence,' said the printer, and pressed the note dry between two pieces of blotting paper.

They trooped upstairs to an airy, richly furnished office with a pleasant view of the garden in the courtyard below. The RT Hon William Liddesdale, Governor of the Bank of England, rose to his feet and held out his hand, 'I am afraid that a summer Saturday afternoon is not the best of times to have a major financial crisis fall in one's lap,' he remarked with a perfunctory smile.

'Isn't that overstating it, sir?' asked Bragg.

'Not a bit of it. But before we get down to that—the detective who was killed . . . had he any dependants?'

'He has a wife . . . I think his two eldest children are working now, but I would guess he still has some at school.'

'Oh dear! The Bank will see that they lack for nothing, of course, though it is little more than a gesture in the circumstances.' Liddesdale sighed heavily. He had been a working banker all his life, and had won universal admiration with his handling of the financial crisis created by the failure of Barings bank, at the end of eighteen ninety. Now he looked up with a grim expression that would brook no dissent.

'After our discussion I shall be going to see the Chancellor of the Exchequer, and possibly the Prime Minister. Subject to ratification by them, this is the way I intend to deal with the situation. Firstly, I shall require total secrecy from everyone who is presently aware of the existence of this forged note. Secondly, I shall permit that information to be communicated to only those additional people who must have it, and under similar conditions of secrecy. Thirdly, I shall mobilize the forces of the City, in conjunction with those of the police, to track down the source of these forgeries, and see that they are ended.'

'But how shall we be able to investigate, if we cannot ask for public co-operation?' asked Bragg.

'The Bank will offer one thousand pounds reward to any person—and I mean any person, public, police, bank staff—who provides evidence leading to the apprehension of the people, or any of them, connected with the murder of the detective this morning.'

'That would take us part of the way,' said Bragg, 'but I would prefer . . .'

'Your preferences are of small account, sergeant,' said Liddesdale brusquely. 'I am sure that if I could speak as a member of the general public, my sentiments would chime entirely with yours. "Let us have the widest possible publicity, a reward that would tempt a bishop, and get these people behind bars as quickly as posible." Unfortunately, at the Bank we cannot afford the luxury of righteous indignation . . . Am I not right in thinking that you were involved in investigating the Bernstein robbery, three years ago, sergeant?'

'I was indeed, sir.'

'You will remember that two hundred thousand pounds in Bank of England notes formed part of the proceeds.'

'Why yes, that's right.'

'We knew the numbers of the stolen notes from our records. In due course we found ourselves in the invidious position of having to pay them, because they had been tendered to us by members of the public who had received them innocently. We chose not even to institute enquiries into the antecedents of the presentors, lest it should create public unease.'

'I see,' said Bragg.

'My principal responsibility, as Governor,' went on Liddesdale, 'is the management of the country's currency. And perhaps the main element in that task, is the maintenance of world-wide confidence in the pound sterling.'

'I can see that if there are counterfeit notes in circulation that cannot be distinguished from real ones,' remarked Bragg, 'then the ordinary man in the street would switch to gold sovereigns.'

'Exactly,' said Liddesdale. 'There would be an immediate run on the banks—country banks as well as us. No one would have confidence in paper money any longer. The problem, so far as the Bank of England is concerned, is that the number of sovereigns in circulation is relatively small. The gold reserves underlying the bank-note issue—and we alone have twenty-five million pounds worth in circulation—are held here in the form of bullion. It would be physically impossible, as well as economically undesirable, to convert that into coins in the time available. The better proposition would be to make an issue of a different design of note, and declare the present ones no longer legal tender.'

'But what about the genuine notes?' asked Bragg.

'Why, they could be paid, in the new notes, once each one was proved to be genuine . . . But that is mere theory. In practice, by the time it could be carried out half the banks in the country would have closed their doors, and we would have a political crisis of unprecedented proportions on our hands. No, there is no alternative to preserving the most stringent secrecy, until we have caught the forgers and the position is under control.'

'I shall have to make a report to my superiors, sir, and it would help me if I knew what was meant by the City forces you propose to mobilize.'

'Certainly, sergeant. We have in London a bankers' protection committee, which is maintained for the prevention of financial fraud on the City. It also contains representatives of other financial institutions such as broking houses, and its collective influence is considerable.'

'But how can you mobilize them to detect forgeries, if you are not prepared to admit they exist?'

'Leave that to me, sergeant. Leave that to me.'

'I cannot stand these politicians who want to run what is essentially a police operation.' Lt-Col Sir William Sumner CB, Commissioner of the City of London police, leaned back in his chair and gazed truculently at the ceiling. The air of authority produced by his fortuitous resemblance to the Prince of Wales was vitiated by his lack of a police background and by his indecisiveness under pressure. In addition, being dragged from his bed on a Sunday morning for a meeting at the Bank of England, seemed to have made him tetchy.

'Who were the people making all the fuss, Forbes?' he asked.

Chief Inspector Charles Forbes, the functional head of the detective division, smiled to reveal his white, even teeth.

'The man with the whiskers is John Fortescue, sir, a merchant banker in Lombard Street. The little jokey man is Adolphus Merrick. He is a bond broker in Ironmonger Lane.'

'What is he doing on a bankers' protection committee?'

'A bond broker is part of the secondary financial machinery

of the City. I suppose he has more at stake personally, than any of the bankers.'

'You know what they say about big fleas having little fleas on their backs,' remarked Inspector Cotton contemptuously.

'Well, I am not sure that that is a proper attitude to have at this moment,' said the Commissioner gruffly. 'What I want to establish is our procedures for co-operating with these people, since we are not to be allowed to investigate on our own.'

'If I might suggest, sir,' Forbes interposed, his teeth glinting. 'I will undertake the liaison work with the committee, while Inspector Cotton controls the investigation on the ground. He will report to me on his progress and, through the protection committee, I can try to see that nobody gets under his feet.'

'I am unhappy about having to give them prior notice of every move we make, all the same,' the Commissioner complained.

'I'm sure we all are, sir,' replied Forbes smoothly, 'But if the politicians are paying the piper, I suppose it is not unnatural that they should want to call the tune.'

'Huh! I cannot see us getting any useful information out of it. Dammit! The Bank won't even tell us all the steps they propose to take themselves.'

'At least the reward should tempt a few people to blow on the forgers,' said Cotton roughly. 'My concern is to get authority to follow up a tip quickly, before they scarper.'

'I don't think you need to worry too much about that,' said Forbes. 'I will make it my business to expedite action on any worthwhile lead. My only reservation is about the extent to which the Governor can impose his policy of secrecy. From my experience of the City, it will not take long before the banking community jumps to the conclusion that there are forgeries about. But that is the Bank's problem, not ours. For the moment, I think we can go along with them.'

'Very well . . . I take it, Inspector, that you will be using Sergeant Bragg on the case.'

Cotton thrust out his chin belligerently. 'Only if you specifically order me to do so, sir.'

'But he was on duty at the time Constable Walton was shot. He is involved in it already,' protested Sir William.

'I do not think such qualities as he may possess are suited to this operation, sir. He is contemptuous of advice and disci-

pline, his rough country manners are liable to upset the people
we are dealing with here, and, above all, he would never
subordinate his own ideas to a team effort such as we need.'

'But he is our most experienced officer in the investigation
of fraud—outside the senior ranks, of course,' the Commissioner added hurriedly.

'Well, as I shall be taking personal responsibility for this
operation, he will not be missed,' said Cotton brusquely.
'Frankly, sir, I think his reputation has been founded more on
luck than any real ability. I would trade him with the
Metropolitan police for a stick of rock and an old pipe cleaner
any day. No. I shall use Detective Sergeants Roker and Green
for these enquiries. Sergeant Bragg can mind the shop while
we are out.'

'Very well,' said Sir William sombrely, 'I suppose it will be
best.'

CHAPTER _____
_____ TWO

Once his eyes had got accustomed to the gloom, John Williams began to splash down the great brick tunnel. One thing about being promoted to foreman, you didn't have to go to work on a Sunday any more—at least not unless there was an emergency, and then they could call on anyone. All the same, it was as well to be out first thing on Monday, to see everything was all right . . . It was surprising how much you could see, even though the ventilation grids were upwards of two hundred yards apart. He scraped at the wall with the sole of his heavy rubber thigh-boot. He would have to get the scrubbers on this length; give it a bit of a clean up. The brickwork was so smooth, that normally the current was strong enough to scour out the whole sewer. He smiled to himself. He was always telling the children that it smelled just like the seaside down here, but they would never believe it. Perhaps one day he would bring the older boys down to show them . . . but then, he didn't want them working for the Board. He spent his days down here, so that they could have the chance of something better . . . As he approached the big pool of light thrown by a manhole shaft, he thought he detected movement on its further side. That would be the branch of the sewer coming in down Fleet Lane, to the left. As he gazed, it seemed as if he saw a flicker of white, like a hand waving. Whatever it was, it was hard up against the right-hand wall—probably on the platform that ran along from the steps for three or four yards . . . Suppose it was a hand? He began to stumble clumsily through the water . . . Rats! Bloody rats! There weren't supposed to be any in the Fleet—it was normally too clean. The guv'nor wouldn't be best pleased, but with the flow as low as this, what could he expect? Now he was nearer, Williams could see a heaving mass of large bedraggled rats, some of them a foot long and more. He gave a thunderous shout which echoed down the tunnel, but none of them so much as lifted its head. The flicker of white came when the struggling heap broke apart, exposing whatever it was they were feeding on. As he came up to them he shouted once more and began to rain blows on them with his stave. Reluctantly they gave way and withdrew down the tunnel. He followed them as far as the Ludgate Circus junction in the hope that they would keep on going, to the Thames. Then he went back . . . It was certainly flesh that they had been eating and a big chunk at that. At a guess, it looked like the best part of a side of bacon. Maybe it had gone off, and some porter from the Smithfield market had shoved it down here. They weren't supposed to do that; better tell the guv'nor. Williams turned the lump of flesh over with his stave. Yes, there was skin on this side all right, though it looked softer than bacon rind—it was half a side of pork, that's what it was . . . But why was there only one nipple? . . . Oh God! . . . With the bile rising in his throat, he blundered back up the tunnel for help.

Bragg grunted as he tugged off the thigh-boots they had lent him. As he'd suspected, they were too small, and the top of his big toe had been skinned. He accepted a mug of tea gratefully. It was warm here inside the canvas screens they had erected round the manhole.

'In all my twenty-one years in the force,' he remarked, 'I have never been down the sewers before.'

'Impressive, aren't they?' replied Morton. 'The workman-ship in that great chamber under Ludgate Circus would do credit to a cathedral.'

Williams smiled in gratification. 'They'll last for ever, they will,' he said.

'Well now,' said Bragg, 'what I would like from you is your best opinion about where these bits and pieces were put in the sewer.'

Williams scratched the back of his neck slowly. 'Not far from here, I reckon. The land-water is not much more than a trickle at the moment, so it's got to have been carried by the sewage.'

'Land-water?'

'This is the old Fleet river, that they put in a tunnel and built a road on top.'

'River? Where does it come from?'

'Hampstead way. Get a thunder-storm up there, and you run for it. The level here can rise six feet in a quarter of an hour.'

'Where does the sewer proper begin?' asked Bragg.

'St Pancras. It runs west of St Pancras Road and Farringdon Road, then under Farringdon Street, here, to the Thames at Blackfriars.'

'And are you saying that because the river itself is so low, they must have been put in nearby for the sewage flow alone to have carried them?'

'That's right. There are only two manholes to consider, I'd say. This one and the next one up, at the Charterhouse Street junction . . . I suppose that's why I thought it was from the market.'

'Surely it would have been a bit too busy anywhere near Smithfield, last night? When did your chaps finish work?'

'At six o'clock.'

'And dark by half past nine, say. I suppose it would be possible. One hand-cart would be much like another around there.'

'Would there have been any marked increase in flow after six o'clock?' asked Morton.

'I shouldn't think so, not on a Sunday night. Most people are as clean as they are ever going to be by then.'

'I know that the ledge on which you discovered the first portion was barely above the level of the water,' went on Morton, 'but it would have needed a considerable increase in flow for it to have floated there.'

'So you think they were tipped down this manhole?' asked Bragg.

'I think it is at least feasible.'

Bragg swung round. 'How easy is it to open?'

'As you can see, the cover is in two separate castings,' said Williams. 'We normally have two men to lift each, but a big man could do it on his own.'

'And why do you reckon we found only the one piece here, lad?'

'I think the others were swung outwards, and released so that they fell into the current,' replied Morton.

'Well, as a theory it will do to be going on with,' said Bragg. 'How many have we so far?'

'The upper left quarter, which Mr Williams found,' said Morton, glancing at his pad. 'The left lower quarter with thigh, the right lower quarter with thigh, and the right lower leg and foot—significantly, all found down-stream from here.'

'Can you get a couple of your men to trundle them up on a barrow to the mortuary, Mr Williams? As you can see, we are very short-handed at the moment.'

'Yes, I'll do that, sergeant.'

'Keep them well covered, mind . . . And could someone take a note to the coroner at his chambers in the Temple?'

'Of course.'

Bragg tore a sheet out of his note-book and scribbled rapidly. He then folded it small, till it assumed the appearance of a *billet-doux*. 'There you are,' he remarked. 'That will spoil his lunch for him.'

'Interesting,' remarked Bragg as they sauntered towards the cab-rank.

'Perhaps, though I think I shall have to burn these clothes,' replied Morton. 'I doubt if they will ever lose the smell of sewers.'

'Some people are too soft for their own good,' said Bragg sardonically. 'No, I was thinking about the dismembered corpse, and wondering whether we were meant to find the bit on the step.'

'But how could that possibly be in the interests of whoever perpetrated it?'

'I suppose you are right, lad. I'm always being told by Inspector Cotton that I look for connections that aren't there. It's just that I have this feeling . . .' He climbed into a hansom and pushed up the trap-door in the roof. 'Wapping police station, for a start, cabby,' he called crisply, then settled back in his corner, deep in thought. His reverie lasted throughout the journey, indeed he seemed irritated to be jerked out of it as their horse came to a stop outside the Thames Police headquarters.

'Wait for us, cabby,' he called. 'Come on, lad.'

They walked up some newly scrubbed granite steps, and entered a large room smelling of paint. A bulky man in shirt sleeves lounged behind a desk in the corner.

'You want to watch it, mate, or they'll have you polishing the eight bells . . . Detective Sergeant Bragg, City police.'

'So the swell mob's got itself a comedian, has it?' asked the man good-naturedly. 'Well, what's up now?'

'We've mislaid a few parts of an adult male, that's all. At least, we think the bits we have are from the same jig-saw, but who knows? We found most of him in the Fleet sewer this morning, but we think some have been carried into the Thames.'

'Like what?'

'Like one leg, two forearms, one head . . .'

'Right, we'll keep an eye open. Anything else?'

'Yes, how long do you have to serve before you get a rum ration in this lot?'

'Piss off mate, will you? I can't be bothered . . .'

Bragg seemed in a brighter mood as they regained the cab. 'Spelman Street, driver,' he called, then chuckled to himself, and looked across at Morton. 'Childish, isn't it? And yet it's better than the way the good book says it should be done. The official machinery is a waste of time. Far better to have an understanding with someone on the ground, who will remember you. And that way, your superiors don't know what you are up to.'

'So where are we going?' asked Morton.

'We are coursing a hare, lad. At worst it can do no harm, at best we could have some fun.'

The cab rattled into Whitechapel High Street, then swinging right, under the nose of a plodding van-horse, it swooped through a low archway into a street of dingy clapboard houses. They clattered along the cobbles, past a school built like a fort and a lavish Board of Works depot.

'Jock McGregor's pop-shop, on the corner,' called Bragg, and the cab deposited them outside a building even more dejected than those around it. No gleam of brass touched the three spheres that dangled drunkenly above the corner. The paint was peeling from the woodwork, the windows were so encrusted with dirt that it was impossible to see whether merchandise was displayed there or not. Bragg burst through the door and banged the bell on the scuffed oak counter. There came stealthy scraping noises, and a curtain at the back of the shop was pulled aside to allow a yellow rheumy eyeball to observe them.

'Come out, Jock,' growled Bragg belligerently. 'You've got to the end of your rope.'

The curtain was twitched open, and a red-mottled face appeared, framed by matted yellow-grey hair.

'Why, it's Sergeant Bragg,' he cried in a hoarse Scotch voice. 'It's a pleasure to see you again.'

'Turn it off, Jock,' shouted Bragg wrathfully, 'I'm bloody sick of you. I'm going to close you down this time. Constable, lock the front door, and any exit at the back.'

The pawn-broker made an involuntary darting movement towards the drawer under the counter.

'Aha! So we've come at the wrong time, have we, Jock?' Bragg levered himself on to the counter, and dropped down by the cringing figure. He wrenched open the drawer and pulled out a handful of gold watches. 'Still christening them, are you?' he asked contemptuously, as he spread them on the counter.

'They are pledges, Mr Bragg,' wailed Jock. 'They are in the book.'

Bragg hunched his shoulders and advanced menacingly on the man. 'Do you know, Jock,' he growled, seizing him by the shirt front, 'every time I come within a mile of you I feel soiled. For two pins I'd bloody choke you now, and do society a favour.' He thrust his face within an inch of Jock's. 'Why shouldn't I, eh? What sodding good are you to the world?'

'I never done anybody any harm,' whined the pawn-broker.

'You'd sell your mother, you miserable Scotch bastard, if you could get tuppence for her bones.'

'I've always tried to help . . .'

'Help? When was the last time I got anything decent from you?' Bragg lifted the old man by the shirt till he was standing on tip-toe. 'It's only because of me that the Met haven't taken you long ago. And you know something? I'm tired of protecting you. They can bloody have you.' He dropped Jock in a heap in the corner. 'You thought you could retire on me, didn't you? A "nice to see you, Sergeant Bragg" now and again, and then it's sell up and a villa in Bournemouth. Well, you've bloody run out of time!' He turned back to the counter and extracted a twist of paper from the back of the drawer. As he did so, a look of alarm crossed the old man's face.

'Here you are, constable,' called Bragg, tossing the paper to Morton. 'See what's in there for us, will you?'

Morton unrolled it and let a large jewel trickle into his palm.

'What have we got, constable?' Bragg's eyes were fixed gloatingly on the face of the pawn-broker.

'A large diamond,' said Morton, 'brilliant cut, and weighing, I suppose, three carats or more.'

'Surprise you, did it, Jock?' asked Bragg sarcastically. 'Forgotten it, had you?'

The old man's face had become haggard, and a dribble of saliva was running from the corner of his mouth.

'This one a pledge, Jock?' demanded Bragg. 'Is it in the book?'

McGregor's head shook almost imperceptibly. 'I was doing a friend a good turn,' he mumbled shrilly. 'It isn't mine.'

'Nothing in this shit-heap is yours,' snarled Bragg. 'Where was it prigged from?'

'I don't know . . . I don't know whether it was prigged or not.'

'Whose is it?'

There was dread in the bleary old eyes. 'If I told you, they'd do me in. Even in choky I wouldn't last a week.'

'The Met might have ideas,' said Bragg speculatively.

Jock shook his head. 'Prigged from abroad, I reckon,' he said. 'Brought here to be cut up.'

Bragg laughed harshly. 'That's a good one! Do you really expect me to go along with that? . . . I'd need a big favour, to swallow that one.'

'I'll do anything I can.'

Bragg looked across thoughtfully, then shook his head. 'I doubt if I could trust you, Jock.'

'I've never let you down yet, Mr Bragg.'

'That's what you'd like to think . . . I don't know, that stone would put me in good with the Met till I retire.'

'Please, Mr Bragg,' the old man whined.

Bragg considered a moment. 'All right,' he said. 'One last chance. And if you let me down, I'll cut you up myself.'

'I won't let you down,' said Jock with pathetic eagerness.

'Right, then. I want to know where a gang of counterfeiters is hanging out in London at the moment. And I don't want the fact sung from the roof-tops. If I don't lay them by the heels, you're finished.'

'I can only keep an ear open, sergeant,' said Jock, his face troubled.

'Right. And don't mention it to any of your police pals either. Just between you and me, eh?'

'Yes, sergeant, I'll remember.'

Next morning, when Bragg swung into the entrance-hall of the old Georgian mansion that served the City police for a headquarters, he could see Morton leaning on the duty sergeant's desk.

'Just a minute, Joe!'

'What is it?' asked Bragg, strolling over.

'A present for you.' The sergeant stooped, and plonked a large cardboard box on the desk.

'Looks like a lifetime's supply of Colman's mustard,' said Bragg, peering at the label. ' "Sergeant Bragg, Old Jewry. Happy Birthday",' he read.

'I reckon it's a cake,' said the sergeant, 'from Bertha at the pub . . . She would have to send it here, wouldn't she? Your landlady would have her eyes out if she knew.'

Morton grinned, but Bragg ignored the sally. 'Certainly it's heavy enough,' he remarked. 'The only trouble is, it's not my birthday. Shall we have a look?' He took out his knife, and, cutting the twine around the box, opened the top. A carefully folded sheet from the *Sporting Life* covered the contents and, below it, the box was filled with screwed-up balls of newspaper. Bragg began to shovel them out on to the desk, then stopped. Protruding from the next layer was a damp lock of blond hair.

'You are welcome to a piece of this cake, George,' he said. 'There are bits all over London. Here, spread some of that paper out, will you? I wouldn't want to spoil your nice clean desk.'

Bragg held the head at arm's length by the hair. The mouth

sagged open, and from the putty-coloured face blue eyes stared out in surprise and alarm.

'Not pretty,' said George. 'Some of your friends have a queer sense of humour.'

Bragg re-packed the head. 'I shall have to get it to the mortuary. We'll be back as soon as we can. Here you are, constable, you might as well be the donkey.' They went out into the warm sunshine, and turned northwards towards Gresham Street. Then Bragg checked. 'Give it to me, lad. We might as well save a bit of time. Go to the Bank and find Gibson the cashier, then bring him up to Golden Lane.'

'I would be surprised if he has arrived yet,' said Morton with a smile, 'but I will get him over as soon as I can.'

Bragg quickened his pace, for the box was pulling at an awkward angle, and he was glad when he saw the mortuary ahead. He ran up the front steps into the main hall. It was empty. He went into the lean-to at the back, where one of the assistants was reading a newspaper.

'Is Dr Burney around?' Bragg asked.

The man looked up briefly. 'In the examination room.'

Bragg crossed the mortuary with its grey slate slabs ranged along each wall, and, pushing open a door in the corner, entered a small laboratory. Along the outside wall was a window and under it a long table, with a white porcelain sink at one end. The middle of the room was taken up with a mortuary slab, on which lay the portions of the body which had been fished from the sewer. Dr Burney was bending over them, taking measurements with a ruler.

'I've brought you another bit, sir,' said Bragg.

Dr Burney, the chief police-surgeon for the city, was also professor of pathology at St Bartholomew's Hospital and the author of a formidable treatise on the subject. He seized Bragg's parcel, his loose mouth hanging open in anticipation.

'The head!' he chortled. 'I doubt if they took the trouble to get out the brains . . . At least I shall have some internal tissue to examine.' He took it over to the sink, and ran the tap on it.

'What is going on at Old Jewry, sergeant?' boomed a voice.

Bragg swung round. In front of the small empty fireplace on the back wall, stood Sir Rufus Stone QC, coroner for the City of London. His hands were clasped behind his back, and he rocked himself slowly on the balls of his feet.

'I understand from the newspapers,' he went on, 'that you were at the scene of the murder in the Bank on Saturday, and yet you have not been put forward as coroner's officer. Why is the usual system of finders keepers not operating?'

'I think Inspector Cotton felt it should be investigated by the sergeant in charge of the victim's own section,' Bragg replied mildly.

'You are a poor liar, sergeant,' said Sir Rufus aggressively. 'If I am being kept in the dark about something within my sphere of authority, there will be the devil to pay.'

'I don't think anyone would consider it for a moment, sir,' said Bragg deferentially.

'No?'

'I believe it is being dealt with at the highest level.'

'Is it now?' Sir Rufus glared suspiciously at Bragg. 'Well at least you are my officer for this one, thank God.' He swung round to the pathologist, who was engaged in trying to fit the head against the two halves of the neck. 'I suppose, Burney, that there is no possibility of these revolting exhibits having been pickled?'

'Pickled?'

'I recall that, on occasion, those unruly students of yours at Bart's have deposited, up and down the City, pieces of the bodies they use for dissection. Their puerile idea of a prank, no doubt.'

'I see.' Burney gave a lop-sided grin. 'No, Sir Rufus. There would be a strong smell of formalin, even after a period of immersion.' To confirm the fact, to himself at least, he went round the slab sniffing powerfully.

'My immediate concern,' said Sir Rufus, 'is to decide whether or not an inquest is appropriate in this case. At the very least that means I must satisfy myself that he met an untimely death.'

'I may be able to help you, sir,' said Bragg. 'I am hoping that Constable Morton will be bringing along someone who saw him on Saturday. If the identification is made, it will establish that he was at least hale and hearty then.'

'And so far as the exhibits I have here are concerned,' said Burney, 'I am of the opinion that he was a normally healthy individual. The muscle-bulk is average, and there is no evidence of excessive weight which could have strained the heart.'

'Can you tell us anything more about him, sir?' asked
Bragg.

'Well, now we have the head, it is obvious that he was
around thirty years of age. Although we are unable to examine
his hands, it is clear that there was no muscular development of
the biceps such as one would associate with heavy manual
labour. And, of course, he was six foot three in height—which
is very tall indeed.'

There was a tap at the door, and the mortuary assistant poked
his head in. 'An officer has brought a man to identify that one,'
he said, nodding towards the slab.

'Very well, Noakes,' said Burney. 'Cover him up. I imagine
it is only a facial identification, sergeant?'

'That's it, sir.'

Noakes threw a white twill sheet over the grisly remains,
covering the slab completely. Then he went to the door. 'Right,
you can bring him in now,' he called.

Morton ushered Gibson through the door. He looked white
and dazed, and beads of perspiration stood on his forehead. In
a clumsy act of reverence he took off his top-hat, then allowed
himself to be stationed level with the body's shoulder.

'Now, all I want you to say is whether or not this is the same
man you saw last Saturday morning, ' said Bragg. 'Do you
understand?'

Gibson passed his tongue over his lips, and nodded.

'Right.'

Noakes and Bragg pulled the sheet down gently, till its edge
just cleared the chin.

'Well?'

Gibson was staring in fascination at the grey features.

'Well?' demanded Bragg.

'Yes, yes, it is him. I can tell by the mole on the
cheek-bone.'

'Right, lad,' said Bragg, 'get him a cup of tea, and put his
head between his knees to stop him fainting . . . And see that
he keeps quiet about this.' He hurried Morton and Gibson out
of the room.

'Who is this build-a-body set, then?' asked the coroner.

'Mr Gibson did not know who he was, they happened to be
at the same place, that's all.'

'Damn you, Bragg! You are keeping me in the dark about
something. That young man was never in danger of fainting.'

'There are times, sir, when it's best for all the evidence to be presented together,' said Bragg smoothly.

'Maybe, but I am technically directing the investigation into the death—more than technically, dammit! I am directing it!'

'Yes, sir.' An anxious look settled on Bragg's rugged features. 'It's the kind of situation that brought about the resignation of your predecessor. There are those in the City who would be glad if you made the same mistake.'

The coroner's eyes narrowed. 'Are you saying you believe me capable of partiality?'

'I would prefer it if you were not exposed to even a suspicion of it, sir.'

'What the devil is this, Bragg?' asked Sir Rufus warily.

'Let me just say that it involves the reputation of an old lady you would be certain to know.'

'Ah,' the coroner pursed his lips reflectively. 'Then it must be the Duchess of Horsham . . . though Lady Alice Henson has been threatening to publish her memoirs for years . . . '

'You see what I mean, sir? In the circumstances, I would much rather put the complete report on your desk, and be able to say that you had stood apart.'

'But what if you do not have enough resources?'

'I shall have Constable Morton; but if I need more, I will certainly come to you.'

'Very well, Bragg. Though I do not care for it in the least, and I'm damned if I know why I should trust you.'

At that moment the door opened and Morton returned. He was taken aback to receive a truculent glare from Sir Rufus and retired to a corner by the window.

'Well, can we proceed, Burney?' asked the coroner abruptly.

'Why, certainly.' The pathologist twitched the sheet away from the slab, and dropped it on to the floor. 'You were concerned as to whether there was any foul play involved in the death. I think I can answer that in the affirmative, with a certain amount of confidence.' He turned the left upper quarter to expose the back, and took up a probe. 'You see this wound between the fifth and sixth rib? In my view, that was made by a narrow and exceedingly sharp knife. Placed as it is, such a knife would certainly have penetrated the heart, and led to rapid death.'

'How long a blade?' asked Bragg.

'Bear with me until you have heard me out, since my

speculations hang together, then you can either accept them or reject them as one . . . As to the time of death, we have four major portions of the body which are affected to a minor degree with water, and one which escaped immersion. It is a great handicap to have to proceed without entrails and organs, and indeed I have to admit that I am unable to arrive at any precise conclusions as to the time of death. From the wrinkling of the skin and the washing out of the surface tissues, I deduce that the pieces of the body were in the sewer for some twelve hours only. So he was certainly dead and dismembered by, let us say, nine o'clock last night.'

'Why did they chop him up?' asked Sir Rufus. 'To make identification more difficult?'

'I suppose so,' said Bragg. 'Though it didn't work very well.'

The coroner gave him an irritated glance. 'I would have thought it would be safer to slip him in the bottom of a foundation trench somewhere and cover him over,' he said.

'It had crossed my mind,' Morton interposed, 'that they may have put the head into the Thames itself, well away from the Fleet. They might have felt that it would give them complete security. After all, we do not yet know where the river police found it.'

'Have you any ideas about the murderer, sir?' asked Bragg.

'Well,' replied Burney, with a bashful grin, 'if we are prepared to assume that the killer was also the man who dismembered the body, I can offer some speculations that might be helpful . . . If your constable would hold this portion so that the light falls on it . . . Just so. Now, ignore the breast-bone and look at the bones of the spine. You can see that they have been cut down along the line of the spinal cord. Now look at the surface of the cut bone. Can you see these ridges running across, every inch or so? The distances are not regular, indeed where the vertebrae are less massive, the intervals are greater . . . Has no one tumbled to it?' He looked at the puzzled faces around him. 'Then perhaps my imagination has been running away with me. But let me continue. Constable, look at the position of the cut severing the upper and lower left quarters. Would you have made the incision there?'

'I really cannot say,' said Morton, white-faced.

'You can see that, divided as it is at present, there is one rib on the lower quarter and all the others on the upper. Would you not have cut below all the ribs, into the soft tissue?'

'I suppose I would.'

'I think so. Now, the most revealing exhibit is this lower leg.' He brought it from the side-table into the light. 'First of all, consider the knee. You see that chip out of the cartilage of the tibial plateau? That was caused by a knife, twisting to sever the cruciate ligaments. Again a sharp knife, but much stiffer than the one which caused the wound in the back . . . Then let us look at the foot. That wound above the heel was caused not by cutting, but by tearing through the flesh behind the Achilles tendon . . . No?'

'Dammit, Burney,' said Sir Rufus crossly, 'I studied medicine at St Thomas's, and even I can't follow you.'

'Very well, gentlemen.' Burney's face assumed so serious an aspect, that even his smile was eclipsed. 'When Jack the Ripper was still perpetrating his repellent murders, some three years ago, there was a suggestion that they must have been carried out by someone with medical knowledge, or someone used to slaughtering animals.'

There was a horrified intake of breath around him.

'You will remember that a slaughterman, christened "Leather Apron" by the press, was actually arrested and then released for lack of evidence.'

'Are you saying this might have been done by Jack the Ripper?' expostulated the coroner. 'But he only killed loose women . . . Ah! I see what you meant, Bragg. Lady Alice . . .'

Burney waited for Sir Rufus to subside. 'After the Eddowes murder I made a study of the methods of slaughtermen to test the theory. Then I had to give a verdict of not proven. But here we have an absolutely copy-book example. The hook in the heel, the longitudinal severing of the carcass into two halves with a sharp two-handed cleaver; above all the quartering. A slaughterman always leaves eleven ribs on the upper quarter. In a bullock that would leave three ribs on the hind quarter—here it has left only one.'

'God in heaven!' exclaimed Sir Rufus. 'Jack the Ripper!'

'I would not go so far,' said Burney, 'but a slaughterman, certainly.'

There was a brooding silence for a while, then Bragg broke it. 'What will you be doing about an inquest, sir?'

'Well, there will have to be one,' said the coroner firmly.

'It would be most helpful to me, sir, if it could be kept quiet, and held as late as possible,' said Bragg.

'Hmn. Well, I suppose I could suspend it for a while. I would not want to be opening up a new inquest every time a stray finger or thumb turned up, would I?'

'Jack the Ripper?' exclaimed the Commissioner in consternation. He had come into Bragg's room to enquire about the cardboard box and had been told of Burney's theories.

'He didn't exactly say that, sir,' replied Morton.

'Even a faint possibility is enough to send a shiver up my spine. At all events, it is clear that it was the dead man who succeeded in changing the forged note on Saturday?'

'That much is certain,' said Bragg.

'I suppose they murdered him because he killed a policeman and might be recognized,' Sir William mused.

'If so, it makes them ruthless in anybody's book.'

'I have never been faced with quite so intractable a problem in my life, Bragg. The Governor of the Bank sets the stability of the currency and the economic health of the nation, no less, on our capturing these forgers quickly.'

'Indeed, sir?'

'I would be a great deal happier if the politicians were not pulling the strings. The least breath of failure, and they disown you without compunction . . . And I don't relish putting all our eggs in one basket, like this.' He shot a plaintive look at Bragg. 'In this forgery case we have committed disproportionately large forces on the say-so of the City, and we seem to be blundering about after rumours and informers without achieving anything. I know that seniority is important in the police as much as in the army, but I have always preferred to pick the man for the job, regardless of his rank. I would give my pension, at the moment, for an independent raiding party, as it were, operating behind the enemy lines.'

Bragg gazed stolidly at his blotter.

'If you were given the task of setting up such a parallel operation, Bragg, how would you set about it?'

'I haven't given it any thought, sir,' said Bragg with a hint of smugness in his voice. 'You are right in saying the two should be separate, or they might get under each other's feet.

I think they ought to be operationally independent, so that they can attack the problem in different ways.'

'Exactly my thoughts, Bragg. Go on.'

'I would see it as a precondition, sir, that the leader of the small force should be told precisely what the main force is doing, but that the reverse should not apply.'

'Normally a raiding party is under the overall control of the main body,' objected Sir William.

'You were asking what I would want, if I were setting it up, sir.'

'I understand,' said the Commissioner unhappily. 'I wish personalities did not obtrude into the public service so much, but I suppose it is inevitable.'

'Then,' went on Bragg, 'I would try to discover the enemy's weak points and exploit them. Now, we know that they panicked after Saturday's murder; and since they chopped up one of their own gang, the stakes must be high indeed. I believe that when they come to the conclusion that the forgery has not been detected, they will begin operations again.'

'And how do we exploit that?' asked the Commissioner glumly.

'If the counterfeits are as good as they say, sir, I don't think the Governor's idea of having someone in every bank and office to make a routine examination of all notes received, will ever enable us to catch the putter-down. He will have changed the note for good ones and have gone long ago. At best, all we shall achieve is a nice collection of forgeries. I think you have hit on the right strategy, sir, although I would be tempted to take it even further, and get someone inside the gang itself.'

'But how would you do that?' asked Sir William in surprise.

'Their weakness at the moment is that they have got rid of their putter-down. Now, no matter how good the counterfeit, he is the man who actually converts it into profit. It is he who risks arrest and a long spell in prison, by walking up to a bank counter and asking for the note to be changed into smaller denominations. What they must be looking for is a personable young man with a confident manner, to take over. There can't be too many who would be able to lull the suspicions of a Bank of England cashier.'

'And how would we find such a person, if they cannot?' asked the Commissioner.

'If I wasn't fairly well convinced that the Governor is right about the gravity of this case, I wouldn't even think of risking a policeman's life in such a dangerous venture—for it would have to be a policeman . . . But since it must be done, I would explain all the risks as fairly as I could, and ask for a volunteer.'

'A volunteer?' exclaimed Sir William.

'This is far beyond the line of duty, sir, even to save the nation's currency.'

'I doubt if we have any men in our force who come up to your specification, even without giving them the right to refuse,' the Commissioner complained.

'I can only think of one, myself,' said Bragg, looking at the ceiling.

'Who is that?' asked Sir William. Then his eyes drifted from Bragg to Morton. 'Oh, I see . . . But dammit, Bragg, I am on terms of friendship with his parents.'

'I am sure General Morton would understand, at least. It's what the lad joined the police for. But as I say, he has to be a volunteer.'

There was an uneasy pause.

'I would volunteer,' said Morton doubtfully, 'if I thought I had the remotest chance of succeeding. But I have never done anything like that in my life—I even pay all my bills by cheque.'

'I don't want to seem to over-persuade you, constable,' said Bragg, 'but I think it would be like offering a plump maggot to a trout. They would not expect to find somebody who was already a putter-down. In fact, they would want a man who was completely new to the game. They would train you.'

'Part of the problem,' began Morton '—and I do not wish to give the impression that I am afraid—is that I am fairly well known in London, through playing cricket at the Oval and Lord's.'

'We could change your appearance a bit,' said Bragg. 'And we would have to give you a completely new past.'

'I might be able to help there,' said Sir William cautiously. 'I went down to my old school, in June, to present the prizes. The headmaster was a reasonable enough chap, for a parson. I think he would be prepared to help.'

'What school is that, sir?' asked Bragg.

'The Wells Cathedral Grammar School—I was a chorister in the cathedral choir,' he added bashfully.

'Were you, indeed, sir? Then if you hadn't climbed to the top in the army, you might have been a bishop now?'

The Commissioner looked at Bragg for any sign of ridicule, but his face was a composition of good-natured interest and admiration. 'Yes, well, if need be I could send him a telegraph to arrange a meeting.'

Bragg switched his gaze to Morton, and there was silence for a space. Then Morton turned to Sir William. 'Firstly, sir, I would want you to give me a letter for my family solicitors, to be opened in case of my death, saying that I was acting under your orders entirely.'

'But I would never dream of allowing any stain to remain on your character, my boy.'

'I know that, sir. But only we three will be aware of this operation, and no one is immortal.'

Sir William cleared his throat. 'Very well,' he said reluctantly.

'The next requirement would be that I should publicly be seen to sever my connections with the force—a formal resignation, removal from the roster, everything; though I would want to have the option of rejoining, once this insane enterprise is over.'

'Your resignation would probably be an advantage,' said Sir William, brightening. 'Then any criminal acts you became involved in, would not have been committed by a policeman. For some reason the British are not over-fond of *agents provocateurs*. Anything else?'

'I cannot think of anything at the moment,' said Morton. 'It looks as if I have talked myself into a mixture of a schoolboy prank and a mission of self-destruction.'

'I hope your country is worthy of you, lad,' said Bragg sardonically.

'I expect I shall never know,' replied Morton lightly.

CHAPTER ——————
—————— THREE

'He is going to have to hurry, if we are to catch the train,' said Bragg, peering at this watch for the umpteenth time. 'And there is no point in our going without him.'

'I suspect we are already too late,' replied Morton. 'There is hardly enough time to board the train now, and he will have to buy a ticket.'

'I suppose that clock is right?' Bragg muttered.

'There is another by platform four,' said Morton. 'I will see what it says. After all, it is their time they run the railway by!' Morton vanished into the early-morning crowds.

Bragg looked down at his boots. It was always a mistake to go on a long trip in new boots. They were drawing his feet already. He had thought it was an ideal opportunity to break them in—plenty of sitting and not much walking—but he would be sorry before the day was out.

'Ah, there you are, Bragg!' Sir William was waving his umbrella at him. 'Hurry up, or we shall be late. Where is Morton?'

'Gone to platform four, sir.'

'We will have to leave him if he doesn't hurry.'

'But haven't you got to buy a ticket, sir?'

'No, I got one from a railway agent on the way . . . Where is the boy?' he exclaimed testily.

'Here he comes,' said Bragg, glimpsing Morton pushing his way towards them.

'About time, too . . . Right, men, I shall be travelling first class, of course, so I will see you at Witham junction.' As the Commissioner hurried through the ticket barrier, Bragg and Morton looked at each other and burst into astonished laughter.

They found an empty second-class compartment. Taking out his pipe, Bragg settled into a corner by the window. Soon they were pulling smoothly through the rain-drenched outer suburbs of London, towards the west. Morton watched as Bragg lovingly cut thin slices of twist and began to rub them between his palms.

'That was a diabolical piece of manipulation yesterday,' he remarked with a smile.

'How do you mean, lad?' asked Bragg innocently.

'You picked up a stray phrase from the Commissioner and led him to believe that you were merely embellishing his own idea.'

'Just tactics.' Bragg began to feed the tobacco into the bowl of his pipe.

'You already had it all worked out, hadn't you? And you created that opportunity to manoeuvre Sir William into letting you do it on your own terms.'

'There was no other way we were going to get in on the case. I don't suppose you know it, but Inspector Cotton refused to have us involved in the operation, even though the Commissioner asked him to.'

'Did he?'

'It's my guess that this could be the most important case for donkey's years. You have seen Liddesdale. I wouldn't think he is given to exaggeration or panic, would you? That being so, I wasn't going to be kept out of it by that grudging bugger Cotton.' Bragg struck a match, and sucked at the flame greedily.

'I also remember that the notion of a volunteer and of explaining the dangers fully, got pretty short shrift.'

'Do you think I wouldn't relish it, lad, if I could do it?' asked Bragg sharply. 'No, occasionally police work is like the army; it's an honour I'm conferring on you, the privilege of leading the charge.'

'The more I hear of this uncharacteristic drivel, sergeant, the more I begin to worry.' Morton smiled wryly.

'Well, let's put it another way.' Bragg puffed smoke into a haze around his head. 'For reasons I can only guess at, you, right out of the top drawer of society, decide to spend your young manhood playing at policemen. I can think of a hundred things you are better bred to do, but this is how you want it. All right, but you won't just be a fair-weather policeman. You will be just as committed to the job as any other copper—more so, as long as you are with me.' Bragg took his pipe out of his mouth, and jabbed the stem at Morton to emphasize his words.

'The only bit I am taking on trust in this lot, is the assessment of how important it all is. After that, I am relying on my own judgement and experience. And that tells me that this is the only way to lay them by the heels. You are an imaginative man; you don't need me to tell you of the dangers, after yesterday. But you are the only man we have who could carry this off. And you are a good policeman. If I said ten times over that you needn't do it, it would not change your decision.'

'I suppose not.'

Bragg settled behind the pages of the *Daily Graphic*, and Morton drifted into a restless reverie. Up to now he had never thought about his death: though when he had considered his life, he had generally found it profoundly unsatisfactory. He had often thought, dispassionately, of the changes that the death of his invalid elder brother would bring. Then he could take over the running of the estates in Kent; then his parents would be prepared to acknowledge that he would inherit the title, and ultimately live at The Priory; then he really would consider marriage . . . But his own death . . . just dropping out of the fabric of things. How much would it matter? His mother would be distraught. Perhaps then, she would regret the empty pretence that his brother was capable of running the estates—which was the most important factor that had kept him away. His father would mourn, as well, the approaching end of a line which had occupied The Priory for hundreds of years. His sister Emily would weep inconsolably for a week, then would be fretting that black clothes did not suit her complexion. In America, his cousin Violet might shed a tear of sorrow; but outside the family who would give a toss?

His death might rate a couple of lines in the newspapers—
Death of a promising England batsman—something like that.
He would be sucked below the surface with barely a ripple. On
any rational assessment it meant that his present existence was
virtually without significance. In view of what he had undertaken, that was probably just as well . . . He decided that, if
he came out of this escapade, he would reassess his mode of
life before deciding whether or not to rejoin the police. Then he
closed his eyes and pretended to sleep.

Indeed, he must have slept, for he was jolted into wakeful-
ness as the train pulled up at Frome station. He glanced out of
the window, and saw a bearded porter on the platform calling
'Witham only, this carriage!'

'That is a bit of luck,' he remarked.

'You make your own luck in this life, lad,' replied Bragg.
'This is the line I use when I go home to Dorset, so I know full
well that the Witham coach is the last. No sense in having to
disturb yourself more than you need. I expect his nibs will be
joining us in a minute. There's no first class in this coach!'

He had scarcely finished speaking when the irate face of the
Commissioner appeared. Bragg opened the door for him.

'What is all this about, Bragg?' he demanded, dropping on
to the unyielding horsehair cushion. 'They told me at Padding-
ton I was all right till Witham.'

'This is the slip-coach for Witham,' said Bragg, as the guard
waved his flag.

'What on earth does that mean?'

'Why, the train itself doesn't stop there—it just drops this
coach off.'

'You mean that it releases us when it is actually moving?'

'A friend of mine on the railway, says that it gets to a steady
sixty miles an hour, then at the right moment the driver slows
down a fraction—to ease the strain on the linkage—and the
guard slips the shackle.'

'But good God, man, we might crash!' exclaimed the
Commissioner in alarm.

'We have our own guard, sir. No need to worry. We just
coast in, and he applies the brake to bring us to a gentle halt at
the platform.'

'Have you ever experienced this, Bragg?'

'Only once, sir. It was perfect, a real work of art.'

'Huh!' grunted Sir William. 'What are we stopping for now?'

Bragg dropped the window and leaned out. 'There is a signal against us. Perhaps we have a local train ahead of us.'

'That would make sense,' Morton observed. 'The good people of Witham must be served by some trains.'

After a delay during which the Commissioner pulled out his gold half-hunter at least three times, the train began to move again. With great gasping heaves it slowly increased its speed, but the gradient was against it. White clouds of steam were being spewed out by the pistons, but still it had not regained its original momentum.

'This is going to be tricky,' said Bragg. 'The marker for the release point is just around this bend, and we are not going nearly fast enough . . . There it is! Do you see?'

They felt a slight easing of the engine's pull, heard a metallic clang, and gradually the sound of the train receded.

'We should be able to see the station down the line,' said Bragg, dropping the window. He and Morton poked their heads out, Sir William followed suit at the other end of the compartment.

The carriage was coasting silently down the track at a comfortable speed and all seemed well. Then it came to an adverse incline and its speed dropped perceptibly. It coasted a further twenty yards, it trickled another seven, and came to a stop still two hundred yards from the station. The guard dropped down on to the track, and bustled importantly away.

'What the devil happens now, Bragg?' asked the Commissioner in an accusatory tone.

'They'll be bringing down one of the horses from the coal-yard to pull us in, I dare say.'

'I'll be brought in by no Horse!' exclaimed Sir William wrathfully. 'We shall already be late. See, they are backing our train from the sidings.' With that he opened the door and lowered himself grunting to the ground. 'Come on, you men!' he ordered, and Bragg and Morton followed reluctantly.

They marched in single file, the Commissioner leading, his umbrella held like a sabre. As they approached the station they could see a uniformed figure gesticulating and shouting at them: 'Get back on the train!'

Sir William marched intrepidly on, his brolly at the ready

and, reaching the platform, confronted the frenzied station-master.

'There seems singularly little point in remaining in a carriage which has been abandoned by you in the middle of the countryside,' he said firmly.

'But you are not allowed on the permanent way! It's against the bye-laws!'

'I am the Commissioner of Police for the City of London, my man. Your bye-laws do not apply to me—or my officers. And so that I do not misrepresent the facts when I make my complaint to your board, I would like you to tell me what it is, besides innate stupidity, which prevents your from backing that train down the line to pick up the carriage, instead of sending that singularly puny horse.'

The station-master's voice had lost its hectoring tone. 'It can't, because of the catch-points,' he said surlily.

'Then I suggest that the train should be allowed to proceed. I have an appointment in Wells in twenty minutes, for which, through your inefficiency, I shall inevitably be late.'

A sly smile crossed the station-master's face. 'I'm not allowed to send it off without that coach, sir,' he said. 'There's mail in the guard's van. Perhaps you would like to take some refreshment while you wait.'

Although they were an hour late in arriving at Wells, the Commissioner was unaccountably cheerful. Perhaps, thought Morton, he felt he had had the better of the joust with the railway authorities. And he was evidently enjoying being back in Wells—as a figure of some importance, moreover. He insisted on walking from the station, as he used to as a boy—to save the cab fare for tuck. As they came to the cathedral green, he became quite animated, pointing out the roof of the choir's practice room, south of the cloisters, and admitting to having been caught sucking a large bull's eye when he was supposed to be singing a solo. Certainly Morton could see plenty of reason for his enthusiasm. The town was compact amid rounded hills, the scale of the buildings that of a small market town, the inhabitants cheerful, the pace of life slow—and all dominated by the mellow beauty of the great cathedral in its oasis of green lawns. The intricacy of the carving on its west front was beyond belief, the harmony of the whole breath-stopping.

'Good, isn't it?' remarked the Commissioner, seeing Morton check.

'It is quite the most superlative building I have ever seen,' replied Morton warmly.

'Wait till you see inside!'

They approached a medieval bridge of sighs, spanning the road, and Sir William stepped through an archway in the wall, just beyond it. They found themselves in a long cobbled court, with a uniform row of small stone houses on either side; quaint, Morton decided, with their tall chimneys straining for an up-draught.

'This is Vicars' Close,' said the Commissioner.

'Why would he want so many houses?' asked Bragg in mystification.

'It goes back to the fourteenth century, when the cathedral services were sung by vicars choral. They lived in these little houses, and they could get to the cathedral over the bridge there, without ever going into the world. An odd idea, is it not?'

As they approached the top of the close, Morton could see that there was one considerable house on the left. The Commissioner led the way up the short path and rang the doorbell. A round-faced maid appeared, and showed them into the headmaster's study. A few moments later the Rev. Archibald Truscott himself appeared, a white linen napkin still tucked into the top of his waistcoat. He advanced, beaming, his hand outstretched.

'My dear Sir William, I am sorry that we did not stay luncheon. We feared some mishap must have overtaken you.'

'We did have a small contretemps at Witham, when our slip-coach failed to reach the platform. But no matter, we found the refreshment room was sufficient for our needs.'

'I thought something of the kind must have happened. Then if you will not take luncheon, I will have some coffee sent in.'

He hurried out and shortly reappeared, minus his napkin. He seated himself comfortably in the tall leather chair behind the desk, and looked appraisingly at the three men opposite him.

'And how can I be of service to the school's most distinguished old boy?' he asked with a smile.

Sir William cleared his throat self-consciously. 'It is a police matter,' he said, 'and one demanding the highest degree of delicacy and secrecy. I regret that I can give you no information concerning the operation itself, beyond saying that our national interests are gravely threatened.'

'I quite understand,' said Truscott earnestly.

'It is some measure of the gravity of the situation, and perhaps of our desperation, that this young man is going to risk his life in trying to infiltrate the criminal organization we are endeavouring to wipe out. His name is James Morton, and he is a constable in my force.'

'Not Jim Morton?' asked Truscott, with interest.

'Yes,' Morton admitted.

'I thought I had seen you somewhere. You played for Kent against Somerset at Taunton, a few weeks back. I remember that splendid catch you made on the long-on boundary. We thought it was a certain six, and instead we lost a wicket.'

Sir William shot an exultant glance at Bragg, but he was engaged in studying the garden through the window.

'Your recognition of him, headmaster, has precisely highlighted our difficulty,' he went on. 'His face is moderately well known to cricket followers around London, and it is also public knowledge that Jim Morton is an officer in the City police. We therefore need to arrange for him to disappear and acquire a new character. If you are able to assist us, he will resign from the police force, and it will be given out that he has gone abroad, perhaps permanently.'

'And you wish me to assist you with this fresh identity?' asked Truscott.

'In any way you can.'

'What kind of person is this *alter ego* to be?'

'Personable, self-assured, of good middle-class background, well spoken; at the same time someone who is indolent yet attracted by luxury, and thus easily tempted towards criminality.'

'A concoction of worldly virtues, with just a flavour of vice?'

'Just so, headmaster.'

'And why, precisely, did you come to me?'

'I was hoping that you could invent a plausible history for him at the school, and perhaps give us some advice on an appropriate family background.'

The headmaster gazed at Morton for a time, his chubby pink cheeks the picture of sad benevolence. Then he turned to Sir William. 'I must clearly accept your judgement of the importance of this affair, and it is my obvious duty to help you as far as I am able. It is, therefore, up to me to salve my own conscience in the matter. But tell me, will there be any publicizing of this young man's role in the affair, particularly of his new character?'

'If we succeed in catching them through his efforts,' Bragg interposed, 'some of the story might come out at the trial, because he would have to give evidence.'

'And otherwise?'

'He will be dead,' said Bragg shortly.

'Yes,' Truscott dropped his eyes. 'That puts the issue in the starkest possible terms . . .' He sighed, and wriggled his neck around inside his collar. 'I have to say,' he began, 'that I see the gravest peril in his assuming an entirely imaginary background. The dangers of inconsistency and over-elaboration in such a course would be considerable, and could prove fatal. Far better to fasten on to some real person with the characteristics you require, learn his background and then impersonate him.'

'Then you cannot help us, headmaster?' asked Sir William in disappointment.

'I am indeed sorry to say, that I can. I had just such a boy through my hands when I first came here, and since he is now in New Zealand, he is hardly likely to be harmed by whatever happens here. I would be prepared to assist your young man to impersonate him, though I fear it will sorely trouble my conscience.'

'We will protect your former pupil as far as we can,' said sir William gruffly.

'Yes. Well let me outline the circumstances of that young man, and you will be able to decide if he is what you are seeking.' Truscott rose from his desk, and took a large register book from the drawer of a bookcase. He carried it back to his desk, and turned a few pages.

'His name is Frederick Reginald Thorburn,' he said, 'and he was born on the tenth of July eighteen sixty-six in Waipara, which is a remote agricultural community near Canterbury in the South Island of New Zealand. I imagine, therefore, that he is of much the same age as your constable.'

'That is correct, sir,' murmured Morton.

'I should explain,' went on Truscott, 'that his parents came from Somerset farming stock, and that they emigrated to New

Zealand before he was born. They prospered and, to their credit, decided that their son should have a good education. They entered the boy in this school and charged the relatives still living in the county with a general responsibility for him, during holidays and so forth. In fact, the school should have been ideal for him. Our boys—excluding the choristers, of course—are drawn from the families of yeoman farmers around the town, with a good sprinkling from the local professional classes. Unfortunately, the outcome was far from satisfactory.' He contemplated the register sadly.

'Thorburn was a senior boy when I was appointed headmaster,' he went on, 'and already very difficult. I suppose, as a colonial, he may have been looked down on by the English boys—though his accent and manners were indistinguishable from their own. He did not take readily to discipline, and by my time was impervious to punishment. Indeed, I have to admit that he was contemptuous of both authority and religion . . . I cannot say whether the outcome would have been different had I had him for the whole period of his schooling, or not. But such speculation is profitless. As is often the perverse way of nature, Thorburn excelled at sport, particularly rugby football. He consequently became the idol of the younger boys— an influence that he did not exert for good. He was idle and spendthrift, and became involved with the girls of the town. I would gladly have expelled him; and for the protection of the other boys, it is a course I certainly should have followed. But I could hardly turn him loose in a hostile world, and he adamantly refused to go back to Waipara. I consulted with his uncles, but they had had enough of him also. So, perforce, we all had to endure until he was old enough to leave school. By this time he was virtually estranged from his family in England, and I persuaded him to make a career in the army, hoping that the more rigorous discipline would be his salvation. His outstanding leadership qualities ensured that he was accepted as an officer, and he was posted as a subaltern to the second battalion of the Dorset Regiment, stationed at Dorchester.'

'And did he do well?' asked Sir William.

'At first that seemed to be the case. The open-air life, the physical activity, the responsibility and the feeling of maturity seemed to work together for good. I even received a letter from him, following his promotion to captain, thanking me in the warmest possible terms for my perseverance and guidance. The next time I saw him was at his court martial, last year.'

Sir William's ears pricked up.

'It seems,' said the headmaster, 'that as junior captain in the battalion, he was put in charge of the affairs of the officers' mess—including its funds. He was charged with converting some of the mess's money to his own use. And, since his servant had already pleaded guilty to conspiring with him to that end, the defence was perfunctory in the extreme. I became involved because, against my better judgement, I was brought in as a witness to his character. I fear I may have done the boy more harm than good. I spoke for him as far as my Christian conscience would allow, but unfortunately the prosecution elicited from me the information that he had been strongly suspected of stealing other boys' pocket-money at school.'

'And what was the verdict?' asked Sir William.

'He was found guilty, and cashiered . . . The experience clearly chastened him. His uncles clubbed together, bought him a passage to New Zealand and off he went. Not surprisingly, I never heard from him again.'

'What did Thorburn look like?' asked Bragg.

'Of similar height and build to Constable Morton. The face a little longer, the hair perhaps a shade darker—and he had a moustache then, of course.'

'Do you have a photograph of him?' asked Morton.

'No. Perhaps his relatives in Cheddar might have one— though it is unlikely to have been taken recently.'

'We dare not risk approaching them,' said Bragg firmly.

Sir William cleared his throat. 'Well, constable, does it sound feasible'

'I am grateful for Mr Truscott's help,' said Morton with a smile. 'All in all, Thorburn seems quite an engaging character . . . Yes, he will do very well!'

CHAPTER ———— ———— FOUR

Morton came back from shopping to find a large trunk in the hallway of his rooms in Alderman's Walk. On hearing the door, his manservant appeared, his face a picture of bewilderment.

'I have packed your warm things on top, Master James, because it will still be winter in Australia when you get there.'

'Have you put a return address inside and out?'

'Yes, I have. And I have left you to pack your cricket gear, but your flannels, sweaters and shirts are at the bottom.'

'Very good, Chambers.' Morton crossed to an inlaid escritoire, and took out a letter he had written during the night. 'Give this to my mother, when you get to The Priory. It will explain everything. And tell her I will write to her when I am settled in Australia.'

'It seems odd, Master James, you throwing up everything like this, and going off,' said Chambers querulously.

'It makes life exciting! Now, I will put the labels on the bags myself, when I get them from the shipping office. So why don't you and Mrs Chambers get off to Kent right away?'

'She is still putting the kitchen to rights, sir. She was taken by surprise.'

Morton felt a violent urge to be alone. 'Oh, tell her to leave it! We are not likely to come back here again,' he said savagely. Immediately he regretted it, realizing from Chambers's shocked face that he was throwing their life into turmoil. 'I have asked Lady Morton to see that you have a nice cottage on the estate, near your daughter, so you will be quite comfortable.'

'Yes, sir,' said Chambers bleakly. 'Then I will tell my wife to pack our things.'

Damnation! thought Morton. These kindly people, who had been more like indulgent parents to him than servants, suddenly uprooted and deprived of a purpose in life, after caring for him here for four years. It was all abominable—and likely to be futile, moreover. He cursed Bragg and his machinations, then sat down to write a long letter to his solicitor, which he would send with the official vindication from Sir William. In it he intended to recount at length the reasons for entering into a venture which must have led to his death, if the letter was to be read at all . . . Certainly it was not patriotism. He had been educated privately, before going up to Cambridge, and thus had escaped the worst of such pressures. And having his brother's life shattered in the Sudan campaign had more than outweighed his family's military tradition. Nor was it the adventurous spirit of youth driving him on. At twenty-five he was too old for that, he reflected ruefully . . . No, he was a victim of Bragg's Machiavellian manipulations like everyone else. The sergeant had found his weak spot. All that man-to-man stuff in the train had been a lure, and he had snatched at it. His elders and betters had decided what was needed, and he was the only man who could carry it out. It was as simple as that—straightforward flattery. Morton crumpled up the half-written page, and began instead a simple statement of regret and condolences to his family.

As he finished, there was a discreet tap on the door and Mr and Mrs Chambers stood there in their travelling clothes. Morton enfolded his housekeeper in a bear-like hug, then, pressing a twenty-pound note on Chambers, shook his hand warmly. It was a jolt to see them go. She had been crying, of course. Blast Bragg!

Yet their going somehow signalled the beginning of the operation. He walked briskly to the post-office with his letter. There was no going back now, no point in recrimination. No point, either, in holding it against Bragg; he was a grown man, and had he refused, that refusal would have been accepted. Besides, a harmonious relationship with the sergeant could be vital over the coming weeks. He tramped off to St Paul's Cathedral and wandered around its vastness. Perhaps he was seeking some divine reassurance that what he proposed to do was right; or perhaps he was trying to simulate the dedication of a crusader. Whatever it was he sought, the earth-bound grandeur of the building failed to provide it. Then he walked to the Tower, squatting on the bank of the river, guardian of the City for nine hundred years. Somehow its uncompromising bulk, its permanence, raised a response in him and he marched back to his rooms in exhilaration at the prospect of joining battle.

He packed his cricket gear and his small travelling bag. Tomorrow would be time enough to put them into store. Then he found a piece of a stand-pie in the larder and ate it for his lunch. As he finished, there was a peremptory knocking at the street door. He opened it to find Bragg standing there.

'Come on, lad. I have a cab waiting. I thought you might like some fresh air.'

'I notice that my resignation from the police has not changed our relationship,' replied Morton with a smile.

Bragg looked round, startled. 'Nor will it,' he growled. 'You will come back—Spelman Street, cabby! . . . You know, when you first came to me, there was a rumour that they were grooming you to be the next Commissioner. Taffy Davis told me that, in a couple of years, you would be my boss. Well, if ever you are, I shall still call you "lad".'

Morton laughed. 'And where are we going?' he asked.

'I had a message that Foxy Jock wanted to see me. It can only mean he's got a whisper. It's all happening a bit too quickly for comfort. I would have preferred you to have had a week or so in a doss-house first, so the dirt got properly engrained.'

'I am always taken aback by the consideration you have for the welfare of your men, sergeant.'

Bragg's teeth flashed behind his nicotine-stained moustache. 'You forget. You are general public now. You don't count!'

Before long they were drawing up outside Jack's pawn-shop. When they went in he was sorting through a pile of well-worn clothes, while a scraggy hard-faced woman watched

keenly. Eventually the amount of the loan was agreed, an entry
was made in a ledger, and she tucked the coins and pawn-ticket
into her purse with an air of triumph.

'Ah, Mr Bragg,' said Jock, hoarsely, as she went out.

'What have you got for me?' asked Bragg roughly.

'The Black Horse in Shoe Lane,' muttered Jock behind his
hand.

'Is that where they are operating from?'

'I don't know, Mr Bragg. That was all I could get . . .
They said if I wanted to get in touch, that was the place . . .'

'All right. And remember,' growled Bragg menacingly, 'not
a word to anyone, or you're finished.'

Jock laid a dirty finger along his nose. 'I'll remember, Mr
Bragg,' he croaked. 'I'll remember . . .'

When Catherine Marsden was shown into Bragg's sitting
room, she was surprised to find that Morton was there also.

'I hope you have a story for my paper,' she said with a
sparkling smile. 'The City is rife with rumours of forged
currency notes, and it is said that all the newspaper editors are
under pressure from the authorities not to publish them.'

'Now where did they pick up that nonsense?' asked Bragg.

'It must be true,' said Catherine spiritedly. 'They say the
information came from the police themselves.'

'It was I who asked Sergeant Bragg to invite you here, Miss
Marsden,' said Morton, 'on a quite different matter. I wanted
to give you a present.' Morton fished in his pocket and laid a
small jewel-case on the table beside her. 'I have known you
now for almost a year and the cut and thrust, not to say rough
and tumble, of our professional relationship has given me
unfailing delight. I wanted you to have this small token of my
admiration.'

She looked at him suspiciously.

'Go on, open it,' he said with a mischievous grin.

She glanced at Bragg, but he was busy easing his bootlaces.

'Very well.' She drew off her gloves, and pushed up the lid.
There, nestling on the silk, was a most beautiful cameo brooch.

'But I could not possibly accept such a valuable present from
you,' she exclaimed. 'It might be misconstrued!'

'You know I would never put anyone's honour in jeopardy,'
he said teasingly. 'That is why Sergeant Bragg is here as my

chaperon!' Then his face took on a serious cast. 'It is by way of being a farewell present,' he said lamely.

'Farewell? . . .' Her head jerked up in consternation.

'I have resigned from the police force, and am about to embark for Australia.'

'But why?' she asked, floundering.

'I hope to play a lot of cricket—and perhaps learn something from our Aussie friends . . . and there is the possibility that I shall be married.'

'Married?' she asked flatly. 'To whom?'

'Either Mary Graham from Melbourne, or Carrie Weston from Sydney.'

Catherine looked up at him guardedly. 'You are teasing me,' she said crossly.

Morton pulled a comic face. 'Alas, I am as an open book to you.'

'Sergeant,' she demanded, 'can you please put an end to this charade, and tell me why you asked me to come here?'

'Well, miss,' said Bragg heavily, 'the fact is that we are going to ask for your help—to a degree that you might find burdensome, or even dangerous. In return I can promise you first bite at a story that will put you right at the top of your profession.'

'What is it this time?' asked Catherine warily.

'Well, the rumours of forged notes are correct—though it was all supposed to be highly secret, and the fact that it has leaked out will make Morton's job more difficult.'

'So it was all a fabrication about his going to Australia?' A faint colour rose to her cheeks.

'That part of it was, miss. But he is disappearing from public view, and he has resigned from the police . . . I know you will treat this in the strictest confidence. The truth is that he is going to work underground. We are hoping to infiltrate him into the gang of forgers to facilitate their arrest.'

'You make it sound very simple.'

'It is far from simple and it is exceedingly dangerous. The man who shot the bank cashier last Saturday had just uttered a forged one-thousand pound note. On Monday we found his chopped-up body—or parts of it—in a sewer.'

'But this is absurd!' cried Catherine. 'James could be killed!'

'We have to accept that it is possible.'

'You make it seem like one of those stupid adventure stories,' she said angrily. 'Why cannot someone else do it? You are not even a policeman now, James!'

'There is no one else who can,' said Morton calmly.

'You see, miss,' explained Bragg, 'our coppers are either country bumpkins like me, or rough diamonds out of the army. For this job we need a young chap with a bit of social class.'

'But why do it at all?' she cried wildly. 'What does it matter?'

'The forgeries are virtually undetectable,' said Bragg patiently. 'And they won't stop at the thousand-pound note. Soon you might find your salary being paid in notes that are worthless.'

'It could reduce the economy to ruins,' Morton said quietly. 'I have no choice.'

'And what about your parents?' asked Catherine rebelliously.

'I have written to them, saying that I have resigned, and am going to Australia. I have hinted that a broken love-affair is the reason.'

'Do not ask me to help you with that,' said Catherine. 'I do not want my friendship with Emily to be affected by your stupid antics.'

'We all know you are wedded to your career,' said Morton with a slow smile.

'So you will do it, whether I help or not?'

'It will just make it more difficult, if you don't,' said Bragg, 'and more dangerous.'

'What is it that you want me to do?' asked Catherine irritably.

'Well, let's deal with the easy bit first. We are going to make out that Morton has resigned, and gone to Australia. But somebody who is a public figure because he can knock a little leather ball over a pavilion, isn't able to disappear all that easily. What I would like you to do is to drop a word in the ear of the *Star's* cricket correspondent, that Jim Morton is going down under. Now, at this time of year it would seem a bit odd, so we thought you might hint at a romantic entanglement. These things happen—and you seemed to swallow it all right.'

Catherine gave him a withering look, and reached in her bag for her note-pad. 'Those girls you mentioned, James,' she asked in a matter-of-fact tone, 'were they real? . . . We have to be careful not to libel anyone.'

'I just made them up,' said Morton innocently.

'And what other steps are you taking?' she asked.

'Why, none. Chambers packed up a trunk of clothes for me, which will go into store tomorrow with my cricket gear. He and his wife have gone home to Kent, and I shall lock up my rooms for the time being.'

Catherine snorted. 'You underestimate the resourcefulness of the press, and the public interest in England's batsman-hero of the moment,' she said sardonically. 'You will have to be a deal more thorough, if you do not want your stratagem to be exposed.'

'Such as?'

'You must really buy a passage to Australia, actually send your luggage onboard the boat. That is the only way you can put the press off the scent.'

'Surely that is going further than is needed?' protested Morton.

'By no means. The story might not get more than a passing reference in the *Star* or *The Times*, but it will be meat and drink to *Tit-Bits*,' Catherine said scathingly.

'Very well,' replied Morton with a mocking smile, 'I will do as you say—and you shall come to see me off, to ensure that you are fully satisfied.'

'Yes, I will.' Catherine tossed her head assertively. 'Now what was the other favour you wanted?'

'I would call it much more than a favour,' rumbled Bragg.

'In that case,' said Catherine quickly, 'I think I shall have earned this.' She picked up the jewel-case and slipped it into her bag.

'Once Morton has made contact with the gang,' went on Bragg, 'he has got to keep in touch with me. Obviously he can't walk into Old Jewry, or come here. We need to set up a safe means of communication; somebody who can come here without exciting comment.'

'Such as I?'

'In all honesty, miss, you are the only person I can think of—and it's not for want of trying. I know you are a newspaper reporter, but I would stake my life on your integrity. And it is no unusual thing for you to pop in here. Added to which, you do know the man at the sticky end of this operation, which will give it more . . . interest.'

'So what precisely is it that you are asking?'

'Morton will re-emerge as Frederick Reginald Thorburn, a New Zealander and cashiered army officer from a county regiment. The real Thorburn has gone back to New Zealand, so he won't mind us pinching his character—such as it is.'

'Will you be able to manage the accent?' Catherine asked with a sceptical smile.

'He is said to speak like a west-countryman. He went to school in Wells,' said Morton.

'Now, what more natural than that a personable young man should write letters to his girlfriend; or even to see her now and then?' asked Bragg persuasively.

'Oh no! Not me! Not with a shady ex-officer,' said Catherine firmly.

'Why not?' asked Morton.

'I have my own position to think of. Much as I would like to help, I have no intention of sullying my own reputation in the process.'

'How should we do it, then?' asked Bragg, discomfited.

Catherine pondered for a time, scrawling aimlessly on the top of her pad. Then she looked up. 'A person such as you describe would hardly be involved with someone like me, but he could be interested in a maidservant,' she said. 'I would be prepared to have Thorburn send letters to me at Park Lane under the guise of a housemaid. Let us think of a name . . . "Ada", that sounds right. "Ada Smith"—remember that, James. I will tell cook that they are to be kept for me. Then I can bring them here on the night that I receive them.'

'Splendid, miss,' exclaimed Bragg warmly. 'We could do with somebody like you in the police. Now, we had thought that we ought to have some device in the letters, so that we can tell they are genuine. We don't want to take false information as true.'

'I suggested that I should put a number into the second line of every letter, either as whole word, or part of a word,' said Morton.

'That seems a little excessive,' replied Catherine indulgently. 'I think I know your writing well enough.'

'You must not forget that we are dealing with a gang of forgers, miss,' said Bragg.

'Very well. It can do no harm . . . Now the meetings are more difficult, much more difficult. Obviously, I cannot stand around on street corners waiting for you. Let me think . . . It ought to be a place where we could meet casually, almost accidentally, and where either of us could wait without being obtrusive.'

'A tea-shop?' suggested Morton.

'Not in the evening,' said Catherine dismissively. 'No, a church or charitable function would be better . . . I know! Every Wednesday evening, they open the vestry hall of St James's church, Piccadilly, for the benefit of the indigent. They give them a cup of tea and provide them with clothes. That would be perfect. I shall be free by eight, and the hall stays open till ten. We should be able to meet in those two hours . . . And no one could look askance at my being involved in charitable work, could they?'

CHAPTER ———————

———————— FIVE

'Please, gentlemen,' said the Governor, rapping on the table with the end of a gold pencil. 'May we begin?'

The committee room was too small for the number of people wedged in it, the afternoon was hot and the air already thick with cigar smoke.

'Tomorrow morning,' went on Liddesdale, 'it will be a whole week since the regrettable incident which gave rise to this current crisis; I therefore felt it appropriate that we should review the situation. Firstly, I suggest that we examine the effectiveness of the measures we have already taken and then, if necessary, decide on whatever further action is appropriate. You will see that Chief Inspector Forbes and Inspector Cotton of the City of London police are in attendance, and you will in due course receive a report from them.'

He opened a leather folder in front of him and consulted a pad on which he had jotted a few words. 'I would like you to address yourselves first to the counterfeit currency. You will recall that having imposed stringent secrecy as to the existence of last Saturday's forgery, we decided to set up a mechanism in each bank branch or financial institution to scrutinize every note received. I would like to hear from you as to how that has fared.'

'Point of information, Mr Chairman,' cried a bibulous-looking man, holding up his hand.

Liddesdale frowned in irritation. 'What is that, Mr Townsend?'

'As to this secrecy business,' the man said in an aggrieved voice, 'a chap came up to me in the club last night, and asked me if it was true that there were forged bank-notes about.'

'You denied it, I trust,' said Liddesdale.

'Of course, but as to whether he believed me, I cannot say.'

'Mr Chairman.' A man rose to his feet, not to indicate deference, but to dominate the meeting. Liddesdale looked at him warily, as to a near-equal. 'Yes, Mr Radford?'

'I have something to add on that subject, and to show how seriously I view developments, I am going to impart to the committee some information which I would have much preferred not to release for a month yet.' He paused until the murmur of interest had subsided. 'My bank had planned to invite public subscription for a new issue of shares—a large issue. This morning I received a telephonic communication from my stockbrokers, advising that we should delay or abandon the issue, on account of these self-same rumours.'

There was a babble of excited conversation, which Liddesdale tried to quell. As it ebbed away, Townsend pulled himself to his feet.

'Mr Chairman, may I suggest that we are no longer faced with the situation of last Sunday, but one that has deteriorated considerably. In my opinion, there could well be a run on bank shares in the next few days; and that would hit us all.'

There was a shocked silence, each man looking at his neighbour, wondering who was the most vulnerable, which shares should be quietly unloaded.

'I am aware,' said Liddesdale, 'of these rumours, and have so far been successful in persuading the Fleet Street editors that their duty lay in not retailing them. It is the press that gives substance to people's fears and to that extent the situation has been contained. Let us therefore address ourselves to the effectiveness of the measures so far taken. Has any other counterfeit note been discovered?'

There was a murmur and a general shaking of heads.

'Then does it not indicate that we are on the right track?' asked Liddesdale rhetorically.

'Not necessarily, Mr Chairman.' A bewhiskered man with a peevish face stood up. 'In my view the measures you have imposed on us—yes, sir, imposed on us—are a complete waste of time. You order a scrutiny, and yet you do not entrust us with the details of the defects which would make that scrutiny effective. Our clerks have to be given the job in a casual way, so as not to excite suspicion. As a result they regard it as a finicky piece of routine—like having new blotting paper every Monday morning. Frankly, sir, this strategy is totally misconceived, and imposes unwarranted strains on the staffing of our branches which we cannot sustain indefinitely. I would like to hear what the police are doing to capture these people.'

'All in good time, Mr Fortescue,' cried Liddesdale over the buzz of support. 'Let me say that the Bank of England—which has examined all suspect notes at the highest technical level—has found no more counterfeits. That, to me, shows that our strategy is succeeding. I would suggest that we continue it, without elaboration, until our next meeting.'

'Why not scrap it all now, if there has only been that one?' remarked a benign-looking man. 'With the police combing London so thoroughly, I would have thought all self-respecting counterfeiters would have fled long ago.'

'I cannot be as sanguine as Mr Merrick,' a large bearded man intervened. 'Certainly our bank has not identified any further bad notes, but we have encountered a rash of forged cheques over the last month. They were so perfectly executed that even signatories to the accounts were convinced that they must be genuine. One of our professional clients suffered losses in excess of twenty thousand pounds in a week, and is totally unable to understand how it could have happened.'

'Perhaps it would be best if you were to discuss these forgeries with Chief Inspector Forbes or Inspector Cotton, after the meeting,' said Liddesdale. 'And now it might be appropriate, at this point, to ask the Chief Inspector to report on his progress.'

Forbes rose to his feet with a confident smile, resting his hand on the corner of the table.

'Mr Chairman, gentlemen,' he began. 'You will remember that last Monday's newspapers contained the announcement of a reward of one thousand pounds for information leading to the arrest of any person connected with the murder of the detective constable in the Bank last Saturday morning. We have since distributed many thousands of hand-bills throughout the poorer districts of London, giving a description of the murderer. As a result, we have received a flood of information from people who have seen a tall man with fair hair. I have set up a section at headquarters to sift out the letters from obvious cranks; the rest are being sorted by district and street, and passed to the operational section.'

'How do you know when one is from a crank?' asked a voice from the back.

Forbes smiled smugly. 'Experience, sir, experience. After a few years you can pick them out all right.'

'And what do the operational sections do with them?' called someone else.

'I will ask Inspector Cotton to report on that, gentlemen, since he is in charge of them.'

Cotton got up slowly, and looked around him belligerently. There were beads of sweat on his brow. 'You will appreciate that there are difficulties involved in any large-scale operation such as this,' he began defensively. 'Not least, is the fact that most of the information so far received has involved premises in the Metropolitan Police area. Now, the normal arrangement is that officers of the City force can pursue enquiries and make arrests within the Metropolitan and Home Counties police areas, without any prior permission having to be obtained. This, however, does not apply to large-scale searches of particular districts, such as our present operations entail. We are thus compelled to liaise with the Metropolitan Police, who in an exercise of the present kind, prefer to use their own men.'

'I'm not surprised, with a thousand pounds for the copper who catches him!' cried a voice.

'At least you will have all your men for the ones in the City area,' called another. 'What about them?'

Cotton began to look harassed. 'On Wednesday night we carried out a search of a lodging-house in Blackfriars, but no one answering he description of the murderer was discovered.'

'I would have thought it singularly unlikely that a gentleman who did not excite the curiosity of a bank cashier, would spend his nights in a doss-house, Inspector,' said Merrick with an impish smile.

'It would be just the place for him to hide up,' countered

Cotton dogmatically. 'On Thursday, following information received, we apprehended a blond young man in a Lower Thames Street rooming-house. Our informant insisted that he had seen him with printer's ink on his fingers. After interrogating him, however, we came to the conclusion that there was rivalry between the two men over the affections of a young woman, and there was no truth in the allegation. Since the young man did not have a mole on his cheek, we released him.'

'It seems a ridiculous waste of manpower,' muttered Fortescue.

'We have to take any information we receive seriously,' replied Cotton doggedly. 'Anyway, all these operations are cleared in advance with your committee, through its liaison man at Old Jewry.'

'So we bear a joint responsibility, do we?' asked the bearded banker. 'I am not at all sure, Mr Chairman, that it is a proper position for us to take.'

'I would prefer it to continue for the time being, Mr Jacobson,' said Liddesdale shortly.

'And what is on the programme for tonight?' quipped Merrick.

Cotton looked round for support, but neither the Governor nor Forbes came to his rescue.

'Tonight, in conjunction with the Metropolitan Police, we are carrying out a raid on some factory premises in Spitalfields.'

'Buy your tickets on the way out,' came a voice.

Liddesdale flushed with anger at the general laughter, and rapped the desk with his pencil.

'In view of the level of puerile badinage to which this meeting has descended,' he said icily, 'I presume that no one has anything further of substance to contribute. I judge the feeling of the meeting to be in favour of continuing the present tactics in relation to counterfeit notes, and of ensuring that the police are made aware of the existence of any other forged instruments with the utmost possible expedition. I declare the meeting closed.'

The train from Fenchurch Street to Tilbury was crowded, and Morton and Catherine could do no more than exchange occasional smiles across the compartment. Even after they had alighted and secured a cab, this constraint continued; both lost in their own thoughts. But as they clattered through the gates of the dock, Morton roused himself.

'I am most grateful to you, Miss Marsden, for falling in with my jest and coming to launch me into the unknown,' he said flippantly.

'You forget,' she said with an acid smile, 'it was part of my contract to secure the scoop of the century. I am not likely to let you spoil it at this juncture.'

Morton leaned to one side and pretended to inspect her. 'You would have made a very good Amazon,' he said, 'if they were still in fashion—though thank God, they are not!'

'Enough of that!' she admonished him. 'There is a man, who looks very much like a reporter, standing at the foot of the gangway. Have your wits about you!'

Morton handed Catherine down, and turned to pay the cabby.

'Surely you are Miss Marsden of the *City Press*?' A burly man with raddled features was raising his hat to Catherine. 'I'm Wardle of *The Times*. I saw you at the union jamboree the other week. I have been wanting to meet you ever since you wrote that piece about Sir Walter and Lady Greville. Fine work, that.'

'From you, that is praise indeed,' replied Catherine, purring with pleasure.

'Now, Mr Morton,' said Wardle, licking his thumb and turning the pages of a thick note-book. 'I wonder if you can confirm the rumour that you have resigned from the police and given up your membership of the Kent County Cricket Club?'

'As to the former,' said Morton cautiously, 'it is certainly true. As to the latter—never!'

'Why have you resigned from the force?'

'Let us just say, that I felt a change would be beneficial.'

'But why Australia?'

'Why not?'

'I gather you are taking your cricket gear with you.'

'Ah! Then you have already made the acquaintance of my steward.'

Wardle shrugged. 'Will you be playing **some** cricket there?'

Morton grinned in capitulation. 'If **they will** let me. After all, they did win the series last winter. We have a lot to learn from them.'

'Will you be coming back in time to play for England against them, next summer?'

'That is something I cannot comment on,' said Morton shortly.

'It is rumoured that you have a romantic reason for going. Are you prepared to say anything about that?'

Morton took Catherine's arm and drew her close to him. 'If this young lady were not so committed to a journalistic career,' he said with a smile, 'there might be compelling reasons for staying.'

Wardle looked up, as Catherine pushed Morton away. 'May I quote you?' he asked.

'Certainly not! I would not want to embarrass either of you.'

Wardle closed his note-book, and raised his hat. 'Then may I wish you—both of you—all the best,' he said, and turned on his heel.

'Idiot!' Catherine hissed as they hurried up the gangway. Morton produced his ticket, and they were shown to a large cabin on the upper deck. In the middle of the floor were his trunk and bags. A spruce middle-aged steward followed them in.

'Mr Morton, sir? My name is Jones, sir. I shall be your steward for the voyage. Now, if you will let me have your keys, I will unpack the clothes you will need and have the rest put down in the hold.'

'Ah no, Jones,' said Morton conspiratorially, holding out a ten-pound note. 'I would rather you did not do that.'

Jones glanced from Morton to Catherine. 'Of course not, sir,' he said, tucking the money into his waistcoat pocket. 'I will see you are not disturbed. Shall I give you a knock, twenty minutes before we sail?'

'No, no! You quite misunderstand me,' said Morton hurriedly. 'I want you to perform a very particular service for me.'

'Oh yes, sir?' said Jones, poker-faced.

'For reasons which need not concern you, I want to appear to go to Australia on this ship, while in fact remaining in England.'

'I see, sir,' said the steward in a matter-of-fact tone.

'Can you pretend that I am ill, or something, and confined to my cabin, until you have cleared British waters? By the time you get to Australia, it will no longer matter.'

'Don't worry, sir, I will have your baggage stowed, and keep the cabin locked . . . Will you be wanting the baggage brought back again?—I see there is a return address label.'

'Please.' Morton handed over another note. 'That should

cover the freight back. And there will be another twenty for you when you get back, if the deception is not discovered.'

The steward gave a small smile. 'Then it's as good as mine, sir . . . Now if you will take my advice, you will go down to C deck and along to the third-class section, then down the gangway at the stern.'

They followed his directions, plunging down steep steps into the bowels of the ship, and along a narrow passage which unaccountably seemed to sway, despite the fact that the vessel was still firmly tied to the quay. They slunk down the rear gangway and, walking the short distance to the station, took second-class tickets to London. For the first part of the journey there was also an elderly couple in their compartment, but even when they had alighted, Catherine observed an outraged silence. Morton tried to catch her eye, but she would have none of it.

'Have I made you angry, Miss Marsden?' he asked contritely. 'If so, I am sorry.'

'Angry!' she burst out. 'I have never felt so humiliated in my life. That . . . that steward man actually thought I was your strumpet!'

'No, I don't think so for a moment,' said Morton with a disarming smile. 'I am sure he thought you were my wife, and that we wanted a few moments of privacy before you left.'

For a moment Catherine seemed to be somewhat mollified, then: 'And why did you say that to the reporter?' she cried.

'What was that?'

'Hinting at a relationship between us!'

'As I recall it, I was suggesting quite the converse.'

'Well, it was stupid and unnecessary!'

'You may well be right, but it suddenly struck me that to Wardle's eye there was no very good reason for you to be seeing me off, and it was better for me to implant the idea that there never could be a relationship between us, before his imagination got to work.'

'You didn't have to do it in that way,' she exclaimed crossly.

'I'm sorry. My mind does not work as quickly as yours in these situations.'

The train groaned to a halt at the terminus, and suddenly Catherine's irritation was overlaid with foreboding. Morton walked her to the cab-rank.

'I have some old clothes in the left-luggage office here,' he said. 'So in ten minutes, I shall start my new existence as Thorburn. I am quite looking forward to it!' He paused, and turned to face her. 'Will you look after these for me, Miss Marsden? The keys are for the street door of my rooms, and there is enough money in the pocket-book to meet any immediate expenses, in case things should go wrong. If they do, give my love to my parents.' He handed her up into the cab, and raised his hat. 'See you on Wednesday,' he said with a jaunty smile, and was gone.

'And what can I do for you, Mr Merrick?' said Inspector Cotton, brusquely.

The benign face looked careworn, there was not a flicker of waggish humour left.

'First of all, Inspector, I wish most sincerely to apologize for my conduct towards you this morning. It was quite unforgiveable in me, the more so in that, as a public servant, you were in no position to hit back . . . All that I can advance by way of extenuation is that one acquires a reputation as a kind of licensed clown and one is expected to live up to it.'

'I see, sir,' replied Cotton non-committally.

'The second purpose of my visit is to show you this bill of exchange.'

Cotton stretched out his hand for the piece of paper and studied it carefully. 'And what about it then, sir?'

'It is a forgery, Inspector. You will see that it is a four-month bill, drawn payable on the nineteenth of July this year. I discounted it in May, and paid out nineteen hundred pounds to the presentor. In strictness I ought to have sent it for acceptance before making payment, but that is a procedure more honoured in the breach, nowadays. On the due date, it was, of course, sent by my clerk for payment by the drawee, and was repudiated. I naturally approached the drawer, to obtain his support, and he denied any knowledge of the transaction. He maintained that the signature was a forgery. He even opened his books to me, and demonstrated that there had been no such transaction anywhere around the relevant date.'

'So you are nineteen hundred pounds to the bad, are you sir?' said Cotton with ill-concealed satisfaction.

'I am. But that is not the whole point. What I am concerned about, Inspector, is that there may be many more such bills in circulation.'

CHAPTER ———————

——————— SIX

Morton changed into Thorburn's clothes in the public lavatory at the station. He had been to the clothes exchange off Cutler Street and had bought a good black morning-coat that was somewhat shiny at the elbows, a pair of grey checked trousers that were slightly too short for him and a reasonable-looking bowler hat. His shirt and collar were a dingy white and half a size too large, and his tie a blue silk bow. He had kept his own socks and boots, arguing that, for his own safety's sake, comfort must have priority over verisimilitude there. He looked at himself in the mirror. Not bad! The garments gave him the desired air of an out-of-work clerk, but the fresh confident face above them was still that of James Morton. It was too late to grow a moustache or sideboards now and if he merely neglected to shave, no one would look upon him as a prospective putter-down. He took out his comb, and parted his hair on the left side instead of in the middle. It made some difference, certainly, enough to deceive the proverbial man on the galloping horse, but no more. It would have to be spectacles. He put two sovereigns and some loose change in his pocket, and locked the rest in his bag. This he deposited in the left-luggage office, and posted the key and ticket to his rooms. Now, with a spare shirt and socks in a cloth bag, he was Frederick Thorburn, devil-may-care, womanizer, down on his luck. 'Frederick?' . . . 'Fred?' No, 'Fred' didn't have the right kind of ring; it was too solid, too honest.

Morton realized that although he had thought through the character he was assuming, he had not had any time for rehearsal. He tried to recall the background voices he had heard in Wells. It was not the broad accent of the pantomime hayseed, sounding like a long mangled vowel with an occasional grunt for a consonant. Anyway, he was supposed to be from a comfortable middle-class background. Thorburn's New Zealand origin worried him a little; he had scarcely ever heard a New Zealander speak, and he suspected that it was a noticeably different accent from that of the Australians. Far better not to attempt it. If Waipara was as remote as the headmaster had indicated, Thorburn's parents would have retained their native intonations and passed them on to their son. And Truscott had said that his accent was the same as that of the other boys at the school. He would stick, then, to a slight broadening of the vowels. He walked slowly down the street, muttering to himself in his new tongue, till he received a suspicious look from a police constable and desisted.

A hundred yards ahead was an optician's sign. This would be a perfect opportunity to try out his accent. He marched through the door into the empty shop. Eventually, the wildly tinkling bell brought a short brisk man from the room at the back. He was balding, with grey mutton-chop whiskers, and as he advanced he dabbed at his chest in an effort to find the string of his prince-nez.

'Yes, young man?' he enquired sharply, settling them on his nose at the second attempt.

'I want some spectacles,' said Morton in a broad slow voice.

'Of course you do,' snapped the optician, 'or you would not be here. Can I have a look at your present ones?'

'Oi haaven't haad any afore,' said Morton. That was even broader—too much so—and the optician had given him a startled look.

'Sit down in this chair, and I will test your eyes . . . Now, you see that card over there, with the letters on?' he asked, pointing vaguely towards the opposite wall.

'Noa,' said Morton.

'Goodness gracious, they must be bad,' muttered the optician. 'Here, let me examine your eyes.' He crossed to a desk and, stooping low, located a large magnifying-glass. He advanced on Morton brandishing it, and began to peer into his left eye.

'Look over my shoulder, not at me,' he snapped.

It was grotesque, thought Morton, a short-sighted optician, that huge blurred pupil blinking down at him, the tobacco-stale breath . . .

'Now the other one,' said the little man, bustling round the chair. 'They seem perfectly all right to me,' he said in vexation. 'Can you see the card now?'

'Where is it supposed to be?' asked Morton in his normal accent.

'Why, it's propped on the table there, of course.'

Morton got up and, groping behind the table, retrieved the card and set it in its proper place.

'You didn't read any of the letters, did you?' asked the optician accusingly.

'Noa, I ded noat,' replied Morton.

'Very well, cover your left eye with this paper, and read me the fourth line of letters.'

'A Q U H Y'

'Good, What is the last line you can see clearly?'

'Z B G O K'

'Try the one below that.'

'There isn't one,' said Morton

'Goodness me! That is very good . . . Now cover the right eye . . . That's it. Will you read from the third line?'

Morton began to make up a sequence of letters of his own. 'First there's an O, and then there's an R, and after that there's an I, then an A . . .' He mumbled on, giving the vowels different tone values. It was the O's and A's that had to be lengthened, he decided, with a touch of a burr on terminal R's.

'Is that the end of the card?' asked the optician.

'Yes.'

'Well, what is wrong with your eyes?' he demanded.

'Nothing, it would seem.'

'See you here, young man,' he said angrily. 'I will not have you coming into my shop, obtaining a free sight-test on the pretext of needing glasses—and, moreover, behaving in a thoroughly boorish way. If you do not leave immediately, I shall call the police!'

'But I do want spectacles,' expostulated Morton. 'I am trying for a position as a librarian, and I am told I shall stand a better chance if I look a bit more studious. Surely you can put plain glass in some frames for me?'

The optician regarded him with irritated suspicion, then, apparently deciding to indulge him, vanished into the room at the back and returned with a box of frames. With his help, Morton chose a pair of round gold-framed spectacles, which were duly furnished with plain lenses. When the wire springs snapped around his ears, he felt the metamorphosis was complete.

But they had cost him a half-sovereign, and suddenly his store of money looked meagre indeed. Well, Bragg had joked about a week in a doss-house, he might as well find out what one was like. After all, Thorburn could well have had a spell of living rough. Morton paid a penny for a tram-ride to Stepney and trudged around the shops. He attempted to beg a stale bun from the back of a baker's shop, and was sent about his business with a torrent of abuse. Clearly he would not be much of a success at being poor. Perhaps he was not down-at-heel enough to excite pity. What was it the woman at the baker's had said? Something about a ragged service at the mission hall? He asked directions of a passer-by, and was sent down a side street where an assertive red-brick Methodist church stood. Beside it was a long, low building with open doors, from which issued the doleful sound of hymn-singing. He went up the steps and entered the hall. It contained row upon row of hard wooden benches without backs. No allowances for the weakness of the flesh here. Most of the forms were occupied by a dejected mass of men, huddled together despite the warmth of the evening. One or two had an overcoat draped across their knees, many were still wearing a cap or hat. Morton was surprised that this near-blasphemy was tolerated by the hard-faced, self-righteous stewards who stood around the edge of the hall. At the top end was a lectern, where a plump man in a black frock-coat led the singing. Near him a middle-aged woman pedalled vigorously at a harmonium.

Morton moved up the hall to take a vacant place at the end of a row, but retreated in the face of the frowsty smell of dirty clothes. He took a seat in the empty area at the rear, and realized from the look on a steward's face that he had somehow earned a black mark. Above the head of the plump man, a huge brown board had been secured to the wall. On it had been painted a long cream ribbon, which bore the assurance that those who hungered and thirsted after righteousness should be filled. At the back of the hall, on either side of the double doors, were two smaller boards, one bearing the legend CASTING ALL YOUR CARE UPON HIM, the other, HE CARETH FOR YOU.

The plump man was now extemporizing a long prayer; largely, it seemed, asking forgiveness for the dreadful sins, whose existence the evident destitution of the congregation so conclusively demonstrated. Most men had their heads bowed, one or two stared stonily ahead of them. Morton looked around him, and received a baleful glare from one of the stewards until he dropped his head. Then another hymn was announced and the harmonium began to wheeze. The tuneless moan arose again from the congregation, and Morton joined in as best he could. Some men were singing with a will, as if they enjoyed it, some were merely mumbling in tune to the music; but all had their lips moving. This, then, was the way to the kingdom of heaven; the rousing celebration of eternal life, which was supposed to dull the pain of living.

The end of the hymn seemed to mark a significant stage in the proceedings, for the congregation began to look around with something approaching animation. The plump man retired, and several stewards came from the back of the hall with trays containing lumps of bread and mugs of cocoa. Once they had been consumed, the ragged men shuffled off quickly. Morton stuffed his piece of bread in his pocket and forced himself to drink the sweet muddy liquid. Then he moved to go.

'Will you want a bed?' enquired a steward.

'Please.'

'There is a casual ward in Ship Street. Turn left at the furniture warehouse.'

'Thank you, sir.' Morton raised his hat and the man gave him a curt nod of dismissal.

Morton followed his directions. By now he was beginning to feel weary, and the fine sense of adventure had dwindled into resignation. He trailed along Ship Street, until he came to a building that was barely distinguishable from the warehouses around it. A queue of men was waiting by the front door, stretching down the steps and a little way along the pavement.

'Is this the casual ward?' Morton enquired of the last man in the line.

'This is the dosser, mate,' he asserted gruffly.

Morton took up station behind him, and before long the front door was flung open. The file of men pressed through and, as Morton passed over the threshold, he could see one of the dormitories through a door on the right. Instead of bedsteads, there were taut pieces of canvas stretched between iron bars running six inches or so above the bare wooden floor. There could not have been more than eighteen inches between one bed and the next in the row. A twill sheet and a blanket had been dropped on every bed.

While Morton had been gazing, the queue had moved on, and he was being nudged from behind. He moved forward, and numbly paid his tuppence. This gave him access to a large room, about the size of the dormitory he had seen. Near the door there were some benches; the people who had been in front of him in the queue were busy taking off their clothes and stuffing them into canvas sacks. These were labelled by an officious-looking man and taken off to a side room. The men then proceeded to wash themselves in a communal bath that reminded Morton of nothing so much as the sheep-dipping tank at the home farm. Once out of the bath, they dried themselves and were given a rough cotton night-shirt. They then hurried through to the dormitory—presumably with the aim of getting the best beds.

'Come on, get your clothes off!' commanded the officious man.

Suddenly Morton's resolve revolted against the humiliation that was to be visited on him. He turned round and elbowed his way through the press, to the fresh air.

'Hey, come back!' someone shouted. He took to his heels to escape them. They had his tuppence, hadn't they? What were they complaining about?

Morton's financial resources were further depleted by the tram fare back to the City, where he found a bed in a Rowton House shelter in Clerkenwell. Here, his sixpence at least furnished him with a proper bed in a small dormitory, the use of reasonable washing facilities and the promise of an adequate breakfast.

By eight o'clock next morning he was walking briskly towards the river. His dejection of the previous night was behind him;

so too was the euphoria. Now he felt the confident optimism which was natural to him—and to Thorburn. But he would have to watch himself like a hawk; an unguarded moment could spoil it all. He muttered to himself as he went, until he had got his intonation right, and suddenly realized that he had come into Farringdon Street, above the Fleet sewer. Was it still a few hours short of a week since Walton had been murdered at the Bank? So much had happened in the meantime, so much frenetic activity, that he had hardly had time to think. Well, this was scarcely the time to begin. He turned down Stonecutter Street and into Shoe Lane.

The Black Horse was a large double-fronted property with a central door. It was probably Georgian, from its severe soot-stained front. Above the ground floor were three further storeys. A narrow board ran from the pediment down to the doorway, proclaiming the purveyance of wines, spirits, Whitbread's beers and stout. The pub door was already open, and Morton could see that there were two further doors in the passage-way, giving entrance to the bars. On one side of the pub was a tobacconist and on the other an eel and pie shop. As he crossed the road, Morton could see that the trapdoors in the pavement had been opened and a paunchy red-faced man was busy securing a rope across the uplifted ends, to keep the public away from the hole. Morton approached him.

'Any chance of a job, sir?' he asked deferentially.

The red-faced man looked him up and down appraisingly.

'Could be,' he replied tersely.

'To start now?' asked Morton.

'You ever worked in the licensed trade before?'

'Only in the country,' replied Morton, hoping that this would excuse any shortcomings on his part.

'Well, you are a big fellow. I could do with some help. There's a delivery due, and the cellarman is sick . . . All right, we'll see how you do today. The steps to the cellar are at the end of the passage. When the dray's gone, you can collect the glasses in the four-ale bar. There'll be a rush at noon, being Saturday.'

Morton went smartly down the passage and groped his way down the cellar steps. Two gas brackets were already burning, but by far the greatest source of light was the hole above the delivery bay. He wondered what he was expected to do in preparation. He supposed that they would have to take the old barrels out first, or there would be no room for the new. By tapping them sharply with his boot, he managed to identify the empty ones, and putting on a heavy sail-cloth apron in place of his coat, he began to roll them to a convenient place. Then he swept the floor vigorously—too vigorously it seemed, for clouds of dust rose into the air and settled anew where he had swept. Still, sounds of activity were more important than proficiency of technique at this juncture. Morton had managed to acquire a small heap of the heavier debris, and was standing back in satisfaction, when he heard the noise of the dray horses, and shouts of 'Whoa! Steady! Whoa!' He dashed upstairs to display his eagerness and greeted the draymen. They gave him a perfunctory ''Morning', as to an inferior breed. The driver hung a nosebag round the head of each of the big shire horses, then went in to seek the landlord. One of the draymen unhooked a heavy wooden slide from the side of the lorry and casually pushed it down the hole in the pavement.

'Well, come on, mate,' he said to Morton good-humouredly. 'We haven't got all day.'

Morton had time to see the other drayman setting a thick rope mat like a ship's fender on the pavement, before he followed down to the cellar. The whole operation seemed to go like a well-rehearsed ballet. The co-ordination between the two men was amazing. First the empty barrels were rolled a little way up the slide, then drawn up with two hooks on a chain. When they had been cleared, the man Morton had been helping went outside again, and soon there was a series of heavy thumps. Fearful of betraying his ignorance, Morton went upstairs and leaned against the door-jamb. One man was on the dray, rolling the full barrels to the edge and dropping them precisely on to the mat. As they rolled away, the other man spun them slightly with a touch of his foot and their impetus carried them to where the others had collected. And all the time the four horses stood placidly, stabbing at the road occasionally, or shaking their heads to disturb the flies, but heedless of the work going on behind them. When the dray was empty, one of the men rolled a barrel to the top of the slide and looked at Morton expectantly.

'Are we ready then?' he asked.

Morton dashed down the steps to find that a barrel was already half-way down the slide, restrained from above by the two draymen. He waited in some trepidation. This, if any, was

the moment when he would be revealed as a novice. But as the
barrel touched the cellar floor, the draymen gave the chain a
flick and the hooks fell away, leaving the barrel a little impetus
to clear the end of the slide. So it was just a matter of rolling
them away? Morton gave the barrel a shove and it moved a
mere foot. Who would have thought beer was so heavy?
Already he could hear a rumble as the next barrel was trundled
along the pavement. He bent down and, exerting all his
strength, rolled the barrel into the corner, then turned as
another hit the cellar floor. For the next half-hour he endured
the most back-breaking labour he could ever have imagined. It
must be every bit as bad as the treadmill—worse, probably,
though there was a wage at the end of it. Half way through he
realized that the trick was to utilize the dying momentum as the
barrel rolled clear of the slide and keep it going. That removed
the worst of the physical strain. Why was it that one learnt the
most important of life's lessons too late to be of use? Still, if
Thorburn was a rugby-player, he would think nothing of this
mindless shoving; it would be like any one of a hundred scrums
to him. Morton toiled on until, to his relief, he heard the slide
being withdrawn and the thud as the trapdoors closed. He
straightened up, his fingers scraped and sore; then, mindful of
the need to display his zeal, he swept the floor again, put on his
coat and dragged himself upstairs. The three men from the
brewery were standing in the doorway of the four-ale bar,
talking to the landlord, great foaming glasses of beer in their
hands.

'Draw yourself a pint,' said the landlord, nodding affably at
Morton.

Morton thanked him, and made for the bar. Dear Lord was
his trial never to end? How did they do it? He took a glass and
held it under the tap, then grasped the lever of the pump firmly.
He glanced up and saw that mine host was looking absently in
his direction. If he got a glass full of froth now, he was as good
as finished. He pulled the lever steadily and strongly. Nothing
came out! But he'd seen this happen scores of times. There was
plenty of pressure on the lever, so he was not merely pumping
air. The trick must be not to snatch it. Another controlled
pull . . . and another. At last, a jet of amber liquid hit the
bottom of the glass and was transmogrified into white foam.
Steady! . . . slowly does it! Not too much head. The inch of
foam crept up the glass and reached the rim. Morton raised it

in salute and received an answering smile from the landlord. He had passed the first test, anyway!

It seemed that no sooner had he drawn breath, than the bar was invaded by a horde of clerks, fighting for a quick drink before catching the train home to the suburbs. For an hour he was kept busy collecting the sticky glasses, washing them in a mahogany sink behind the bar, and polishing them dry. Working at top speed, he managed to keep ahead of the demand. Then, as if by magic, the elbowing throng evaporated, leaving a handful of regulars behind. For a while Morton coasted, gathering his wits. Then the landlord came over to him.

'What's your name, then?' he asked.

'Thorburn, Fred Thorburn,' So much for advance planning!

'Well, I'm prepared to take you on. How much work do you want to do? We are open from six in the morning till past midnight, weekdays.'

'As much as you can let me have—I need the money,' Morton said with a rueful smile.

'What I really need is a waiter in the parlour. If you could work from eleven in the morning till eleven at night, that would suit me.'

'It would be perfect.'

'Sunday it's noon to eleven.'

'Right. So can I work on now, till eleven tonight?'

'Yes.' The man paused with a quizzical look on his face. 'You're a queer one,' he remarked. 'Don't you want to know what your pay is?'

Morton mentally kicked himself. 'I assumed it would be much as other places,' he replied.

'You would have a half-hour off for lunch form two to half past, and another from half past six to seven for supper. So you would be working eleven hours at eleven pence an hour. All right?'

'Yes, fine.'

Morton went through to the parlour, wondering whether he ought to have haggled. He was greeted by a barmaid who, propped against the counter, was lifting one tired foot after the other to rest them.

'You are the new waiter, are you?' she asked amiably. 'We could have done with you just now. Saturday lunch-time is a real mad scramble.'

'I can imagine,' said Morton. 'I was in the four-ale bar.'

'There won't be much to do now, till round eight tonight—the Sundays, you know.'

Morton looked blankly at her.

'We get a lot of newspaper folk here, especially when they've got their copy in.'

Morton was taken aback. He had not remotely considered this possibility. He looked at himself in the mirror behind the bar. Thorburn looked back at him, hair disheveled, eyes red-rimmed behind the ridiculous spectacles. No. He would have to be very unlucky to be recognized.

Morton did not find his duties onerous for the rest of Saturday and was able to achieve tentative mastery of a tin tray full of drinks. Around eight o'clock, there was a reasonable crowd of customers, most of them oldish men content to talk and make a pint last an hour. More lively were the men who had brought their wives in for a weekly treat. They would gang up till there were about ten of them around a small oval table drinking shorts, and going into shouts of laughter over some risqué remark or other. Around nine a young woman came in and took a seat on a banquette at the side of the bar, near to where Morton was standing. She was on her own, which probably meant she was a street girl or a kept woman, but she was plump and pretty, with dark brown hair and white even teeth.

'What can I get for you, madam?' Morton asked.

'A small port, please.' Her voice had a warm teasing quality that threatened to break into laughter.

He brought her drink and, since no one was signalling for him, took up his station near her.

'Do you come here often, madam?' he asked, mindful of Thorburn's reputation.

'You are new here,' she laughed, 'or you would know I do . . . And less of the "madam". That's one thing I'm not, more's the pity.'

A man waved at him from the other side of the room, and he went over with alacrity to take his order. He stayed chatting for a few moments and when he came back to the bar, the woman was gone.

They had scarcely opened on Sunday, however, when she was in again.

'A small port?' he asked with a smile.

'It's nice to be remembered,' she said happily.

'There's a bottle of quite good Taylor's there,' said Morton solicitously. 'I am sure you would prefer that.'

'It's all the same to me, love,' she said.

'What heresy! Just try it, for my sake, and see whether I am right or not.'

'If you insist.'

He brought the drink and hovered anxiously over her while she sipped it.

'Am I not right?' he asked.

'It's not quite as sweet, is it?' she pronounced. 'I like it sweet.'

'Then milady is assuredly right.'

'You are a funny waiter,' she observed, 'with your long words and your going on about port.'

'The fates can be cruel—but they have sent me a small consolation.'

'What's that?'

'They have placed me where I can look upon you.'

'Don't be bloody silly!' She gurgled with laughter and Morton joined in. She ordered an ordinary port for comparison and declared she would never enjoy it again, thanks to her ill-luck in meeting him. Then she gathered up her bag, and went out.

The next day was busy from morning till night. Morton constantly watched the customers as discreetly as he could. He did not quite know what he was looking for, but he maintained an air of confidence and relaxed bonhomie the whole day. Fairly certainly, he was in the right place. No self-respecting forger would look for a putter-down in a four-ale bar. By the time the young woman came in again, he was feeling thoroughly jaded, but put on his act for her sake.

'A small port?' he asked.

'Can I have some of that stuff you gave me last night?'

'Certainly, your grace.'

'What are you on about?' she asked.

'Your grace forbade me to call you "madam".'

'You silly devil,' she said with a ripple of laughter. 'Call me Lily, it's my name.'

'Then Lily it shall be, your highness.'

He set the drink down before her and she sipped it delicately. 'I can see what you mean,' she said. 'It is less like sugar water—but I still don't like it.' She drank it off at a swallow and began to cough. 'You'll be the death of me,' she complained. 'Get me one of the other stuff.'

He brought it to her table. 'Sit down, and take the weight off your feet,' she suggested.

'I can't do that,' he said, 'I would get the sack if the guv'nor caught me.'

'Does it matter all that much?' she asked scornfully.

'Matter? It's the best job I've had for months.'

'What have you been doing, then?'

'Oh, this and that—a lot of this and very little of that,' he grinned lubriciously.

'Like what?' she smiled in return.

'I worked on a farm for a while—that was damned hard labour—piling hay on carts, spreading manure in the fields. Then I came to London and tried all manner of things. I sold books for a wholesaler once. That was interesting. But once Christmas was over, trade went slack; so I gave it up. Then I had a spell as a plumber's mate . . . I did, honestly! That's the trade to be in. Think of all the miles of bog-houses in London waiting to be modernized.'

'You're a vulgar devil,' she said, chidingly.

'That's because of my upbringing. I was sent to Wells Cathedral choir-school. I ask you! I had to go to the bad, after that.'

'So what happened to the plumbing?'

'The union found out about me and I got thrown out.'

'And was this the best you could do?' she asked.

'Hey! Stop pouring scorn on my profession! I gauge the value of a job by where it lets me sleep. This one has allowed me to move from the dosser in Stepney to a Rowton House in Clerkenwell, so by my lights it's a good one.'

'What do you do, when you finish here?' Lily asked brightly.

'Go home to bed, of course.'

'Full of fun, aren't you?'

'Steady on! I only finish at eleven.'

'I thought we might do something . . . together,' she said provocatively.

'Honestly, I'd like to,' he said. 'But by the time I was done last night, I couldn't have raised a smile.'

'Suit yourself,' she said pertly. 'See you tomorrow,' she called as she went through the door.

When he got up on Tuesday morning, Morton persuaded himself that this was going to be the crucial day. If he were not approached today, it would be because they had already found a putter-down; either that, or he was doing something wrong. He thought through every aspect of the character he had created for Thorburn, to see if there was something that did not ring true. But Truscott's advice had been sound; it was based on a real person, so it ought to be convincing. In any case it was already too late to make changes. Perhaps he was going to fail. The only person he had held even the most desultory chat with was Lily. He resolved to project the Thorburn character for all he was worth for another week. If nothing had happened by then, he would go back to Bragg and report his failure. He refused to let his mind consider whether such an eventuality would cause him disappointment or relief, and he strode along above the Fleet sewer in a state of self-induced elation.

Lunch-time was frantic, as usual, and there was little opportunity to display his potential as a putter-down, amongst the heaving mass of clerks. About two o'clock, Lily came in. He found he was delighted to see her. She was warm, human and bubbling with fun. At least he would have something pleasurable to look back on when Thorburn was laid to rest.

'Hello, Fred,' she greeted him. 'Surprised to see me?'

'Transported to the seventh heaven of joy.'

'You ought to get a job in the music halls,' she smiled.

'Perhaps I'll try. How did you know my name, anyway?'

'A little bird told me,' she said archly.

'The landlord, I suppose. He's not a little bird, he's a greater red-faced beer-swiller.'

'S-sh!' Lily laid her finger across her lips. 'He might hear you.'

'Why did you bother to find out?'

'Because I like you.'

'I'm bad luck, my girl,' Morton said with mock sternness. 'Steer clear of me.'

'I'm in no danger, thanks.'

'Have you got a man-friend, then?'

'What, me? No fear!' she said scornfully. 'I can look after myself. I've got a proper job, too—I'm not on the streets.'

'Not a bad job, either, if it allows you to drink port at the rate you do.'

'Well, I deserve it, don't I?'

'None more, I'd say.'

'Your parents must have been well-off,' she remarked speculatively.

'Why do you say that?'

'Paying all that money for you to go to school.'

'I suppose they are—but little good will it do me.'

'Have they given you the order of the boot, then?'

'Years ago. I've almost forgotten what they look like.'

'What for?' she asked ingenuously.

'It happened when I lost my first job,' said Morton shortly.

'What was that?' she pressed him.

'It's not something that I want to talk about. I was in the army, but it didn't suit me, so I left.'

'Are you married?'

'Never have been, never will be,' he answered lightly.

The reply seemed to satisfy her and she sipped her port thoughtfully. At that moment she was far from being her own jolly unaffected self. The notion struck him that Lily might in some way be connected with the gang of counterfeiters. Certainly she was the only person who had exchanged more than superficial pleasantries with him. It seemed absurd! And yet she had been persistent with her questioning. She caught him staring at her.

'Have I got two heads or something?' she asked pertly.

'I was just thinking about your offer the other night,' he said insinuatingly.

She tossed her head. 'You men! You think you can have it just when it suits you. Well, I'm busy at the moment.' She settled her hat on her curls and, with a conspiratorial smile, went jauntily out.

The afternoon wore on without incident. Then at seven o'clock a group of men came in.

'A bottle of claret, and a scotch and polly,' called a voice he seemed to recognize. The man turned to hang his hat up. In consternation Morton realized that it was Wardle, the *Times* reporter.

'No Apollinaris left, sir,' he said apologetically.

'A jug of water, then.'

'Very good, sir.'

Morton took the drinks over, and was relieved to see that Wardle was sitting with his back to the bar. At least he had not been recognized instantly. He kept out of sight as much as possible and, when he had to go near their table, he sidled around it to keep his face turned away. After half an hour they left and the dull routine of the evening supervened. Nobody approached him; nobody showed the slightest interest in him. He began to feel deflated. About nine, Lily came in with a man. He was wiry, of medium height, with mousy hair and clean-cut features. Morton served them without being acknowledged by Lily. Perhaps he was some relative. They certainly did very little talking; sitting there with their drinks in companionable silence. He had been wrong about her being with the gang. This was the protector she wouldn't acknowledge, the man who really could have it when he wanted it.

CHAPTER _____

_____ SEVEN

Wednesday was a blank day also; just meaningless drudgery. Morton felt his mask was beginning to slip—but he doubted if the real Thorburn could have sustained his bonhomie with this job. He looked forward to Lily's arrival for some light relief, but she did not come.

At eight o'clock he complained of feeling unwell and was allowed to go. He walked quickly down Fleet Street and along the Strand; past the delicate stone cross that a doting King had raised to his dead wife, and on to the massive granite column that a besotted nation had erected in memory of a flamboyant admiral. He pulled out the scratched metal watch that had replaced his own. If Catherine's predictions were right, she would be at St James's church any time now. He eased the springs of his spectacles away from his ears for a few moments. It seemed that you either had to have the bridge of your nose crushed, or your ears torn off. Diabolical! He crossed Piccadilly Circus, dodging between the horses of omnibuses and growlers, and hurried along until he saw the railings of the churchyard. He then adopted what he had learned was the mien of indigence most likely to stir a

charitable chord in the hearts of the wealthy. He unbuttoned his
morning-coat, allowed his body to sag and his head to slump
forward; his gait became an aimless shuffle. Had he been able
to refrain from shaving it would have been better, and he
perhaps smelled too wholesome to be authentic—but it would
have to do. The church was restrained, with red-brick walls
and clear elegant windows; and embodiment of the refined
understatement of seventeenth-century taste. It was a strange
quirk of fate that it should have become the fashionable church
of modern ostentation. He turned towards the east end, and
went through a narrow doorway into the vestry hall. There
were only two gas-jets burning, but in the gloom he could see
Catherine talking to a man in clerical garb. Along one side of
the hall were trestle tables with discarded shirts, blouses and
underwear on them; on the other were racks of trousers, dresses
and coats. Some of the dresses were ridiculously elaborate for
the needs of the clientèle. Several women were turning over the
cotton shirts and blouses with an appraising eye. No doubt
some would find their way to the clothing exchange next
morning. Well and good! If they got a few pence for them, it
would relieve their poverty by so much. Morton sidled along
the table, stooping over it, till he got to within a yard of
Catherine. Then he waited for her to excuse herself from the
parson and approach him. He gave her a sidelong glance. He
was clearly in her field of vision, yet she was still looking
towards the doorway. The rector went off to talk to another
helper and Morton picked up a shirt.

'What size is this, mum?' he asked in a cockney voice.

'I am sorry,' said Catherine, 'I am afraid I do not
know . . . James!' she squeaked as he turned his head round.
'Don't do that! You surprised me.'

'Would you be able to have a cup of tea with me at the back,
there?' asked Morton quietly.

'I think so,' replied Catherine with some hesitation. 'So long
as we don't appear familiar.'

A woman poured them two cups of strong tea from an
enameled jug and they took them to chairs in the corner.

'Your disguise is very good,' said Catherine admiringly.

'It is mostly fatigue,' replied Morton with a brief smile. 'I
am working as a waiter in a pub and it's no easy matter, I can
tell you. Yesterday, Wardle from *The Times* came in. I was
terrified in case he would recognize me, but he didn't. I hope

he does not come in too often, or the penny is bound to drop.'

'Have you made any progress?' asked Catherine.

'Nothing specific has happened as yet, but I have a feeling that if any approach is to be made, it will be within the next couple of days.'

Catherine shivered. 'I wish you did not have to do it,' she said.

'You know my answer to that.'

'I suppose I do.' She bit her lower lip unhappily. 'Is there anything I should tell Sergeant Bragg?'

'It is hardly worth conveying a mere presentiment to him. However, since next Wednesday is so far off, I may well have to send some letters to Ada Smith.'

'I will keep an eye open!'

Morton drained his cup and wiped his mouth on the back of his hand. 'Much as I would like to stay with you,' he muttered, 'I must go. One day it may be important to have a longer time with you.' He rose defeatedly to his feet, and shuffled off.

Next morning, as the bar settled down after the rush of office-bound clerks, Morton was beckoned by the landlord.

'You can have a break now,' he said. 'Take this up to room number three, above the tobacconist's, next door.' He indicated a tray bearing a bottle of champagne in a bucket of ice and four glasses.

'Someone is making an early start,' Morton said with a smile.

'Can you open the bottle, in case they ask you?'

'I've opened a good few in my time.'

'Right. Be off then . . . and I want you back by noon.'

It was vaguely continental, thought Morton, to be carrying bottles of wine along the pavement. In this weather they ought to have tables on the pavements, like Paris or Vienna—but he wouldn't fancy it in these narrow streets, with the dust and the smell of horse dung. He found a doorway beyond the tobacconist's shop, with a flight of stairs leading upwards. At a half-landing, a short passage went off to the back. In it were brown-painted doors, numbered one and two in cream paint. Morton ascended the next short flight and was brought to the front of the building again. Number three was evidently the room directly over the shop. He rapped at the door and heard a woman's voice call. He turned the knob, the tray expertly balanced above his shoulder, and went in. The room was light and high-ceilinged, and filled with shabbily comfortable furniture. On a bed in the corner reclined Lily, clad in a thin wrap with a frill at the throat.

'It's my birthday,' she gurgled. 'Turn the key, will you, love?'

'Sounds as if it might be mine too,' replied Morton with a grin.

'Well? Aren't you going to open it?'

'Don't tell me you need it to get you going.'

'Saucy!' she admonished. 'I like it. Why shouldn't we have a little fun?'

'Why indeed?' Morton twisted off the wire cage and, placing the bottle between his thighs with the neck pointing towards Lily, began sensually to ease out the cork.

'You are a wicked devil, Fred,' she giggled.

The cork came out with a satisfying pop, and closing his eyes, Morton exhaled lasciviously. 'I enjoyed that,' he said, joining in her laughter.

'Bring them over here,' she ordered, patting the bed beside her. She hoisted herself into a sitting position, modestly covering her ankles.

Morton placed a glass in her hand and raised his own. 'Here's to a mutually satisfying connection,' he said.

'What's that supposed to mean?' she asked.

'Happy birthday, Lily. A happy birthday to both of us.'

He squatted on the bed facing her. She was not as plump as he had thought. Her waist was tiny, her hips broad. If she had been taller, she would have had a most elegant figure.

'Your eyes will pop out in a minute!' Lily exclaimed.

'Are you surprised? By God! You're good to look at, Lily. I've never seen such a luscious body as yours.'

She preened herself with pleasure. 'Can I have some more?' She looked towards the champagne. 'Pity to let it go flat.'

'I know something that feels it will never be flat again.'

'Want to bet?' she asked coquettishly.

He carried the glasses across and this time sat beside her. He kissed her softly on the mouth and felt the tip of her tongue against his lips. He pulled back and emptying his glass, set it on the floor. Then he turned to Lily and slipped his hand inside her robe. Her breast was firm and rounded, the nipple erect. He took her glass from her hand, parting her robe, began to suck her breast. She gasped and, wriggling her shoulders, allowed the wrap to fall away from her body.

'Why don't your take your clothes off?' she murmured.

Morton tore his clothes, dropping them in a heap on the floor.

'Oh my God!' cried Lily in a strangled voice. 'Look at him! He's like a barber's pole! You don't think you can get that inside me, do you?'

'It's your birthday present, Lily.' He wriggled in bed beside her, pressing himself against the soft curves of her body.

Their congress was satisfactory; carried out conscientiously on Morton's part, and on hers with virtuosity and a convincing simulation of passion. Afterwards they lay contentedly in each others arms for a long time. Then Lily roused herself.

'Fred?' she said.

'Yes?'

'I could get you a good job, if you wanted.'

'What's that?'

'In finance.'

'That sounds a bit high-flown for me,' said Morton doubtfully.

'It wouldn't mean figure-work, or anything like that.'

'Is the pay good?'

'Better than that stupid job you've got now.'

Morton looked across at the clock. 'Well, since I should have been back half an hour ago, I reckon I've lost that one. All right, I'll give it a go, if that's what you want.'

Lily smiled warmly. 'Well, if you will get your great carcass out of my bed, I'll make arrangements for you to see the boss.'

'Where is his office?'

'Oh, he doesn't have an office. He works from home. I'll try to fix for you to meet him here, tomorrow—say ten o'clock in the morning. Then if he can't come . . . well, I might just have another birthday!'

When Morton knocked on Lily's door next morning, it was answered by the mousy-haired man who had accompanied her to the Black Horse, two nights earlier.

'Mr Thorburn?' he asked in a warm musical voice. 'My name is Beasley, Herbert Beasley.'

'How do you do?'

The handshake was firm and friendly; the smile ingratiating

without obsequiousness. The man ought to be selling life-assurance policies, thought Morton.

'I understand that you are interested in the possibility of working for me.'

'If I can do the job, yes.'

'We would give you a trial,' said Beasley with his warm smile. 'If you were not suitable, we would part with no hard feelings.'

Morton felt the hairs prickle on the back of his neck. It was difficult to have hard feelings, when you were floating in bits down the river.

'I must say,' went on Beasley, 'that the person I am looking for has to have very special qualities. The post I am offering is as my personal assistant. It demands great integrity, and an ability to create confidence in the minds of our clients . . . I gather that Miss Curtis has satisfied herself that you are, so to speak, a real man.'

Morton turned with a half-smile to Lily, but her face was impassive.

'I cannot employ a nancy-boy,' said Beasley. 'They put clients' backs up—it's a matter of instinct. Well, now, can you give me some information about yourself?'

Morton looked uncomfortable. 'I was born on a sheep-station at Waipara in New Zealand,' he began hesitantly. 'My parents emigrated there from Cheddar in Somerset and they sent me back there to school.'

'That was in Wells?' Beasley commented.

'Yes.'

'Did you acquire any particular distinctions there?'

'Not unless being caned every day for three years is a distinction! No, I was captain of the rugby team, but that is about all.'

'Nevertheless, from your manner and address, they would appear to have civilized you to some extent.'

'Oh, I'm civilized all right—just not qualified for anything.'

'Ah, but you could be qualified for something very special, Mr Thorburn . . . Fred isn't it?'

'That's right, sir.'

'I gather from Miss Curtis, that you have no dependents, or indeed close family in this country.'

'Right.'

'What is your employment history?'

'I've just been bumming about, from one job to the next, all over England.'

'But I gather that, for a period, you were a soldier.'

'That is true,' said Morton shortly. 'I went into the army straight from school.'

'What regiment?'

'The Dorset Regiment.'

'And what was your rank?'

Morton stared straight in front of him. 'Captain,' he said.

Beasley laid down his pencil, and leaned back in his chair. 'Most people would be proud of the fact,' he remarked.

A dogged look settled on Morton's face. 'I'll tell you the truth,' he said, 'though it will mean I shall not get the job . . . It was over mess funds. It was my own stupid fault; I signed for all the money and stock from my predecessor, without doing a proper check. Honour of a gentleman, and all that rubbish. Then, when the deficiency came to light, I was stuck with it. The previous treasurer swore it was all there when he handed over, and he had my signature to back him up. So I had no defence.'

'And what happened?' asked Beasley silkily.

'I was cashiered, thrown out, with a black against my name for ever.'

Beasley pondered for a time, with a smile playing over his lips. Then he looked up. 'Well, Mr Thorburn, your candour does you credit, indeed you appear to have borne your tribulations with admirable resilience. Yes, I think we can proceed as far as the probationary stage.'

'Thank you, sir.'

'Be outside the Mansion House at eleven o'clock tomorrow morning and I will meet you there.'

As the *City Press* was published on Wednesdays and Saturdays only, Catherine had finished her working week by late Friday evening. Only the accounts and advertisement sections were really active on a Saturday morning, so when Catherine had suggested that she could be equally well employed at home, preparing for the coming week, the editor had readily agreed. She had been offered a temporary post, as a reporter on the paper, some fourteen months ago. Then, Mr Tranter had been sceptical. The idea of a woman writing for a City paper concerned primarily with economic movements and business

personalities had seemed to appall him. But the owner—no
doubt under gentle pressure from her father—had insisted, and
she had been appointed. She had been eager to learn, able to
work as hard as any man, and gradually the editor had been
charmed into grudging approval. Initially she had been given
assignments that might interest women, such as social and
charity affairs. Then, to satisfy a moralistic self-righteous
streak in her, she had taken a tilt or two at sharp practice in the
police and corruption in the City. As a result, she had been
caught up in a scandal which had almost cost her life. It was
James Morton and Sergeant Bragg who had rescued her then,
and ever since she had been involved with them in what
seemed to her a preponderantly one-sided relationship.
Though, to be fair, it had led to her being appointed as the
Star's occasional correspondent on City affairs, which was
another small step up the ladder. And here she was, sitting in
Bragg's room at Old Jewry, watching him read James's letter.

She had got up at her usual workaday hour that morning,
determined to intercept the post. It was well that she had done
so, for the family letters had been placed on the breakfast table,
including one addressed to Ada Smith. She had scolded the
cook roundly, then retired to her bedroom to read the letter.
She could have wept with vexation. It was full of trite
expressions of affection, trivial bits of gossip, and even an
occasional lapse of grammar. Surely he could have written
better than this? She would certainly have no desire to keep it!

'It's a bit difficult to tell where the message ends and the
padding begins, isn't it, miss?' said Bragg, scratching his
temple with his pipe-stem.

'It is mostly padding, if you ask me,' replied Catherine
crossly.

'At all events, there is a number in the second line, so it is
authentic . . . And when he wrote it, which was yesterday
afternoon, he was hoping to "start work" today—whatever that
means.'

'He had a feeling that he would be contacted, when I saw
him on Wednesday.'

'How did he look?'

'Dreadful! He was shabby and stooping, and his face was
pale and strained. I hated it!'

'Now, miss,' said Bragg, in gentle reproof, 'you must not
bring your own emotions into this. It won't help you, and it
could be fatal for him.'

Catherine flushed. 'I only hope no one else sees that letter!'

'Get away with you! Ada Smith would love it.'

'Is there anything I should tell him, if I see him on Wednesday?' asked Catherine coolly.

Bragg pondered. 'I don't think so. There is no point in lumbering his mind with useless information. He is holding the reins at the moment, we can do nothing but wait.'

Catherine decided to walk to the cab rank in King William Street; the exercise might work off some of her ill-temper. She was thoroughly irritated with herself. Nowadays she was perpetually cross and edgy. She certainly had not inherited it from her mother, who was vague and charming, and allowed nothing to ruffle her. Nor did she get it from her father. A successful portrait painter, he loved the social round for its own sake, though it was also a fruitful source of commissions. Perhaps their minds were too frail to stand the acquisition of learning, and their bodies too weak to cope with the strains of employment. The very thought made her more annoyed than ever and she glanced across the street to distract herself . . . and there was James Morton! Outside the Mansion House. It was certainly him, talking to two other men. He was looking better this morning, erect and cheerful. He seemed to be listening intently to what the older man was saying. On an impulse she lifted the hem of her skirt and raced back to Old Jewry. She gasped something to the duty-sergeant in the hall, and stumbled up the stairs to Bragg's room.

'They are there' she cried. 'Outside the Mansion House!'

'Steady on, miss,' said Bragg in concern. 'Sit down and get your breath back.'

'There is no time! You can capture them now!'

Bragg set a chair for her, and she reluctantly sat down.

'Now first of all, tell me who "they" are,' said Bragg in a matter-of-fact tone.

'James Morton and two men. They were talking together, on the pavement. James seemed to be taking instructions from one of them.'

'And you suggest that I should arrest them? What for?'

'Well, for . . . Well, at least you could be on hand for when the crime has been committed!' she spluttered.

Bragg took out his pipe and began to poke at the contents of the bowl with a spike on his knife.

'In some ways,' he said in a fatherly tone, 'you have got the

worst part in all this. I'm sorry, miss. I know you won't agree
with me, but this business is more important than any one
person's life, however appealing he may be. All I can say is
that if I could have done it myself, I wouldn't have let him
anywhere near it . . . Now don't concern yourself. He is a
fine policeman, and a sight cleverer than anyone he's likely to
be up against. He has a fair chance.'

'Fair?' Catherine exclaimed indignantly. 'You are not hand-
icapping race-horses! His life is at stake!'

'I told you he is in the driving seat,' said Bragg firmly. 'I
shall not intervene until he lets me know he's ready. Now why
don't you go home, and write some letters?'

'Just the kind of patronizing thing a man would say!' cried
Catherine, and flounced angrily out of the room.

To Morton it seemed odd to be waiting outside the Mansion
House for a business appointment. He wondered if Thorburn
would find it so. Presumably not, if he were used to operating
on the fringe of the underworld. He watched as a cab stopped
some distance away, in Queen Victoria Street, and saw Beasley
alight. Proper professional caution, thought Morton in approval. He was accompanied by another man, short and slim,
not much more than a youth. They crossed the road and, on
seeing Morton, Beasley held out his hand.

'Good morning,' he said. 'This is George Snell, one of my
assistants . . . Well now, Fred, your job would entail carrying out financial transactions with various City institutions, so
I thought a simple practical example would be a good idea. Are
you familiar with the workings of a bank?'

'I had an account with one, when I was in the army,' said
Morton.

'Then you will be familiar with paying sums in and
encashing cheques?'

'Yes.'

'Good, good! Well, as I indicated yesterday morning, for the
purpose of this trial I am less concerned with the mechanics of
the transactions, than with the relationship you can establish
with the other party. Now George is outstanding in his ability
to achieve a rapport with someone. He is going to cash a
cheque for me in the Union Bank over there. I would like you
to observe him and note his approach. And so as not to
influence the outcome, I suggest that you go into the bank first

and stand some distance apart. After George has completed his transaction, I want you to meet me in front of St Stephen's Walbrook, round the back here, and I will explain what you will be required to do.'

Morton sauntered across the road, in what he hoped was a relaxed manner, and entered the bank. The counters were moderately busy, so he took a seat at a table nearby and began to fill up a paying-in slip. A few moments later he saw Snell hurry through the door. There was a half-smile on his fresh face and a hint of swagger in his bearing. He looked around easily, as if seeking acquaintances, then crossed to one of the counters where there was a short queue. Before long, someone took up station behind him and Snell turned round with a flippant remark. He was every inch a young City clerk, thought Morton, cheerful, brisk, cheeky. When it was his turn at the counter, Snell held the cheque in full view, but made some remark before passing it over, thus drawing the cashier's gaze to his smiling, innocent face. Then he handed over the cheque confidently and leaned with one elbow on the counter. The clerk put a squiggle on the cheque and rubber-stamped it, then counted out ten ten-pound notes and pushed them under the grille. Snell picked them up with a brief word, and walked casually away.

When Morton followed, a few moments later, Snell was nowhere to be seen. He crossed the street and found the church Beasley had mentioned. He took up a position near the door and looked around him. Then he heard Beasley's voice calling him from inside the porch. He went into the church and followed Beasley to a pew below the organ.

'Useful places, churches,' said Beasley slyly, 'away from the world's din . . . Did you see Snell cash the cheque?'

'Yes.'

'Do you understand what I mean about the rapport with the cashier?'

'Yes,' said Morton doubtfully. 'but he is a typical clerk. I'm not.'

'Everyone has his own methods,' said Beasley. 'Now this is what I want you to do. Here is a cheque for nine hundred pounds, drawn on an account at Smith's bank over there. I would like you to encash it for nine one-hundred pound notes. But first you will have to pay in this note.' He passed over a bank-note folded in half and a paying-in slip for a thousand pounds.

'It should be simple enough,' remarked Morton.

'Yes, of course. But it is the relationship with the cashier that I want you to concentrate on . . . Now when you have completed the transaction, take the money back to Miss Curtis's room in Shoe Lane. I will meet you there.'

Morton walked at a measured pace towards the bank. He seemed preternaturally aware of his body. His head was too stiff and he was holding his right arm rigidly, as if to cover the contents of his pocket. He stopped at the kerb, while a cart rumbled by, and made a conscious effort to relax. Then he crossed the road, and went into the bank. It was almost empty and he was able to go straight to the counter.

'Good morning,' he said pleasantly.

The cashier looked up. 'Good morning, sir.'

Morton drew the papers from his pocket. He passed over the paying-in slip and opened out the bank-note as a courtesy . . . It had been issued by the Hull branch of the Bank of England, and was dated the twenty-ninth of March eighteen eighty-nine. He pushed it under the grille, his heart thumping. The cashier initialled the paying-in slip, then put it in a box on the counter. The note he placed in a division of his cash-drawer. Then he looked up with an enquiring smile.

Morton pushed the cheque under the grille nonchalantly. 'Hundreds, please,' he said.

The cashier looked at the cheque, then closed his drawer and locked it. 'One moment, please,' he said and went into a cubicle at the back of the banking-hall.

Morton could feel a constriction across his chest. Dammit, the man was going to check on the signature. Surely to God that would be genuine? He turned away from the grille and, leaning on the counter, idly surveyed his surroundings. It was not until he heard the cashier unlock his drawer, that he allowed himself to turn round.

'There we are, sir,' said the cashier, pushing the notes towards him. Morton heard in the distance his voice giving thanks, his hands fumbled the notes into his pocket and with studied casualness he walked out of the bank.

When he gained the street, Beasley was nowhere to be seen. Morton took a hansom as far as Ludgate Circus and walked the rest of the way to Lily's room. Snell was already there, and she greeted him with restraint, frowning a warning. He made friendly overtures to Snell and was snapped at in return. They sat in uneasy silence until there was a rap at the door and Beasley entered.

'I saw you return,' he said to Morton. 'Did all go well?'

'Of course,' said Morton airily.

'Good, good! May I have the money?'

Morton handed over his nine hundred pounds, and Snell his hundred. Beasley was beaming, his voice mellifluous, as he counted out five sovereigns and gave them to Snell, then forty-five pounds for Morton.

'What is this for?' exclaimed Morton with a laugh of disbelief.

'The putter-down always gets five per cent of the proceeds,' said Beasley.

'What is a putter-down?' asked Morton.

'One who utters a counterfeit note.'

'A counterfeit note? . . . You're kidding?'

'The thousand-pound note you paid into the bank was a counterfeit,' said Beasley, watching Morton intently.

'Well I'm buggered!' Morton allowed his puzzlement to dissolve into excited laughter. 'As easy as that, is it? My God, if I'd known, I would have shit my trousers! . . . Forty-five quid! It's the easiest money I've ever earned in my life!'

'Then the idea is not morally repugnant to you?'

'Not bloody likely! . . . Get my own back on those sods!'

Snell rose, his lip drawn back in dislike, and went out.

'Very good. Then shall we say that your employment will continue so long as it is mutually profitable?'

'Yes, indeed! . . . I can't think why you trusted me! After all, I might have decamped with the cash.'

'As to the trust, I pride myself on being a good judge of character; as to the money, you were closely followed by one of my associates and any attempt to do as you suggest, would have been . . . discouraged.'

Morton raised his eyebrows, then nodded. 'Fair enough,' he said.

Beasley got up. 'I suggest that you use your commission to buy some good clothes. I see you as a very wealthy young landowner, with all the confidence and assertiveness that high social position brings with it. Try to dress the part. When you are appropriately provided, Miss Curtis will take you to the quarters which you will occupy. I will see you there in due course.'

Morton winked at Lily, and followed Beasley out. He had hopes of tailing him to wherever he lived, but this was frustrated by Beasley's taking the only cab in sight. Instead, Morton strolled to the West End. He had an amusing vision of going to his Savile Row tailor, and asking for a putter-down's outfit. In the end he spent a good deal of the forty-five pounds on a lounging suit, a well-cut morning-coat and trousers, plus various shirts and ties, at a shop in Jermyn Street. Then he wandered slowly back towards the City. So far Bragg had been absolutely right. It was as if he were a puppeteer, sitting above, pulling the strings. He wondered what would happen when the new counterfeit was discovered. Would Bragg still be able to keep control of the situation? Well, all he could do was to act out his part to the best of his ability . . . Beasley was a thoroughly unpleasant individual. He clearly enjoyed uttering veiled threats—even when the recipient could not be expected to understand. There was a hint of violence in him—though probably vicarious. He could well have ordered the butchering of his predecessor, but someone else would have had to carry it out. No doubt it was the man who had shadowed him back. Had he tried to bolt, it would have been a quick knife between the ribs, and away.

When he got back to Shoe Lane, he found Lily sitting with an ice-bucket on the table by her.

'I decided you would like to buy me some champagne to celebrate,' she said, a little defensively.

Morton kissed her on the forehead, and dropped a sovereign down the front of her blouse. 'You've done me a good turn, Lily, and no mistake,' he said with a smile. 'It should have been a crate.'

'I thought you might be against it,' she said with relief.

'Not me!' said Morton airily, handing her the bubbling glass. 'At this rate I shall be rich in a year.'

'Don't count on it going on that long.'

'Ah well! Be grateful for what comes, as the bishop said to the actress . . . What's the matter with Snell?'

'What do you mean?'

'Every time he looks at me, you would think he had a pain in his guts.'

'You want to watch out for him, he's a miserable little devil.'

'Why?'

'Don't be stupid! From what he said when he came back, he had done something every bit as difficult and risky as you did; yet he gets a fiver for it, and you get forty-five.'

'Understood. Anyone else to look out for?'

'Not that I know of.'

'Right. I'd better change into my new aristocratic clothes, then we can be off.'

'I have a better idea,' she said with a cheeky look. 'Why don't we have another birthday?'

Morton wondered if he dared risk alienating his only ally.

'It's all right,' she said accusingly, 'I'm clean. I told you, I haven't been on the streets in months.'

'It wasn't that,' said Morton cautiously. 'I just thought you were Beasley's girl.'

'My body's my own,' she asserted sharply. 'He doesn't bleedin' own me . . . Come on,' she put her arms around Morton's neck and pressed against him. 'You're the best I've ever been with. Last time, I thought you were after my back teeth.'

'Come off it, Lily, you're not a street-girl now.'

'Bloody pig,' she countered good-naturedly. 'Anyway, I like you.'

'And I you, Lil.' He bent down and kissed her on the lips.

CHAPTER —————

————————— EIGHT

Early next morning they left Shoe Lane and walked down to Fleet Street. Morton was carrying his old clothes in a bag he had borrowed from Lily. The streets were almost deserted, just the clip-clop of a trotting cab-horse broke the silence—apart from the church bells, which seemed to be pealing at them from every direction.

'Do you fancy going to church, first?' asked Morton with a grin.

'Not me!' replied Lily scoffingly. 'They'd all die of shame, if I went in . . . Now, where are we going? I can't keep up with all these moves.'

She fished in her bag and brought out a small piece of paper. "Ah, yes. We want a cab as far as Beech Street.'

Morton signalled a passing hansom and they ambled gently northwards. To Morton it was a wholly unlooked for interlude; the warm rays of the sun, the pretty girl beside him, the joyous sound of the bells. But at the end of the journey, what?

They came to the corner of Beech Street at last, and Morton paid off the cab. It was all very well, he thought, having to act like a lord; but he had precious little money in his pocket. He wondered idly if he ought to keep an account of his earnings and expenses for Bragg; whether there would ever be a balance struck between the people he had defrauded and the losses he had saved.

Lily tugged at his arm and he realized they were walking along Golden Lane. He glanced across the road and could see the mortuary ahead of them. The last time he had been there, was to view the remains of a blond putter-down who had made a mistake. He shivered at the thought.

'What's the matter?' asked Lily. 'Are you cold?'

'Just short of sleep, that's all.' He grinned, and slid his arm round Lily's waist.

'Now, stop it, and act proper. You'll draw attention to us.'

'You don't need anyone to draw attention to you, Lil.'

She pushed him away with a happy smile. 'Come on, we turn up here.'

'Cupid's Court, eh? Should be all right for us!'

'You've had your lot for the moment,' she said, rapping at a door on the right hand side. There came a clumping noise from within and the door was flung open. The man standing there was so enormous that he filled the passage-way. He had craggy features and red hair, and his shirt sleeves were rolled up his knotted arms.

'Where've you been?' he asked in a hoarse, strangled voice. 'You should 'ave been 'ere last night.'

'We were delayed,' said Lily airily. 'We couldn't complete his lordship's wardrobe, till Petticoat Lane market opened this morning . . . Fred, this is Albert Goulter.'

Goulter nodded mistrustfully at Morton, then led the way to a kitchen at the back. He sat down in a chair by the table end and, taking up a piece of wood, began whittling it with a clasp-knife.

'Mr Thorburn is to stay here with you for the time being, Albert,' said Lily.

'I know.'

'Right, well I'll be off, then.' Lily smiled briefly at Morton, and hurried out.

Morton walked to the window. There was a small yard at the back, but no means of egress. There was a seven-foot wall on the left, which separated it from what was presumably an identical yard next door; and both were surrounded by the blank towering walls of warehouses. All well and good. The

house itself was a typical two-up, two-down and gave directly
on to the street. It should be easy enough to take by
storm . . . It was a couple of streets inside the Met area,
though. Pity!

'Wot you lookin' at?' growled Goulter menacingly.

Blast it! thought Morton. He really must be on his guard
every moment. 'Lines of escape,' he said. 'I was in the army.
It's the first thing you should think of.'

'Are you criticizin' me?' Goulter heaved himself to his feet,
threateningly.

'I didn't know it was your responsibility.'

'Well, it is.'

Morton looked at Goulter, feigning indifference. He was
clearly immensely strong, but probably not too quick on his
feet. In a straight wrestling match Goulter would always win;
one might be able to catch him off balance, to give one an
opportunity of escape, but no more.

'If this was the best you could do,' said Morton, 'then it isn't
your fault.'

Goulter looked at him uncertainly, then sat down again. 'It's
always, "Find somewhere else, Albert". This is the third place
in a week,' he complained hoarsely.

'You want to have a few up your sleeve,' Morton said with
a smile.

Goulter's look hovered between resentment and toleration.
'It's not easy, with all these blue-bottles swarming around.'

'Who are they looking for? . . . Us?' asked Morton.

'No! Some cove who knocked off a copper . . . 'ere,' he
asked truculently, 'd'you smoke?'

'No.'

'You can bunk in with me, then. Otherwise you'd have had
to share with Snell.'

For the first time, Morton regretted that he had not acquired
the habit. 'I'll go and settle in, then,' he said.

'Front room,' rasped Goulter and began to cut smaller
slivers from near one end of the stick with his knife, digging
into the wood, shaping a groove, a neck . . .

The bedroom was small, and made awkward to furnish by
the chimney breast. There was a cupboard in the left alcove;
the right was occupied by the head of an iron bed, stretching to
the door. From the crumpled bedclothes this must be Goulter's.
Morton's own bed was on the opposite wall, with the foot

under the sash window. He made it up with the sheets and blankets placed on it. Then he gently tried to lift the bottom window; it moved with a slight squeak. The drop was no more than ten feet; it would suffice at a pinch. He must try to free that window, if he got the chance.

Just before nine o'clock on the Monday morning Bragg found himself sitting outside the clerk's room of Sir Rufus Stone's chambers. Bewigged barristers were already bustling about, calling for briefs and looking for books in the row of shelves that filled one wall of the corridor. Precisely on nine o'clock the clerk approached him.

'Sir Rufus will see you now, sir. I think you know the way.'

Bragg went down the corridor and tapped on the coroner's door.

'Come in.'

He entered the room, to see Sir Rufus tying up a bundle of documents with green tape, a grim smile on his face. Although he glanced in Bragg's direction, he did not greet him. He crossed to the side table, dropped the bundle on it, then swung round.

'I have a distinct impression, Bragg, that you have been avoiding me,' he said sarcastically.

'I've been rather busy, sir,' said Bragg deferentially.

'Well, I hope it will not inconvenience you too much if I confer with you, as my officer on the jig-saw man case.'

'It is going quite . . .'

'Enough!' He held up his hand. 'In my conferences, I speak and my clients pay for the privilege of listening. We will conform to at least the first part of that proposition.'

'Yes, sir.'

'It is seldom, Bragg, that I am outwitted, in court or out. And I am incensed at the growing conviction that I have been comprehensively duped by you.'

'Not duped, sir.'

'Yes, sir. Duped! You took advantage of the trust which has built up between us over the last several months, and induced me to take no part in the investigation of this case—which, moreover, it is my sworn duty to direct . . . What have you to say?'

'I can promise you that the investigation is proceeding, Sir Rufus. As to not keeping you informed, I am still convinced that you would be gravely embarrassed if your superiors asked you about it.'

'Superiors?' trumpeted the coroner. 'I'll have you know, Bragg, that I acknowledge no superior save the Queen, and beyond her my own conscience.'

'Yes, sir.'

'Now Bragg, I have kept my ears open in the club and listened, for a change, to my wife's foolish gossip, and not one whiff of scandal can I detect. From which I deduce that you have been lying to me—no doubt for weighty reasons, but lying nevertheless. Unless, therefore, you terminate this duplicity voluntarily, I shall apply *force majeure* to compel it.'

'I see, sir,' said Bragg in a neutral voice.

'Yes, Bragg, I shall remove you from the case.' He glared at Bragg, with a smile of triumph forming at the corners of his mouth.

'You put me in a difficult position, sir.'

'I know. I intend to. As I argue the point, you would not adopt so devious a course, unless the case were of considerable personal interest to you. Therefore, the most direct way of forcing your hand, is to propose to dismiss you from it.'

'I shall be breaking a solemn undertaking given at the highest level, if I do,' urged Bragg.

'That is a small matter, compared to your duty to me. Come now, stop shilly-shallying. Who is this old lady?'

'The Old Lady of Threadneedle Street, sir,' said Bragg baldly.

'The Bank of England? Great Heavens!' Sir Rufus crossed to his chair, swivelling it round to face Bragg. 'And why is her reputation at stake?' he asked suspiciously.

'To get the full picture, you will have to consider two cases together, the murder of Constable Walton and the dismembered body in the sewer. Operationally, the two are being dealt with separately.'

'I know,' interrupted Sir Rufus. 'Sergeant Roker is my officer for the first, and you for the second.'

'It is vitally important that the two are kept apart, in my view.'

'Your views are of no account, Bragg. Nevertheless, I am prepared to listen to what you have to say, before I make up my own mind. But there must be no holding back! Understand?'

'Yes, sir.'

'Well, then?'

'I said there are two cases, but they are closely linked. The man who shot Constable Walton is the same man we fished out of the Fleet. He had just cashed in a counterfeit note for one thousand pounds at the Bank.'

Sir Rufus whistled.

'The case is being investigated from two angles; the search for Walton's murderer is being handled by Chief Inspector Forbes, while I am looking for the murderer of the putter-down.'

The coroner rose from his desk with a frown, and took up his favourite pose before the fireplace.

'I begin to think,' he pronounced, 'that you have but a passing acquaintance with Truth, if you have ever met her. Are you telling me that you are prepared to allow half the police-forces of London to go blundering around, at great public expense, while you know Walton's murderer is lying on a slab in the mortuary? . . . No, don't answer! I should have the greatest difficulty in believing anything you said.' His eyes narrowed and he threw back his leonine head, 'I have it!' he exclaimed triumphantly. 'It all derives from some ridiculous internal rivalry in the City force. I could not understand how you would so tamely allow yourself to be supplanted as my officer for the Walton case. But of course you have the jump on them, and you are investigating the whole affair unknown to anyone else.'

'You are wrong, sir,' said Bragg quietly.

'Wrong?' exclaimed the coroner wrathfully. 'How am I wrong?'

'I have been charged by the Commissioner to investigate the central issue of the forgery gang; and it has been made clear that my activities are to be kept secret—particularly from the other investigating team.'

'I can't see what all the fuss is about,' exclaimed Sir Rufus. 'There have always been forgeries, always will be. What is so special about this one?'

'It is so perfect, that the only person at the Bank of England who could say for certain it was a counterfeit, was the head printer.'

'Hmn.' Sir Rufus pursed his lips.

'The Governor has seen the Chancellor of the Exchequer and their considered view is that, if the public became aware of the quality of these forgeries, there would be a run on the banks that could cause the economy to collapse. The whole existence of the forgeries is to be kept secret.'

'Pshaw!' snorted the coroner. 'These politicians are afraid of their own shadows. What harm would it do to go back to barter for a bit?—they do it all the time in the country. Come to think of it, now that income tax is at this iniquitous level of sixpence in the pound, I would be better off if some of my clients paid me in cases of port!'

'The situation is, sir, that the Bank of England insists its primary duty is to protect the currency. The two murder enquiries have been subordinated to that.'

'Are you saying that the Governor and the Chancellor are prepared to acquiesce in this monstrous waste of public money on a police exercise which can only put the public on enquiry, and which you would have me believe is part of an operation to keep the existence of the forgeries secret? . . . By God, it is impossible to plumb the black depth of your mind, Bragg!'

'I don't know about the Governor, sir. I took my orders direct from the Commissioner. You could ask him—though I'd be glad if you didn't. He easily gets worried.'

The coroner gave a snort of laughter. 'Very well, Bragg, I will give you all the time you need. But God help you if you fail!'

Morton woke up on the Monday morning feeling dull and jaded. Even washing himself down with cold water failed to restore any feeling of well-being to his tired body. The previous afternoon Goulter had brought in a dozen bottles of stout and, during the course of a tense and mistrustful evening, he had consumed most of them. Not that he had become drunk. He had sat by the window, morosely carving his mannikin. When it was finished, he turned it in his fingers for a while. Then with a sudden flare of anger, he snapped off the head and threw the pieces into the fireplace. Several times Morton had tried to initiate a conversation, only to be answered by a sneering grunt, or a snarled comment that killed the attempt. When dusk fell, Morton went upstairs to bed. He took the opportunity to try the windows and managed to drag the top one down by four or five inches; the bottom one refused to move more than half an inch . . . It was after the church clocks had struck twelve, that Goulter came up. He made no attempt to be quiet. He blundered about the room, pulling off his clothes; then seeing the opened window, slammed it shut. He fell asleep instantly and began to snore like the last trump. Morton was sure he could hear the roof-tiles rattling. He tossed and turned in the sweltering heat, only falling asleep in the early hours, when Goulter's snoring abated. Now he felt drained and dull—a dangerous state to be in.

Since breakfast Goulter had been sharpening his clasp-knife on a whetstone; tenderly stroking oil on to its surface and massaging the blade along it in a slow circular motion. Morton wondered if Dr Burney was right about the weapon that had killed the blond man. The blade of this knife was four inches long. It would easily penetrate the chest cavity. At length Goulter appeared satisfied. He tore a piece out of a newspaper and, holding it vertically, drew the knife gently across its edge. The severed piece dropped, then fluttered to the floor. Goulter grunted in satisfaction. He rose to take the stone to the dresser, as Beasley entered.

'Don't go, Albert. I may need you,' he said curtly. He sat down opposite Morton and began to scrutinize him minutely.

'Take off your glasses, Fred,' he ordered. Morton complied, his heart thumping.

'Yes, I thought so,' muttered Beasley.

Morton realized that Goulter had gone over to the window behind him.

'Now suppose,' said Beasley silkily, 'that you are really a nob—one of the élite . . . How would you talk?'

Morton could feel the hairs on his scalp prickling, his throat had gone dry. He forced a smile.

'I suppose I would speak something after this fashion,' he said in his normal voice.

'Excellent! excellent! Can you keep it up?'

'I can try.'

'Practise it, Fred. It is a great improvement for our purposes. Can you manage without your glasses?'

'I am only slightly short-sighted,' replied Morton.

'Good. I think you should dispense with them when you are working. They make you look too much like a clerk.'

'Very well.' Morton was feeling sick with relief.

'I like your new clothes,' said Beasley with a snigger. 'You obviously have good taste.'

'I just asked for the best,' replied Morton shortly.

'An authentic accent is very important,' observed Beasley. 'I spent a few years in America in my twenties,' he went on with a confiding smile, 'and I have never regretted it. In particular, my familiarity with the accent has often stood me in good stead over here.' His smile took on an engaging youthfulness. 'Once I went into Childs & Co in Gresham Street and said I was one of the Vanderbilt family, over on vacation. I was taken to the manager's office and given brandy and cigars. Then I explained that I had spent rather more than I intended and had wired home for more funds.' Beasley's voice had taken on the clipped, slightly nasal tones of a wealthy New Yorker. 'I asked if he could accommodate me for a few days to the extent of five thousand pounds, and took out of my bag a bundle of share certificates—all counterfeit, of course. His eyes nearly popped out of his head as I turned them over. I suggested he take a certificate for a hundred thousand shares in a Pennsylvania coal mine as collateral, and within ten minutes I had my five thousand.' He laughed exultantly, 'I would have liked to see his face when he realized the advance had not been repaid and the certificate was worthless!'

Morton summoned up a murmur of admiration.

'Well now,' went on Beasley, 'there are two things I want you to do this morning. Then this afternoon I would like you to help George and Miss Curtis in the West End—they will show you what to do.'

'Fine.'

'Now this is the first thing. I want you to select a firm of solicitors and ask to see the senior partner—that's important. Then instruct the firm to collect a debt of one thousand pounds from these people.' Beasley gave Morton a slip of paper with a name and address in the East End on it. 'This is who you are.' he passed over a white oblong of pasteboard, beautifully engraved in black copper-plate. 'The loan transaction is perfectly genuine, as this agreement will testify. You may leave it with him, if he so desires.'

'What is the point of it, then?'

Beasley beamed. 'Casting our bread upon the waters, Fred . . . but be sure it is a large firm of solicitors.'

'I'll call at the Guildhall library, and find the biggest from the *Law List*.'

'No! Don't do that!' Beasley threw up his hands in consternation. 'The first rule of this game is never to over-elaborate.

It increases the risk of being caught. The solicitor describes you to the police, the police make enquiries and find someone who remembers seeing you that same day, looking at the *Law List*. That has doubled the number of people who can identify you. Far better to pick your mark by using your own judgement. When you have finished, come back here.'

Morton took a hansom from the Barbican to the Bank. He felt oddly exposed without his spectacles. They had been the major element of his new appearance, and with them he had felt proof against recognition. Now his friends were more of a threat than his enemies. But at least it was good to be free of those clawing springs! The accent business was a relief, too, though he had become quite attached to his rolling Rs. Now he could concentrate on his major problem, without being fearful that a slip of the tongue would give him away. He selected a firm of solicitors in Throgmorton Street. From the external paintwork it appeared to occupy two adjacent premises, and although the paint was dusty, the brass plate had been so relentlessly polished as practically to obliterate the firm's name. He pushed open the door and found himself in a small reception area. A young woman was sitting behind the desk— that made it a very progressive firm! She smiled at him brightly.

'I would like to see the senior partner,' Morton said in warm, measured tones.

'I am afraid that I have just taken a gentleman up to see Mr Prothero. Can anyone else help?'

'No, I prefer to deal with principals. Can you tell me for how long Mr Prothero will be engaged?'

'I would not think for more than half an hour.'

'In that case,' said Morton with a smile, 'I shall take the opportunity to look around St Mary-le-Bow. It is one of the few City churches I have not yet visited.'

The girl looked surprised, but approving. Perhaps Beasley was right about over-elaboration, Morton thought as he reached the street. No doubt the remark had contributed to the picture of an upright, serious-minded citizen, but because of it, she would remember him more clearly. In expiation, he did walk along to the church and spent a few moments relaxing in its cool shadows. Then he strolled back.

'Mr Prothero is free now,' the young woman greeted him, and beckoned him to follow her. She led him up a narrow staircase and Morton's heart was lightened by the sight of her trim ankles beneath the hem of her skirt. She showed him into a pleasant room overlooking the street. Prothero was already standing and leaned over his desk to shake hands. He was a vigorous man in his early fifties, with a firm handclasp and a shrewd countenance.

'This is a trifling matter, Mr Prothero,' said Morton, 'and one with which I would not normally trouble a firm of your eminence. However, I am looking for a solicitor to take over the family's affairs, and I felt this would be an excellent opportunity to get to know one another.' He passed over the business card.

'Excellent, Mr . . . er, Ballard.' Prothero was almost purring. 'And in what can we be of assistance, this morning?'

'It is a small matter of a loan. I advanced a thousand pounds to a friend of a friend, and it has not been repaid on time. As you will readily understand, I do not wish to pursue the matter myself, but I hope that a letter from you will produce the desired outcome.'

'Of course,' said Prothero. 'Was there a formal agreement?'

Morton passed over the contract and Prothero skimmed through it. 'It seems all in order,' he commented.

'Here is the man's private address,' said Morton, passing over the slip of paper. 'I would prefer you to write to him there, in case he is embarrassed by having your letter opened by his secretary.'

'Certainly.' Prothero rose to his feet. 'I will get a letter off today.'

Another firm handshake, and Morton regained the open air. He was bubbling with exhilaration, almost wanting to laugh out loud. Whatever was at the back of this ploy, it was exciting to draw people into these imaginary situations. He had been pretending to do something which he might well have done in real life; but it was all a fantasy, all pretence . . . Penal servitude for five years; that was the sentence for false pretences. It was a sobering thought. He decided to walk back to Cupid's Court, to clear his system of this dangerous elation.

Morton hammered on the door of the house, and it was flung open by Goulter.

'Is Mr Beasley here?' asked Morton.

'No,' growled Goulter, 'he don't stay long in one place.' He strode back to the kitchen, and picked up a knife from the table. It had a fixed blade some seven inches long, with a thick back to strengthen it, and was rivetted through the tang to a stout wooden handle. Goulter tested the sharpness of the blade on his thumb, then he began to whet it lovingly on the oil-stone. At his feet was kind of holster on a belt, in which were two similar knives.

'What is that for?' asked Morton interestedly.

'The first copper as shows 'is bloody nose in 'ere, that's wot.' He kept on whetting the blade, drawing it in a slow loop down the length of the stone. Morton could see that its surface was burnished to a pearly silver. It must be sharp as a razor already, and yet he kept on with this sensuous, manic sharpening.

Morton crossed to the dresser and took one of Goulter's remaining bottles of stout. He watched him intently out of the corner of his eye, lest this larceny should trigger an assault.

'I'll buy you another,' he said as he prised up the cap. Goulter merely grunted. So he was not touchy about his possessions. And yet there was an insane streak within him that could erupt into unpredictable violence. His musings were interrupted by the return of Beasley. He listened to Morton's report with approval, and then gave instructions for him to discount a bill of exchange at Stephen Kirby & Co. It was drawn in a sum of two thousand pounds, and was payable almost three months hence.

Morton was beginning to lose his fear and he joined the queue at the counter with only a moderate quickening of the pulse. Of course, it was easy for him; discovery could never lead to a gaol sentence—but it would mean the failure of his mission. Fortunately, it was nearing one o'clock and the clerk was under pressure. He glanced at the bill, stamped it and made out a cash slip. Morton strolled over· to the cashier's desk, collected his money and went slowly out. Nineteen hundred and seventy-five pounds! Money for old rope. There was no doubt a great deal of skill and flair needed in the forging of these instruments, but once that was done, there seemed to be little difficulty in negotiating them. Everybody in the City was too busy to worry whether they were genuine or not. No, that was not right. They proceeded on the unquestioned assumption that they were genuine. Once there was substantial cause to think that any note or bill they received could be forged, then the City would suddenly cease to function, like a

steam engine with a burst boiler. It gave Morton a perverse
satisfaction. The Governor was right, and the risks he was
taking were justified.

He met Beasley in St Peter's Cornhill and handed over the
proceeds. Beasley seemed relaxed and gratified. He gave a
one-hundred pound note back to Morton. 'You owe me a quid,'
he said with a smile. 'Now go back to the house, and Snell will
come to pick you up.'

Morton had a dozen oysters and a glass of champagne in a
hotel bar, as befitted his appearance; then he scribbled a note
for Ada Smith and posted it. He took a cab to Beech Street,
smiling at the thought of the bank-note nestling amongst his
meagre reserve of small change.

When he got to the house, Snell had not yet arrived. Goulter
was lugubriously sharpening a second knife. It was longer than
the first and he adopted a different technique, caressing one
section of the blade at a time over the stone. Morton stood and
watched him, wondering at his total absorption in the task.
There was a knock at the door and Morton answered it. Snell
came in, with a sneer on his face and a cigarette dangling from
the corner of his mouth. Morton closed the door and followed
him down the passage. As Snell entered the kitchen there was
a hoarse shout from Goulter.

'Put that fucking fag out!'

Snell gave a pert reply and Goulter lashed out with the knife,
narrowly missing Snell and burying the point in the table. He
rose to his feet angrily, dragging at the handle. There was a
sharp 'ping'. Goulter looked at the knife in anguish. A quarter
of an inch of the blade had snapped off. He gave a roar like a
bull elephant, and began to lumber round the table in pursuit of
the white-faced Snell. While Morton was standing in the
doorway there was no means of escape, though the table was
big enough for Snell to elude his pursuer—unless Goulter
should take it into his head to overturn it.

Snell was alternately swearing and begging Goulter to lay
off, but it was only a matter of time before the big man
cornered him. Deciding that bloodshed in the gang would not
suit his purposes, Morton moved slightly to one side. Snell saw
the gap and shot through it like a rat up a drainpipe. Goulter
heaved Morton aside as they heard the door bang.

'You let 'im get away!' Goulter shouted menacingly.

'I didn't want you to cut him up, that's all,' replied Morton quietly, 'Beasley wouldn't like it.'

'Fuck Beasley! I don't take no lip from 'im . . . Look wot the little runt made me do.' Goulter gazed sorrowfully at the broken knife.

'Never mind,' said Morton clapping him on the shoulder. 'You'll be able to grind a new point, won't you? It'll be as good as new.'

He caught up with Snell at the corner of Golden Lane. He was leaning against the wall, dragging on another cigarette to calm his nerves.

'He nearly did for me,' he babbled. 'Bloody lunatic! That's the second time he's been at me—and all over a bleedin' fag.'

'Some people find them objectionable,' Morton observed mildly.

'Some people are stupid. But I'll do for him, straight I will. I'll get a gun, and next time I'll shoot the bastard.'

'I doubt if they would give you a license,' said Morton straight-faced.

'Are you being funny, mister?'

'Apparently not,' Morton grinned. 'Now perhaps you would tell me where we are going?'

'Lily's place, for a start.'

'Right.' Morton hailed a hansom that was cruising by on the other side of the road, and soon they were clattering down the street towards Ludgate Circus. Morton felt in his trouser pocket for the fare. 'I don't suppose you could change this for me, could you?' he asked, pulling out the hundred-pound note. 'I have very little change.'

'What do you bloody think?' replied Snell with a resentful sneer.

They put together a shilling in pennies and threepenny bits, and paid off the cab; then made their way separately to Shoe Lane. Morton hurried past the Black Horse, and hovered in the doorway of the tobacconist's until Snell had been inside for five minutes.

'Real bundle of fun, you two,' Lily greeted him.

'Albert Goulter is not the most relaxing of companions,' said Morton lightly.

Lily shivered theatrically. 'He gives me the creeps. He'll kill somebody one day, with those knives of his.'

Snell looked up quickly as if to add something, then thought better of it.

'Well, we haven't much time,' said Lily in a businesslike way, 'so let's get on. Beasley tells me you are to help me and George this afternoon. Have you ever done the trip up lay, Fred?'

Morton shook his head in puzzlement.

'It's how I earn my living,' said Lily with a giggle.

'Sounds a damn risky way to go at it!' replied Morton grinning.

Lily gave him a warning look. 'Not if it's done properly.'

'All right,' said Morton, 'tell me what it's about.'

'George knocks into our mark and pushes him against me. I lift his pocket book and walk off. Now this is where you come in. If the mark realizes he's been robbed before we are properly away, and makes a fuss, you come up saying you are a policeman and wanting a statement and so on.'

'Me?' exclaimed Morton. 'Me a copper? That's a laugh!'

'You'd make a lovely one.'

'I couldn't carry it off in these clothes.'

'Don't worry. The dicks are posh up West.' Lily crossed to the mantel-piece, and handed him a note-book and a grubby piece of pasteboard.

'Beasley said I was to give you these.'

It was a more than passable imitation of a Metropolitan police constable's warrant-card.

'So my job is to keep you both in sight, and shove my oar in if there's a fuss.'

'Yes. We'll start in Piccadilly Circus, go up Regent Street and then left along Oxford Street. All right, George?'

'As good as any,' Snell mumbled.

'Oh, and in case anyone gets any ideas,' said Lily pertly, 'you boys help me with this for free!'

They took separate cabs to different streets around the Circus and it was some time before Morton located his accomplices. He took off his hat, wiped the brim as a signal and began to stroll slowly along the pavement. Lily and Snell were at no time together, and yet they had an uncanny understanding of each other's reactions. Several times Lily positioned herself near a potential mark, only to draw away as she sensed that Snell was dissatisfied.

They drifted into Regent Street. When they were halfway

up, Morton perceived a new pattern in their movements. Snell went into a shop doorway, Lily turned round and began to walk slowly back in the middle of the pavement. Morton glanced up the street. An elderly man was wandering towards them, his frock-coat open in the heat. From his appearance he was wealthy, and he looked as if he had lunched well. As he passed the shop, Snell emerged and walked to the edge of the pavement, as if he wanted to cross the street. There were plenty of cabs and vans coming towards them, their horses labouring because of the incline. It was all a matter of timing, Morton realized. Lily would glance in the shop-windows as she strolled along, and presumably had a good idea of how close the mark had come to her. Snell trailed along behind, still peering between the gaps in the traffic . . . It all happened in a twinkling. Lily imperceptibly increased her pace as the man overtook her. Snell jumped from the gutter on to the pavement to avoid a delivery van, cannoned into the mark, swinging him round so that he was pushed into Lily. Morton heard Snell's off-hand apology as he darted across the street. The mark was glaring angrily after him, while at the same time expressing his regrets to Lily. She murmured something to him and smiled—then she was gone. The man continued on his way grumpily and after five minutes Morton turned back.

He caught up with them in Oxford Street. They seemed already to have selected their mark, a prosperous-seeming man who was looking intently at the watches in the window of an expensive jeweler. Snell was a hundred yards to the west of him, Lily about the same distance to the east. They were both hovering aimlessly. Then the man left the window and began to walk slowly towards Lily. This time she could see her victim all the time, and Morton could only admire the skill with which she controlled the situation. There was a knot of people just behind her, and she slowed her pace till they came almost level with her shoulder and some three feet away. The mark changed course to pass through the gap, just as Snell accelerated for it. The man was jostled into Lily, his shouts of protest following the retreating Snell. Again there was the apology to Lily—this time with a polite raising of the hat at her gracious smile.

But Lily had barely vanished into the side street, when the man clutched at his breast in consternation. 'I've been robbed!' he cried angrily. 'Help! Police! I've been robbed!' Morton counted to ten, then rushed up to the scene. He took his forged warrant-card from his pocket-book and waved it under the man's nose.

'I am a police officer,' he said authoritatively. 'Can you tell me what you have lost?'

'My pocket-book and cheque-book! I had them in my pocket outside the jeweller's, I know.'

'And when were they stolen, sir?' Morton slowly took the note-book from his pocket and turned to a fresh page.

'Well, it must have been just now. I've only come fifty yards, man!'

'Constable,' Morton corrected him. 'Are you sure you didn't leave them on the shop counter, sir? It often happens.'

'I told you, constable, I didn't go into the jeweller's.'

Morton looked at his notes. 'No, you didn't say that, sir,' he replied stolidly. 'You said you had them outside the jeweller's. That could have been before you went in, sir.'

'Well, I will tell you now, constable. I did not go into the shop.'

'Very good, sir. What is your full name?'

'John Alfred Bramley.' Morton wrote it down slowly.

'And your address?'

'Ten, Church Street, St John's Wood.'

'I shall have to ask you to come to the police station and make a full statement, sir,' said Morton. 'Now, if you will just stay here, I will see if I can find a cab. I don't expect you feel like walking to Marlborough Street in this heat.'

He put away his note-book, touched his hat to the man and strode purposefully away. Once out of sight, he dived down a side street, and came back on to Oxford Street several blocks nearer Marble Arch. Then, snapping on his spectacles and carrying his hat in his hand, he began to prospect around for his accomplices. After a few minutes he saw Snell, leaning against a lamp-post, reading a newspaper. As he approached, Snell shook his head slowly, folded up the paper and wandered away.

So that was it. Work finished for the day. Morton left the main street and took off his spectacles. He might as well enjoy the sunshine. There were some benches on the green outside St George's church. He could see the square from here, the shadows of the plane trees dappling the grass. As he strolled towards the square, a young woman was just leaving one of the benches. That would be admirable, if no one got there first.

Still, it was too hot to hurry. She was pretty and demure as she came up to him, a young married woman, perhaps, with the housework finished and no children to occupy her. She was looking up at him with a half-smile, when a man came dashing round the corner. He tried to avoid them, but his boot slipped on the smooth paving stones and he collided with Morton. He muttered something and ran on; but Morton was more concerned about the girl.

'Stupid idiot!' he exclaimed. 'People shouldn't run about like that in a city.'

'It's all right,' she laughed unsteadily, smoothing her dress. 'It was not your fault. Anyway, you didn't hurt me.' She smiled at him and walked on.

Moments later Morton heard a shrill 'Oh shit!' He ran back, to see the girl scampering up a side street for her life. On the pavement lay a small grubby oblong of pasteboard.

CHAPTER _____

_____ NINE

'Ah, there you are, Bragg.' The Commissioner sank into the chair by Bragg's desk and mopped his brow. 'Damned hot,' he grumbled, 'and not yet ten o'clock.'

'You ought to get some tropical suits made, sir,' said Bragg with a smile.

Sir William looked up sharply to see if Bragg was roasting him, then cleared his throat, 'I've come to see how you are getting on with the you-know-what,' he said in a conspiratorial tone. 'Not easy to come down here without the others seeing.'

'Things are going according to plan, sir,' said Bragg confidently. 'I had intelligence this morning from a reliable source, that our friend has taken up the post we hoped for, and that he has been involved in two transactions.'

'Has he now? Well done! . . . This reliable source?'

Bragg hesitated. If the Commissioner were told that a newspaper reporter was involved, he would probably have a heart attack. 'I am sure you would prefer not to be aware of it, sir,' he said.

'Oh? Why is that?'

'It could be embarrassing to you, sir.'

'Ah! I see . . . yes.'

'How is the main attack going, sir?'

'Not well,' said Sir William despondently. 'Not well.'

'How's that, sir?' asked Bragg suppressing a smile of satisfaction.

'At first we got a good deal of information as a result of the reward offered—far more then could be dealt with. That which we have followed up, has turned out to be worthless. Either that, or too much time had elapsed before we could mount our operation . . . The Bank is still keeping a tight hold on the campaign, and with so much political support, I cannot disregard the Governor's wishes . . . But if you ask me, it was a mistake from the start. Offering a king's ransom for information, meant every clown and crack-pot in London has been writing in.'

'But the Bank are satisfied, are they?' asked Bragg.

'They have damned little to be satisfied about,' said the Commissioner glumly. 'But the Governor refuses to change his policy . . . And you know what will happen. This forgery business will come out, and the newspapers will be howling for my head on a platter.'

'They wouldn't do that, would they, sir?' asked Bragg, in shocked tones.

'It's only just round the corner. The rank and file in the City are already preparing to disengage. The CI and Inspector Cotton were given a very rough ride by the protection committee yesterday. There has also been a spate of forged bills and cheques and what-have-you. The financial people are determined to link that with the counterfeit notes, and argue that it is the same gang. The Governor insists that there is no connection.'

'And who is winning?' asked Bragg.

'One might say the Governor still has his nose in front, but is tiring badly,' said Sir William with a foxy smile. 'Yesterday, he had to admit that they had received another forged thousand-pound note, just like the first.'

'The same date as well?'

'Yes.'

'That means the forgers only have the one plate. At least the banks should be relieved at that.'

'The Bank of England is still refusing to give details of the flaws—perhaps because they are not such as an ordinary bank cashier would spot. As you can imagine, the committee put the

Governor under pressure on that. And now he has undertaken to pay out on any counterfeit note the institutions may receive— however high its value—rather than give way on the secrecy.'

'At only one a week, I suppose they can afford it,' said Bragg.

'Yes.' The Commissioner sat scrutinizing his nails for some moments, then lifted his head. 'I don't suppose you can say when you will have some news for me, Bragg?' he asked in a pleading tone.

Bragg pretended to consult the calendar pinned to the wall. 'Well now, let's see . . . Today is Wednesday the tenth. I think my source could well have some further news for me by tomorrow.'

'Now you won't forget what I've told you?' Lily admonished Morton, playfully. 'Sometimes you fool about a bit too much for my liking.'

'Not when I'm working, Lil. You can't say that. I did all right yesterday, didn't I?'

'Yes.'

'And so did you. It was a pleasure to watch. What did you get?'

'A couple of cheque books and a pocket book. I get to keep any cash I take, and Beasley pays me five pounds for every cheque I give him.'

'So I'm talking to a rich young woman, this morning?' He turned towards the mirror. 'May I have your daughter's hand in marriage, madam?' he asked in deep tones. 'Yes,' he screeched back in a harsh falsetto, 'take her quickly, before she blows it all!'

Lily took him by the arm and squeezed it. 'You are an idiot, Fred!'

'And doesn't Snell want part of it? He seemed pretty good himself.'

'No. Cheques aren't easy to come by. George gets his, after Beasley has done his bit.'

'You mean, when he cashes them?'

'That's right.'

'But I don't get anything out of it,' exclaimed Morton in comic petulance.

'You get a hundred times more than Snell, that's why he's so

jealous. Beasley won't let him near the bank-notes. He would
shop you, if he had half a chance.'

'Are there only thousand-pounders, then?' asked Morton.

'I think so.'

'Where does Beaze get them from?'

'Now you're wanting to know more than is good for you.
Come on, before the shops shut for lunch—and I promise I'll
talk posh!'

They took a growler to Bond Street and Lily was handed
down by a uniformed commissionaire. They strolled purposefully into the jeweller's and went up to one of the counters.

'We would like to see some musical boxes,' Morton
announced.

'Yes sir,' replied the assistant effusively. 'What kind of price
did you have in mind?'

'The price is immaterial, if I can find what I am looking for.'

'I see. Yes, sir.' He hurried away, and brought back four
richly inlaid boxes.

'These are the best available, sir. This one was made in
Germany, the other three are from Switzerland.'

'Excellent.' Morton turned to Lily. 'She would want to keep
it on that Sheraton work-table in her boudoir, would she not,
my dear?'

'Almost certainly,' replied Lily in carefully modulated
tones.

'Then, I think we should eliminate this one, it really is rather
large . . . Now may we hear the other three?'

'Certainly, sir.' The assistant wound them up, and Lily lifted
the lid of each in turn. She looked quizzically at Morton.

'What do you think, dear?' she asked.

'Well, I know it is her taste we should consider,' said
Morton pompously, 'but I could not bear to think we had given
anyone a present that sounded like the last one.'

The assistant took it in his hands and, at Lily's nod, removed
it. She played the other two several times.

'I like the first,' she said.

'And I the second,' Morton retorted. '*The Trout*, is it not?'

'But I am sure mother would prefer the first.'

'Nonsense. She loves Schubert.'

'Yes,' Lily persisted. 'But not while dressing.'

'Perhaps she should resolve our difficulty.' Morton turned to
the assistant. 'May we take both of them? I will pay for them,

of course. Then my mother-in-law can make her own choice.
We are going down there directly.'

'I see, sir.'

'Whichever one she does not wish to keep, I will send back
to you. You can let me have a cheque for the amount I have
overpaid—less expenses you may have in the matter, of
course.'

'I shall have to ask the manager,' said the assistant, 'but I am
sure it will be acceptable.' He hurried away to a desk at the
back of the shop, where a severe-looking man was working.
He looked as if he ought to disapprove of anything so
inconsequential as jewellery and objets d'art.

'I love shopping with you, darling,' Morton murmured with
a smile. 'Is there anything else you would like to see, while we
are here?'

'Wouldn't it be lovely, if it was all true?' she whispered,
brushing his lapel in a wifely gesture.

'Yes, sir, that will be quite all right.' The assistant began
wrapping up the boxes. 'Do you have an account with us, sir?'

'I will pay cash.'

'Very good, sir. The one with the mother-of-pearl inlay is
thirty-eight pounds, and the other forty-two. So that will be
eighty pounds in all.'

Morton gave him a one-hundred pound note.

'Now, here is my card,' he said. 'With any luck, I may be
able to send a servant round with the rejected one, before you
close this evening. Whom should he ask for?'

'My name is Cribbings, sir!'

'Very good, Mr Cribbings, and you will let me have a
cheque for the balance, as I requested?'

'Of course, sir. By the same evening's post.'

'Excellent. And may I thank you for your help?'

That evening, Snell ventured back to Cupid's Court. He was
wary and subdued, but Goulter took little or no notice of him.
He was wholly absorbed in grinding a new point on his knife.
The operation involved reducing the thickness of the back of
the blade, from the handle to the new point. During the course
of the day he had ground away both sides, until the point had
been roughly formed. Then he had scratched the new outline of
the blade with a pencil. A good deal of it would have to be
removed, if the point was not to be rounded. From time to

time, Goulter would wipe the knife carefully and look at it; turning it in his hands lovingly and whistling through his teeth.

Morton wondered what excuse he could make to cover his meeting with Catherine. He even wondered whether Goulter would allow him to go—worse still, whether he would try to follow. Snell seemed to come and go as he pleased. But he was an established member of the gang, while Morton was still an initiate. And some of Snell's absences might be on Beasley's orders. It was fairly clear that Beasley was not himself the counterfeiter, from Lily's reaction to Morton's question. But presumably it was he who maintained a liaison between the two sides of the operation.

At seven o'clock Morton picked up the newspaper and clumped off upstairs. He dropped his books noisily on the floor and lay on his bed. A quarter of an hour later Goulter came up. He went to the cupboard in the alcove opposite. Morton observed him round the edge of the paper. There was a clink of coins as Goulter reached to the back of the shelf at the top. Then the door swung wide open. Propped against the back of the cupboard was a huge two-handed cleaver! Goulter re-locked the door and after gazing suspiciously at Morton for a moment went downstairs again. After a few minutes Morton heard the bang of the front door. He peered through the window, to see Goulter swinging down the street like an elephant.

Morton hurriedly changed into his old clothes, then, calling out to Snell that he was going for a breath of fresh air, he went out. At first he was afraid to hurry, lest he should overtake Goulter; but once he was out of Golden Lane, he struck west and broke into an easy-paced run. As a result he arrived at St James's before Catherine. He browsed through the cast-off clothing for a few minutes, then accepted a cup of tea and sat down with it in the corner. He took out the note-book which Beasley had provided, and began to sketch the faces of the members of the gang. He was just wondering whether he ought to add a portrait of Lily, when he saw Catherine come in. She was dressed in the blue tailor-made and white jabot which constituted her working clothes, and a little feathered hat nestled on top of her curls. She chatted briefly with the rector and took a cup of tea. Then affecting to recognize Morton, no doubt as a worthy down-and-out, she strolled over to him.

'Goodness!' she said, as she sat down by him, 'I was not aware you could draw . . . Really, those are rather good!'

'I've told you that my cricketing skills are not so very far removed from your father's painting ability. I expect he could play a fine cover-drive if he tried.'

'I am sorry for belittling you,' she said contritely. Then impelled by a compulsion to justify herself, added, 'it is just that excelling at a game seems to lack *gravitas*.'

'Well, there is enough *gravitas* in this rogues' gallery,' said Morton shortly. 'I have put the names and descriptions underneath. Beasley seems to be the leader. He is a forger and confidence trickster. He spent some years in New York, so the American police may be interested in him. Snell just cashes the bills and cheques that Beasley forges, so far as I can discover . . . Perhaps that means Beasley is known to the police here, since he no longer seems to act as his own putter-down. Get Sergeant Bragg to sound out the Met . . . Goulter, here, is a really nasty bag of tricks. He is undoubtedly the man who murdered and dismembered my predecessor. He keeps his cleaver in our bedroom cupboard, and he plays with knives compulsively. He has a holster, with three slaughterman's knives in it, around his waist; and he bears a grudge against coppers. Tell Sergeant Bragg he will need three men to take him.'

Catherine's face had paled. 'I did not think it would be like this,' she said in alarm. 'Why do you not give the whole stupid business up?'

'What? And play cricket for my excitement?'

'Don't be irritating! You know perfectly well what I mean.'

'But you are forgetting,' said Morton teasingly, 'this stupid business is going to put you at the head of your chosen profession.'

'That is nothing, compared with your life.'

'Ah, but then it was never the primary purpose of the operation.' His eyes dwelled mockingly on her and she could feel her colour rising.

'I cannot be seen here, talking to someone as disreputable-looking as you are,' she said crossly. 'Is there anything else for Sergeant Bragg?'

'Yes.' He drew a few lines on a page of his note-book. 'Here is a plan of the house we are in at present. See, there is no exit from the back, except into the yard of the adjoining house . . . Now, tell him that I have not yet found out who the counterfeiters are, though they must be part of Beasley's gang. I seem to be slowly gaining acceptance, but it will be some time before they really trust me.'

'Is that everything?'

'Well, you could give him my regards.'

The next morning was dull, with rain clouds scudding before a westerly breeze. When Morton came downstairs, he found that the other two had already left. Goulter's knife lay on the dresser, with the sharpening-stone. It was nearly finished. Morton pushed the kettle on the fire and made himself some tea. There was bread and cheese on the table, which would make an adequate breakfast. As he ate, Morton tried to analyse what he had discovered. His involvement was oddly spas-modic. Monday had been hectic—his so-called training. Tuesday had been blank. Wednesday had seen the odd business of the musical boxes. He still did not understand it. Snell had duly taken one of them back to the jeweller's, that same afternoon. Lily had been told to sell the other to a dealer—which probably meant a fence. So, on the face of it, they had incurred a considerable loss. Morton wondered, idly, why it had been necessary to go to such an exclusive shop, where prices were sky-high just because of their name. But there would be a reason; Beasley was no fool.

Morton picked up Goulter's *Tit-Bits*. He was mildly piqued to discover that Catherine's prediction about their interest in him had not been fulfilled. He was engrossed in a snippet about a woman from Cardiff, who had been widowed seven times, when the door burst open.

'We're clearin' out,' Goulter shouted hoarsely. 'Quick, the bloody rozzers are comin' round 'ere.'

'Where are we going?'

'Twelve, Gun Street—off Artillery Lane.'

'Behind Bishopsgate?'

'That's it . . . Go on! Scarper!'

Morton dashed upstairs, thankful that his possessions were already packed in Lily's bag. He was down again directly.

'Which way are they coming?' he asked.

'I dunno,' Goulter grunted, stowing their utensils into a large sack. 'That's the blow—sometime this mornin'."

'What about Snell?'

'That little snot,' sneered Goulter. 'Mister piss-in-your-pocket.'

'If he gets caught, he'll give us all away,' said Morton anxiously.

'I'll bring the little bugger with me. Don't you fret.'

Morton dashed out of the house. It would most likely be a raid by the Met. If so, his best way out was over the boundary, into the City. He sprinted to the bottom of Golden Lane, then walked swiftly along Chiswell Street, past the brewery, and mingled with the crowds in Finsbury Square. He then worked his way through side streets, reaching the eastern end of Artillery Lane without any indication that he had been followed. He loitered for a time, to make doubly sure, then sauntered down the narrow cobbled thoroughfare, and turned up Gun Street. It was no more than a dank gloomy alley; nothing bigger then a handcart could possibly go up it. At the far end, a passage led out to another street— perhaps the lines of escape were better this time! Glancing around to see that it was safe, Morton went to the door of number twelve, then knocked gently. Nothing happened. He waited for a couple of minutes, then knocked again. This time he heard an upper window being eased open. He stepped back, to see Beasley peering at him. The window was closed quietly, and shortly afterwards, the door opened.

'I'm glad you got here safely,' Beasley said unctuously. 'Go upstairs. You are in a little room of your own at the back. Unpack, then come down for a word with me.'

The room gave on to a noisome court, with a stagnant drain running down the middle. A ten-foot drop and into the isolation ward! Apart from that, the room would serve well. There was a bed and a low chest of drawers, and Morton treated himself to the unexpected luxury of hanging out his clothes on hooks behind the door. Then he went in search of Beasley.

He found him sitting at a table against the kitchen window, painstakingly filling in a cheque.

'Come in, Fred, come in,' he greeted him. 'Thanks to your undoubted flair for this work and the efficiency of our postal system, the bread we cast upon the waters was returned to us after very few days!'

Morton crossed to the table, and pulled up a chair. 'What are you doing?' he asked.

'The solicitor you instructed on Monday . . .'

'Oh, yes?'

'He wrote to your debtor, as promised, on that same day, and I caused the loan to be repaid immediately. So this morning we received a cheque for the money recovered—less their charges of thirty pounds.'

'That is pretty steep!'

'Now, now! Do not begrudge them their dues. That is another rule of this game—never be too greedy, never look as if you are scooping the pool. You remember the cheque you cashed on Saturday? If you had drawn out the whole of the thousand pounds you paid in, it might have made the cashier wonder—particularly had it been a cheque you were depositing. Much better to lose a hundred and allay any suspicion.'

'So you will not use that account again?'

'No. I opened it several months ago, and put through a few transactions to generate confidence. You can always afford to lose a little, when the stakes are high.'

'What was the purpose of the loan transaction?'

'Why, the loan was repaid by cheque—perfectly genuine, I may say. Because of their charges, however, the solicitors could not simply endorse it over. They deducted their thirty pounds, and sent you one of their own cheques for nine hundred and seventy.'

'So?'

'So we have a cheque signed by their senior partner. And thanks to our inventive German friends I have been able to erase the name of the payee and amount payable from the cheque.' He picked up a bottle of colourless fluid, and shook it vigorously. 'Made in Hamburg,' he said with a delighted smile. 'I do not think even the German police realize its significance yet! In a few moments more, I shall have turned it into a cheque for five thousand pounds, payable to "Cash".'

Morton whistled in appreciation.

'George will cash it, I am afraid,' said Beasley apologetically. 'We could not run the risk of your being recognized.'

'That's all right . . . And will the same happen to the cheque from the jeweller, for the music box?'

'You learn quickly, Fred. Yes, we shall have lost the best part of twenty pounds, but . . . well, that business should stand, say, four thousand.'

'It is obviously important to prepare a coup well in advance,' observed Morton.

'The best one I ever did took me six months,' said Beasley with a complacent smile. 'I started off by buying a letter of credit on Anstruther's bank, in the market. That cost me a hundred pounds. Then I made half a dozen copies in large amounts. The difficult bit came next. I wanted to get hold of a letter from the bank, with its private markings and special endorsement seal on it. That took me three months, and cost me another two hundred . . . Once I had it, I got dies made, and I wrote letters to the main banks in France. They were all the same—I was a valued client of Anstruther's, I was on an important business trip in Europe, and anything the French bank could do to assist me would be appreciated.'

'And did it work?' asked Morton in wonderment.

'Like a charm,' said Beasley smugly. 'I presented a letter of credit at every bank I had written to, and they paid out as if I was doing them a favour! I cleaned up fifteen thousand in that six months. That's three times as much as the Governor of the Bank of England would have been paid!'

'Why don't you do it again?' asked Morton with an encouraging smile.

'That's another thing to learn, Fred. Never overdo a ploy; variety is your greatest protection.'

'Is that why we haven't had any more bank-notes?' asked Morton innocently.

'No, that's rather different,' said Beasley with a secretive smile. 'That's rather different.'

As soon as Catherine arrived at the *City Press* office, she was sent to interview an important Australian contralto, who was passing through London on her way to the Continent. So it was noon before she could slip away to Bragg's office. She laid the portraits and the plan on his desk.

Bragg looked at them intently. 'I don't recognize any of them,' he said. 'But then, this lot's got to be a bit out of the ordinary.'

'Perhaps they are not very good likenesses?' suggested Catherine.

'Oh, he's a lively lad with a pencil, is Morton . . . I nearly called him "constable"!'

'I hope I never hear him called that again!' exclaimed Catherine pettishly.

'Are you wishing him dead, miss?' asked Bragg quietly.

'Oh, no!' She sank back in her chair dejectedly.

Bragg picked up the sketch of Goulter. 'I would think the Met might have something on this bludger. I'll show it to one of my cronies, on the side.'

'James says he is certainly the murderer of the blond-haired man.'

'Is he now? I wonder if we ought to pull him in.'

'Then do be careful. James says he has a whole armoury of knives. He said it would need three men to capture him.'

'Hmn . . . Did he tell you to ask us to do anything?'

'No. I think he only sent the plan because he had the opportunity. He seemed to be hoping to find out something about the counterfeiters soon—oh, and he said that Beasley had spent some time in New York.'

'Good, I'll send a telegraph to their police department and ask if they have come across him. Anything else?'

'He sent his regards to you,' said Catherine, her voice faltering.

'Did he now? He's still got his pecker up, then . . . That's a brave man,' he said slowly, 'and far too intelligent for any dim-witted slaughterman to best . . . Remember that.'

That evening Morton was told to help Lily with a job. He went down to Shoe Lane and found her oddly restrained. She greeted him with a kiss, but seemed far from her normal ebullient self.

'Are you scared of this one, Lil?' he asked.

'No, of course not!' she replied scornfully.

'What's the matter, then?'

'Oh, nothing . . . I just bloody hate people.'

'Not me, is it?' he asked.

'No, it's not you . . . Come on, we must be going, or we shall be too late.'

They took a cab to Oxford Circus, then Lily led him through several back streets, until she stopped at the gate to a yard.

'Where are we?' whispered Morton.

'This is the back of some accountants' offices. Is there anybody in sight?'

'No.'

She pushed open the gate and they hurried through.

'Close it quietly,' she instructed.

She led him quickly along the wall, to a door at the other end of the yard. It was also open. They passed through it, into a corridor leading to a staircase. The bottom flight was being assiduously scrubbed by a cleaner in a large flowered apron and dust-cap. Morton shrank back.

'It's all right,' said Lily, advancing to meet her. There was a murmur of conversation, a sovereign changed hands and Lily beckoned him furiously.

'We only have an hour,' she said as she ran upstairs.

'What are we looking for?' asked Morton.

'Cheques, of course. Cheque books would be nice, but paid cheques would be as good, if they're not too old.'

'I saw Beasley with his erasing fluid, yesterday,' said Morton with a laugh.

'S-s-sh!' She pushed her way through a swing door, into what seemed to be the general office of a large accountancy practice. There were piles of books, and cardboard boxes filled with invoices, everywhere.

'See if you can find some paid cheques, while I have a look in the bosses' rooms,' whispered Lily.

Morton decided that he should participate to the best of his ability, particularly in view of Lily's unlooked-for moodiness. Presumably Beasley would be able to remove any date on the cheque, so it must be the bank's printed serial number which would arouse suspicion. As to which boxes to plunder, there would be far less risk of discovery if he took cheques only from boxes which had already been audited. After a while, he realized that those cases were stacked along the back wall of the office, awaiting collection. He selected ten cheques, of recent date, from each of six large concerns, then went in search of Lily.

He found her going through the drawers of a large mahogany desk. She smiled triumphantly at him. 'A new cheque-book,' she exclaimed, 'with fifty in it; and I bet they'll think they mislaid it!'

They tiptoed through the empty office again, and down the back stairs. The cleaning woman was nowhere to be seen. Five minutes later, they were hailing a cab in Regent Street.

'You'll come in, Fred?' she asked in a subdued voice, when they arrived in Shoe Lane.

'Give me half a chance!'

They went into her room and Lily began to unpin her bonnet.

'No champagne tonight, Fred. I've decided it's a waste of money.'

'When did we ever need it?' asked Morton, taking her into his arms.

They came together in a friendly, companionable fashion,

and afterwards lay side by side. Morton gazed at her chubby good-natured face, her rosy cheeks and unlined forehead.

'However did you get into all this?' he asked.

'On the streets, you mean?'

'Well, yes. You are so pretty and . . . wholesome, and you speak so nicely.'

Lily's eyes sparkled and she laughed with her old bravado. 'I was a lady's maid, once,' she said, 'till the master laid me over my bed and showed me there were other things in life beside curling tongs! It was months before the mistress found out. You should have seen her face! She blamed me, of course. Threw me out without a character. So what else was there? . . . But I was never one of your common tarts. My beat was round St James's. Many's the sovereign I've earned up against a tree in the park, and the bloke's got no nearer then my thighs!'

Irrationally, Morton was irked by her words. 'You are too good for this life,' he said.

'Are you trying to reform me, Mr Gladstone?' she asked perkily. 'It's the ones that say they want to help you, that do the wickedest things!'

'You could have done better, with your talents, Lil,' Morton said in a lighter tone.

'I might, at that,' she laughed. 'I might have had six kids by now and a husband that beat me.'

'I would never beat you, Lil.'

'I might like a bit, from you.'

Morton slapped her bare buttock with his hand, and she twisted on top of him, gripping his wrists with her hands.

'What d'you do now, mister?' she gasped.

'Surrender unconditionally,'

She laughed uncertainly, then slid down and put her hand on his chest.

'I like you, Fred,' she said. 'The one they had before you was a pain. Made out he was real upper-crust—but he wasn't.'

'What happened to him?'

'He went to America. I'd been over to see my mum for the weekend, in Romford. When I got back he'd cleared out.'

'Without saying anything?'

'He wouldn't have said anything to me, anyway. But they showed me the note he left. Stupid sod!'

'Come on, Lil. You must have liked him a bit. I wager you had to prove he wasn't a sodomite, for Beasley.'

'Huh! You'd have thought he'd never had it up anybody lower than a countess.'

Morton laughed delightedly, and kissed her on the cheek.

'Never mind,' he said. 'You've got me now.'

'Yes,' she relapsed into moody silence. Then: 'Fred?'

'Lil?'

'What will you do when this business is over?'

'Over? I thought it was good for a bit, yet.'

'I suppose it is.'

'You've done well today, haven't you?'

'Yes. I'll get a small fortune from Beasley. And I'm going to put away every little bit of it.'

'As the actress said . . .'

Lily thumped him in the ribs. 'That's the trouble with you, Fred,' she complained. 'You don't take anything seriously.'

'What do you want, then?'

'I'm not sure,' She traced a pattern on his chest with her finger. 'I think I'd like to live in the country; get away from this stinking place. Maybe a little shop—a grocer's or a tobacconist's. I've always fancied that . . .'

'Sounds nice,' said Morton sleepily. 'Yes, that would be good . . .'

CHAPTER ——————

—————————— TEN

Lily surveyed the station yard at Wells with distaste. There were great piles of coal at the far end, and a cool wind was whipping the dust into her eyes. More knowledgeable passengers had rushed off the train with their bags, and deposited them on the pavement to secure their turn for a cab. Now they were drinking tea in the refreshment room, with a line of baggage seven yards long for other people to trip over. The trouble was that there did not seem to be any cabs. When she and Beasley had been standing in the shelter of the booking office for ten minutes, a trap trotted into the yard and, after making a wide sweep, pulled up on the pavement. The red-faced driver got creakily down and inspected the luggage. He picked up three bags, placed them slowly in the bottom of his trap, then went into the tea-room in search of their owners. After some conversation he was apparently invited to have a cup himself, so that it was a further ten minutes before his passengers were installed and he could drive away.

'For God's sake, Herbert, can't you get a cab?' she asked irritably.

'I'll go into the town and see what I can find,' Beasley replied, and strode briskly away.

A few moments later a light farm-cart arrived, and collected two more passengers. Then the whole station seemed to drift into slumber. Lily eased her feet and looked at the little silver watch on her lapel. She wondered whether to have a cup of tea herself, and leave Beasley to get on with it; but she stayed where she was. At length he reappeared, a broad smile on his face.

'Have you got one?' asked Lily abruptly.

'No, there doesn't seem to be a cab in the place,' he said brightly. 'But I went right into the middle of the town; it isn't far to walk.'

'Walk!' she cried. 'You must be off your rocker! In these shoes? . . . Dress up posh, he says. Look the part, he says. And now he wants me to bleedin' walk.'

'Honestly, Lily, it's only a few hundred yards. I actually found the Swan. It looks nice—you'll like it.'

With her nose in the air, Lily began to walk gingerly out of the station, while Beasley tramped behind her with the bags. She glanced perfunctorily in the shop windows, a rebellious scowl on her face.

'Bloody farce, this is,' she hissed, as they waited by a crossing for a hay-cart to rumble by.

'Now, I've told you we can't take any chances,' replied Beasley plaintively. 'Don't spoil everything.'

'When have I ever spoiled anything?' she snapped, and walked on.

She stood disdainfully while Beasley signed the register, and followed the porter with reluctance to their room.

'What time is the appointment?' she asked, when he had gone.

'Three o'clock,' replied Beasley.

'Two hours to wait! . . . Get us some champagne,' she asked in a wheedling voice.

'It wouldn't be in character.'

'Some port, then.'

'Nor that, either.'

'I shall need something to get me through this,' she said petulantly.

'We will go down for some lunch in a little while. You can have a glass of wine then, if you must.'

Lily crossed to the window and stared out moodily. It overlooked the yard. She could see some stables on the right, and a trap by the wall, with its shafts pointing to the sky. In the opposite corner an area had been fenced off with wire netting. Inside it some hens and a cock were scratching in the dirt.

'What a hole this is,' Lily exclaimed.

'Did you expect anything else?' asked Beasley.

'I thought it might be something a bit special.'

'Never mind,' Beasley walked across and put his hand on her shoulder. 'We'll have a special time tonight.'

She shook off his advances. 'I don't want to get there looking as if I've been fumbled by the footman,' she said irritably—then burst into a giggle. 'That was good, wasn't it?' "Fumbled by the footman"!'

'That's more like you, Lily. Come on, let's go and have lunch.'

An hour and a half later, they were following the route traversed by the three policemen some two weeks earlier. Lily gazed at the cathedral in puzzled wonder.

'It's as big as Westminister Abbey,' she exclaimed. 'What do they want to build a thing like that for in a little dump like Wells?'

'I expect that it was here first, Lil,' said Beasley indulgently. 'Here, do you think we ought to have gone in to look at it? They might expect it.'

'It's hard enough to pass myself off as a mother and a married woman,' replied Lily acidly, 'without turning me into a bloody nun as well.'

'Well, we'll say we are going to look round tomorrow.'

'I wonder you ever go to bed, Herbert, in case you forget to button your flies next morning.'

'There's no chance of me staying up tonight,' Beasley nudged her slyly.

'That's enough! You're a respectable married man, remember.'

'Quite right, Lily,' he said abashed. 'Quite right.'

They turned into Vicars' Close, and the mantle of middle-class sobriety seemed to fall on Lily. She walked demurely at Beasley's side, her hand in the crook of his arm, pointing out the medieval chapel at the top and exclaiming in wonder at the cottages. Beasley knocked at the door of the school house and they were shown to the headmaster's study.

'I am delighted to meet you, Mr Pettifer, Mrs Pettifer,' said

Truscott, shaking hands and seeing Lily settled in a comfortable chair.

'Thank you for your letter and telegraph,' he went on. 'I am glad you could come down to see the school for yourselves . . . I hope that next time you come, you will bring your son with you. I think it is important that he should feel he is helping to make the decision. After all, it is quite a wrench to leave home at eleven.'

Lily murmured solicitously.

'We teach grammar, history, geography, mathematics, the sciences, Latin, Greek, and French,' said Truscott. 'And we play rugby-football and cricket. In addition, the boys can go riding, or sailing at Weston-super-Mare. Since, however, those activities involve instruction from people who are not on the school's staff, additional fees are payable in respect of them.'

'Plenty of time to worry about that,' said Beasley with a warm smile. 'I hope that the boys are given a thorough moral and religious grounding.'

'Oh, most assuredly. As you can see, I am of the cloth myself, and in addition we have a chaplain, who also teaches history to the lower forms.'

'Is that your chapel, at the top of the close?' asked Lily.

'No,' replied Truscott. 'That belongs to the cathedral and, happily, would be too small for our needs. All our boys go to matins in the cathedral every Sunday morning, and those taking classics to evensong as well—they mostly go into the ministry, you see.'

Beasley smiled in approbation.

'Now, I have arranged for one of the senior boys to take you round the school in a few minutes. I can answer any further questions you have, when you return—unless anything springs to mind immediately.'

'What about his uniform?' asked Lily. 'Will he have to bring his own sheets?'

'Matron will send you a list, once you have decided to place your son with us,' said Truscott reassuringly. 'But our requirements are much the same as those of any other school.'

'It all seems very satisfactory,' said Beasley with a gratified smile. 'Even better than we had been led to expect.'

'I confess I have been wondering what caused you to select Wells,' said Truscott. 'Welwyn Garden City seems a very long way off. Have you a connection with the school?'

'Not a connection exactly,' said Beasley smoothly. 'We have become friendly with the man next door, and his nephew came here. He recommended it highly.'

'Excellent! And what is the boy's name?'

'Thorburn. Frederick Reginald Thorburn. He looks to be about twenty-five or so. I expect you remember him.'

'Indeed I do, Mr Pettifer,' the headmaster said cautiously. 'If I seemed taken aback, it was because I did not expect that the young man would have a good word to say about the school.'

'Oh, but he has,' said Beasley with a reassuring smile. 'I have spoken to him at length about it.'

'But I thought he was back in New Zealand.'

'He has come to England again, and is staying with his uncle. He seems a presentable, self-assured young man; I have almost made up my mind to offer him a post in my business.'

An embarrassed look crossed Truscott's face. 'Assurance and address are qualities we seldom fail to inculcate,' he said hesitantly.

'How do you mean?' asked Beasley, puzzled.

Truscott sighed. 'It is difficult for me to comment on the young man's character as it is now. But when a prospective parent is involved . . .'

'Are you saying he is no good?' asked Beasley in alarm.

'For all I know, he may be genuinely seeking a new start. I would urge you to judge anything I say in the light of Christian charity and forbearance.'

'I will, you may be sure.'

'Then I may safely admit to you that Thorburn was a disappointment to me. He was an attractive boy and a born leader—but not always in the paths of righteousness. There were suggestions that he used to take other boys' pocket money from the locker-room, though it was never proved . . . Even worse, in his last year he became involved with the school maids. We had to dispense with the services of one, who was said to be with child.'

'Good gracious!' exclaimed Lily, covertly digging Beasley in the ribs.

'I used to think it was a phase he would grow out of,' said Truscott sombrely. 'But my hopes were rudely shattered. I had urged him to take a commission in the army, and he seemed to have found his métier . . . Then he fell into temptation again and was cashiered for stealing mess funds.'

'Are you sure we are talking about the same young man?' asked Beasley in astonishment. 'Do you have a picture of him?'

'I am happy to say that we have not yet succumbed to the modern fashion for school photographs,' relied Truscott pompously.

'Well, I was told nothing of this,' said Beasley in dismay.

'Of that I am sure,' Truscott gave a deprecating smile. 'I do not know the nature of your business enterprise, Mr Pettifer, but I feel it would not be in the young man's best interest, if you gave him too free a hand with money.'

'Well, thank you, headmaster. I will not dismiss the idea of employing him, out of hand. But I will certainly bear in mind what you have told me.'

'Mamma! You are knitting! Whatever for?' Catherine had wandered into the drawing room, to find her mother laboriously trying to pick up a dropped stitch.

'We are all knitting for the poor,' her mother replied vaguely. 'It is the new vicar's idea. He says that it is important to make a personal sacrifice, and that contributing money is merely buying immunity from involvement . . . I cannot think he will last long.'

'But you are hopeless at knitting, Mamma!'

'I know. In my view, he is merely denying the poor the benefit of what we do best. Lady Ellesmere says it is some kind of penance for having been born comfortably off.'

'And what is the garment supposed to be?' asked Catherine.

'The trousers of a woolly suit for winter.'

'But Mamma, one leg is much longer than the other!'

Her mother held the needles at arm's length and gazed at her work. 'I suppose you are right, dear. Oh well, I expect they will be able to find a child to fit it . . . What I ought to be doing,' she pronounced, 'is knitting clothes for my grandchild.'

'So you think that I would be able to produce a child of that shape?' asked Catherine with a laugh.

'At the very least, you ought to be married at your age.'

'Yes, Mamma,' said Catherine off-handedly, as she flopped into a chair.

'Have you seen any more of that nice young underwriter man recently?' her mother went on relentlessly.

'Thomas Tipping? No, Mamma. Not for months.' She picked up a magazine in the hope of fending off the impending catechism.

'At least you seem to have dropped your policeman. I am glad of that. He was most undesirable.'

'But Mamma, surely you married beneath you? Why shouldn't I?' said Catherine teasingly.

'Beneath me?' exclaimed her mother in astonishment.

'Papa was only a struggling painter, and you were the daughter of a wealthy gentleman.'

'Oh, but everyone said that he would rise to the top,' her mother assured her. 'He was so handsome. If I had not caught him, your aunt Phoebe would have done. There was never any question of his not being good enough for us. It just did not occur to anyone.'

'Well, I am glad to hear that romance sometimes enters into this disgusting marriage-market.'

'There is nothing at all disgusting about it, dear. Your father and I are concerned that you should marry someone who is of our own kind, and able to keep you in some style.'

'And if I do not love him?'

'Oh, one's feelings are changing all the time. However you begin, you end up at best with an easy-going tolerance of each other.'

'Well, if you are concerned about my policeman, I can set your mind at rest. He has gone to Australia and is likely to stay there.'

'Has he really?' remarked her mother indifferently. 'Oh well, I expect they need policemen out there, with all those transported criminals running about.'

'Mamma, you really are the limit! . . . In any case, in your book he would have been in the highest degree desirable. His father is a baronet and the Lord Lieutenant of Kent; he is unattached, aged twenty-five and, through the American side of his family, probably a millionaire.'

'Really!' her mother castigated her. 'Sometimes Catherine, I think you just do not try!'

'However much I cared for someone,' said Catherine with asperity, 'I would never throw myself at his head if he did not reciprocate.'

'But you must know him quite well, by now. To my knowledge he has brought you home twice. That must mean something.'

'We had a gratifyingly static relationship. I called him "James" whenever I could; he invariably responded with "Miss Marsden".'

'I suppose propriety would allow you to write to him?' her mother wondered.

'My dear Mamma, he is not remotely interested in marriage. If I tried very hard, he might consent to take me as his mistress. You could have your grandchild then. Would that satisfy you?'

'You know perfectly well it would be a disaster,' replied her mother in a shocked tone.

'Then please stop nagging me, and leave me to run my own life.'

It was inevitable, Morton supposed, that Sunday would be a void, with all the banks closed. But he had never spent such a boring day in his whole life. Normally he would have gone to church, if he were off-duty. But that was out of the question. He dared not even take a walk, lest he should bump into one of his colleagues—ex-colleagues, rather—from Bishopsgate station. He doubted if his spectacles would protect him, in a close encounter on familiar ground. Anyway, the knife-man might have orders to stop him going out.

Goulter had been in an unpredictable mood all day. It was Snell who had set him off. He had defiantly slapped his packet of cigarettes on the table at breakfast, before pouring himself a second mug of tea. Goulter had been turning his refurbished knife over and over in his hands, and Snell had moved the packet about the table, between gulps of his tea. It was like a confrontation between a mongoose and a python, grotesquely un-matched, yet ordained by compulsive antipathy. Morton wondered if Snell had obtained his revolver, and was picking this quarrel to give justification for his revenge. If so, his own course must be to run at the first shot, and get out of the area. He could always find Beasley again through Lily.

The confrontation ended without serious bloodshed. Snell had pushed the open cigarette packet across the table till it was within a foot of Goulter, near enough for him to smell the tobacco; near enough, too, for Snell's head to be in range. Goulter had fetched him a blow with the back of his hand, knocking him to the floor, with blood pouring from his nose. He had gone to lie down on his bed and had remained there. Goulter had replaced his knife in the holster, and was sitting morosely in an armchair staring into space.

That had been the highlight of the day. It was as if life was suspended. There was no sound in the house, or in the alley outside, and only occasionally the grating crunch of an iron-bound cart-wheel on the main road. The blessed day of rest! . . . Once or twice, Morton had attempted to engage Goulter in conversation, in the hope of finding out something about the counterfeiting. But all he had achieved was to make Goulter irritable and suspicious.

Towards evening, Morton was tempted to steal out of the house and walk the few hundred yards down Bishopsgate to his rooms. He could have a couple of hours in the real world, in his proper setting. And a bath—even a cold bath—would be an untold luxury . . . But it would be folly. Already he was conscious that his disguise was wearing thin. The new clothes, Beasley's request that he should speak without an accent, and the instruction to dispense with his spectacles all conspired to make him feel like James Morton, rather than Fred Thorburn. A visit to his rooms would complete the process, perhaps to his undoing. Anyway, Catherine had the keys . . .

The thought warmed him. It was just boredom, coupled with a certain degree of loneliness; it would pass. He decided to write to her. The very act would direct his mind towards pleasanter things—and, anyway, it would let them know he was still alive, even if he had nothing to tell them. He went upstairs and began to write. He carefully placed the number code in the second line, then wrote a farrago of sentimental nonsense such as Ada Smith would sigh over, but including a few digs that the prickly Miss Marsden would pick up. He smiled to himself as he addressed the envelope. It would be amusing to look back on this pantomime in the years to come. He licked the flap and was just sticking it down, when he heard a noise on the landing outside. He thrust the letter into his pocket, as Lily entered.

'Hello, Fred,' she said with a mischievous smile. 'I thought I'd come to see where you hang out.'

'Not up to your standards, Lil,' said Morton apologetically.

'That's a fact!' She looked round the damp-stained walls and grimy floorboards, then turned towards him. 'Aren't you going to give me a kiss, then?'

Morton put his hands under her armpits and swung her round like a little girl, then planted a kiss on her lips and set her down.

She giggled and, retreating to the door, half-opened it. Then, like a conjurer at the Empire, she produced Morton's letter from behind her back.

'What have we here?' she asked archly. ' "Miss Ada Smith, care of Ninety-five Park Lane". Ooh! that's a posh address!' She waved the envelope at him and he made a dart for it, grinning. With a screech of laughter she clattered down the stairs into the kitchen, with Morton in pursuit.

At the doorway Morton pulled up short. Beasley was there, talking to Goulter. Lily sidled round behind Beasley's chair and tore open the envelope savagely. ' "My dear, darling Ada",' she read. ' "Although we cannot spend much time together, I think of you often, every day." Bloody lying devil, you are, Fred.' She glared at him, the smile fading on her lips. Then she cocked her head on one side, and held the letter in the air.

'Listen to this, Herbert,' she cried. ' "I remember the beauty of your face, the sweetness of your voice. You have been very good to me, Ada." ' Lily broke off and glared at Morton, then began to read again in a high mincing voice. ' "I do not deserve to have your affection, my dear. It should be enough for any man, merely to be close to such a generous and uncritical nature. Yet you hold out your hand to me, and say you would do anything for me!!" There are two bloody exclamation marks,' exclaimed Lily. 'Shit!' She crumpled the letter and flung it from her angrily.

Beasley retrieved it and quickly scanned the pages. 'Who is she, Fred?' he asked quietly.

'She's a housemaid in Park Lane. I've known her for eight months. She's a damned good shag!'

'Bastard!' hissed Lily from between clenched teeth.

'Why have you written it as from Catford?' asked Beasley.

'She thinks I am still selling books. I tell her I'm moving round London, doing one district, then another. She's a bit hoity-toity; she wouldn't have anything to do with me, if she thought I'd been living in dossers. She thinks I'm going to marry her!' Morton's laugh sounded harsh and strained in his ears.

'I see. And where do you meet her, Fred?'

'Hyde Park, when it's not raining. Up West, when it is.'

'She knows where you are, then?' Beasley asked slyly.

'No! She doesn't know anything about this business. We just meet Wednesday, either in the park opposite her place, or in Piccadilly.'

'Hmm. I am not sure this is wise, Fred,' Beasley frowned.

'Come off it!' exclaimed Morton. 'She's only a flaming dolly-mop. I can't see what all the fuss is about.'

'The fuss,' said Beasley with a forced smile, 'is because Lily fancies you.'

Morton burst into laughter. 'So what's against me having it off with a doxy? Lily'll drop her drawers to anybody for a shilling!'

Lily exploded with rage, and seizing her handbag swung it viciously at Morton's head.

'You lying bastard!' she shouted, then with a look of hate at Beasley, stalked out of the room.

CHAPTER _____

_____ ELEVEN

To Morton's surprise, nothing was said about Ada Smith next day. No questions, no insinuating remarks; nothing. He had expected some chaff from Snell, but he was out of sorts and went back to bed after breakfast. Beasley left early, saying he was going to see Lily; but when he returned, he said nothing to Morton about her. It was as if the incident had never occurred. That, of course, would be the sensible way of dealing with it; treat it like a row in the family, ignore it until it had blown over and normal relations were re-established. But this wasn't a family; it was a group of disparate people, associating for a criminal purpose and kept together only by the expectation of profit. On that footing, it was careless of Beasley to be so trusting, to take him at face value and be satisfied with the explanation he had given. Morton wondered whether he ought to raise the subject himself, to draw the enemy's fire; but he had given his explanation and more questioning might create an unwelcome interest in Ada Smith. It was best to let it lie.

Even so, he wandered into the kitchen in the middle of the morning, where Beasley was working. He was relieved to find that, for once, Goulter was out and he drew a chair up to the table. Beasley had been removing the bank cancellation stamps, and the dates and payees' names, from the cheques that had been filched from the accounts' office.

'Magical isn't it?' he remarked, leaning back with a satisfied smile.

'I only took cheques made out for large amounts,' said Morton. 'I thought it would reduce your labours!'

'I wish everyone was as intelligent, Fred. You are a natural for this, do you know?'

Morton gave a gratified smile. 'I don't seem to have any trouble,' he said.

'When this rig is over, you could do worse than team up with me permanently.'

'When would that be?'

'It is not altogether in my hands; but soon.'

'And what about Snell and Goulter?' asked Morton.

Beasley let the questions hang in the air and took one of the cheques. He studied the remaining writing intently, then with smooth flowing strokes wrote in that day's date and made it payable to 'cash'. Looking over his shoulder, Morton was unable to tell that the new entries had not been made by the original hand.

'What do you think?' asked Beasley, relaxing again.

'I think it is incredible,' replied Morton warmly. 'I could never do that.'

'It takes a certain flair,' said Beasley with a smirk. 'However, my question was concerned with Snell and Goulter.'

'It is hardly for me to say,' replied Morton hesitantly. 'I have only known them for a few days.'

'Nevertheless, you must have formed some views.'

'Well, I cannot say that I am comfortable with either of them. Snell is brilliant, whether he is working on his own, or with Lily. At the same time, he seems moody and dissatisfied; I would not regard him as wholly reliable.'

'So you would rather leave him to pick pockets with Miss Curtis?'

'Yes,' said Morton, with a grin.

Beasley did not respond. He gazed out of the window for a time, in thought. Then he looked around. 'And what about Goulter?' he asked.

'I have never been entirely clear as to Goulter's function,' replied Morton slowly. 'I gather he finds our quarters; and should the need arise, I imagine he could hold off the police while we made our escape. I do not see his being able to take a more active part then that in your kind of operation. In addition, there seems to be a streak of instability in him, which could make him difficult to control. In my view we would be better off without him.'

'That is very acutely observed,' remarked Beasley with a sly smile. 'Your experience in the army has not been lost on you. However, that is for the future. At present, I would like you to deputize for Snell and encash this cheque during the lunch hour—there are fewer cashiers then and streams of clerks drawing out a few pounds.'

'Do I get the commission?'

'Of course.' Beasley passed over the cheque.

'Five thousand seven hundred and twenty-three pounds!' exclaimed Morton. 'Phew! How do you want it?'

'Mainly in five-hundreds.'

'Right. If I asked for thousands, we might get our own back!' Morton grinned and went out jauntily.

But even though the cashier paid him without hesitation, Morton could not shake off a feeling of unease. Perhaps he had underestimated Beasley. After all, why should he offer him a permanent partnership on the basis of his having put down a few bank-notes. Snell was far more experienced. Furthermore, there seemed to be no firm foundation for Beasley's preferring him to Snell where the bank-notes were concerned. In the last few days, he had seen plenty of junior clerks changing large notes. Perhaps Beasley was a snob at heart, and Thorburn conformed more closely than Snell to his idea of a rich young man . . . He was, of course, right. All other things apart, he was exactly that. Perhaps it was not too bizarre to suppose that, in his profession, Beasley might have become hyper-sensitive to wealth and developed an instinct for it. That might account for the easy relationship that seemed to have developed between them. But if he ever rationalized that affinity, he would realize that it was at odds with Thorburn's background. Morton chided himself for being fanciful. Yet he had been foolish to pontificate about Snell and Goulter. His views on them could not possibly have been of immediate importance to Beasley, even if his proposals had been genuine. Once again, he had been flattered and opened his stupid mouth. Now it was obvious that he was taking a close analytical interest in the operation—perhaps an undue interest. He just could not afford to take avoidable risks. Yet what was he supposed to do? He was nowhere near the stage where he could take the initiative. Morton marched irritably back to the house, only to find it locked. He shinned up the drainpipe and climbed through his bedroom window, expecting to discover that everyone had moved on. But no, his things were still there. He went downstairs. Everything was as it had been; even Goulter's holster of knives was in its customary place on the dresser. He made a rapid search of Beasley's room. It had a wardrobe and a chest of drawers but the clothes they held were in no way sufficient for a prolonged stay. So he had a bolt-hole elsewhere? . . . The top drawer held an assortment of pens and ink, and a couple of unopened bottles of erasing fluid; but no cheques. There was nothing that even hinted at criminal activity.

That night Morton lay awake, listening, till well after midnight and he was certain that Beasley had not come in. Perhaps he was spending the night with Lily? Morton put the thought behind him in irritation. He was becoming far too involved with the people in the gang. His objective was clear; to stay with them until he had discovered the counterfeiters, then get word to Bragg so that he could take them.

About ten o'clock next morning Beasley arrived in a high good humour.

'Good morning, Fred,' he clapped Morton on the shoulder.

'Good morning, Albert. Is George better?'

'Better than he was,' Goulter grunted.

'Is he still in bed?'

'Yer.'

'Ah well, I shall have to trouble you, Fred, to undertake a small commission—for no commission.' Beasley laughed at a witticism that was not yet apparent to Morton.

'I would like you to present this letter at the Provincial Bank branch in Cornhill. It is merely a request for a new cheque-book, but perhaps you should read it.'

Morton scanned it rapidly. 'That is a splendid letter-heading,' he remarked. 'Who did it?'

'Curiosity killed the cat, Fred,' replied Beasley smugly.

'It is the heading of the lawyers who recovered the loan for us, isn't it?'

'That is right. Nothing is impossible in this business, if it is properly organized. But of course, the overheads are high. To have a plate engraved for one letter is a costly business!'

'Not if you get fifty blank cheques out of it,' replied Morton in an admiring tone.

'Now, you will remember to wait for the cheque-book, won't you Fred? Don't let them send it by post!'

Morton laughed. 'There is something else I must remember.' He delved into his pocket and placed a roll of notes in front of Beasley. 'Don't tell me you had forgotten about five thousand odd pounds! I was tempted to do a bunk with it.'

'I have you sized up, Fred,' replied Beasley with an unctuous smile. 'You wouldn't betray anybody for a measley five thou.'

'One would think you didn't need it!'

'Oh, I need it all right.' Beasley counted out two hundred and eighty-five pounds in notes and, dropping a sovereign on to the pile, pushed it over to Morton. 'We have a big coup coming up. But it was as well in your pocket as mine.'

Morton took a hansom to the Royal Exchange, wondering yet again if Beasley was playing with him. On the basis that he was trustworthy, it was less of a personal risk to Beasley if he acted as a walking banker. Anybody with five thousand pounds in his pocket would have some explaining to do, if the police searched him. But behind the badinage had been the implication, perhaps unrealized, that Morton could be an enemy. Once that feeling crystallized, he was as good as dead.

He entered the ecclesiastical gloom of the banking hall and passed the letter over the counter. The cashier slit open the envelope and read it.

'And who might you be, sir?'

'My name is Partridge,' replied Morton amiably. 'I am the most junior of junior partners in the firm. So recent am I, that my name does not yet appear on the letter-head. But since we could not wait for you to despatch the cheque-book by post, and since only partners are allowed access to them, behold I am here.' Morton pulled a wry face, and the cashier smiled in return.

He went to the back of the room and shortly returned with a thick cheque-book, which he passed under the grille. Morton thanked him, carefully deposited it in his inside pocket, and walked purposefully away.

Wednesday was another empty day. Snell got up from his sick-bed and went out early. From the attention he had paid to his toilet, Morton surmised that he was going to cash cheques for Beasley. For some reason, the cohesion of the gang seemed to be breaking up. Was it something to do with the big coup that Beasley had hinted at? Certainly he seemed to need a great deal of money; and he was prepared to disregard his own professional canons to get it. It was bordering on the reckless for Beasley to send him for the new cheque-book, when it had been he who had seen Prothero, the senior partner. It argued that they were up against a time-limit of some kind. Added to which, the cheques being encashed were for staggeringly large amounts. Even allowing for the possibility that Snell's cheques would be smaller, Beasley must be amassing a very considerable sum. Perhaps the coup was nothing more than this spate of cheques, with Beasley's flight abroad at the end of it. But it had not sounded like that; and when he had spoken of it, he had shown the smug excitement that had characterized his accounts of the impersonation of Vanderbilt and the foray into France. Yet if it was to be a gang operation, one would think he would want to maintain their collective identity. . . . But perhaps that cohesion was a figment of his own imagination. Goulter was surly and distrustful of everyone—including Beasley; Snell was perpetually resentful and hostile. He only had a close relationship with Lily, and that was probably damaged beyond hope of repair . . .

When Goulter went out for more beer, Morton made a careful survey of the house and drew a plan on a piece of paper taken from Beasley's room. He dressed in his old clothes, and put it in his trouser pocket, just in case Lily should return and propose a reconciliation! Then he lay on his bed and waited for the time to pass.

At half past seven, he put on his spectacles and slipped out of the house. He walked rapidly to Piccadilly, and arrived at the church before Catherine. He accepted a cup of tea, and stood in the corner watching the door.

'Young man! Young man!'

A pleasant well-dressed woman was hurrying towards him, her hand raised to attract his attention. Morton took off his hat and raised a tired smile.

'Young man, would you like some work?'

He was completely taken aback. Anyone using this place

was likely to be out of work, of course. Indeed a man with a job would probably scorn charity—particularly from the idle rich . . . She was looking at him expectantly, an encouraging smile on her face.

'Yes'm,' he said in his west-country voice.

'Good, good. What is your name?'

'Fred, mum.'

'Well, Fred, I could not engage you permanently, but I could give you work from time to time.'

'What kind of work, mum?' asked Morton, seeing out of the corner of his eye that Catherine had come into the hall.

'Oh, getting coal up, cleaning windows—I have a flat in Berkeley Square, there are always things that need doing there.' She plunged her hand into her bag and, glancing up, Morton could see a frown of displeasure on Catherine's face.

'There!' The woman gave him a visiting-card. 'Come tomorrow morning at ten o'clock. I am sure I can find you something to do.' She gave him an oddly girlish smile and bustled out.

Catherine took a cup of tea and came towards him.

'What are you doing, talking to her?' she asked angrily.

'The lady has found me some work,' replied Morton in a broad country accent.

Catherine recollected herself. 'She is a wanton,' she hissed.

'I know. She is a-wantin' me to clean her windows tomorrow.'

'Don't you dare!'

'But I can't let a chance of a job go so easy,' said Morton with a glimmer of a smile.

'Then never speak to me again!'

'You rich folk just toy with us poor,' Morton complained.

'Stop fooling, and concentrate on what we are here for,' said Catherine crossly.

'Yes, mum.' He gestured towards the chairs and they sat down in the corner. Morton pushed his hand into his pocket.

'Here is a plan of our present hide-out,' he said. 'It would be rather more complicated to raid than the last one, because they could escape through the properties at the back. It would need a cordon round the whole block.'

'Do you want Sergeant Bragg to move in on the gang?' asked Catherine hopefully.

'By no means. I begin to feel that I have won Beasley's confidence. He has even offered me a partnership!'

'Partnership?'

'With him only, once this present episode is finished.'

'When will that be?'

'Oddly enough, when I asked him that question, he said it was not wholly in his hands. He may have meant that he could only start it when he had amassed enough money.'

'I thought they made their own money.'

Morton laughed. 'He obviously needs real money, in quantity, for some reason. But I think it is connected with the counterfeiting operation. I am chary of questioning him about it, because once when I raised it, he was very coy. But the other day he told me that there is a big coup afoot. I think I may be getting close.'

'You will be careful, won't you?' Catherine urged him.

'I think that applies to both of us. For no real reason, beyond feeling down in the dumps, I wrote to Ada Smith on Sunday.'

'Your stupid letters!' said Catherine with a grateful smile.

'It was precisely that—and a good thing too, or you would have been in real danger.'

'Danger?' she exclaimed in alarm.

'As I was sealing the envelope, they came in and caught me at it. They read the letter and questioned me about you—I mean about Ada Smith, of course. I said she was a dolly-mop housemaid, who did not even know where I lived, let alone what I was doing now. I think they believed me. They certainly have not mentioned it again. Still, you should take care yourself.'

Morton was playing cricket. He recognized the place. It was in the spinney, down by the river at home. The other wicket was a large elm tree. He gripped his bat firmly and patted the crease a few times. Then suddenly, the Commissioner appeared from behind the tree and, running halfway down the pitch, threw the ball at his head. It was going much too fast for him to hit it. He ducked and the ball was transformed into a great white bank-note, wrapping itself round his head, stifling him. He struck at it with his bat and it became a seagull fluttering at him, pecking at his eyes with its bright yellow beak. He tried to fight it off, and could hear the roars of disapproval from the crowd. Sergeant Bragg was fielding, in white trousers and red braces. He ran across angrily and grabbed him by the shoulder.

'Gerrup! . . . Gerrup!' Goulter was standing by his bed. 'Stir yerself. We're off.'

'Wh . . . where?' Morton mumbled stupefied.

'Get bloody dressed!'

Morton huddled on his clothes, stuffed the remainder of his possessions into Lily's bag and ran down the stairs. Goulter and Snell were in the hallway, waiting impatiently for him. Goulter slammed the door shut after them and set off at a shambling trot. They kept it up until they were beyond Spitalfields market; then Goulter pushed them into an alley. They waited there for five minutes, Goulter peering suspiciously out. Then, apparently satisfied that they had not been pursued, he led them on a wide detour around the market. Finally he turned into a cul-de-sac, with a brewery at the end. It was lined with mean terraced houses on either side, but as they neared the bottom, Morton could see a substantial double-fronted house, set back some twenty yards from the pavement. There were high brick walls along the sides and back of the grounds; the front was enclosed by a straggly yew hedge behind rusting iron railings. Although the lawns had been recently mown, the flower beds were overgrown. The house itself was dejected. It looked as if some long-dead brewer had built this monument to his wealth at the gates of its source, then abandoned it.

Goulter took them round to the back door, through the kitchen and into the main hall of the house. The staircase was massively handsome, the frieze elaborate under its thick coating of dust. Goulter commandeered the room on one side of the front door and put Snell in the other. Following his instructions, Morton mounted the stairs. As he did so, he thought he detected a movement on the landing above. He found his room, and was relieved to see that it was reasonably furnished. He threw open the window and peered out. It gave on to the back garden. Below the sill was the bow window of a ground-floor room. Its leaded roof was a mere four feet away and a drain-pipe ran from it to the ground. There was even a breach in the garden wall, where the foundations had sunk. It should be possible to find a way through the undergrowth beyond. The line of escape would have been satisfactory, even to Thorboun. He closed the window and turned round. Lily was standing in the doorway, her eyes cold and hostile.

'Hello, Lil,' Morton greeted her warmly. 'Surely you've not forsaken your cozy room, for this place?'

'The bleedin' rozzers were around,' she said grudgingly.

'They can't have been after you,' exclaimed Morton with a grin.

'Some bloke who killed a copper; but they don't care who they put their hands on—or where they put them.'

'Couldn't blame them, though, could you?'

Lily refused to be drawn further. 'Beasley says you are to help Percy Kemp,' she said. 'He's downstairs, at the back.' She tossed her head and went out.

Morton unpacked his things, then went down to the servants' quarters. He discovered that the kitchen gave on to a short corridor, and that there was a door at the end of it. He knocked and went in.

'Mr Kemp?' he asked.

The room had been a butler's pantry. There were cupboards along two walls, a sink, and a long wooden bench covered with a litter of tools, rags and paper. In the corner was a contraption that looked like the prototype of a mangle. A grey-haired man was sitting at a table by the window. He was short and plump, with a chubby face and twinkling eyes. His hands were soft, with thick stubby fingers, his clothes rumpled and shabby.

'You are the new putter-down, are you?' he asked in a genial, cultured voice.

'Yes, Fred Thorburn. Lily says I have been deputed to assist you.'

'I'm not what I used to be,' Kemp replied with a short laugh. 'Have you got a hundred-pound note? . . . It's all right,' he said, noting Morton's consternation, 'you shall have it back.'

Morton pulled out a roll of notes and Kemp selected the newest. He carefully straightened it in his fingers, then, taking a small oblong of tracing paper, he pinned them both on to a piece of cork.

'Do you know anything about engraving?' he asked, as he began to trace the pattern of the note.

'I have never been artistic,' Morton replied obtusely.

Kemp looked up with a smile. 'Pass me that knife, will you? . . . For this job we need a very soft pencil, but we have to keep it sharp.' He scraped rapidly at the point, then resumed his tracing.

'If you have no immediate need of me,' Morton said, 'I will

get some hot water and have a shave. And mind you don't run off with my hundred quid!'

When Morton returned, the tracing was nearly completed and Kemp was gazing at it dolefully.

'Have you broken your pencil?' Morton asked chirpily.

'The bastards did for me at college,' said Kemp. 'Look!' He lifted his right hand from his knee, and Morton could see that it was trembling. 'Go and get me some half-and-half will you, my boy?'

Morton went to the pub near the gates of the brewery, and came back with several bottles of ale and stout. He poured one of each into a pint glass and Kemp gulped at it greedily, till it was half gone.

'I did a three-year stretch in the Scrubs,' he announced. 'And for all that it's supposed to be one of the new humane prisons, the cold got into my bones . . . and all through a woman.'

'How was that?' asked Morton with a smile.

'My father wanted me to become a lawyer, like him. I wanted to be a painter . . . I do not know what my father had done to cross his sister, but they were at loggerheads all the time. It was enough that my father was against my going to art school; my aunt was determined to help me. And she did God bless the old dearie!' A smile enveloped Kemp's genial face. 'She paid my fees at the Royal Academy, and gave me something to live on. I had a tremendous time—till it stopped. She thought being an artist was like any other job; you did your training, then you earned your living at it. And I suppose by then, she had found some other way of spiting my father. Anyway, the money stopped . . . Looking back, I was as naïve as she was. I trailed my paintings round the dealers, but no one was interested. I had some cards printed and left them at all the best houses, but I could not persuade anyone to let me paint their portrait.' He took another swallow from his glass and smiled ruefully.

'All this Bohemian business is nonsense,' he went on, wiping the froth from his lips with his sleeve. 'You need money to set up as a starving artist. I had none. I would have gladly attached myself to some patron, in return for board and lodging, but I was born a hundred years too late. If some rich old woman had asked me to be her lap-dog, I would have done, so long as I could paint—but I was not built to excite interest in the ladies!' He began to titter and his whole body quivered. 'Soon I could afford neither food nor canvas. I went crawling back home, with my tail between my legs. But my father did not conceive that the parable of the prodigal son could apply to him. It was just something to read to the servants, at morning prayers . . . That was the last time I saw my family.' He paused reflectively, then emptied his glass.

'I got a job with a print-seller, doing etchings of London street-scenes. In the early days we sometimes got a commission to do a big country-house, but photography ruined all that. Etchings have been affected more by it than paintings, oddly enough; the rich still want something to hang on their walls. Anyway, a few years ago, I really hit the bottom. I was reduced to doing etchings of other people's paintings—and not just the classics, either—paintings by Landseer, Frith and Tissot. What an affront to an artistic soul!' He gave a sly grin. 'That was the top of the slippery slope, for me.'

'What did they send you to prison for?' asked Morton.

'Blasphemy!' Kemp began to gurgle with laughter again.

'Blasphemy?'

'It was a bit naughty!' He wiped his eyes on a grubby handkerchief and stifled his giggles.

'I was asked by a bookseller in Jermyn Street to do some etchings for him. He was, if you understand me, a very special kind of bookseller, with some very special clients. I did a series which he called, *Gods and Man*. It included *Leda and the Swan*, *Europa and the Bull*, that kind of thing. It was what we called *The Immaculate Conception* that did it.'

'In all the pictures I have seen,' remarked Morton, 'Mary has been standing demurely on a cloud, surrounded by cherubs.'

'This one was concerned with St Luke, chapter one, my boy,' Kemp said with a boyish grin, 'the bit that goes, "the Holy Ghost shall come upon thee". In my picture she was a luscious, provocative young girl, lying back naked on a bed.'

'And the Holy Ghost?'

'A dammed great disembodied John Thomas!' Kemp dissolved into giggles again.

'So what did you expect?' asked Morton.

'Not that,' said Kemp in a pained tone. 'They were just ordinary indecent pictures, for ordinary licentious gentlemen, and they can't get you for that . . . But if you affront the religious susceptibilities of this hypocritical generation, they will bend all the rules to bring you to book. I was sent for trial to the Assize; you would have thought it was the Spanish Inquisition.'

'What happened to the bookseller?'

'The magistrate's court ordered the etchings to be destroyed and fined him twenty-five pounds.'

'And his clients?'

'They were protected, of course. My judge would not even let them be named in court, although the police knew who they were. There's justice for you.' Kemp lifted his arm and, satisfied that it had stopped trembling, resumed his tracing.

Morton sat and watched him. He drew with a series of short strokes, stopping frequently to sharpen his pencil. Bit by bit the design of the note appeared on the surface of the tracing-paper, its outline black and sharp. At last Kemp leaned back with a sigh of satisfaction.

'Now for the tricky bit,' he said, and reaching into the back of a cupboard, brought out a copper printing plate. He polished it with metal-polish, until all the oxidation had gone and the surface shone brightly. Then he laid the tracing-paper face down on the plate.

'Can you drag the press out a bit?' he asked, gesturing towards the contraption in the corner.

Morton saw that between the two rollers was a flat metal bed, which meshed with a gear on the end of the top roller. At the other end of that roller was an array of spokes like a capstan. Kemp placed some folded tissue paper on the bed of the machine, then put the plate and the tracing-paper on it, and covered them with a blanket.

'You are to be my pressman, Fred,' said Kemp. 'The trick is to turn the cross steadily, so that the bed rolls through at an even speed. You will feel some increase in resistance when the plate begins to go through.'

Morton turned the windlass and the end of the blanket was swallowed up by the roller. At first it went easily, but even after Kemp's warning, he had difficulty in keeping a steady momentum when the roller began to bit on the plate. Then it carried through evenly again, until the end of the plate was reached, and he had to hold the machine back to stop the roller snapping down on to the bed. He rolled it through completely, and Kemp peeled the tracing-paper off the plate. On the burnished copper surface was a perfect representation of a hundred-pound note, in reverse.

'Splendid!' said Kemp with a gratified smile. 'Now all I have to do is engrave it.'

'All!' exclaimed Morton. 'I should thing it would be impossible. Have you done one before?'

Kemp went over to the bench and poured ale and stout into his glass.

'Just to steady my hand,' he remarked. 'Do you want some?'

'No thank you.'

Kemp took a long gulp. 'I did a plate for the fiver, some years ago. It wasn't any good. I did it for my own amusement, really. It was never used, but I knew that if I spent enough time, I could make a perfect one. Then this chap asked me to do a plate for him—offered me two hundred quid. So I did.'

'Oh, these things leak out. I expect it came from the man whose press I used. Anyway, I had barely finished it, when they jugged me for my etching, so it had to stay hidden while I was inside.'

'And was it any good?' asked Morton.

For an answer, Kemp pulled the table away from the window and, lifting up a floor-board, thrust his arm into the cavity. With a grunt he brought up a bundle of rags, which he proceeded to unroll. He took out a copper plate which he gave to Morton.

'I am not used to reading these things backwards,' said Morton. 'Good Lord! It's for a thousand-pound note. Incredible! . . . What is this? . . . Hull? Why did you put that on?'

'I think the idea was that cashiers in London would not have seen many. Any uneasiness they felt, they would put down to that.'

'Twenty-ninth of March, eighteen eighty-nine,' remarked Morton. 'Was that when you got the chop?'

'No, in May. That date was on the note I was given to trace.'

'And the serial numbers?'

'Yes.'

'I didn't notice you tracing the serial **numbers** from my note?'

Kemp beamed. 'I didn't.'

'Why not?

'Wait and see!'

Morton felt he dared not press Kemp any further. He turned
back to the plate. 'I should think the real thing isn't any better,'
he said admiringly.

'Ah, but this is my masterpiece.' Kemp unrolled the rag
further and produced another plate for Morton's inspection.

'I don't recognize this,' said Morton. 'It's mainly wavy
lines. What do the letters say? . . . "Bank of
England . . . Thousand" . . . I have never seen a note like
this.'

'It is the plate for the water-mark,' said Kemp proudly. 'You
print it, just as you print the ink design.'

'But what do you use to make the markings?'

'Spermaceti from the sperm-whale and linseed oil, melted
together over hot water. The plate holds it a treat. It's a pity we
shall not be using it this time.'

'You don't expect me to put down a note without a
watermark, surely?' exclaimed Morton.

'Ah,' said Kemp mysteriously. 'You will have a surprise in
a day or two. We have got hold of a piece of genuine Bank of
England paper. I ran two thousand-pound notes off yesterday.
They are drying in my bedroom.'

Morton watched the landau coming towards him down Park
Lane, the liveried groom erect on his box. It was a magnificent
equipage, the beautifully matched pair of chestnuts picking up
their feet proudly. For all that it was nine o'clock, with the last
flush of sunset showing through the trees, the hoods were still
down. No wonder, on such an evening. A man in a silk top-hat
was sitting with his back to the driver. Opposite him was a
young woman in a green brocade evening dress. They were
probably going out to dinner, thought Morton. She was most
beautiful, her complexion soft and white. A tiara was perched
on her brown curls, and a necklace sparkled through a filmy
wrap thrown over her shoulders. Morton let his eyes follow her
as the carriage trotted past, then gave a start. There had been
a sudden movement on the other side of the road. He turned to
resume his walk, peering at the spot out of the corner of his
eye. The woman was pivoting round again, looking towards
him . . . it was Lily!

How the devil had she picked him up? She must have
followed him all the way from Spitalfields. Not that it would
have been difficult. He had slipped out of the house as soon as

the coast was clear, and he had taken the best part of an hour to stroll here. She could easily have followed him in a hansom as far as Hyde Park Corner, then walked along the edge of the park, keeping just behind him. What a fool he was! If he had not been so preoccupied with the implications of what Kemp had told him, he would have been able to throw her off the scent. Now, it was impossible. She would know perfectly well where he was going, and any attempt to get rid of her would only increase her suspicions. He sighed with vexation, as he turned down the area steps of number ninety-five and knocked on the door. It was opened by a smart young maid.

'I have to speak to Ada Smith,' Morton mumbled.

'Who shall I say?' she asked pertly.

'Fred Thorburn.'

She gave him a knowing smile. 'Will you wait a moment, please?' She disappeared, leaving the door ajar, and Morton heard raised voices. Then a buxom woman came to the door.

'I'm the cook,' she announced sourly, surveying his crumpled clothes. 'Who is it you want?'

'Ada Smith.'

'Are you sure you have the right house?'

'Quite sure, she gave me the address herself.'

'And what do you want with her?'

'I'm afraid I am not at liberty to say, but tell her it is extremely important.'

The cook sniffed suspiciously. 'Wait there,' she ordered, and closed the door.

Morton kicked his heels for some minutes, willing himself not to look up, in case Lily had crossed the road.

Eventually the door opened and Catherine appeared.

'I could not leave the dinner table,' she said apologetically.

'Keep back! Stay in the shadow. I have been followed,' exclaimed Morton. 'I must talk to you. I will wait for you opposite, just inside the park. Come as Ada Smith.'

'I shall have to change,' said Catherine in a bewildered voice.

'Well, don't be long.'

Morton turned on his heel and went up the steps to the street. Blast it! Why did it have to be so light! He dodged across to the other side and took up position under a tree. A few yards away, a path ran across the park at right-angles to the road. It was flanked by trees and every so often there was a bench. Well, so far at least, the location was appropriate to this story of meeting a frisky-tailed doxy there. He wondered where Lily was. Not far away, if he judged her right. He overcame the urge to look around for her and stared at the house opposite, until he saw Catherine emerge from the area steps. He walked to meet her. She had changed into a black skirt and thrown a shawl over her white blouse.

'Who followed you?' she greeted him in perturbation.

'One of the gang. I was not aware of it, until it was too late. We shall have to act out what I told you of the relationship between Thorburn and Ada Smith.'

'Where is he?' Catherine whispered.

'I don't know. Just forget it, if you can . . . And look pleased! I am your boyfriend, turned up unexpectedly.'

Catherine gave a shaky laugh and, taking Morton's arm, began to pace slowly along the path.

'I want you to go to Sergeant Bragg as soon as possible,' said Morton quietly. 'Tell him that the gang has got hold of a piece of genuine Bank of England paper and he is to look out for Hull thousands. I dare not probe any further, in case I arouse suspicion. I expect him to follow that up. I can stay with the gang until he is ready to move. Right?'

'Yes . . . Do you have to, James?'

'I do.' Morton said abruptly. 'I have met the counterfeiter, indeed I am helping him to prepare a plate for a one-hundred pound note! His name is Percy Kemp, and he has done time. He showed me the plate for the thousand-pound note this afternoon.'

'Oh dear, this is such a jumble,' Catherine complained. 'I wish I had brought my note-book.'

'Housemaids don't take notes,' said Morton grimly. 'Tell the sergeant that there may be other members of the gang I have not yet met.'

'Where are you?' asked Catherine anxiously.

'In a big old house at the bottom of Rupert Street in Spitalfields—near the brewery. Don't worry. I am in no danger . . . And now, for your own sake, we must convince them that you are the dolly-mop I said you were.'

He pulled her down on to a bench and, wrapping his arms around her, began to kiss her roughly. She tried to shout her outrage, but it was smothered. 'Stop fighting,' he mumbled through his teeth. 'Your life may depend on it.'

In a fright she submitted, even to putting her arm round his waist. Her head was tipped back on his arm, their mouths joined.

'Sorry,' he murmured . . . 'our spy is coming closer.' She felt a fumbling at her blouse, the shock of his hand against her breast.

'Oh, no!' she gasped in alarm.

Even though he was now holding his hand away from her flesh, she could feel her breast tingling. She twisted her face away from him. 'My reputation . . .'

'Good God, woman,' he muttered, 'don't you realize that, beside you, every other female is an insipid ninny?'

'Woman? . . . How dare you!' she hissed.

'Well you are one, aren't you?'

'I am only twenty-one.'

'What does that make you?'

With a sudden surge of anger she struck out at his face and struggled free. She ran down the path homewards, ignoring his repeated calls of 'Ada! Ada!'

She went in through the basement and, slinking upstairs, flung herself on her bed. She was angry as much with herself, as with him. Why had she believed him? Why had she ever thought herself safe with him? Beastly men! . . . What if someone had seen her? She would be a pariah! Cast out from society. Would he want her then? . . . But perhaps it had been too dark . . . Oh! It wasn't fair! How could he force her? Making it a grubby furtive business, when it ought to be sublime. And her wretched tumescent nipple might have given him the idea that she was fond of him, while he'd been fumbling her like a trull!

Numbly she changed back into her two-piece and took a cab to the City. Nothing seemed to matter, now. Even if it did not become public knowledge, she would never be able to forget it; never throw off the outrage, the feeling of degradation. Nor would he forget it. He probably would exult in it—another young woman to his tally . . . 'Woman!' How dare he address her so, as if she were his chattel . . . How dare he?

She dully ordered the cabby to wait for her and hammered on Bragg's door. His landlady, Mrs Jenks, came down in curl-papers and a wrap over her nightdress. She put Catherine in Bragg's sitting-room, while she roused him, then went down to make coffee.

Bragg appeared soon afterwards, his nightshirt stuffed into his trousers.

'Whatever brings you here at this time of night?' he asked in perturbation.

She repeated everything that Morton had told her, while Bragg sliced tobacco and filled his pipe.

'You are not worried about him, are you, miss?' he asked, when she had finished.

'No, I am not!' she cried angrily.

'Then what is upsetting you?'

Catherine bit her lip. 'He . . . he violated me!'

Bragg looked at her incredulously. 'I find that hard to believe,' he said gently. 'I would have staked my life he was way above that.'

'He said that one of the gang had followed him, and he forced me on to a bench and kissed me, on the pretext of convincing them I was a dolly-mop.'

'I doubt if it was just a pretext, miss,' said Bragg quietly. 'They have been down to Wells school and asked the head-master about him. They are a thorough lot.'

'It was no excuse for . . . for pawing my breast.'

Bragg lit a match, and puffed a haze of smoke about them.

'How old are you, miss?' he asked absently.

'Don't you start, sergeant!' she cried.

'You know, things are different where I come from,' he said reflectively. 'I suppose the lads and lasses are let run wild, by your standards. None of them would turn their nose up at a cuddle behind the haystack. In our village, I reckon at least half the brides are three months pregnant. A farm is finished, you see, if there are no children to follow on.'

'I am not a country bumpkin, sergeant,' Catherine replied coldly. 'In my circle, merely going unchaperoned with him into the park was enough to taint my honour.'

'I am sure Morton would never say a word about it,' replied Bragg with conviction.

'I do not want my reputation to lie in his hands, thank you.'

'I cannot think of better,' said Bragg gruffly. 'If you don't mind me saying so, miss, your trouble is that you want it all ends up. You want to be one of these new career women, and cock a snook at the traditions of your class; and at the same time you want the comfort of belonging to it. You want a good home, children, a husband . . . You can't have it every way, miss.'

Catherine rose to her feet. 'Why should I not?' she asked haughtily. 'Why not?'

CHAPTER ———————
——————— TWELVE

'I have asked for this meeting, Mr Liddesdale, because I have received a somewhat startling piece of information relating to the counterfeiting case.'

The Commissioner and Bragg were seated in the Governor's opulent room at the Bank.

'I am, however, only prepared to divulge it,' went on Sir William, 'if you will give me a strict undertaking that it will go no further.'

Liddesdale looked at him speculatively. 'Will you tell me why you wish to impose this secrecy on me?' he asked.

'Because I regard the present operation as a futile waste of time. I have in mind a new approach, and I have no intention of allowing its development to be prejudiced.'

'And how do you reconcile this reticence with your duty as a public servant?' asked Liddesdale coldly.

Sir William flushed. 'I have decided to carry out my duty as a policeman, and leave the public posturing to others,' he said angrily.

'Since your continued employment depends on those posturers,' Liddesdale said abrasively, 'are you not attitudinizing, yourself?'

'I am prepared to resign over it,' Sir William retorted with asperity. 'I have lost one man already. I am not going to have another murdered.'

Liddesdale gazed out of the window for a moment, frowning. Then he turned back to the Commissioner. 'Very well,' he said quietly. 'You have my word that it will go no further.'

'And you will undertake not to interfere in any consequential actions I choose to take?'

Surprisingly, the Governor smiled amiably. 'I can see nothing but benefit from having any further initiative under your exclusive control,' he said, 'and I will do all in my power to assist you.'

Sir William seemed deflated by the sudden capitulation. 'Right.' He cleared his throat uncertainly. 'We have it on good authority that the counterfeiters have obtained at least one piece of genuine Bank of England paper.'

A tolerant smile crept over Liddesdale's features. 'This "good authority", am I to be allowed to know its nature?' he asked.

The Commissioner glanced across at Bragg. 'Yes,' he replied . . . 'We have infiltrated the counterfeiting gang. The young constable whom you saw on the morning of Walton's murder, is now a putter-down with them.'

'Is he, by God?' exclaimed the Governor. 'Then why do you not arrest them?'

'We have to take the whole gang, or they will merely set up again. The constable feels there are others still unidentified. And, of course, we now have to investigate the source of the paper.'

'Has your constable seen this allegedly genuine paper.'

'Not so far as I am aware. He was told that they had obtained it, and had printed two notes using the Hull branch plate.'

'Well, if it is true, they will lose no time in presenting them,' Liddesdale observed. 'In the meantime, I see no harm in your discreetly probing the Bank's procedures.'

'Have you any idea where the paper might have come from, sir?' asked Bragg.

'Assuming it is indeed genuine, sergeant, it must have been obtained either at the manufactory, during transit thence, or from this building.'

'That about covers everything,' remarked Bragg gloomily.

Liddesdale smiled. 'We are not so lax in matters of security

as your remark would imply. We have our own officer at the
works in Hampshire. His sole function is to ensure that every
piece of completed paper is accounted for and duly despatched
to us. The paper, on its receipt here, is checked by the Chief
Cashier's department, and any discrepancy with the invoiced
quantities would immediately become apparent.'

'And where is it kept?' asked Bragg.

'In the vaults, as are the printed notes still unissued. So you
understand, Sir William, my scepticism as to the validity of
your information . . . However, I recognize your concern,
and I appreciate that we should lose no time in establishing the
position. What I would ask is that you consent to my taking
May into our confidence. We could hardly take any meaningful
action without his co-operation.'

'I would agree to that,' said the Commissioner gruffly.

'I imagine that it would be in both our interests, if the
sergeant were to carry out his enquiries surreptitiously. I will
therefore ask May to put it about that he is running his eye over
our security arrangements.'

'And the factory?' asked Bragg.

'I will give you a personal letter of introduction to Obadiah
Crutwell, the owner of the works. You can use it as you think
best.'

Morton was reading the paper on his bed, next morning, when
he heard the door open and stealthy steps approaching him. He
affected not to hear and went on reading for a few moments.
Then he made to turn the page.

'Lily! . . . You gave me a fright!' he exclaimed.

She was standing at the foot of the bed, looking at him
steadily. She did not seem to be hostile. If anything, her gaze
was empty of emotion. He wriggled over to the wall and patted
the mattress beside him, but she made no move to sit down.

'I followed you on Thursday night,' she said flatly. 'Did you
know?'

'Followed me? Whatever for?' he said with an incredulous
laugh.

'She's as common as dirt, your girl, walking down the path
doing her buttons up.'

'I know she's not your class, Lil, but . . .'

'But what?' she asked, suddenly fierce.

'If I had met you first, I would never have taken up with her, but I've known her a long time, now.'

'So why don't you forget her?'

'It wouldn't be hard to. She's not any fun, compared to you.'

'Well, then?'

'Be reasonable, Lily . . . All right, I didn't mean what I said about you the other night, and I'm sorry . . . But although Ada is not much, she is my girl. She doesn't go out with any other fellows, and she spends all her free time with me.'

'I thought Wednesday was her evening off,' said Lily sharply.

'It is, but she didn't come. They'd had an unexpected dinner-party that night and she had to help. But I thought she was ill or something, so I went along the next night, to find out.'

'I didn't notice you getting much,' she scoffed.

'She said she had come on early this month.'

Lily gave a contemptuous laugh. 'You men! You will swallow anything. She's just tired of you.'

'Tired of me?' exclaimed Morton in disbelief.

'If she will lift her skirts for you, she'll do it for plenty more.'

'Now, she's not like that.'

'How do you know? How can you be sure there was a dinner-party on Wednesday?'

'I suppose I don't know,' Morton admitted.

'She was stringing you on, that's what she was doing,' said Lily with a sneering smile. 'If she was roped in for a dinner-party, it must have been big. You can't arrange one that size in a hurry. It takes weeks.'

'I suppose you know, Lil,' said Morton thoughtfully.

''Course I bloody know!'

'Perhaps she wouldn't miss me, after all.'

'Miss you?' she exclaimed derisively. 'You are two of a kind, and no mistake. You think you are having it for free because she's hawking her mutton round anybody who will give her a good time. I know these bitches, they hang around in the park, taking bread out of working girl's mouths. They will go with any man who winks at them.'

'Do you really think so?' asked Morton slowly.

'I'm sure of it. You don't think she'd be serious about marrying a man, when she doesn't even know where he lives? You're stupid, Fred.'

'I suppose I am, Lil . . . So you reckon I could let her go, with no hard feelings?'

'Feelings? That trollop? Flashing her tits in the park!'

'I'd better have it out with her, though. I can't just not turn up any more.'

'Suit yourself.' She turned disdainfully. 'Beasley wants to see you in the kitchen,' she said over her shoulder.

Morton put on his coat and followed her down the stairs.

Beasley seemed to be elated. 'What do you think of that?' he asked slyly, pointing at a thousand-pound note lying on the table.

Morton picked it up and looked at it perfunctorily.

'Why, it's just the same as the others,' he said.

'Not quite the same, Fred, not quite the same.'

Morton affected to examine it more closely. 'I give up,' he said finally. 'What is different about it?'

'It's real paper, Fred. The real McCoy!'

Morton whistled. 'How did you get hold of that?' he asked admiringly.

'Never you mind! And there's more where that came from,' he exclaimed exultantly.

'You're a wizard,' said Morton.

'I think it would end the week on a fitting note,' he dwelt on the pun, 'if you were to change that for me this morning. Why not try the Bank of England? There can't be any risk now.'

'So you are looking at our security?' remarked the chief printer. 'Not before time, in my opinion.'

'I cannot say that I was over-impressed by the clerks in the cashier's store,' said Bragg.

'It's odd, isn't it? Twenty years ago, my predecessor persuaded the court of directors to adopt a procedure that reduced staff, and they went and employed them elsewhere.'

'I don't follow you.'

'Up to eighteen seventy, every cashier personally signed the notes he issued. As you can imagine, that took a great deal of time, and it did not really reduce the risk of forgery. So we got them to allow us to print the signature of the Chief Cashier on the notes, instead. As a result we had a surplus of cashiers . . . So they found them a billet in the store! It is the old story, every man under-employed, boredom and slackness setting in, no new blood.'

'Have you made representations, then?'

'What me?' John exclaimed. 'That's Frank May's department. I would not tolerate his interfering in my printing!'

'I see. Well, I have a couple of cashiers doing some checking in the store, so I thought I would come and see what happened to the paper at this end.'

'No bank-note paper whatever is kept here overnight,' said John. 'We stop printing at three o'clock, so that everything can be back in the vaults by four. Because of that, our procedures are designed to account for whatever paper has been drawn from the stores that day.'

'Do you carry out a physical count on the paper issued to you in the morning?' asked Bragg.

'No. It comes to us already checked, in boxes holding a ream.'

'How much is that?'

'Five hundred sheets.'

'What happens then?'

John led the way to a large printing machine, being driven by a belt from an overhead shaft.

'The paper is stacked in this feeder,' he explained, raising his voice above the din. 'It is carried along here to the first cylinder, where a plate prints the main design, then it goes to the second cylinder, where the date of the printing and the serial numbers are added.'

'And when it comes out?'

'It goes to the guillotine, for the notes to be separated, then down to the vaults.'

'Back to the cashier's store?' asked Bragg.

'No, into what we call the treasury.'

'I see. So you don't know exactly how many sheets of paper you start with. You take that on trust.'

'Yes.'

'How do you know how many you have processed?'

John motioned Bragg to follow him round to the other side of the machine. 'Do you see this dial?' he asked. 'It records the number of impressions made by the first plate.'

'That is before the role is complete?' asked Bragg.

'Yes, but don't forget there is a correlation with the serial numbers printed by the second plate.'

"And how do you control the notes when they leave the machine?"

'The divided notes are put in the same box, and the serial numbers are noted on the outside.'

'Do you count the notes?'

'Every now and then we do a sample check.'

'Have you discovered any discrepancies?'

'Not yet, thank God!'

'But the machine can't work perfectly all the time. What happens when a note is spoiled?'

'There will be a gap in the serial numbers, then. We make a note of it in our production records and also on the outside of the box.'

'So you always know the number of notes you are sending down to the treasury?'

'Yes.'

'What about the spoilt paper?'

'That is returned to the cashier's store.'

'And what do they do with it?'

'I have no idea.'

'Is it possible that a piece of paper returned by you as spoilt, could be introduced into a box of paper for future processing?'

The printer hesitated. 'Most of the spoilt sheets are torn, or would have already have an impression on them. It does happen, however, that an occasional sheet is picked out of the feeder because it has a flaw. I suppose that could be sent round again.'

'And somebody, somewhere, could dispose of a perfect piece of Bank of England paper.'

'Yes . . . Not good enough, is it?'

Tarnation! thought the cook. She never did learn. Every year it was the same. She would give in to the knife-grinder's blandishments and agree to her vegetable knives' being sharpened. And every year she would cut herself straight afterwards. She plunged her hands into the bowl to wash the lettuce, and a brown wisp rose from the bloodied rag round her finger. A good thing it was only for garnish . . . It would have to be on a Saturday, with the young mistress at home, and a proper lunch to cook. Usually Mr Marsden had a try in his studio and madam made do with an omelette, or something light. She darted across to the gas stove, and just managed to catch the milk before it boiled over. The master had been very proud of it when he'd had it installed; but all it had brought her, was more work. They seemed to think that now she could get through twice the amount of work; luncheon parties, dinners— and her with still only the one pair of hands. She lifted the lid of the big pan simmering on the coal range—they could keep their new-fangled gas contraptions, for her. Then she went to the sink and lifted out two blue-black lobsters. She ran them under the tap, then, carefully avoiding their pinioned claws, dropped them into the simmering water. They should be a treat, with mayonnaise, for dinner. There was a rapping on the area door.

'Just a minute,' she called. She watched the surface of the water begin to bubble again, and balanced the lid on the pan so that enough steam would escape to keep it from racing. Then she opened the door. A slightly-built young man was standing there. He was dressed like a clerk and was smiling in a knowing sort of way.

'Morning ma'am,' he said brightly. 'I hope you are going to be able to help me, or I shall be working overtime for no pay.'

'What is it?' she asked, warming to him.

'I'm a clerk at the post office, on the "inadequately addressed" section.'

'Oh, yes?'

'We've had this letter, addressed to "Miss Ada Smith, Park Lane". The postman doesn't recognize the name, and he can't deliver it without a number; so it has landed on my desk. I've been knocking on every door in the street.' He pulled a comical face.

'It's for here,' said the cook.

'Does Miss Smith live here?' asked the man.

'I've told you it's for here.'

'Only, I am supposed to see her myself.'

'Well, you can't.'

'Why not?'

'You just can't.'

He scratched his jaw. 'I'm not supposed to deliver it, except to her personally.'

The cook could hear the hiss of her lobsters boiling over.

'It's for the young mistress,' she said hurriedly. 'She's a bit of a card. She is always up to some mischief or other.'

'That would be Miss Marsden, would it?'

'Yes. Give it to me. I'll see she gets it.'

'Well, will you ask her to see that her correspondents put the number on her letters? It will save us a lot of trouble.' He handed over the letter, saluted cheekily, and strode off.

The cook put the letter on the dresser, and it was only after lunch was over, and the washing-up finished, that she noticed it again. She sent the housemaid upstairs and the young mistress came hurrying down. The cook recounted as much as she could remember of the interview.

'What did he look like?' demanded Catherine.

'Young and cheeky, I'd say.'

'You are quite sure it was not the same gentleman who called on Thursday evening?' asked Catherine, in some embarrassment.

'Quite sure. That one was much taller.'

'I do wish you had not said it was for me.'

'You wouldn't have got it at all, if I hadn't, miss.'

Catherine took it to her room, full of foreboding. It was inconceivable that James would not have put the house number. She slit open the envelope, and read it quickly. It was short, and pure drivel, with none of his mocking tone. Slipping into a coat and hat, she ran downstairs and took a cab to Tan House Lane.

Bragg was spraying the spindly roses with soap-suds, so Mrs Jenks took her to him in the garden. He leaned against the wall and read the letter carefully.

'You would swear it was his writing, wouldn't you, miss?' he said slowly. 'And yet he has not put the number code in the second line. If he wrote it at all, he wrote it under duress.'

'Oh!' cried Catherine, 'I had not thought . . . I assumed it was a forgery. But since they took away one of his letters to me, they must know the house number perfectly well.'

'I think you were right first time,' said Bragg soothingly. 'They left off the number to give themselves an excuse to call. From the description, I would say that it was Snell, wouldn't you?'

'But what have they gained?'

Bragg looked at her steadily. 'I would say that they are not satisfied with the Ada Smith story, and they were checking it.'

Catherine shivered. 'And now they know that she doesn't exist, that James is in contact with a reporter . . . Oh, I wish I had never agreed to help you!'

'You musn't blame yourself, miss. Nothing ever goes just as you had planned it; but that doesn't mean it was wrong from the start. The information he has given us already would enable us to cripple the gang, even if we weren't able to wipe it out.'

'You talk as if he were already as good as dead!' cried Catherine wildly.

'No. I am not saying that, miss.'

'Then why not let me tell him to abandon it all?'

'He wouldn't, even if I asked him to. He knows how important it is—he would never have taken the risk on Thursday otherwise. And he is very near to the heart of the conspiracy. No, I think it is you that may be in greater danger. You must be very careful from now on.'

CHAPTER _____
_____ THIRTEEN

Bragg took off the jacket of his new tweed lounge-suit, and mopped the back of his neck. When he had set off it had been dull, with a damp breeze from the east. But as the train panted its way into Hampshire, it was a glorious summer day. He had lunched off beer and sandwiches at the Railway Inn, and then set off to walk to the house, which was visible over the valley. 'Only a couple of miles', they had said. Well, they must be damned long miles! Part of the trouble was the rutted surface of the road. You could turn your ankle, if you didn't keep a wary eye open. And the verges were overgrown with tangled grass and cow-parsley. If you ploughed through that instead, like as not you'd blunder into the ditch . . . Blast it! He was becoming too much of a towny. Instead of wallowing in the smell of drying hay, and the sound of the bees in the honeysuckle, he was intent on rushing there as if a minute wasted was a pound lost. He plodded on again. The house had long since been swallowed up by the trees, and the hill was steeper than it had seemed from the railway station. Not that he'd had any choice. Although everybody has known where Crutwell's place was, no one seemed anxious to take him

there . . . On this stretch he was in the full sun, and he was
sweating like a pig. That would be the ale. If you poured it in,
it had to come out one way or another. He ought to cut down
on it. The bulge over his waist-band might disappear then. He
rounded a bend and saw a pair of splendid iron gates on the
left. This must be it. He went up the long gravelled drive, to an
imposing house marooned in a green sea of closely mown
grass.

His knock was answered by a maid, who told him to wait
while she enquired if the master was in. A few minutes later an
elderly man appeared, his hair tousled as if he had been
napping.

'I don't see commercial travellers on a Sunday,' he said
abruptly.

'I have a personal letter for you from Mr Liddesdale, sir,'
said Bragg quietly.

'Oh. Then you had better come in.'

Crutwell led the way down a dark passage, into a study at the
back of the house. He motioned Bragg to a chair, then, taking
a silver paper-knife from the desk, carefully slit the envelope.
He read the letter in growing perplexity.

'It says that the bearer is a member of the City police force,
and that I am to afford him all the assistance and facilities he
may require to further his enquiries.' He looked up sharply. 'I
suppose you have some proof of your identity.'

Bragg handed over his warrant-card, and Crutwell stared at
it for some moments.

'What is it all about, then?' he asked brusquely.

'The Governor said I should pretend that I am checking on
the Bank's security procedures, but it's more than that, and I
can't see any point in trying to deceive you.'

'Then you have more sense than he has, sergeant,' Crutwell
remarked frostily.

'According to a very reliable informant, some bank-note
paper has gone missing and has fallen into the hands of
counterfeiters.'

Crutwell looked up sharply. 'Go on,' he said.

'I have examined the security arrangements at the Bank and,
while there are still some checks to finish, it is already clear
that their procedures need overhauling. So I have come down
here, to have a quick look at this end.'

'How much is missing?' asked Crutwell.

'One piece only, that we know about.'

'Hmn. That could be worth two thousand pounds, if they had a good plate.'

'They have,' said Bragg shortly.

'Then, what do you want of me?'

'My concern is to arrest everyone involved, including the people who are stealing the paper. So I don't want to alert any of them, until we are ready. What I would like at the moment, is a description of the manufacturing process, and the methods used to control the paper once it has been made. Then I should be able to decide if there are any weaknesses that should be rectified.'

'You mean, whether it was taken from here or not,' said Crutwell flatly. 'Well, you will not get any idea of it by sitting here. I'll just go and find my keys.'

Bragg spent an enjoyable ten minutes helping the old man to harness the horse to the trap, then they were rattling along the road, towards the village of Lovington. Just before they reached the first houses, they stopped outside a large works. It was surrounded by a massive ten-foot-high wall, and Bragg noted with approval that no trees were allowed to grow near it. Crutwell drove in and re-locked the heavy wooden gate behind them. The main factory was one great single-storey building. It had no windows in its walls. Instead, the roof had been designed as a series of ridges, running across the building, one side of each ridge being slated and the other glazed. Crutwell nodded to the watchman, then unlocked a stout oak door and led Bragg into the plant. The floor was filled with ranks of large machines, with narrow passage-ways between them. Bragg stopped to admire one which was in the process of being installed.

'You don't need to worry about that one,' Crutwell said. 'It is a new continuous-flow machine, for making postal-order paper. The paper for Bank of England notes is made in the old way.' He walked down to the other end of the building.

'Pfou!' exclaimed Bragg. 'What a stink! Have you got some rotting corpses in there?'

'That's the steeping tanks,' said Crutwell with a chuckle. 'We use white linen rags and offcuts. The first part of the process is to let them ferment in warm water till they begin to disintegrate.'

'My God! I'll stick to beer, thanks.'

'It's not so bad, once they are washed; the odour is tolerable then.'

'What happens after that?'

'The rags are put into one of those Hollander beaters. It has rotating bronze blades in the tank, which draw the contents against a bed-plate and pull the fibres apart. The more the individual fibres are teased out, the stronger will be the finished paper.'

'Why is that?'

'Well, paper is little more than vegetable fibres, matted together and pressed. The longer the fibres, the greater the degree of entanglement. When it is finished, a sheet of our Bank of England paper will bear a load of half a hundred-weight.'

Crutwell passed on to a large tank, with wooden decking across it. 'This is where the skill lies.' He picked up a wooden frame backed with wire mesh. 'I used to be able to do this, many a year ago,' he said with a smile. He dipped the frame into the tank and scooped up a quantity of fibrous liquid. Most of the stock ran back into the tank, but while there was still some liquid in the frame, Crutwell shook it sharply sideways.

'You see what has happened?' he asked. 'The water has drained out through the wires of the mould, leaving the linen fibres behind. That shaking action is done to matt the fibres together. You are supposed to do it from back to front, as well as sideways, but I daren't risk my back.' He removed the frame from the base of the mould. 'The vatman would put this deckle on another mould, to make the next sheet while the first was draining, but I think that is enough for this afternoon.'

'I thought the deckle was the edge of the paper,' said Bragg.

'That is true.' He turned to the mould which was draining. 'There is your piece of paper. You can see the straight edges formed by the frame, which are still quite thick at this stage. The irregular frill outside them, is caused by stock seeping under the frame. That is the deckle you are talking about.'

'So that is a piece of paper?' remarked Bragg in surprise.

'Complete with Bank of England watermark.'

'Obviously, a lot has still to happen to it,' said Bragg.

'Why, yes. It is turned out on to a piece of felt. When they have a stack of them, each separated by felt, they go to be pressed. Let me just get rid of this . . .' He tipped the embryonic piece of paper back into the vat. 'I would not want

John Popham to see my apprentice efforts, tomorrow morning!'

'When do you start accounting for the paper?' asked Bragg.

'Not yet. My goodness me, no! We discard about twenty per cent in processing. Even when it has been pressed several times, it is still easy to damage it while it is damp; and there are always holes, blurred water-marks and so on, to contend with.'

'It sounds a very expensive business.'

'In terms of labour, yes; but the spoilt paper just goes back in the vat.'

'At all events, there is nothing approaching a finished piece of paper, yet.'

'I suppose once the pressed paper has been through the drying machine, you could describe it as finished in one sense, though it still has to be sized.'

'How many sheets of paper go in the press at once?'

'A hundred and forty-four sheets—what we call a "post".'

'So we know there is that number in every stack at the pressing stage?'

'No. Not necessarily. The full number would be in the post when it left the vat; but if some were removed, because of defects, they would not be replaced.'

'Hmn.' Bragg pursed his lips. 'What happens in the drying stage?'

"Each individual piece is passed through heated rollers.'

'And bundled up again into posts?'

'No. We still do tub-sizing for the Bank of England. The sizer can only handle around a hundred sheets at once, so he just takes a batch at a time from the pile.'

'I don't understand this,' complained Bragg. 'You start off with a precise number, but by the end of the process you don't care how many sheets are in the pile.'

'You've got hold of the wrong end of the stick, sergeant. The number in the post is determined by the capacity of the press. You don't keep track of the sheets at that stage, because you don't know how many you will lose. Anyway, from a security angle, there is no point in counting until finished paper is being produced.'

'And when is that?'

Crutwell crossed over to a machine beyond the sizing tub. 'This little beauty dries and glazes the whole of the output of bank-note paper.' He pushed aside an inspection flap and gestured to Bragg to look in. 'Made in Winterthur and goes like a Swiss watch.' He walked to the end of the machine. 'This is where Langton, the Bank's officer, stands.'

'And what is his function?' asked Bragg.

'Why, he has to ensure that every last piece of finished paper goes into the strong-room, there.'

Bragg looked across and saw a heavy metal door let into the brickwork, with locks at top and bottom.

'The Bank sent their own contractors down to build it.'

'Who has the keys?' asked Bragg.

'Langton has one set, the works manager has another.'

'Any other sets?'

'No, only the two.'

'This works manager, is he trustworthy?'

'He'd better be,' said Crutwell brusquely. 'He's my own son.'

'And does Langton count the sheets?'

'Good Heavens, no! He's an important man around here— the representative of our biggest customer. They bought him a house not much smaller than mine!'

'I see. How long has he been here?'

'Eighteen years, come Michaelmas.'

'Is he well thought of?'

'Why, yes. He's a nice man. You won't find anyone with a bad word to say against him.'

'I like a watch-dog that growls,' observed Bragg darkly. 'So, who does count them?'

'This finishing machine. It batches them in five hundreds, when they have been processed. All the storeman has to do, is pick up a batch and put it in the box. Then it's straight into the strong-room.'

'And Langton watches him do it?'

'That's right.'

'How does the paper get to the Bank?'

'By train. It's put in damned great steel chests and taken to the station by the Bank's own wagon. I believe an armed guard travels with it to London, but Langton could tell you more about that.'

'I might come down another time and have a word with him; but for the moment, don't tell anyone at all about my visit.'

'Just as you wish.'

Bragg pondered for a moment. 'Tell me, sir. If I wanted to

come down on a working day and watch what was going on, unobserved, could you arrange it?'

'Why, yes. Just send me a telegram, and come.'

'Ah, May. I was just about to send for you,' the Governor said irritably. 'Have you seen this report in today's *Manchester Guardian*?'

'No, sir.'

'It amounts to a complete account of all the forgeries that have been discovered in the City recently.'

'Not the counterfeit notes!' exclaimed May apprehensively.

'Not those, thank God! But they have the forged cheques, bills of exchange, promissary notes—in many cases with the amounts and the names of the banks and brokers involved . . . And for good measure, they have a historical assessment, showing that in monetary terms, this is far worse than any previous episode of the kind. Only two more months of my term of office to go, and this has to happen!'

'I fear that I bring you no comfort,' said May glumly. 'This Hull thousand-pound note was paid out on Saturday. It is the same plate as the other two—only, on this occasion, the paper is undoubtedly genuine.'

Liddesdale took the cancelled note, and held it up to the light. 'Has John seen it?' he asked.

'Yes. Naturally, he was the only person I consulted.'

'Give it to Sergeant Bragg, will you, May? I would like him to get absolute confirmation from Obadiah Crutwell.'

'Of course. In fact he has only just left my room . . . I fear that my own reputation will not emerge unsullied from this affair.'

'How is that?' asked the Governor sharply.

'At the sergeant's request, I sent three cashiers down to the store-room on Friday. He particularly insisted that I should require the clerks down there to undergo a test of their efficiency. Accordingly, we took a few sheets out of a ream of paper and got each one to count it, unawares. We were carrying out a physical check of sample boxes, so it was not difficult to arrange. Of the eight clerks involved, seven reported a total of five hundred—which is what they would expect to find. And the man who detected a shortfall still got the total wrong.'

'Then we shall have to move them,' said Liddesdale unhappily.

'There is no post of responsibility within the Bank, Governor, which can be safely entrusted to a man who can no longer count,' said May firmly.

Liddesdale sighed. 'Very well, I will speak to the directors about letting them go . . . Thank goodness that is the worst of it.'

May looked down at the carpet. 'I am sorry to say that there is more. Over the weekend, my cashiers have done a physical check of every box in the store—and one piece of paper is missing.'

'So it came from here?' exclaimed the Governor.

'Sergeant Bragg does not seem prepared to assume that, at the moment,' said May hesitantly.

Liddesdale glanced at the note on his desk. 'Well, if there really is only one more to come, it will be a small price to pay for a salutary lesson. What steps are you taking?'

'Quite apart from the efficiency of staff, the sergeant has high-lighted some deficiencies in our procedures. I imagine that when you receive his report, you will wish to institute a review of all security matters.'

'You do not exactly fill me with joy, May.'

'No, sir.'

'Ah well, it will be a task for my successor . . .' His glance strayed to the newspaper at his elbow. 'How do these people get hold of their information?' he asked irritably.

'There must be plenty of people in the City with the necessary knowledge,' said May. 'Not least, the police.'

'I wish they would get on and make some arrests,' Liddesdale said testily.

'How long do you think we can maintain our present policy, sir? There has been a significant increase in the demand for sovereigns, in the last few days.'

'Has there, indeed?'

'I fear that rumours of counterfeit notes are no longer confined to the business community. I am told that it is a common topic of conversation in the ale-houses, all over London.'

'Then God help us, May . . . God help us.'

Morton could not shake off a persistent feeling of disquiet. After a weekend of idleness, Monday had usually begun with a burst of activity. Today there had been nothing—for him, anyway. Snell had been given the job of putting down the second 'genuine' note, and he was visibly cock-a-hoop about it. Ever since his return, he was smiling provocatively—almost maliciously—in Morton's direction. Well, he had earned fifty pounds that he had not expected. Surely that was enough to make anyone elated? Except that it was not just elation. There was a vindictiveness about him that went beyond merely getting his own back. Of the others, Beasley had been his usual smarmy self and, after giving Snell his instructions, had disappeared; Lily was still keeping her distance; Goulter had embarked on a manic sharpening of his knives.

After lunch, Morton went to see how Kemp was progressing. He was preoccupied, concentrating on engraving his plate. He had spent a great deal of time measuring, and minutely adjusting the pencil outline on the plate, before cutting it.

'Why do you cut it on that leather cushion?' Morton asked, while Kemp was replenishing his system with half-and-half.

'If you notice, I am cutting it from right to left,' he said. 'The reverse of the way you write. I do that, to ensure it is nothing more than a pattern to me. Now look . . . It's mainly loops, isn't it? You cannot cut a loop on a table; you have to be able to turn the plate into the cut, without it slipping.' He glanced at Morton's bank-note on the bench. 'It looks deceptively simple, doesn't it? The kind of writing they teach any kid at board-school. But I'll tell you what, I would rather cut a plate for the most elaborate-seeming foreign note, than a Bank of England note . . . Pass me that oil-stone, will you?'

He began to sharpen the point of his burin, his mind once more involved with the task before him.

'I will get you some more beer,' said Morton, and wandered pensively out.

When he returned, Kemp was engrossed in cutting a loop, his tongue protruding from the corner of his mouth. Morton deposited the bottles on the bench, then strolled into the kitchen. Beasley had returned, and was busy forging yet another cheque. Morton drew a chair up to the table and, as he did so, Snell slipped out. He watched Beasley for a while, and became aware that Lily had entered. She hovered by the door, then crossed over and stood by the dresser. A few moments after, Snell came back with Goulter. Snell leaned on the door and Goulter took up a position by the fireplace, behind Morton. It was all done without a word. They all seemed detached from

one another, watching Beasley's careful calligraphy without
moving a muscle. The tension in the room had become almost
palpable. Morton glanced towards the dresser. One of
Goulter's knives was missing . . . He felt panic rising in
him. What had gone wrong? What had they discovered? He
had a sudden urge to spring to his feet and hurl himself through
the window. But before he had gone a step, Goulter's knife
would be in his back. Instead, he affected not to notice; but
pretending to stretch, he swivelled round slightly, so that his
legs were no longer under the table. Now, at least, he would be
able to react quickly, if the opportunity arose.

'Fred?' Beasley laid down his pen with a sigh of satisfaction.

'Yes?' replied Morton lazily.

'What would you say, if I told you Ada Smith doesn't exist?'

'Don't be daft,' Morton's tone was good-humoured. 'Ask
Lily. She's seen her.'

'I am well aware of what Miss Curtis saw,' replied Beasley
silkily. 'Nevertheless, I tell you that she does not exist.'

'I don't follow you,' said Morton in a troubled voice. 'Are
you saying somebody has knocked her off?'

'I am saying that she has never existed.'

'Go on! You are pulling my leg!'

'I have never been more serious.' The smile faded from
Beasley's face, leaving a hint of menace.

'But I saw her on Thursday,' Morton expostulated. 'So did
Lily.'

'You may have seen someone you thought was Ada Smith.
But you were wrong.'

'You've got me baffled,' said Morton with an uneasy laugh.
'Who is she then?'

'She is Miss Marsden, the daughter of the house.'

'The daughter . . . You are joking! What, somebody rich
enough to live in Park Lane? Get away with you! She talks just
the same as Lily, her clothes are ordinary, she has no
finery . . . Somebody is having you on!'

'No, Fred. It has come from the house itself.'

Morton's jaw dropped in disbelief. He glanced across at
Lily, but her face was blank.

'We have to decide what to do about it,' said Beasley curtly.

Morton shifted in his chair and suddenly Goulter's great
hand clamped on his shoulder, holding him down.

'What is this?' cried Morton wrathfully, pushing away the hand. 'What if it is true? I knew nothing about it.'

'Are you sure, Fred?' Beasley's voice had a sinister edge of expectation . . . of hope.

'Of course I'm sure! Ask Lily.' He turned towards her. 'You saw her from near enough. Would you have believed she was a toff?'

To his relief, Beasley waited for her answer.

'No,' she replied uncomfortably. 'No. I would have said she was a housemaid, all right.'

'There you are, then,' said Morton in an injured tone.

'How did you come to meet her, Fred?' Beasley's voice was a little more normal.

'It was up round Marble Arch, where the cranks get up on soap boxes and spout. That day, there was a man from the Temperance Society going on about the evils of drink. I was having a bit of fun—you know, heckling him. She was standing beside me and she joined in. After it was over, we walked down the park—and it went on from there.'

'You got to know her very well, Fred?'

Morton gave a snort. 'That's true enough!'

'And yet in all that time, you never got a hint that she was upper-class and well-educated?'

Morton wrinkled his brow in recollection. 'No . . . No, not once. She spoke with an east-London accent, and . . . well, we didn't talk much. I once tried to explain the intricacies of book-selling to her, but she was not interested—and there were better things to do!'

'She was amorous, was she?' asked Beasley.

'Couldn't get enough! We would jig-a-jig down by Stanhope Gate, and by the time we'd got back to the Arch, she'd be wanting it again.'

'But when it was wet, you used to meet in Piccadilly. Surely you used to talk then?'

'Not really. We'd have it up against a wall, in an alley.'

'I have heard of women like this,' said Beasley meditatively.

'Cock-smitten!' asserted Goulter in a hoarse bark.

'Obviously, you could not have been the only one,' said Beasley.

'That's what Lily told me.'

'Not if you only met her once a week . . . They call it

nymphomania,' he added. 'Think yourself lucky you didn't marry her, Fred!'

'Too much hole in that corner,' Snell chipped in, with a sneer.

Morton gave a harsh chuckle.

'You must not see her again, Fred,' said Beasley.

'I wouldn't want to. The nobs are no friends of mine.'

'And to ensure that she does not seek you out, you will write a valedictory letter—to my dictation.' The menace was back in the voice.

'Fine. It's all the same to me.'

Beasley pushed the pen and paper across the table.

'We can hardly begin "Dear Ada", can we?' Beasley chuckled. 'But why not? We do not know her real Christian name, and it would be a pity to be formal after such an intimate relationship.'

Morton dipped the pen in the ink bottle, and began to write.

' "I now know that you are not Ada Smith",' Beasley dictated.

Morton transcribed it. The next line was the tricky one.

' "Also, I know I was not alone in enjoying your favours".'

Blast it! thought Morton. He had to get rid of that 'alone', or Bragg would think the letter was genuine. He dared not spread the earlier words out, because it would look absurd, and Beasley was watching him intently. There was still two inches of the line left. He dipped his pen deeply in the ink, and pressed hard on the nib. To his relief a large blob of ink formed on the page. He managed to spread it laterally a little, before Beasley passed him some blotting-paper. He blotted it delicately. He must not make too much of a mess of it, or he might have to start afresh. He took up the pen, and wrote 'alown', then crossed it out neatly, and wrote 'alone' at the beginning of the next line. Then he completed the sentence. Beasley did not seem to have noticed the deletion.

' "You are the best screw I have ever had",' he dictated.

'Isn't that a bit coarse?' asked Morton. 'You say she's educated.'

'Becoming squeamish, Fred?'

'No, not that. It just seems unnecessary.'

'You know what they say about a woman scorned,' replied Beasley. 'You have to let her know that you appreciated her talents.'

Morton shrugged and wrote the sentence down. Any reluctance would be taken as proof that his story was untrue.

' "But I cannot forgive you for deceiving me".'

Morton glanced across at Lily. She was absently twisting a ringlet round her finger, her face impassive.

' "So you will have to find someone else to touch you up" . . . Then another paragraph, "Thank you for the good times you have given me".'

Morton transcribed it carefully, and looked up.

'Then sign your name.'

Was it another trap? Morton wondered. Beasley was watching him like a hawk. He signed 'Fred' with a flourish, and handed the letter across.

Beasley read it, shaking his head over the blot and the mistake. 'You will never make a penman, Fred. Now the envelope.'

Morton addressed it to Ada Smith at Ninety-five, Park Lane, and put down his pen.

Beasley folded up the letter and sealed it in the envelope.

'And to ensure that it is properly despatched,' he remarked with a malicious smile, 'let us ask Miss Curtis to post it for us, shall we?'

CHAPTER _____

_____ FOURTEEN

Next morning, Kemp looked into Morton's room and asked for his assistance.

'I have finished the plate and inked it up,' he said, 'and I want to run it through the press.'

When they went down to the butler's pantry, the plate and paper were already on the press, smothered with their protective blankets.

'Nice and easy,' said Kemp. 'Remember to keep it going steadily.'

Morton turned the cross and managed to roll the bed through to Kemp's satisfaction.

'Now let us see . . .' Kemp's jovial face was pink with excitement. He removed the blankets and the tissue paper underneath; then taking a fold of card, he gently peeled the trial bank-note off the plate. He laid it carefully on the table and put the genuine note beside it. Morton peered over his shoulder. The vignette of Britannia, with its elaborately scrolled cartouche, stood out boldly; the complex woven pattern on the sum piece was faithfully reproduced. It was perfection!

'Hmn . . .' murmured Kemp. 'Not quite enough out of the

bottom curve of the pound sign. Pass me the burin, will you, Fred?'

He made a cut that was imperceptible to Morton, then peered at the result through a magnifying glass. 'Yes . . . That should do the trick. Let's take another print before lunch.'

He lit the gas-ring and warmed the plate gently. Then rubbed thick black ink into the grooves with a pad of muslin. He roughly cleaned the surface, then stood back.

'Now we have to wait for it to cool,' he said, turning to the bench and filling his glass. 'Do you want a drink?'

'No thank you,' said Morton. 'I see that on this plate you have not engraved the serial numbers.'

'That's right, it makes it a deal easier. With the numbers being placed over the "I promise", and "Demand", you get some very complex cutting indeed. I was relieved when I knew it was not going to be necessary.'

'I see,' said Morton, once more deciding against the straight question. 'And likewise, there is no date of issue or branch on the plate.'

'That will be done later. I will say this for Beasley, he's a good quartermaster.'

'Do you not rate him highly as a penman?' asked Morton with a smile.

'I have not seen enough of his work to form an opinion, though what I have seen is all right,' he said grudgingly. 'But cheques are apprentice stuff.'

'Have you not known him long?'

'Three months. Shortly after I came out of stir.' He took a long pull at his glass. 'I hear you've been making ends meet with an upper-crust wench,' he said, his round face lighting up with mischief.

'Without knowing it,' said Morton shortly.

'These nobby bits of crumpet take some beating, they say.'

'She was all right.'

'I shared a cell in clink with a chimney-sweep, turned burglar. He told me about one woman who used to have her bedroom chimney swept every month. Upper-class widow she was, with pots of money. He had to be there prompt at eight o'clock in the morning. She would be lying on her bed in a silk wrap, watching him. When he'd finished, he got his bonus— and the dirtier and sweatier he was, the better she liked it.'

He crossed to the table, and tested the temperature of the

plate, then with a rapid circular movement polished its surface with muslin. He carried it to the window, and scrutinized it intently, whistling under his breath.

'I am pleased with this one,' he said with a broad smile. 'It will stand for a few thousand.' He powdered the edge of his hand with french chalk and drew it lightly across the face of the plate. 'There we are. Let's try it, shall we?'

He carefully set the plate on the press, placing a piece of dampened paper on it; then covered it with tissue and the blankets. Morton took hold of the cross with a flourish, and rolled it through. Kemp examined the new print with a grunt of satisfaction, and compared it minutely with the genuine note.

'I do not think even an expert could tell it was counterfeit,' said Morton admiringly. 'What a pity we will not be using genuine paper.'

'Oh, but we will,' replied Kemp in surprise. 'Did Beasley not tell you? He is expecting a large quantity in the next few days.'

Mrs Marsden walked down the stairs into the hall and ran her finger along the giltwood console table. A little dust adhered to its tip. Was it enough to make a fuss about? she wondered. Really, servants were the limit! They did not take pride in their work, nowadays. If there had been dust on the furniture, when she was young, the housekeeper would have sent the servant concerned packing. But this was London, not Winchester, and twenty-five years later, moreover . . . If only she could be more forceful. Some of her friends had only to raise an eyebrow and their domestics would quail. But she was not made like that—she hated scenes, whatever the justification. No doubt the servants sensed this, and took advantage. She started, guiltily, as Joan came through the baize door, bobbed a perfunctory curtsy and went upstairs. Oh, dear. She would never be able to exert her authority. She would have to continue as she had always done—currying favour with her servants, asking them to do things as if soliciting a concession. But they did not respect her for it. It just made them slacker than ever.

She crossed to the window and rearranged the drape of the curtain. It was even more difficult, now that William had taken to inviting prospective clients for lunch or dinner. Somehow it had not seemed to matter, when it was only her friends calling in for tea. But he said it was helpful to have them look around his studio, see work actually in progress; and she could not let him down. She looked back up the hall. First impressions were so important . . . The roses were wilting by the hour. She would have to send out for some more, before the florist closed. Oh, how she missed living in the country! She would give anything to be able to take a trug into the garden, and snip off some choice blooms herself . . . Joan was coming down the stairs again, her head cocked in the air as usual. What would be the best way to broach it? Joan, I wonder if you would like to . . . A rattle at the door distracted her. It must be the afternoon delivery of post. She turned round, to see a letter fall upon the mat. She stooped to pick it up, and suddenly Joan was at her side, grabbing it before her.

'The post, mum,' she said pertly, beginning to walk away.

'You need not worry about a tray now,' said Mrs Marsden in mild annoyance. 'Just give it to me.'

Joan stopped. 'It isn't for you, mum,' she said, hiding the letter behind her skirts.

'Who is it for, then?'

'It's . . . it's for cook,' Joan said hesitantly.

'Nonsense! Cook does not get letters. Give it to me.'

Unwilling Joan passed the letter over.

'Ada Smith?' exclaimed Mrs Marsden. 'Who is Ada Smith?'

'I was told to give them to cook, mum.'

'Whatever for? Her name is not Ada Smith.'

'No, mum.'

Mrs Marsden was beginning to enjoy the confrontation. For once she had struck the right note of authority and the girl was taking notice.

'We will see what cook has to say about it. Come along.'

She marched down the stairs to the kitchen, with Joan trailing unhappily after her.

'Cook, a letter has arrived addressed to a Miss Ada Smith, at this house. Joan tells me she has instructions to give all such letters to you.'

'That's right, ma'am,' said the cook stolidly.

'And what, pray, do you do with them?'

The cook was looking rebellious, so she drew herself up to her full height, and glared.

Cook dropped her eyes. 'I give them to Miss Catherine, ma'am,' she mumbled.

'Miss Catherine?' exclaimed Mrs Marsden, taken aback. 'But . . . did she say why they were addressed to Ada Smith?'

'No, ma'am. She said they were for her, and I was not to let you see them.'

'Have there been many?' asked Mrs Marsden, flabbergasted.

'No, not many,' said the cook mulishly.

'Who are they from?'

'Last Thursday night,' Joan interposed excitedly, 'a chap . . . sorry mum, a gentleman called asking for Ada Smith.'

'I do not remember that . . .' said Mrs Marsden in perplexity.

'He came to the area door. Miss Catherine got dressed in old clothes, and went out with him into the park.'

Mrs Marsden could feel the ground sinking beneath her feet. 'The park?' she repeated numbly. 'What was he like, this man?'

'Oh, he looked nice, mum,' said Joan enthusiastically, 'tall, and strong-looking, and young.'

'Thank you, cook. I will give the letter to Miss Catherine, myself . . . And make sure that neither of you mentions the matter to anyone.'

She retreated upstairs before her composure crumbled, and went into her boudoir. So the worst was happening after all, just when she seemed to be establishing a comfortable relationship with Catherine. Her friends had said it would—giving in to her demands that she should be allowed to have a career. Please God, it would never get to their ears . . . But going into the park, alone with a man! She felt quite faint. It was reckless, wickedly reckless! Had she no shame? Could she not see what it would do to her reputation, if it became known? She would have to give her a dressing down . . . And then Catherine would get self-righteous and talk about middle-class hypocrisy in that sharp way of hers, and it would develop into a wrangle that would go on, and on . . . Oh, dear! Perhaps she ought to have exercised more control while she was growing up, but she had always been so independent. And her father had indulged her, encouraged her . . . At least, it was not all her fault. William must bear some of the blame, so she ought to have his support when she challenged Catherine. But she dared not tell him tonight. He would be very upset, and the client who was dining with them was important. So it would have to wait until tomorrow . . . Yes, that was best.

She slipped the letter into the drawer of her dressing-table, and closed it.

Towards evening a mist rolled up from the river, shrouding the houses and deadening the sound of the drays going back to the brewery. The more Morton had pondered on what Kemp had told him, the more he realized the urgency of its import. He had got to alert Bragg if he could and it was no longer safe to send a message through Catherine. Now nature seemed to be on his side. He wandered around the house with studied casualness. It was a pity that the front door was nailed up; it meant that the only exit from the building was through the kitchen, and there always seemed to be someone in that area. Sure enough, Lily was washing up some cups in the sink.

'Hello,' he said, picking up a dish-towel. 'Can I help?'

She looked at him briefly, without speaking.

He dried the cups, while she drained away the water and rubbed the pitted porcelain.

'I am thinking of going home, tomorrow,' she said suddenly.

'Oh, why?' he asked. 'Do you have to?'

'This place gives me the creeps; it's full of loonies.'

'Including me?'

She gave him a searching glance. 'No, not you,' she said coolly.

'What about the police?' he asked.

'Oh, they lost interest in Shoe Lane ages ago.'

'I'm sorry you are going,' said Morton seriously. 'I shall miss you . . . Still, perhaps Beaze will send us cheque hunting again soon.'

'We did too well, that last time,' Lily said, pulling a face. 'He's not given me a job for over a week.'

'Don't worry, you still have your nest-egg.'

'Yes, I have that.' She crossed to the door, then turned and looked at him. 'I am sorry I made so much fuss over your girl, Fred . . . I didn't like to see you wasting yourself on such as her.'

'Don't let it bother you, Lil. As I told you, she meant very little to me—even when I thought she was a dolly-mop. Now

I know she's a raving nymphomaniac, I'm grateful to
you! . . . So are we friends again?'

She gave a grudging smile. 'Yes, we're friends again,' she
said and went out.

Morton waited till he heard her feet on the stairs, then
slipped out of the back door. A quick sprint and he was in the
middle of the garden, the house a faint outline in the mist. He
stopped and waited. If he had been seen and they came after
him, he could always fob them off with some excuse or other.
But no, the house remained quiet, hugging its secret in its
slatternly bosom.

He found the breach in the wall and, pushing through the
undergrowth, came to another wall. He clambered over it and
found himself in a narrow alley, running along the back of a
row of workmen's houses. At the end of it, an entry gave
access to a road which he did not recognize. He walked
westwards as quickly as the fog would allow and came to a
wide thoroughfare, which he decided was Commercial Road.
He followed it for several minutes before he got his bearings,
then turned down a side-street that would take him to Tan
House Lane. He was within a few steps of the corner, when the
rashness of his intentions struck him. It was reasonably likely
that Sergeant Bragg would be at his lodgings. But suppose
someone else were with him—perhaps a fellow-policeman who
would recognize him . . . Morton, back from Australia! It
could ruin the whole enterprise. He stood irresolute for a
moment, then deciding on a flanking attack, he retraced his
steps. The gates of the laundry stood open, the watchman was
on his rounds. If Morton calculated aright, the boundary wall
of the works constituted the wall at the back of the Tan House
Lane gardens. Twenty yards along it, was a stack of metal
drums. He dashed inside, climbed up them, swung himself on
to the wall and dropped.

To land on a garden frame would have been worse, he
decided, but only marginally so. He wiped the slimy mixture of
compost and manure from his boots on to the grass, and looked
around him. The fences dividing the gardens were of low
wire-netting, so there would be no difficulty in crossing them.
The problem was to identify Mrs Jenks's garden. He had seen
it often enough from Bragg's sitting-room window, but what
was distinctive about it? Nothing that he could remember. It
was a long narrow oblong, with a path near one side, some

grass, a flower bed, and vegetables at the top end—but so were all the others. He looked up to count the chimneys, but because of the poor visibility, he could only see four. It would be just his luck, to pick the wrong house and be run in for unlawful trespass! Well, it certainly was not this garden, nor the next, because he could see a large goldfish pond there. He crossed over the fences, till he was halfway down the row. It ought to be around here, if his memory of the street frontages was any guide. There was something niggling at the back of his mind, some remark of Bragg's that held the clue to it, if only he could remember it. He looked down towards the row of houses, but they all seemed the same in the gloom. He could easily cross Mrs Jenks' garden . . . that was it—one of Bragg's anecdotes about the late lamented Tommy Jenks. He put the thought from him, in the hope that it would spring full-grown from the womb of his recollection. As he clambered over the next fence he missed his footing on some rockery stones and fell to the ground. The noise disturbed the pigeons in a loft nearby, and they began to flutter their wings and coo. He froze into immobility. That was it! Something to do with a garden shed. There had been trouble with the neighbours over it . . . No, that was not quite right, it involved the neighbours . . . Yes! the house next door had changed hands, and the new neighbours had looked down their noses when they realized they were living next door to a dustman. It had not been long before they had let Tommy know as much. So when he erected his new tool-shed, instead of placing it at the top of the garden like everyone else, he had put it in the middle, where it would overshadow his neighbour's asparagus bed . . . And there it was! Two gardens away. When the pigeons had settled, Morton crossed over and tiptoed down the path. He crept gingerly down the steep steps, to the back area, and knocked softly on the door. There was no response. He knocked again and stood back. This time the door was opened and Mrs Jenks's head appeared. When she saw Morton she uttered a cry of alarm.

'S-sh! Mrs Jenks,' he hissed. 'It's me. Is Sergeant Bragg in?'

'Who are you?' she demanded apprehensively.

'Constable Morton.'

'You're not. He's gone to Australia. Go away, before I call the police!'

'Surely you remember my voice, Mrs Jenks,' he said

persuasively. 'Why not put the door on the chain, so that I can come near enough for you to recognize me?'

'It's all right,' she said sharply. 'I can see who you are, right enough. But you've no call to come in this way, frightening a body.'

'I am sorry, Mrs Jenks, but it is important that I am not seen. Is the sergeant alone?'

'Yes. He was writing in his room, earlier on.'

'May I go up?'

She opened the door reluctantly and he went up the back stairs to Bragg's room.

'God Almighty! What's wrong?' asked Bragg in consternation.

'Nothing. I just dropped in for a chat.'

'You smell as if you dropped in more than that, lad. Now if it had been me, she'd have made me leave my boots on the mat.' He looked at Morton questioningly. 'Taking a chance, aren't you?'

'Yes, but I had to . . . Now, while I get my breath back perhaps you will bring me up to date. I begin to feel somewhat abandoned.'

Bragg looked at him appraisingly, then reached for his pipe.

'Well,' he said, 'Inspector Cotton is still blundering round London, turning over doss-houses and slums. That's about his mark, if you ask me. He enjoys it all the more, because he thinks he's got me stuck at Old Jewry as a dogsbody. I'm told he said to the CI that now you are gone, I'm like an organ-grinder that's lost his monkey—so you know what your superiors think of you!'

'My erstwhile superiors,' said Morton with a smile.

'It is clear that the Commissioner thinks Forbes's operation is a waste of time, but he can't get the Bank to drop it.' Bragg struck a match and applied it to the bowl of his pipe.

'Sometimes I think the counterfeiters know what is going to happen before you do,' said Morton. 'We have moved our base of operations several times at short notice and each time Goulter seems to have had advance warning that the police were coming.'

'I'm not surprised, with the number of people involved,' said Bragg. 'Mind you, while Cotton is huffing and puffing around the place, no one is going to suspect that we've planted you in the gang itself.'

'Let us hope that holds for a little longer!'

'I have spent the last few days following up your information about the genuine paper . . . You know, these bankers are a pompous self-satisfied lot; they can't entertain even a remote possibility that their methods are defective.'

'And are they?'

'Well, we seem to have proved that one piece of paper has not been accounted for at the Bank's own store; and I'm not all that happy about the plant where it's made . . . By the way, the second of the notes printed on genuine paper turned up today. The Chief Cashier seemed almost relieved—queer, aren't they?'

'The reason I have come tonight is to tell you that a large quantity of genuine paper is expected shortly.'

Bragg looked up sharply. 'Is that so? Who did you get the whisper from?'

'Kemp, the engraver. He let it slip inadvertently.'

'Are you satisfied that it's true?'

'Well, he certainly thinks it is,' said Morton. 'He is making no attempt to engrave a plate for the watermark.'

'Hmn. I wonder if it has been stolen already, or if that is still to come? . . . I can't see anyone wanting to hold on to it, can you? If it has not yet been delivered, then I reckon it's not been nicked yet.'

'Should you warn the Bank?'

'I don't know.' Bragg knocked out his pipe in the grate, and propped it against the clock on the mantel-piece. 'If I do, they will want to prevent it. In that case the conspirators might realize we were on to them, and sling their hook . . . No, lad. I want those bastards.'

'Kemp has finished his work on the new hundred-pound plate now,' said Morton. 'We ran off a proof copy on ordinary paper today.'

'A good one, is it?'

'Absolutely perfect.'

'It worries me, does their making a hundred-pounder,' said Bragg. 'More so, now you've told me about the large quantity of paper. It seems as if they may be going for a different layer of society, where bigger notes would be a rarity . . . Suppose they were going to move into the provincial towns and cities—what would Liddesdale's strategy be worth then?'

'If they did that, we would have failed.'

'Do you know the date and branch of the plate, and the serial number?' asked Bragg.

'No. It has not been engraved on it yet. I am afraid I am not sufficiently trusted to be brought into anyone's confidence. I just pick up crumbs of information here and there.'

'You are doing a grand job, lad, make no mistake . . . I wonder if we should pull them in. Are they are in the Rupert Street house now?'

'No. Beasley has not been in all day, and I think Snell went out just before I did.'

'Goulter is the bugger I want,' muttered Bragg savagely.

'Apart from that,' went on Morton, 'I have a growing feeling that there is someone in the background—a putter-up who is planning the whole counterfeiting operation.'

'What makes you say that, lad?' asked Bragg in surprise. 'Beasley would hardly need financing, he can make his own money.'

'Basically, it is that Beasley does not quite match up to the counterfeiting operation. He is a miniaturist, if I can use that analogy. He is capable of meticulous planning, but the exploits he boasts of are small-scale. He is an individualist. I think he would only feel secure working entirely on his own, forging cheques and uttering them himself. The person who is behind the counterfeiting is accustomed to paint on a somewhat broader canvas.'

'Any firm evidence?' asked Bragg.

'A little. Kemp only met Beasley three months ago. He has limited respect for him and refers to him as a "good quarter-master", whatever that may mean. Perhaps more conclusively, Kemp made that Hull plate over three years ago—at the request of an unknown putter-up from, I think, London.'

'Would Kemp split on this man, if we leaned on him a little?'

'Perhaps. But if I am right, the man in the background would flee as soon as we arrested the gang.'

'Have you got any feel for when we shall be able to move in on them?'

'I must confess that there are aspects of what is happening that I do not understand. Beasley is clearly looking towards some kind of climax, whose timing he cannot control. He is amassing a great deal of money from forged instruments and the counterfeit notes we know about. There must be a reason for it.'

'Since when did anyone need a reason for amassing money—particularly when it's someone else's?'

'Ah, but he is breaking his own rules; he is going against the cardinal principles by which he lives. He must be under some considerable pressure.'

'So you are prepared to let it run on, to see if we can bring this shadowy putter-up into the net?'

'Yes. There would be little point in taking the rest, if he were allowed to escape. There is one thing, however. I do not intend to involve Miss Marsden any further, unless it is absolutely vital.'

'I'm glad of that,' said Bragg. 'I think I can safely say, that that makes three of us.'

Morton retraced his steps with some difficulty in the thickening fog. After casting about in the maze of back-streets and entries, he decided to risk going down Rupert Street itself. He slunk through the front gate, then made a wide detour along the hedge and the wall. Since he could hardly distinguish the roof against the sky, he was satisfied that no one inside could have seen him. He crept round to the back door. It was locked! Cursing under his breath, he went round to the bay window. He took off his odiferous boots and, tying them together by the laces, he slung them round his neck. It was something, that the window of his room was open. He took hold of the drainpipe and hauled himself on to the top of the bay. Then, easing up the bottom sash, he clambered through the window. As he straightened up, there was the spurt of a match . . . It was Lily—in his bed!

'Where have you been?' she asked in remonstration. She leaned over to light the candle and Morton could see the white gleam of her naked shoulders.

'I went out,' said Morton briefly.

'I know that, you daft devil. Why didn't you say anything?'

'It was important to me, and I was not going to be prevented by Goulter, or anyone else. Since yesterday, I feel he is just waiting for an excuse to stick one of his revolting knives in me.'

'It wasn't Ada Smith, was it?' Lily asked suspiciously.

Morton laughed. 'No fear! It was something much more interesting. It had to be done tonight, because of your saying you were going back to Shoe Lane tomorrow.'

Lily wriggled over towards the wall. 'Tell me in bed,' she said coquettishly.

Morton undressed and slipped in beside her. She nestled up to him, her head on his shoulder. 'What is it, that's so interesting?' she asked softly.

'Beasley wants me to go into partnership with him, when this is over,' Morton said. 'He would do the forging and I would do the putting-down . . . But I have been thinking about what you said a couple of weeks ago.'

'What was that?'

'You remember—about taking a shop in the country. I don't suppose you would be interested . . .'

'Try me,' she said, her eyes bright in the candle-light.

'I am aware that you were thinking of it for yourself only, but I wondered whether . . .'

'Go on.'

'Well, I know we had a flaming row over the silly bitch in Park Lane, but it wouldn't always be like that. I think we could make a go of it.'

'Together?' she asked archly.

'Well, yes . . .'

'So what has that got to do with you climbing drain-pipes? Are we going in for breaking and entering?'

'No! There is a business-transfer agent in Great Tower Street. I went to see what they had in their window. There is a nice-sounding grocery business in Saffron Waldon and a pub near Ilford. Either of them might do.'

'Hmn. Sounds nice!' She caressed him provocatively.

'Of course, I should have to wait until this present rig was over,' said Morton. 'Do you know when that is likely to be?'

'I know nothing about it,' replied Lily absently, 'except that it's big and is to do with notes.'

'Ah well, if those businesses have gone, there will be plenty more.' He kissed her forehead gently.

'Fred,' she said quietly.

'What?'

'I wouldn't make you marry me, or anything like that.'

'Well, I had wondered . . .'

'Let's try it as we are, for a bit. If I couldn't keep a man without a gold shackle, good riddance to him.'

'And you think you could keep me?' Morton asked teasingly.

In answer, she twisted on top of him. 'I'll have a bloody good try,' she said.

CHAPTER ——————
—————— FIFTEEN

Catherine had been in St James's hall for half an hour already and she was beginning to feel conspicuous. Although she had no acquaintance with the women in charge, she knew the rector slightly. He must, by now, be wondering at her repeated visits . . . She looked through the rack of clothes again. Incongruous as it was, it seemed preferable to just standing around. She touched Morton's cameo on her breast, as if it were a talisman. Why did he not come? He had never been as late as this. She drifted back again towards the door.

'Can I help you, miss?' The woman from the tea urn, was looking at her uncertainly.

'No, thank you . . . I am a journalist. I am gathering material for a series of articles on London's poor.'

The woman looked at her with curiosity bordering on distaste. 'There are not many really poor people in this area,' she said severely. 'I would have thought the East End would be better for your purpose.'

'No, you misunderstand me,' said Catherine hastily. 'My concern is to find out what is being done to relieve their poverty. I have selected five institutions, of which this is one, and I visit them regularly. In that way I hope to avoid distortions.'

'I have seen you in here before,' said the woman suspiciously.

'That is so—every Wednesday,' said Catherine and moved away. Goodness! Did she think that she, too, was seeking complaisant young men? She sat in the corner and, taking her note-pad from her bag, put down a few lines of shorthand.

The time dragged on . . . Now they were piling the clothes into large cardboard boxes . . . till next week, presumably. She heard a clock striking ten and rose to her feet. He would not come now. She felt desolation flooding over her, quickly replaced by sharp anxiety—she hurried out of the hall, and hailed a growler.

'Tan House Lane, in the City,' she directed.

She was on tenterhooks. Would the sergeant think she was panicking unnecessarily? Treat her to one of his homilies? But James had not come, and it had never happened before. Perhaps he had been alienated by her violent reaction when they last met. The very thought of what had caused it, made her feel ashamed. No, that was not strictly true. She had acted without thinking, instinctively . . . except that instinct would have wanted him to go on. Anyway, she had slapped him and he might have taken umbrage . . . but she did not think men were put off so easily. He had said things had gone wrong; he had needed her to play up to him, and she had drawn back. Probably it had left him more exposed than ever. And now, he had not come . . .

She leapt out of the carriage, and rapped on the door.

After what seemed an age, Mrs Jenks opened it.

'I have come to see Sergeant Bragg,' said Catherine urgently.

'He's not here, miss,' replied Mrs. Jenks.

'Where is he?'

'I don't know. He went off this morning, with a change of clothes in a bag. He said he might be away for some days.'

Catherine turned away disconsolately and ordered the cabby to take her home. She had a sharp sense of isolation, of being vulnerable herself. She ran up the steps in near panic, and stood for a moment in the hall to steady herself. Then she began to mount the stairs.

'Catherine?' It was her father, calling from the drawing-room.

'Yes?'

'Come here!' his voice was abrupt, stern.

'Yes, Papa.' She retraced her steps and went into the room. Her mother and father were sitting side by side, on a settee.

'Sit down.' Mr Marsden waved her to a chair opposite them. It had all the hallmarks of an interrogation, thought Catherine; there was even a gas-bracket, shedding its light full on her face!

'Where have you been?' asked her father uncompromisingly.

'I have been working,' said Catherine lightly.

'Since when have journalists worked at eleven o'clock at night? There is no news to be got at this time of night, that is fit to be printed in your paper.'

'I have to maintain my contacts.'

'You have to maintain your good name also,' Mr Marsden retorted angrily. 'You know full well that you should not be out of the house at this hour, unchaperoned and unescorted.'

'I found the cab driver to be quite charming,' said Catherine flippantly.

'That is quite enough of your impudence, young lady,'

'Papa!' cried Catherine in amusement. 'I believe you are being the traditional heavy father.'

'It is time I exerted my authority in this house,' asserted Mr Marsden wrathfully.

'Oh, no!' Catherine said, with an edge to her voice. 'Not over me! You abandoned your authority over me, when you sent me to boarding school because you could not be bothered to bring me up yourselves.'

'I will not have insolence from you in my house!' he shouted.

'Are you going to turn me out into the snow?' asked Catherine coldly.

Instead of giving way to his rage, as she had expected, her father reached into his pocket and took out an envelope.

'There is a letter here addressed to Miss Ada Smith, at this house. Cook says you gave her instructions that such letters were to be given to you—and moreover,' he added sternly, 'that their existence was to be kept secret from us, your parents. Is that correct?'

'Yes.' She felt a wave of relief. He must have written to say that he could not keep this evening's appointment. It was all some silly blunder by cook. He was safe.

'Have you received other letters addressed in this way?'

'Why, yes.' It was hard for her to treat the matter with the solemnity her father seemed to expect.

'Who is the sender of these letters?' His voice was hard, accusing.

'One of my contacts.'

'And why are they not addressed to you openly?'

'I felt it was preferable to use an assumed name for this purpose.'

'I can well believe it.' Her father glared at her angrily, then thrust the letter at her. 'Read it,' he commanded.

She took the envelope with a look of reproach. It was his writing. Thank God! She felt for the flap with her thumb—it had already been unsealed.

'How dare you open my letters!' she cried in outrage.

'Read it!'

In sudden apprehension, she pulled out the fold of paper . . . certainly, it was his writing, but there was none of his teasing ungrammatical ramblings. Just short brutal sentences. She looked anxiously at the second line. The word 'alone' would have caused the letter to be accepted as genuine; he had gone to some lengths to get it on to the beginning of the third line. It had been written under duress.

'Do you know what these words mean?' Her father's voice seemed far away.

'What words?' she asked absently.

'Will you spare your mother nothing?' he exclaimed angrily. 'I refer to the words "screw", and "touch up".'

'I have heard them,' said Catherine coolly.

Her mother gasped. 'Where?' she asked.

'In the dormitory at Cheltenham, to be precise.'

Her mother subsided, aghast, but her father returned to the charge. 'Joan informed your mother that you went into the park alone with this man, when it was almost dark.'

Again the word 'alone'—so short, so invested with menace.

'Answer my question!' her father demanded angrily.

'I was not aware that you had asked a question,' said Catherine icily. 'However, the report that Mamma had from Joan is correct.'

'Have you no shame, hussy?' he exploded. 'Do you care nothing that you have destroyed your own reputation, that you have dragged our name through the mud?'

'I have done neither of those things,' said Catherine with asperity.

'But you have admitted being alone with him,' said her father in exasperation.

'Yes, I have.'

'You did not permit any intimacies, I trust,' said her mother timidly.

'No, Mamma, I did not permit any intimacies,' replied Catherine with fractionally different emphasis.

'Then explain yourself,' Mr Marsden demanded.

'All I can tell you, is that these letters are a clandestine line of communication between my contact and the police. As a result of your stupidity in keeping this letter from me, my contact may well have been murdered.'

In the stunned silence, Catherine rose to her feet and walked slowly upstairs.

'I got your telegraph, sergeant,' said Crutwell tersely. 'Does that mean it's come from here?'

'I've not got so far, sir,' said Bragg, 'but it has come from somewhere.' He took the bank-note from his inside pocket. 'This was presented last Saturday morning. The people at the Bank are sure it is genuine paper, but they asked me to let you have a look at it, to make certain.'

Crutwell passed the note gently through his fingers, then held it to the light. 'It's ours, right enough.'

'Good.'

'It's not good at all, man,' Crutwell said irritably. 'We have been making the paper for Bank of England notes for a hundred and fifty years and more. Never once has a scrap of paper gone astray before.'

'I am not saying that it has been taken from your works,' said Bragg evenly.

'Then what are you here for?'

'In the strictest confidence—and that means you cannot tell your wife, or your son, particularly your son . . .'

'All right, go on.'

'We have received information that more paper is expected by the counterfeiters. This time it is a large amount.'

'Well, we'll just have to put supervisors in the works, to see it doesn't happen.'

'And what good would that do, sir? It would only put your costs up, and you still wouldn't know if there was a villain in your employ.'

'So what is your solution, sergeant?' asked Crutwell sternly.

'Well, I have looked into the procedures at the Bank, and while I can see someone smuggling out the odd piece of paper, I can't see how a great pile could be got out.'

'Except by ones and twos.'

'I agree. But the records have been checked and re-checked. There is still only the one piece missing.'

'So you do think it is going to come from here?'

'If it is, I want to let it happen.'

'I'll see you in hell first!' exclaimed Crutwell, aggressively. 'It would bankrupt us.'

'I have the consent of the Governor to proceed on that basis, Mr Crutwell. It would not be your responsibility.'

'And what about Langton?'

'In his position, he must be a prime suspect,' said Bragg.

'I don't like this, sergeant.'

'Mr Liddesdales's concern is to catch the counterfeiters. It is only because they exist, that people are tempted to steal bank-note paper.'

'I think I should tell you,' said Crutwell defensively, 'that I saw George Langton over the weekend. I pumped him about his records, and from what he said, there is no deficiency there, either.'

'Are you a member of the watch committee, sir?' asked Bragg slowly.

'No . . . No, I'm not,' replied Crutwell nonplussed.

'So you do not know what your local police cells are like?'

'Er . . . No!'

'You will find out, if you betray my confidences again,' said Bragg coldly.

Crutwell looked up arrogantly, and met the sergeant's angry gaze.

'A word out of place could lead to my men being killed.'

Crutwell dropped his eyes. 'I am sorry,' he mumbled. 'I thought I was helping you.'

'You will only hinder, if you proceed on your own initiative, sir.' Bragg allowed the rebuke to fade from his voice. 'Now then, I want to keep observation of your works for a few days. I am afraid that if I am introduced on to the shop floor, it will excite curiosity and alert our quarry.'

'Always assuming it is coming from here,' Crutwell grumbled.

'Always assuming that, yes. Now, you said that the Bank of England sent their own contractors down to build the strong-room. Could I be engaged in a similar way, to do roof repairs?'

'As an outside contractor, you mean?'

'Yes, checking over the structure, or the glazing.'

'I don't see why not . . . My son was saying the other day, that the coping on some of the gables needed re-pointing.'

'Then, can you have a load of sand and some lime delivered, for tomorrow morning?' asked Bragg. 'I will pop into Andover this afternoon for some tools.'

When Bragg turned into the gate of the factory next morning, he was confident he looked the part. He was collarless, his trousers were tied up below the knee, his coat and waistcoat were unkempt, his hat stained. He had been fortunate to find some second-hand tools in Andover market, and a serviceable cloth bag to carry them in. He reported to the watchman on the gate and was directed to the maintenance foreman. He was supplied with a shovel, for mixing mortar, and a long ladder, then left to his own devices. He took the ladder round the side of the building and reared it up at the valley between two gable ends. Then he climbed up and got on to the roof. There was a flat leaded area, some two-foot wide, which would make for comfortable standing. On his left was a long expanse of slates, to his right thick glass sloped away to the ridge. He peered through it cautiously. He could see men preparing a pile of felts and paper for the initial pressing and, almost beneath him, the first drying machine. There was enough noise to drown anything he did and, with any luck, he would soon be forgotten.

He took off his coat, rolled up his sleeves and, going down the ladder again, mixed half a bucket-full of stiffish mortar. He lugged it up on to the roof and put it down out of sight. Then he inserted the long flat slate-ripper under a slate in the middle of the roof, and cut through the pin. Gradually he worked the slate down, until a narrow slit appeared; then he wedged it there. He could lie with his feet in the valley and his belly against the warm slates, and watch the vital area.

That must be Langton, standing at the end of the Swiss finishing machine. He was wearing a top hat and morning-coat, with a gold albert across his middle. In his hand was a clip-board. A man of around thirty-five was standing near him. He seemed to be the storeman. Every time the machine pushed out a bundle of paper, this man would place it in a stout cardboard box and seal it with gummed tape. Langton watched him intently, then made a note of some particulars already printed on the end of the box. This went on all morning. With the exception of a ten-minute break for a cup of tea, the machine churned relentlessly on. Whatever Langton's place might be in the community, Bragg did not envy him his job. A gangling youth was feeding the machine's voracious appetite. It was his job to take the damp piles of paper from the sizing area and place them on the feed-tray. Once he stopped the machine by disengaging the overhead drive-belt, and oiled a bearing. So he was the machine operative? Well, he looked bright enough; why not?

After two hours Bragg was getting weary. The sun was beating down on him, burning the back of his neck and making him feel dizzy. On top of that, his legs were aching, and the unnatural angle of his feet kept inducing cramp in his calf. Perhaps Langton had the better of it, after all. He looked at his battered watch. Ten minutes to twelve . . . but when could he have his lunch? He had brought a pork pie and some cheese, and a bottle of beer; this, on the assumption that he would eat it at his observation-post. But he'd had no idea, then, of the torture keeping watch would involve. He gingerly eased each leg in turn. His neck was aching, too, through holding his head in the same position all morning. It would be a relief to walk about a bit. Suddenly, the air was split by a piercing whistle. Almost immediately, the hum of the machines dropped, then ceased, as the steam was shut off. The men below stopped their work. Some of them walked quickly out of the factory—these would be the ones lucky enough to live nearby. Lucky, that is, if you could forget the stink of the steeping-tanks! Langton strode importantly away and, shortly afterwards, Bragg heard the sound of horse's hooves. Going home for lunch—that was more than Liddesdale could do. The storeman had wandered into the strong-room . . . That was a flagrant breach of security. The keys for both locks were still in the door. It would be simplicity itself, to take a wax impression . . . The gangling youth had picked up a folded newspaper. He looked about him cautiously, then approached the machine. He pushed aside the inspection cover and thrust his skinny arm through the aperture. In a twinkling he had withdrawn it—with a piece of finished bank-note paper in his fingers. He dropped it between the folds of the newspaper and walked casually into the strong-room. Moments later, he emerged and began to read the newspaper while he ate his lunch. Bragg watched him intently. There was no doubt about it. The filched sheet of paper was no longer in the youth's possession; it was in the strong-room!

CHAPTER ———————
——————— SIXTEEN

'Well, gentlemen,' said Beasley, 'the time has come to let you into the secret.' They were sitting in the kitchen at Rupert Street, Beasley at the head of the table, with Morton on one side of him and Snell on the other. Goulter was too restless to sit and stood by the door, on guard.

'You all know,' Beasley continued, 'that Percy Kemp has provided us with a thousand-pound plate, and that both Fred and George have successfully presented notes printed from it. He has now engraved a new plate for a hundred-pound note, which is even more perfect, if that is possible.'

'I don't see why we are coming down from a thousand to a hundred,' said Snell discontentedly. 'It will take us ten times as long to get our money.'

'All will be revealed,' said Beasley unctuously. 'Suffice it to say that we are moving out of the City. We have had rich pickings here, but we are in danger of over-reaching ourselves. It is regrettable that the higher-denomination notes are seldom used outside the capital, and would excite curiosity.'

'As soon as you let me in on it,' grumbled Snell, 'you stop it.'

'Have no fear, George, I am going to give you an opportunity that will satisfy even your avaricious soul.' Beasley smiled blandly. 'I take it that both you and Fred are not averse to making your pile?'

'Just give me the chance,' said Morton.

'Well now, I have arranged for a large quantity of genuine Bank of England paper to be . . . er, made available to us.' He smiled smugly. 'And over the next week, Percy, with the help of Fred here, will print hundred-pound notes with it. That process has to be finished well before Sunday the fourth of September.' He looked around as if expecting questions, but no one spoke.

'This, then, is the rig. I am going to recruit six more putters-down . . .'

'Bloody hell!' Snell interrupted.

Beasley raised his hands like a parson blessing his flock. 'I assure you, George, there is more than enough in it for everybody. You don't want to end up in Pentonville, do you?'

Snell shifted in his chair, a rebellious look on his face.

'Since you will all be operating at the same time, and in the same place, it will be an added safeguard if you do not know the others, nor they you.'

'Where is it to be?' asked Morton innocently.

'Doncaster . . . Yes, boys, I am taking you racing!'

'Racing?' exclaimed Snell.

'It is the St Leger on the seventh. All the toffs will be there, splashing their money about. No one will notice a little extra!'

'That is very clever,' Morton said in admiration. 'The race will draw a lot of interest this year, with Orme coming back.'

'I didn't know you were a racing man,' said Beasley, momentarily distracted.

'I was a groom at Newmarket for a time,' said Morton shortly.

'Excellent! You will no doubt be able to advise us on what tactics to use in placing our bets. Now, I am told that there will be six races, and there will be a great number of bookmakers on the course. By betting with every bookie for every race, and doing a certain amount of doubling up if we get there early enough, you should be able to put down a good proportion of the notes.'

'Are we staying for the whole meeting?' asked Morton.

'No, just the Wednesday. We shall go to another meeting elsewhere, to put the balance.'

'We'll get 'em all down at Doncaster,' said Snell with a wolfish grin.

'Now, now, we will have no rashness, George.' Beasley admonished him. 'It could well be that you will have far more than you could safely get rid of in a day.'

'Suppose one of us is taken?' asked Morton.

'I will see that whoever it is will get compensation. The important thing is to give the police no information until two or three days have elapsed . . . Now, once we have left, we shall not return here. You will be able to contact me through the Black Horse in Shoe Lane.'

'Is Lily in on this?' asked Snell.

'No,' Beasley replied, with a smirk at Morton. 'It is sad to think that we have no further use for Miss Curtis's undoubted talents . . . Now then, the usual five-per-cent commission will apply. And take care to have some genuine notes on you, in case anyone tumbles to what is going on.'

'I don't see how that can happen,' said Snell, 'if they are as good as you say. We shall be in and out, before they get near a bank.'

'You will go far, George,' murmured Beasley, 'unless your greed gets the better of you . . . Now, when you are placing your bets I want you to go, in the main, for a pony. To give a hundred for a five-pound bet would seem odd. Equally, we do not want to cut down our profit. Twenty-five pounds is about right; and fortunately for us, it is a very popular stake. Don't forget to keep the change you receive separate from the notes you are putting. We don't want to be laying out real money!'

'What about winnings?' asked Snell. 'Do we claim them?'

'We will decide that on the day. It might look odd if a large number of winning bets was unclaimed. On the other hand, collecting them would increase the chance of being apprehended.'

'But we can keep our winnings?'

'I suppose so. But this operation is not about betting. I would much prefer it if winning could be avoided. Not being knowledgeable in this field, I shall have to rely on your collective judgement. I am moving in here today. Although I shall have to be out a good bit, making arrangements, you will be able to get hold of me and tell me what you have decided.'

'What do we do with the money we get?' asked Morton.

'I am renting a house near the race-course for the whole of the meeting. I will let you have the address later.'

'What is Goulter getting out of this?' asked Snell suddenly.

'Oh, Albert will get his reward, never fear.' Beasley got to his feet with a sinister smile. 'And now that you have been given details of the rig, no one will leave this house. Do you understand? No one!'

As Beasley went out, Goulter crossed to the dresser, and pointedly buckled the holster of knives around his waist. Then, to Morton's surprise, he took Beasley's chair.

'The Leger's the only race wot matters,' he asserted hoarsely, 'the rest is rubbish.'

'You mean we can ignore form, and back the field in the others?' asked Snell, with something like respect.

'Yes. La Flèche is the one.'

'Get away with you!' Snell exclaimed. 'It was beaten hands down by Sir Hugo in the Derby and he's no cop.'

'You'll see,' Goulter rasped, 'September's the mares' month.'

'I shall get as much as I can on Orme,' said Snell. 'It's going to walk it. I'm going to squeeze this rig for all it's worth.'

'Yer wastin' yer time,' said Goulter gruffly. 'He's down to evens this morning. He'll be odds-on before the race.'

'If it's a cert, it don't matter,' said Snell perkily. 'Fred agrees with me, don't you Fred?'

'I said Orme was the public's favourite,' replied Morton. 'I did not say he would win.'

'But he won the Eclipse last month, and the Sussex Stakes.'

Morton smiled secretively. 'Not against really top-class horses.'

Snell looked at him narrowly. 'Here, Orme is trained at Newmarket. Have you got a whisper?'

Morton hesitated. 'Orme has had a long lay-off. The punters are going by his form of last year.'

'They said in May he'd been poisoned,' said Snell slyly. 'Was he?'

'The police couldn't prove anything,' Morton replied with a grin. 'Let's say that he's not got the stamina for the St Leger.'

Snell looked long at Morton, then turned to Goulter. 'What's the odds on La Flèche?' he asked.

'Five to one against.'

'Then it's a dollop on that one, for me.'

'I don't think we should concern ourselves with winning,' said Morton. 'I think Beasley is right. It only increases the chances of getting caught. In my view, we ought to spread our bets evenly over the field, so as not to upset the odds. Most of all, we should avoid putting a great deal of money on any unfancied horse. The bookies would be sure to look twice at that.'

'That's sense,' Goulter grunted.

'And I, for one,' added Morton, 'will not be attempting to collect my winnings.'

Bragg was slumped against the roof again, peering through the gap in the slates. After yesterday's long period of immobility, his legs had started off sore and stiff. Thank God it was Saturday, with only half-day working. He lifted his right leg and flexed the ankle. Quarter of an hour to go, then the factory would be securely locked for the weekend and he could relax. None too soon, either. In the last hour grey-black clouds had rolled up from the south and there were ominous rumblings. If it came on to rain, he would have to close his peep-hole, or risk water dripping down and betraying him. Once during the morning, Langton had moved away from the machine—possibly to answer a call of nature. Immediately, the youth's skinny arm had been through the inspection hole, bringing out a fistful this time—and without stopping the machine. At that rate, it would not take long to build up a pile.

The whistle's blast signalled noon and the machines fell idle. The gangling youth removed the damp pieces of paper from the feed tray, then took them back to the size-tub. The storeman removed some finished pieces from the batcher and counted them. Langton watched this process carefully, and noted the result on his clip-board. The part-batch was then put in a cardboard box with a bright red top. This was sealed, as the full boxes had been, and taken into the strong-room. Langton then moved along the side of the machine and looked through the inspection hole. As he did so, the youth crept past him and slipped into the strong room. The storeman pushed the heavy door till it was almost closed, then stood near the aperture picking his nails. Apparently satisfied that there was no paper left in the machine, Langton crossed over, pushed the strong-room door closed and locked it. He put the two keys into his pocket and, after a brief word, hurried away.

The storeman lingered idly for a few minutes, until the last of the other workmen left, then drifted after them. Bragg crawled to the other end of the roof and quickly glanced over the coping. The storeman was standing in the road, watching Langton's trap disappearing in the other direction. Bragg ducked down. When he looked again, the road was deserted except for the storeman, who was dawdling along by the verge. Suddenly he jumped over the ditch and into a copse. Bragg watched for some minutes, but he did not emerge. Below, he could hear the watchman going his rounds. Well, he would not be able to check the strong-room; that would be out of bounds to him. So there was one man inside the factory, and one hiding in the trees beyond the wall. Something was up, that was for sure. A door banged shut, then, after an interval, there came a dull thud as the main gates were locked. Now everything was quiet, except for the rumble of thunder overhead. No doubt the watchman would retire to his hut by the entrance and eat his lunch.

Bragg crept down the valley again, to his peep-hole; that must be his vantage point from now on. He spreadeagled himself on the slates and watched. Nothing happened. The thunder was almost overhead now, and he felt a large drop of water strike the back of his neck. It would be the last straw, to be caught in a thunder-storm up here. His feet would be in a river . . . What was that? At the end of that clap of thunder, there had been an odd scraping sound. Bragg looked around, to see the end of his ladder disappearing. So now he was marooned up here. A fine thing to happen! There was a clunk as the ladder hit the wall further down, then silence. But in the middle of the next thunder-clap there was the unmistakeable sound of breaking glass. Bragg eased down his slate a little, so that he could look across the roof-space. The storeman had kicked in two panes of glass and, having attached a grappling-iron to the glazing bar, was sliding down the rope. In a trice, he was at the strong-room door, unlocking it. The youth emerged with four cardboard boxes already strung together. The door was re-locked, the storeman swarmed up the rope and pulled himself on to the roof. Then he hauled the boxes up after him, before the youth followed. Bragg had a final glimpse of them carrying the boxes towards the ladder.

It had all been so easy. They had been lucky with the thunder, sure enough; lucky too that the rain was keeping off, so the paper would stay dry. But the rest had been the result of expert planning. It had only taken seven minutes, from breaking the glass to escaping with the booty. A real professional job. There was a muffled thump. Bragg cautiously peered over the edge of the coping. The ladder lay on the ground, where they had pushed it as they dropped over the wall. It was not far from where he had left it the night before, Bragg thought wryly. Everything looked completely innocent. Nothing would be discovered until the watchman made his rounds. Well, he didn't want to be around then. Catch him up here, and they'd have him in the nick as soon as spit. And Crutwell would be in no hurry to get him out, either, after his threat to lock him up. He looked down at the ground. It must be all of twenty feet away. With a drop like that, he could easily break his leg. A little to the right was his yard of sand. A pitifully small heap it looked from up here, but it might break his fall. He climbed on to the coping, crouched there for a moment, then launched himself into the air. He struck the pile in the centre and, stumbling sideways, fell heavily. He crawled painfully to his feet. His right shoulder had been bruised as he lurched over, but his limbs still seemed to be functioning. He must have had his mouth open at the moment of impact, and his teeth had cut the inside of his cheek. He spat out the blood and felt his face gingerly. It had not gone right through, it would soon heal. He limped over to the ladder and, propping it against the perimeter wall, climbed up. He crouched on top, gave the ladder a hefty shove, then slithered to the ground.

There was not much doubt about what he should do. The paper had been stolen, and he well knew its destination. It was a matter of getting as much first-hand evidence as he could. Nobody in their right mind would try to transport it sixty miles by trap, or on horseback. It had to be the train. He brushed down his clothes as best he could, untied the strings from his trouser-leg, and put on a collar and tie from his pocket. He then limped down the road to the village. Thank God he didn't have to hobble all the way from Crutwell's place!

The thunder-storm had drifted away to the west and the sun shone warmly again. Damnation! He had left his lunch-bag by the lime pit, and a good bottle of ale with it. He approached the station cautiously. An empty hay-cart straddled the level-crossing and the signalman was leaning out of his box, talking to the driver. There seemed no immediate likelihood of a train. Bragg went into the Railway Inn and, buying a hot meat-and-potato pie and a pint of beer, took them over to a table by the window. No one showed any interest, no one appeared to recognize him from the previous Sunday. The barmaid had smiled warmly at him, as was the way of her kind, and had gone back to polishing glasses without another look in his direction. Well and good. He pushed away his plate and felt in his pocket. Blast it! He had broken his pipe! It must have happened when he rolled off the heap of sand. He could feel the separate pieces; it had snapped off at the stem. It was one of his favourites, too. He sourly bought some cigarettes at the bar and stood by the crossing-gate, smoking one. Then he wandered along to the booking-office and bought a third-class ticket to London. One or two people had gone on to the platform now, and Bragg followed suit. He strolled along it, looking carefully at the intending passengers. No one had luggage with them which could conceal the stolen paper. He walked to the end of the platform, just as the gates were opening, and looked down the street. Approaching in great haste, were the youth and the storeman, pushing a bassinet. A small child, sitting upright in it, was wailing as he was bounced along. Seeing the signal arm drop, the storeman wrenched a sack from the bottom of the perambulator and sprinted for the ticket-office. Bragg forced himself to watch the approaching train and, when it pulled into the station, he boarded it without a backward look.

Nevertheless, he dropped the window at every station and looked out, in case his quarry got off. But nothing unexpected happened. They must think that they had got away with it . . . He liked the bassinet—a lovely touch, that. And the sack would disguise the outline of the boxes; plenty of people would have recognized them otherwise. At Waterloo station, Bragg jumped down quickly and saw the storeman alightning from a compartment near the engine. He hurried after him. This was the tricky bit. Since the man was in all likelihood a professional crook, he would be alive to the possibility of being followed. The sack had now been discarded, and the man was merely holding a large brown-paper parcel that no one would look twice at. Bragg managed to arrive at the cab-rank immediately behind him. Two hansoms came up more or less

together, and they ambled along the river and over Westminster
Bridge in procession. Directly it reached the north bank,
however, the other cab stopped and the storeman got out. He
skipped across the road, and disappeared down the steps
leading to the underground railway. Bragg followed him
cautiously. The man boarded a train going eastward, so he did
likewise. He spent most of the journey hanging out of the
window, looking down the tunnel for the lights of the next
station, in case the man should jump out quickly and he should
lose him. Eventually, the man left the train at Blackfriars and
Bragg, his eyes streaming from the dust and smoke of the
railway, kept on his heels. On reaching the surface, the
storeman walked the few yards to the Black Friar pub and went
into the parlour. After an interval, Bragg followed and stood at
the bar with a pint of beer. His man was sitting on a bench by
the window, the parcel at his side. Twenty minutes went by.
Bragg, washing the soot from his throat, was on his third pint,
the storeman had barely tasted his. Bragg lit another of his
cigarettes and stubbed it out half-smoked, in disgust. Then a
wiry, mouse-coloured man came into the bar. He looked
around, then wandered casually over to the window and sat on
the bench by the storeman—with the parcel between them. It
was Beasley! Morton's sketch come to life. He ordered a drink
from the waiter in the smarmy voice Morton so detested. The
two men did not acknowledge one another. Indeed, after the
first exchange of glances, they studiously avoided contact.
Bragg wondered idly if he should pull them in. He would be
able to pick up the people in Rupert Street easily enough. But
no. Morton was intent on taking this shadowy putter-up of his.
Well, it was up to him. He watched out of the corner of his eye,
as Beasley drew a bulky envelope out of his inside pocket and
surreptitiously placed it on top of the parcel. The storeman
gulped at his beer then, as he stood up, swept the envelope into
his pocket and went out.

Bragg decided that there was no point in following Beasley.
The paper had been delivered. It was time he got home, to see
if Mrs Jenks had anything for his supper.

CHAPTER ——————
————— SEVENTEEN

'Do you mind if I smoke my pipe, sir?'

'If you must, sergeant,' replied Crutwell grudgingly.

'I have really only popped in to say goodbye.' Bragg poked the pristine bowl of his new pipe and lit it.

'So it's all over then, is it?' asked Crutwell, with satisfaction in his voice.

'Yes, I suppose you could say that.' He had bought this one last night in Cheapside; French briar, with rich red-brown graining. He'd decided to get one that fitted snugly in his pocket, and this one had filled the bill perfectly. It looked very smart, too, with the slight curve in the stem—and yet it wasn't quite right somehow.

'We had a real to-do, here, last night,' said Crutwell, smiling broadly. 'The factory must have been struck by lightning in that storm yesterday afternoon. We got off lightly; they say the centre of Whitchurch was flooded . . . Anyway, the watchman found some broken glass on the floor at six o'clock. He thought at first it was a break-in and we all got rousted out. We were buzzing around like blue-arsed flies, I can tell you—police and all. You should have seen Langton's face! But my son and I helped him to do a check of his strong-room, and it was all there. But it was a fright, and no mistake!'

'I'm sure it was. I have just been having a chat with Mr Langton.' It was the bowl, Bragg decided. Somehow it was too small. It seemed as if it was made to hold between finger and thumb, rather than to grab hold of; a pipe for the nobs to play at smoking, after dinner. He knocked it out in Crutwell's ash-tray and put it back in his pocket.

'How much paper could you get in four of those cardboard boxes, Mr Crutwell?' he asked.

'Each one takes a ream, and since the Bank of England make their own rules, that means five hundred sheets.'

'So four would take two thousand?'

'That's right.' Crutwell's eyes narrowed in suspicion.

'Only, I saw two men remove four boxes from the strong-room, yesterday afternoon.'

'You what?' exclaimed Crutwell.

'It was they who broke the roof-glass, not lightning.'

'But . . . but how can that be so?' Crutwell expostulated. 'I tell you, we counted it with Langton, late last night.'

'I am not disputing your word, sir—but it happened, all the same . . . Langton has to bear the blame, for leaving the keys in the locks of the strong-room door. He only had to go for a pee, and anybody could take wax impressions and have duplicates made.'

'But dammit, man, the paper was all there!' cried Crutwell angrily.

'If you mean that the boxes in the strong-room tallied with what should have been there according to Mr Langton's records, then I agree with you,' said Bragg quietly. 'The paper was stolen before it got to Langton—and what better place to hide it, than in the strong-room itself?'

'I've already told you that it is pointless taking any paper till it has gone through the finishing machine,' said Curtwell truculently.

'You have. But you weren't quite right. That inspection-hole in the machine is placed after the glazing rollers, and just before the batching device. Your skinny machine operator could get his arm through that hole, and take out finished pieces of paper that were not in any records anywhere.'

'Jack Tompsett's lad? I don't believe it!'

'I saw him do it, on more than one occasion.'

'My God! After all I've done for that family.'

'The storeman was the prime mover, of course,' said Bragg.

'He's employed by the Bank,' asserted Crutwell.

'I know. He was taken on three months ago.'

'But Langton showed me his references, they were extremely satisfactory.'

'I'm sure it's not beyond the resources of this gang to forge references that the Archangel Gabriel would accept . . . I gather that the storeman lodges with the Tompsetts.'

'Not for much longer,' exclaimed Crutwell wrathfully. 'I'll see they get such a sentence, that they'll be old men by the time they get out.'

'That is what I have come to see you about,' said Bragg firmly. 'I do not want any action taken which would alert them to what we know. Everyone involved in the search last night believes it was the lightning—an act of God, you might say. I want it to stay that way.'

Crutwell looked up incredulously. 'But what if they run away?'

'I don't see that they will. They have no reason to. You said, yourself, that the records show everything is correct. Why should they not repeat the process?'

'And if they do escape?'

'I have more important fish to fry then petty criminals,' said Bragg. 'I want you to carry on as if nothing had happened.'

'I'd better feign an illness, then, and keep away from the place,' replied Crutwell roughly. 'I would never be able to carry it off.'

'As you please, sir. Mr Langton seems to have more composure than you have.'

'It's not Langton paper,' said Crutwell fiercely. 'The most they would do to him, is pension him off. But if the story gets out, I might as well start selling matches on the street corner.'

'And if you reveal it precipitately, by rash action, then the Bank of England will be looking for a new paper supplier, anyway,' said Bragg brusquely. 'I shouldn't think your business would be worth much, after that.'

Crutwell's face was purple with suppressed rage.

'And for your information, sir,' Bragg added equably, 'rather then involve the local police, I have arranged for the police at Winchester to pick up our two Indian rope-trick merchants, when I give the word . . . So if the story gets out, we shall know where it has come from, shall we not, sir?'

'As you may have seen in last Saturday's *Times*,' said Liddesdale, 'my deputy, David Powell, has been appointed to succeed me in October. I think it would be well, if Sergeant Bragg were to make his report on security matters direct to him.'

The Commissioner and Bragg were closeted with the Governor in his office. He looked careworn and dejected.

'I must say that, while not expecting to go out in a blaze of glory,' he went on, 'I had hoped for better than this . . . I just do not understand it. The strategy of withholding information has always been effective in the past. The difference seems to be, that on this occasion, the police have not moved quickly enough to apprehend the counterfeiters.'

Sir William flushed angrily. 'Let me remind you, Mr Liddesdale, that, because of pressure from you and the government, I was not allowed to proceed as I would have wished in the case. I have protested on several occasions about the wasteful use of police time, but to no avail.'

'I know.' The Governor sighed wearily. 'And now the politicians are taking me to task over the lack of progress. In the last fortnight bank shares have fallen to so low a value, that it is virtually impossible to give them away. In addition, it is common gossip that counterfeit thousand-pound notes are in circulation in London.'

'I feel I should tell you,' said the Commissioner, 'that we believe the newly stolen paper will be converted into notes of one hundred pounds.'

'That will be a catastrophe,' said Liddesdale in alarm. 'Up to now, the public have looked on it as something affecting the upper-classes only. There is sure to be a great outcry if forged hundreds appear in circulation . . . I very much regret my agreeing to allow the theft to proceed. In retrospect, it looks like a desperate gamble on my part. It was only my belief that you would be able to bring the case to a satisfactory conclusion, which caused me to agree . . . Do you think it is too late to change course?' he asked plaintively.

Sir William seemed to take pity on the man. 'I will willingly discontinue the operation that is being conducted by Chief Inspector Forbes and his men,' he said briskly. 'But so far as the covert operation is concerned, I will allow no interference with it. In my opinion it is proceeding satisfactorily, and it gives us our best chance of arresting the criminals.'

'Very well,' said the Governor, listlessly fiddling with his pencil. 'It seems as if someone has been working against me all the time. There have been leaks to the press; rumours have spread of large quantities of counterfeit notes, when to our knowledge there have only been four . . .' his voice trailed off despondently.

'It goes beyond that, sir,' said Bragg. 'Our man Morton has told us that there have been several moves of premises, while the gang has been operating. He has only been involved in two, but in each of those cases, they fled just before a police search of the area was due to be carried out. When we untangle the whole story, we may find that secret information was being fed to them, the whole time.'

'From someone in the Bank, you mean?' said Liddesdale sharply.

'Or somebody on the fringes.'

'It could equally be emanating from the police, could it not, Sir William?'

The Commissioner cleared his throat. 'Of course, we do obtain a great deal of useful information from the underworld. I suspect that the upper echelon in the force does not always know about the links their men have with underworld informers; and I suppose that in some cases, there could be a two-way flow of information. But I am told it is a well-established and valuable practice—isn't that so, Bragg?'

'I've been hearing these stories, ever since I joined the force,' said Bragg solemnly, 'and that is twenty years ago. But I would not like to say that it happens.'

For Morton the next week was unremitting drudgery. Although Snell was dragooned into helping, they were working from the first crack of dawn until the light faded. At first Kemp insisted on re-inking the plate for every impression; but at the end of the first day he declared that they would be unable to keep to the timetable Beasley had imposed. Next morning, therefore, he experimented by printing from the plate without re-inking, until the result was unacceptable. Thus, at the notional cost of one hundred pounds, they discovered that three perfect impressions could be taken from the plate at one time. Even so, it was only by back-breaking work that they would achieve their target. Morton's job was to turn the windlass on the press. For three notes, Kemp could be ready again in half a minute. Then he had to re-ink the plate for the next three. While he was doing that, Morton would help Snell with the damping of the paper to be printed. Beasley had provided a guillotine, and Snell's first task was to cut the paper precisely into two pieces. Then a good handful would be soaked in the sink for half an hour. They were then drained off, placed between sheets of clean blotting paper and pressed beneath a heavy piece of glass till they were ready. Every surface in the kitchen and butler's pantry was covered with paper in various stages of preparation.

Once the note had been printed, it had to be dried. They rigged up a series of strings across the bedroom Lily had occupied, and balanced bundles of damp notes on them. Every morning and night they removed the notes which had dried and replaced them with damp ones. So it went on, until Morton's shoulders ached with the effort of turning the cross and his mind was drugged with the monotony. Looking at the fast-emptying boxes, he estimated that they would have printed four thousand notes. That gave them a face value of four hundred thousand pounds. Even if the net return was only seventy-five pounds on every note, that gave a profit of three hundred thousand pounds to Beasley. A fortune! No wonder he had planned for this meticulously. Morton speculated on what his commission would amount to. Assuming that the notes were distributed equally between the eight putters-down, his five-per-cent share of the proceeds would only amount to eighteen hundred and seventy-five pounds. It did not seem much for the risk of a long prison sentence. Beasley would no doubt say it was quite a good rate of pay for one day's work—but the very concentration of activity increased the dangers of detection. Morton wondered why Beasley could be regarded by the rest of the people involved as fairly entitled to the balance. Of course there were other expenses, but even so, a vast sum would remain in his hands.

'How much do you think Kemp gets out of this?' he asked Snell, when they were stacking the dried notes and putting them into the cardboard boxes again.

'I dunno. It's usually seven and half per cent of the divvy. If he's any sense, he'll have had a dollop on the nail.'

'Do you not believe this rig will succeed, then?'

'I shall. I don't know about you lot. I'm making bloody sure I get the notes we printed on the first day.'

'You're a fine ally, I must say,' replied Morton with a grin. 'I would not put it past you to scarper with everything you take.'

Snell started, guiltily. 'It would have to be a bloody great pile, for it to be worth while.'

'You would have over thirty-five thousand pounds.'

'I know, but I couldn't stand the thought of Goulter hunting me for the rest of my life, with his bloody knives.'

Morton laughed heartily. 'What do you think he is paid?' he asked.

'I've never seen Beasley pay him anything. I reckon he does it for the chance of . . .'

'Of what?'

'Nothing. Let's get these sodding notes up.' Snell became his usual surly self again and kept his distance thereafter.

Goulter was certainly taking his role as watchdog-cum-gaoler seriously. He hovered around, watching everyone suspiciously, drawing the curtains against non-existent prying eyes. He even refused to let Morton go for Kemp's half-and-half; marching out early himself, and plonking the bottles down on the bench defiantly. Morton began to wonder how he was going to get word to Bragg about the Doncaster operation. He had quietly opened his bedroom door in the middle of the previous night, and had heard Goulter moving about downstairs. He could not risk slipping out of the house; to be caught on the way would achieve nothing. Even worse, he no longer had any writing paper. He had quickly searched Beasley's room, one evening, but had found neither paper nor envelopes. He would just have to wait for an opportunity to turn up. They had finished printing the notes, and Kemp was supervising their re-damping and pressing, to get rid of the ruckle. But the notes were still incomplete, there was a great space in the middle where the date and branch of issue should go, and there were no serial numbers on them. Perhaps they were going elsewhere to be finished. If so, he might be able to contrive an opportunity.

Even though he had finished the delicate work of engraving, Kemp was still drinking prodigious quantities of ale and stout. No doubt his thirst was intensified by the yeasty smell of brewing, which was wafted towards them on the warm breeze.

So when Goulter went out the next evening, after dire warnings against leaving the house, Morton began to drink bottle for bottle with him. Soon Kemp was looking at his dwindling store apprehensively.

'It's all right, Percy,' said Morton. 'I will get you some more.'

'What about Albert?' muttered Kemp.

'I'll be down to the pub and back, before he returns.'

'Could you?' asked Kemp hopefully.

'Of course.'

Morton slipped out when Snell went up to his room, and walked cautiously down to the pub in the gathering dusk. He went into the parlour.

'Have you any writing paper and envelopes, please?' he asked.

'No love,' said the barmaid indulgently, 'you get them from the stationer's.'

'All right, six bottles of Mackie and six of IPA, please.'

'I'll have to get the stout from the other bar,' she said.

As she went through the hatch, Morton noticed a post-card skewered to the side of the bar with a pin. It had presumably been sent by a customer on holiday, and showed an etching of Dover Castle. Glancing round to see that no one was looking, Morton unpinned it and slipped it into his pocket. At least he now had something he could send through the mail, and there was a post-box at the end of the road. He hurried back and put half the bottles in a cupboard, in case Goulter should notice that there were more than when he had left the house. It turned out to be a needless precaution. It was eleven o'clock before Goulter returned. Then he called to them to help him and went outside again. In the roadway stood a stranger with a horse and cart, on which was a huge wooden packing-case. With a great deal of pushing and pulling, they manoeuvred it into the kitchen, where it was left until next morning.

Morton came down early, but Kemp was there before him, levering at the boards of the packing-case with a jemmy.

'Here you are, Fred,' he said, handing him the implement, 'I told you Beasley was a good quartermaster.'

'What is it?' asked Morton, pulling off the top of the crate.

'A numbering machine,' said Kemp with a crafty grin. 'A very special numbering machine.'

'How is that?' asked Morton, wrenching the sides away.

'A few years ago, the Bank of England started bringing in new presses. Until that time, the main design of the note was printed on one machine, and the dating and numbering was done on another. Once the new presses came in, they no longer needed the separate numbering machines, so they disposed of them, as scrap. They were supposed to be broken up immediately, and a Bank of England man was there to see it happened. However, a far-sighted friend of Beasley re-assembled this one from the bits—original dies and all!'

'And does it work?' asked Morton in disbelief.

'I cannot see Beasley laying out good money for one that did not . . . Of course, it would have been driven by steam-power originally, but I see they have provided a splendid wheel for you to turn!'

'Thank you very much!'

'Since we shall have to put each note in by hand, I shall only require one revolution of the machinery at a time.'

'So are you saying that the notes will no longer have the same number?' asked Morton in surprise.

'That is right. They will run in a series, just like proper notes; they will bear a date in April this year, and will have been issued in London.'

'Amazing!' said Morton warmly. 'Surely you will look back on this as your masterpiece?'

'Not mine,' replied Kemp, 'Beasley's really . . . I'm thinking of digging up my plates of *Gods and Man*, now this job is nearly finished. Do you know any gentlemen who might be interested in saucy pictures? We could easily roll off a few hundred . . .'

By lunch-time, Kemp had got the new machine working to his satisfaction, and they began to over-print the notes. It was a slow and painstaking task and, now that he had ample time at his disposal, Kemp was meticulous in the extreme. The serial numbers had to be printed precisely over a line of the script. The slightest deviation, in any direction, would shout aloud that the note was counterfeit. Kemp took endless trouble, getting each note in exactly the right position—but who could blame him? Every one was a potential fiver in his pocket. Once he was satisfied, Morton turned the wheel and Kemp would scrutinize the note minutely. So the afternoon dragged on, Morton standing watching for the most part; it reminded him of his childhood, when he would steal round to the wash-house,

and the women would indulge him by allowing him to turn the
mangle.

After supper, he went upstairs. Finding it deserted, he
tip-toed into Beasley's room and took one of the bottles of
erasing fluid. He closed the door of his bedroom and, taking
out the postcard, removed all the writing from it. He then
replaced the bottle carefully in Beasley's drawer. He pondered
for a while on what to do. It was always possible that he could
be searched, and the card discovered, before he had a chance
to post it. If he addressed it to Sergeant Bragg—or even Mr
Bragg, it could be his death warrant. On the other hand, if he
sent it to Ada Smith, he might just be able to persuade them
that his lust had got the better of him. After some thought he
composed a short message for Bragg and wrote the card. Then
he put it under his pillow and went to bed.

He was awakened by the birds, when it was barely light. He
dressed hurriedly and stole downstairs. Goulter was standing
by the sink in the kitchen, his shirt neck tucked into his vest,
his braces looping down. He was lathering his face with a
shaving brush.

'Just having a breath of fresh air,' Morton said and walked
out into the garden. He went briskly down to the back wall,
well within Goulter's vision, then began to stroll along it,
stopping from time to time to look around and breathe deeply.
As soon as he got round to the side of the house, he dashed to
the gate and ran down the street to the post-box. When the card
dropped in, he felt an odd sense of relief. It was totally
unjustified, of course. If he had been missed, Goulter could be
waiting for him with his cut-throat. He could not even solace
himself with the thought that, even so, the gang would be
caught and the currency saved. Beasley might change his
plans. He could still die in vain. He ran back to the house and
ducked in through the gate. No one was in sight, but the
evidence of his hasty departure would have been visible to
anyone who had bothered to look out of the window. The path
itself showed no traces, but his footprints were all too plain on
the dewy grass—the tracks of a running man. He dawdled back
the way he had come, eradicating the marks as he went. When
he gained the back garden, he sauntered into the house. Goulter
gave him a surly, suspicious look, but no more. Morton hurried
up the stairs, trying to suppress his excitement. He had
succeeded! All he had to do now was to play his part until the

police moved in. He still had to be cautious, of course, but there was nothing remaining which would force him to take risks. He went back to the drudgery of numbering bank-notes with a light heart.

Mrs Marsden was taking tea on a tray in the sitting-room. She often did this, when William was away in the country, working on a portrait. She could snuggle up with a book and forget the tedious business of deciding what to have for dinner. Catherine did not mind, fortunately. She was going through a phase of despising exotic food and elaborate dinner-parties. Silly girl! Though if the truth were known, she was probably more concerned with keeping her figure. She had really turned into a beautiful young woman, tall and willowy; and the newest fashions enhanced the grace of her body to perfection. Whatever she said about getting rid of her, Cheltenham had turned her into a strong, healthy, poised young lady. She was a daughter to be proud of—if only she were not so headstrong. She got that from her father, of course; but still, it was not quite seemly in a woman . . . There was a rap at the door and Joan advanced with a silver card-tray. Someone had called. How nice!

'Excuse me, mum. Cook said I was to bring you this. She says she's paid the excess post from the kitchen money.'

Mrs Marsden picked up the postcard—a picture of Dover Castle. Who on earth could it be from? Naturally, the servants would know already.

'Thank you, Joan. That will be all.'

She turned over the card, and her heart sank. Not another to Ada Smith from this Fred! Catherine had said he would have been murdered—practically promised it. She had been feeling terribly guilty for days, and here was another one. It was too bad! William would be furious, of course. He had made her promise to give any more Ada Smith letters to him, and he would decide whether Catherine should have them or not . . . In strictness, though, this was not a letter. She read the message again. It was pure gibberish—perhaps it was written in some kind of code. The girl had been reading too much Rider Haggard, she decided, with her clandestine communications. On the surface it seemed innocent enough, but perhaps one could send an obscene message in cipher. Oh dear! It was all a great trouble . . . At any rate, there was no need to make a decision yet. William was not due back home until Saturday evening. And even if she decided not to tell him, she would certainly not give the card to Catherine before Sunday. She did not want her upset for the party at the Osbornes' on Saturday night. Whatever Fred wanted, he would have to wait. Mrs Marsden found herself wishing that the wretched man really had got himself murdered. She dropped the card guiltily between the pages of her book, and turned to a new chapter.

By six o'clock on Saturday evening they had finished numbering the notes, and had packed them into the cardboard boxes in bundles of five hundred. Snell was smoking a cigarette in the garden, while Goulter and Morton were sitting round the kitchen table, drinking beer and relaxing. Looking up, Morton saw that Beasley was talking to Snell. He heard Beasley laugh, then Snell dropped his half-smoked cigarette to the ground and they both came in.

'I hear that the great enterprise is complete,' Beasley said with an expansive smile. 'Are you satisfied with them, Percy?'

'I wouldn't mind popping a few down myself,' said Kemp.

'Now, now, each to his own.' Beasley took two envelopes from his pocket, and passed one to Morton and the other to Snell.

'I want to be ultra-cautious over this operation, gentlemen,' he said. 'It could be that questions might be asked about a note you have paid over for a bet. It is just possible that a bookie might suggest it is counterfeit. You would then, of course, take it back and hand over genuine notes in its place. That ought to be an end of the matter. In the unlikely event of your being questioned further. I want you to have papers which would establish an impeccable social background. They will, of course, be the only papers on your persons. You, Fred, will be a man of substance from Bristol; you, George, will be the son of a well-known trading family in Peckham. You will find the necessary papers in that envelope, with a note of your personal and family history. I want you to absorb the details, so that you can pass yourselves off convincingly.'

'You mean these people exist?' asked Snell.

'Of course. If your word is to be accepted because of your social status, you must be known of, but not known.'

'Bloody hell!' said Snell. 'I hope my bloke doesn't turn up at Doncaster.'

'Do try to get rid of that dreadful accent, George,' said Beasley reprovingly. 'It serves you well as a clerk, but not as the scion of a wealthy family—even if they are in trade.'

'Jolly good, old chap,' Snell mouthed, in a stage public-school accent.

Morton pulled out the contents of his envelope and gave a start. On top was a letter addressed to Charles Forbes Esq.

'What is it?' asked Beasley.

'Nothing. I was going to ask how you managed to get the bank to send a letter detailing my man's investments. But I suppose it would be a stupid question.'

Beasley tapped his forehead, with a smile. 'Planning, my boy, planning,' he said getting to his feet. 'Now, I will relieve you of some of the notes. Are these the boxes?'

'Not that one!' said Snell quickly. 'The other three.'

'Equal shares, are they, George?' asked Beasley suspiciously.

'Yes, 'course.'

'We must be fair, mustn't we?'

Goulter had come alert, his hand down under his coat. But he was not called on to use his knife. Beasley picked up the three boxes and tied them one on top of the other with string.

'Look like shoes, don't they,' he said with a chuckle. 'By the way, I have found five of my extra putters-down and a friend is introducing me to another on Tuesday, so our team will be complete—and just in time.'

Mrs Marsden looked across at Catherine, absorbed in making notes for some article or other, and sighed. This morning, the vicar had taken as his text: 'If thine eye offend thee, pluck it out, and cast it from thee.' On this unpromising foundation, he had built a rambling discourse on deceit of various kinds; and more than once she had seen William glance angrily at Catherine, as if wondering whether he should eject her from his household. That would cause a stir. It would bring about the scandal they had so far managed to avoid. She'd had to bribe cook and Joan with a rise in wages, but it had been worth it. So far there had not even been a breath of rumour—and once it was out, her friends would not be slow to come round and commiserate with her. No, she could not let William spoil it all, as he might well do if she showed him the postcard . . .

Perhaps she ought to destroy it. But that in itself would be a kind of deceit.

'Why are you sighing, Mamma?' asked Catherine.

'I, er . . . I just remembered. A postcard came for Ada Smith,' she said, flustered. 'Now where did I put it?'

Catherine had sprung to her feet, her face tense.

'Oh, I remember. I used it as a bookmark, thinking I would be sure to see it and give it to you.' Mrs Marsden took up her novel and handed over the card.

Catherine read it in agitation.

> *St Leger Wed on course*
> *£100s Last Fling & African*
> *Sun sequential love*
> *Fred.*

'Oh, Mamma!' she cried. 'He's all right, he's safe!'

'Good,' said her mother, conscious that she had now been dragged into a conspiracy against her husband. The vicar had been right. There was no end to deceit.

'When did it come, Mamma?' asked Catherine, her cheeks glowing.

'Yesterday evening,' she lied.

'I shall have to go out for an hour or two,' said Catherine buoyantly. 'I will be back for tea.'

When she came downstairs Mrs Marsden noted, with some disquiet, that she had on the rather nice cameo she had been wearing of late.

At ten o'clock next morning Bragg rapped on the Commissioner's door, and walked in.

'Ah, Bragg,' said Sir William tentatively, 'I hope you have some good news for me.'

'I think I may, sir. This postcard came from Morton, via our intermediary.'

The Commissioner took it and placed it on the desk in front of him.

'Why is Ada Smith so sensitive?' he asked.

'Sensitive? I don't understand you, sir.'

'You said I might be embarrassed if I knew the identity of your go-between.'

'Ah, yes, sir. I see what you mean. Well, "Ada Smith" is what we might call a *nom de guerre*, in the circumstances.'

'Oh? . . . Very well,' said Sir William reluctantly. 'And what does all this mumbo jumbo mean?'

'I have had a word with Sergeant Bliss. He is a great betting man, and he confirmed that the St Leger is due to be run on Wednesday.'

'The day after tomorrow? Where? Epsom?'

'No, sir. At Doncaster.'

'That is in Yorkshire, isn't it?'

'Yes, sir. West Riding.'

'Ah, yes . . . Then, the card suggests that it is being run on a course. I would have thought that was self-evident.'

'Just so, sir. It does seem superfluous. However, we know that the notes they are printing were hundreds. So when Sergeant Bliss suggested it referred to on-course bookmakers, I felt certain he must be right.'

'I see. They are going to bet with the money. Is that what you are saying?'

'Yes sir, with the object of getting as much change as possible.'

'So in a sense, the bookmakers will discount it for them—involuntarily, of course!' Sir William gave a foxy smile. 'Well, they are amongst the least deserving members of society.'

'That may be, sir. But when they pay out to the winners, a good number of counterfeit notes will find their way into the public's hands. And no doubt the rest will be put through the banks in the next few days.'

'How many sheets were stolen, Bragg?'

'Enough to print four thousand notes, we think.'

The Commissioner pondered for a moment. 'I think we will keep this from the Governor, for the time being, Bragg. He seems quite depressed enough, as it is . . . And what do you make of the rest of the message?'

'Sergeant Bliss says that there aren't any racehorses named "Last Fling" or "African Sun"; certainly none running at the Doncaster meeting. It is my opinion that Morton was dressing up the message to look like a racing tip. If we take those groups independently, it suggests to me that the counterfeiters are going to get rid of their notes, as quickly as possible, and flee the country.'

'Hm. Well, it would be sound tactics, Bragg. And what about "sequential"? Is that another racehorse?'

'I don't think it is even intended to be taken as one, sir. It doesn't begin with a capital letter, for one thing. But as to what it means, I'm stumped.'

'Do you think it stands on its own, Bragg? Or do we have to lump it in with "love"?'

'I think we can ignore the "love" bit, sir.'

'Can we?' Sir William looked quizzically at Bragg. 'Right. Then what does "sequential" mean? Pass me the dictionary from the bookcase, will you?'

Bragg placed the heavy tome on the desk. 'No wonder they say your annual reports could have been written by Kipling, sir.'

The Commissioner looked up in delighted surprise. 'Do they say that, Bragg?'

'Oh yes, sir. Most impressive.'

Sir William cleared his throat self-consciously and flipped through the pages. 'Here we are, "sequential" means, "characterized by the regular sequence of its parts". I think we could have guessed that, anyway. Where are we? . . . "sequence". It says "a continuous or connected series".'

'It doesn't seem to get us any further, sir.'

'Yes, yes it does . . . it is on the tip of my tongue. Sequence . . . series . . . series of bank-notes . . . bank-note series . . . That's it! Bank-notes have serial numbers.'

'The counterfeits would have to have a serial number, or they would stick out like a sore thumb.'

'I know,' said Sir William impatiently. 'That is why he must be trying to tell us something else. "Sequential" must mean "numbered in a continuous series".'

'So every note will have a different number?'

'I can see no other interpretation, Bragg. Which means that the Bank of England is going to have a monumental task identifying them . . . We cannot let this happen.'

'Well, I had come round to thinking that this postcard was a signal for us to move in on them, but I think we shall have to be prepared to let them utter some of the notes.'

'What have you in mind, Bragg?'

'Obviously, we shall have to work through the local constabulary, sir, and they will have the last word on how it is done. But it would be my idea to put detectives amongst the crowd. They should be able to identify the putters-down, if they watch the bookies' stands. Then when they think they know them all, we could take them.'

'Yes. I suppose that must be the tactic. Very well, Bragg. Perhaps we ought to consult the Governor after all. Then I will get a telegraph off to the local Chief Constable. When do you intend to go up?'

'Well, sir, I am in a bit of difficulty. I would like to go up today; but since the main hunt for the counterfeiters has been called off, Inspector Cotton has been taking up the reins again . . .'

'I see.' Sir William chuckled. 'In that case, I think a few days of compassionate leave are called for . . . Yes, that should do the trick nicely.'

By Tuesday evening the whole house had been tidied up. They had re-crated the numbering machine and Goulter had taken it away on a cart. The plate-press was to stay until Kemp had printed a few of his indecent etchings, then he would arrange for its disposal and vacate the premises. The rest of them had packed their things, and would leave them at King's Cross station next morning. For the first time, Morton felt relaxed. He had done all he could; it was now up to Bragg. He was playing rummy with Snell and Kemp, while Goulter interminably sharpened his knives. Snell was gleefully totting up his winnings, when the door burst open and Beasley stood on the threshhold, a revolver in his hand. The barrel was pointing straight at Morton's head.

'What kind of game have you been playing, Fred?' he spat out menacingly.

'I don't understand you,' said Morton, seeing Goulter swivel round at the ready.

'You don't eh?' Beasley's lip curled. 'Then let me tell you. Your name is not Fred Thorburn at all. You have lied to me.'

Goulter had sprung to his feet and crossed behind Morton. He could imagine the knife point inches from his back. A vision of the dismembered torso swam into his mind and he thrust it away impatiently. He had got to think . . . If they knew he was a policeman, he would have been dead already . . . But what had gone wrong?

'It's no use playing dumb, Fred. Your game is up.'

'I have never lied to you, Mr Beasley,' said Morton in a hurt tone.

'Oh, but you have. Beyond a shadow of doubt.'

Snell was looking at Morton fascinated, his lips moist, his eyes bright.

'I was introduced to our last putter-down this afternoon, Fred. And you can imagine how surprised I was, to hear that his name was Frederick Reginald Thorburn . . .' Beasley came nearer, till the gun was almost touching Morton's chest. If he jumped him, there was a good chance that the bullet might be deflected—but he would not escape Goulter's knife.

'A coincidence, I thought,' went on Beasley, 'amazing, but still a coincidence.' The sneering sibilants made him seem like a snake poised to strike.

'Then I asked him about himself. Would you believe it, Fred? He told me just the same as you had told me—raised in New Zealand, school in Wells, cashiered from the Dorset Regiment. That was too much, even for silly trusting me . . . So what's it about, Fred?' he rapped out.

'So he's come back to England?' asked Morton in as steady a voice as he could muster. 'He said he would never let me down; but when I got out, they told me he'd gone back to New Zealand.'

'I don't follow you, Fred,' said Beasley in a high, excited voice, his eyes glittering.

Morton allowed a broader accent to creep into his speech. 'There was nothing so gentlemanly as a cashiering, for me. I was a ranker. So for what little I did, I got six months in the glasshouse and a dishonourable discharge. When I came out, I tried to find the Captain, but he'd gone. So I had to rub along on my own. Rotten bastard!'

'Are you saying you know this man, Fred?'

'Know him? I was his batman! He ticed me into this little fiddle. "It will never be discovered", he said . . . I wouldn't trust him, if I were you.'

'And what was this fiddle?' asked Beasley abruptly.

'I don't know all he was up to. I heard they got him for all sorts of things. Me, I used to pinch meat and stuff from the mess store, and sell it to the local traders. Six months I got, for that little bit! And he walks away a free man,' said Morton bitterly.

The madness was fading from Beasley's eyes, there was a

puzzled frown on his brow; but the revolver was still levelled at Morton's head.

'How does it come about that you call yourself by his name?' he asked.

'Well, he'd gone back to New Zealand, and it sounded a nice respectable name.'

'But he wasn't, was he?' said Beasley, staring hard into Morton's eyes. 'He was a known criminal.'

'I didn't hang around Dorset, you can bet. I never came across anybody who knew him. How is the old sod? When did he come back?'

'He never left Europe,' said Beasley curtly. 'He cashed the steamship ticket his family bought for him and went, instead, to France.'

'It'll be good to see him again!' said Morton warmly.

'You still have not explained why you lied to me.'

'I haven't lied to you, Mr Beasley,' Morton said in an injured voice. 'As I said, I just changed my name to his, adopted his character. He was better class, you see. Then when you asked about me, without thinking I gave you his story instead of my own . . . You remember that I hesitated when you gave me the envelope, the other night? Well, I was just wondering how I could keep all these characters separate!'

'So who are you, then?'

'Josiah Hogsflesh, a carpenter's son from Winterbourne Zelston—you can't blame me for wanting to get rid of that name!'

Beasley, looked at him speculatively for some moments. 'All right Fred,' he said flatly, 'we need not decide it yet. Unfortunately, the real Thorburn has gone with the others to Doncaster this evening, so we shall have to wait to find out the truth. You will come up with us tomorrow, and we will see if he recognizes you. In the meantime Goulter will watch you. He will sleep in your room, he will go to the bog with you. The slightest attempt to get away, and he will kill you. Understand?'

Morton shrugged. 'Suits me,' he said carelessly.

'And until your *bona fides* have been established, I will look after your share of the notes.'

CHAPTER ——————
—————— EIGHTEEN

Morton spent a sleepless night. From time to time he heard
Goulter snoring lightly, but if he so much as moved, his gaoler
was wide awake. It was impossible to escape. Goulter had
wedged his bed across the doorway and closed the catch on the
window. To get away, Morton would have to be prepared to
murder him. Some people would say it was a legitimate action,
self-defence; but Morton could not bring himself even to
consider it. What was the point, anyway? If he did so, the
conspirators would certainly cancel their plans, and the opportunity to capture them would be lost. At least, they still seemed
to be intent on going ahead with them . . . Morton shud-
dered. He had been within a hair's breadth of being killed. It
was in Beasley's eyes, Snell had been willing it to happen. His
reaction had been convincing enough to make Beasley think
again, but it was a mere postponement. Once he arrived at
Doncaster, the true Thorburn would disown him and he would
be murdered without compunction. He would have achieved
the prolongation of his life by a few fearful hours . . . Yes,
he was afraid. He had accepted the assignment in a spirit of
bravado, seeing himself as some kind of romantic hero. He had

anticipated the excitement of success, not the loneliness of failure. When he had considered that possibility at all, he had airily told himself that his life was worth little anyway, that he was expendable. Now, with death only a few hours away, he fiercely wanted to live. What immature stupidity, to let himself be cajoled by Bragg into sacrificing his life in this way. He had been behaving like a petulant child paying back his parents for favouring an elder brother. In God's name, Edwin had little enough of life. Morton found it difficult to think about them. His mother would have been deeply hurt by his apparently uncaring departure for Australia. Soon she would be told he was dead, his life wasted in an absurd enterprise . . . Morton found his thoughts drifting to Catherine Marsden, her charm, her liveliness, her determination. There had been more than a grain of truth in his remark to Wardle. He would regret her most of all—if one could have human regrets in the next world . . . He tried to pray, to prepare himself for being hurled into the hereafter. But all he could manage, was a pitiful: 'God help me. Why did I do it?' As dawn broke, he drifted into an uneasy sleep of exhaustion.

Next morning, after due warning of what would happen if he tried to escape and expressions of unconcern on his part, Morton was hurried to the main road and from there, in a growler, to King's Cross station. Wherever they went, Beasley and Goulter were on either side of him and Snell close behind.

The race special left platform seven and when they arrived, some race-horses were being led into boxes at the rear of the train. Beasley selected a compartment halfway along and motioned Morton into a corner seat. Goulter sat beside him, with Beasley and Snell opposite. Although there was a door between them, Morton noted that the handle to open it was on Beasley's side, not his. Nothing was being left to chance—a good quartermaster . . . In a sense it was that remark which had been his undoing—Kemp's slightly disdainful tolerance of Beasley. It had led Morton to propound the theory of the putter-up behind it all. The shadowy figure who must be brought into focus and caught. Well, he had not advanced the idea lightly and he still thought it was valid. But he had not foreseen himself in this predicament. Oddly enough, death was easier to face in the daylight. Even with his executioner by his side, he could feel that he was still a policeman, that Bragg's tactics had been triumphantly vindicated and that even if he must die, he had lured the gang to Doncaster, where they would surely be taken.

When the train hissed to a halt at the station, they remained in the compartment until the other passengers had left the platform. He was given no opportunity to escape. He glanced up at the clock. He had about an hour of life left to him—perhaps two, if they failed to locate Thorburn straight away. Surprisingly, he viewed the matter with a light-headed objectivity. He strolled with his escort along the sunlit street, watching the horses being led to the race-course, observing the jostling cheerful crowds. He ought to be fearful or dejected, desperately wishing to escape, or regretful for things left undone. Instead he was detached from it all, like a minor actor going woodenly through his role, and destined to be slain before the end of the scene.

They were nearly at the entrance to the race-course now. Beasley slowed down still more, till they were swallowed up in an eager crowd coming from behind them.

'Don't think you can get away,' he hissed in Morton's ear. 'Try it, and you're dead!'

'I have no reason to escape,' replied Morton patiently. He even managed a deprecating smile—he might as well act out his part to the end.

They lined up for the turnstile and Morton could feel Goulter pressing close behind him. Beasley bought entrance tickets for the four of them and, once through the gate, he told Snell and Goulter to spread out. Snell shot off in search of the bookmakers, Goulter was keeping pace with them, a dozen yards to the right.

'Don't forget my revolver, Fred,' said Beasley quietly. 'I can easily shoot you and get away in the crowd. Keep moving nice and slowly.'

Morton wondered what his chances were. Now, he only had two to escape from. If he could dispose of Beasley, he could easily outrun Goulter. He cautiously glanced round to see if Sergeant Bragg was in sight, but he was not . . . Perhaps Bragg hadn't received his message, or had misinterpreted it. If so, he would be justified in trying to escape. He felt his body tingling at the idea. Why should he act like a sacrificial lamb? Beasley was a mere two steps behind him, his hand in his coat pocket. The revolver was of a heavy caliber; if a shot hit him it would cause a terrible wound. The image of his brother flashed across his mind, paralysed, resentful, angrily waiting to die. Did he want that? He pushed the thought from him, anything was better than complete extinction . . . It would have to be soon. They were walking away from the grandstand, towards a line of low buildings beyond the second enclosure. Ahead of them, the crowd was thinning out; any moment the real Thorburn might approach Beasley and his fate would be sealed . . . A rapid twist to the left would be best, his arm flung out to knock away the revolver. He glanced to his right. In a few yards they would have cleared that group of young people; the shot would do no harm then. Suddenly, he felt his left arm seized from behind. Then a bulky man pushed between him and Beasley, and grabbed his right.

'We are police officers,' said a voice. 'Frederick Thorburn, I have a warrant for your arrest, on a charge of assault and causing an affray at the Ship Inn, Doncaster, last September. I would advise you to come quietly.' Morton felt his arms twisted up his back, as he was propelled towards the stands.

'I am Charles Forbes, from Bristol,' he protested loudly. 'You have made a mistake! I am not the man you want!'

Beasley had faded out of sight. Morton was hustled down a passage-way to the back of the stand, then unceremoniously pushed into a room with barred windows.

'Well done, men.' Bragg was sitting by a table, contentedly smoking his pipe. He looked at Morton critically. 'You look as if you have been through the mill, lad. It's a good thing we pulled you out, I reckon.'

Morton felt his body going limp from relief. He flopped into a chair. 'In ten minutes I would have been cat's meat,' he said wearily. 'The real Thorburn turned up. He will be acting as a putter-down here today.'

Bragg called for a cup of tea, and while he drank it, Morton gave the gist of what had happened. As he finished, a slim man in uniform came in.

'This is Chief Inspector Gorry,' said Bragg. 'He is co-ordinating the operation on the ground.'

'Everyone is in place, sergeant,' he said cheerfully, sitting down behind the table. 'I have twenty detectives mingling with the crowd, and they have all seen the sketches of the men we are after.'

'There will be six more putters-down now. And Morton

here, has not met them, so he cannot draw you their likenesses.'

'I'll pass the word,' said Gorry. 'We will not make any
arrests, until we have identified them all.'

'If I might make a suggestion, sir,' said Morton, 'I think it
would be better to refrain from arresting them on the race-
course. Beasley has rented a house nearby, and it has been
arranged that all the gang will assemble there after the racing,
to hand over their money. I am almost certain that the
putters-down I have not met, were in fact staying there last
night. If we delay the arrests till they are all present, there
should be no danger of losing any of them.'

Gorry looked across at Bragg. 'It seems sensible,' he said.
'But since it is a City of London matter, you ought to have the
final say, sergeant.'

'I'm prepared to take the chance, sir,' replied Bragg quietly.
'It would be nice and satisfying to pick them all up at once.'

'Where is this house, constable?' asked Gorry.

'I am afraid that I fell under suspicion before I was told, sir.
All I know is that it is near the race-course.'

'It's a common practice for people to let their houses for the
St Leger week,' Gorry said with a frown. 'It could be any one
of a dozen. We shall have to follow them there, then put a
cordon round it . . . For the moment, I suggest that one of
my men should take our prisoner down to the station. You
might like to go as well, sergeant. There is no more for you to
do here, and you could relax down there.'

Accordingly, Morton was handcuffed to one of the detectives who had arrested him, and he was pulled suddenly
through the crowds to the back of the stand, where they were
joined by Bragg. They were conveyed by a police wagonette to
the town and Morton was dragged into the police station. He
was taken into the muster room, where he was released amid a
good deal of chaffing. Then after some food, he went into one
of the cells, where he fell gratefully asleep on the bed.

Bragg spent the afternoon reviewing the situation. Now he
had got Morton out of danger, his perspective had changed.
The Governor of the Bank had agreed to underwrite any losses
which would arise through letting the counterfeiters utter their
notes. Once the serial numbers were known, the banks would
be alerted and a public announcement would be made. So far
as the members of the gang were concerned, they were

virtually certain to arrest Beasley, Snell and Goulter, so at worst it was smashed . . . Unless Morton was right about the shadowy backer. If he existed at all, he was likely to be the man who commissioned Kemp to engrave the thousand-pound plate, three years ago. On that analysis, they would be foolish to be content with Beasley and the others. If the putter-up and Kemp were left at large, they could easily start up again.

At five o'clock, Chief Inspector Gorry came in, a satisfied smile on his face.

'I think we know who they all are,' he said.

'They went ahead with the uttering, then?' asked Bragg.

'Oh yes, like wasps at a jam-pot. They must have got rid of a prodigious number of notes. I withdrew most of my men at the start of the last race. There is a detective shadowing each one of the gang. Any that make for the station will be arrested there. The others will be allowed to proceed to their hide-away, and then we will seal it up and move in.'

'I have been pondering a bit, this afternoon,' said Bragg. 'I think there may be something in the theory of a putter-up in London being behind this. I would like to keep my options open.'

'That should prove no difficulty,' replied Gorry amicably. 'I shall be down there. Once they are in the net, you shall say when we pull the string tight. And now I must go and collect my winnings on the big race!'

'I'd forgotten that,' said Bragg. 'What won?'

'Oh, La Flèche walked it. I got a fiver on when it was still nine to one, so I made a killing.'

'I had half-a-crown each way, on Orme.'

'Not even placed!' Gorry grinned. 'It came in fifth!'

'That's what loyalty does for you,' said Bragg sourly. 'My luck had better improve for tonight.'

Towards six o'clock, word came that nine men had been followed to a house standing in wooded grounds on the edge of the town. Bragg wakened Morton and they went to the location in Gorry's trap. As they approached the driveway, a detective stepped out of the bushes.

'Any change, Inspector?' asked Gorry.

'No, sir. They have been in a room at the back for the last hour. The little weasley man has been counting the takings and paying the others off. They seem to be having a bit of a party.

We might as well let them get a skinful, it will make our job easier.'

'Take care with the big one,' said Morton urgently. 'Alcohol seems to have no effect on him.'

'You are the man who got into the gang, are you?' asked the Inspector with admiration.

'Yes, I can still hardly believe it is over.'

'Is there a cordon round the property?' asked Gorry.

'Yes, sir. Everyone will keep cover until they hear my whistle. If you come through this gap in the hedge, you can get a good view of the house from the shrubbery.'

They settled down to wait. An hour went by, then the front door opened and Beasley emerged. He was dressed in his coat and hat, and was carrying a large Gladstone bag. Immediately behind him came Goulter, the bulge of the knife-holster showing under his coat.

'Well, sergeant?' whispered Gorry. 'What do we do?'

'Let them go,' said Bragg quietly. 'We will follow them. Give us time to get clear, then take the rest.'

'Right . . . And good luck!'

Beasley strode purposefully down the drive and Goulter lumbered after him, peering around him suspiciously. When they had passed through the gates, Bragg and Morton dodged back to the gap in the hedge and glanced out. They were just disappearing round a bend in the road.

'We could have done without the bodyguard,' Bragg grunted. 'I suppose that is your friend Goulter?'

'Indeed. He seems even more massive in the fading light.'

'I'll toss you for him, when the time comes! For the moment we need take no risks; they've got to be going to the station. They know you, so drop behind me. If you see me start to run, come up damned quick!'

Bragg tramped off in pursuit. Soon they were in the middle of the town, the pavements clogged with knots of inebriated race-goers. Goulter was in front now, pushing unceremoni-ously through the crowd; Beasley followed in his wake, clutching his bag in his left hand, his right buried in his coat pocket. He would not let go of his money without bloodshed, that was certain . . . Apart from that precaution, he did not seem particularly concerned. Not once had he glanced back, to see if he was being followed. When they reached the station, he walked casually to the first-class ticket office. Bragg tensed

as he felt Goulter's hostile gaze pass over him, and on to the
people beyond. If Morton were spotted, they would have to
take them there and then—and not a policeman in sight. Bragg
began to regret his arrogance in letting them leave the house.
Once he'd had them all in the bag, he could have found out if
there were a putter-up, all right. Now, with Goulter loose, the
odds were stacked against them. He strolled up to the second-
class window in time to hear Beasley ask for two tickets to
London, then followed them on to the platform, where they
went into the waiting-room. Bragg turned back to meet Morton
at the barrier.

'They will be at the front of the train, in the first-class,' he
said. 'I will get as near to them as I dare. You travel in the rear
and join me smartly when we arrive at King's Cross. At the
stations in between, we had better stick our heads out in case
they do something fancy. All right?'

'Yes. I promise not to go to sleep again!'

Indeed, Morton felt alert and full of vigour once more. As
the train rattled through the dusk, he sat back and wallowed in
the sensation of being alive. At each station, he dropped the
window and gazed along the platform. He half hoped for some
move by Beasley, which would enable him to revenge himself
for the agony of mind he had endured. When they stopped at
Peterborough, the guard came along the train, lighting the
gas-lamps in the carriages. Now the world outside was black,
broken only by the brief tracery of a spark from the engine, or
the glow from the lights of small stations as they rushed
through. Morton began to think again of his narrow escape, but
the delight and relief had evaporated. Thanks to Bragg, he was
no longer on his own, but the most dangerous part of the
operation could still lie ahead. No doubt the sergeant would try
to summon assistance, but neither of them alone would have
any chance of subduing Goulter and Beasley. They would have
to stay together. He took out his watch impatiently. According
to the timetable, they should have been in London by now, yet
the train was dawdling along. He looked for the lights of the
metropolis, but could see nothing. He dropped the window and
was met by the acrid smell of fog. Here was an unlooked-for
complication. It would be ironic if Beasley escaped them now,
through the vagaries of the weather. The train proceeded in fits
and starts for another ten minutes, then finally crawled into
King's Cross station. Before it came to a halt, Morton sprang

down and ran along the platform, dodging between trolleys and
disembarking passengers. When he got to the first-class
carriages, he dropped into a walk and finally came up with
Bragg, who was shuffling along peering into the fog. Ahead of
them was the menacing outline of Goulter, with Beasley in
front, still clutching his Gladstone bag. They made their way
uncertainly to the cab rank, where they took a hansom. Morton
was beckoning for the next one in line, when Bragg restrained
him.

'No, lad. We'll do better on our feet, tonight.'

The cab-horse picked its way tentatively out of the station
forecourt and turned westward at walking pace. Bragg and
Morton had no difficulty in following the red glow from the
lamps. After ten minutes or so, the cab turned left, off the main
road and entered a maze of narrow streets. It was impossible to
discover their names, for the signs were placed high up on the
walls and the feeble light of the street-lamps could not
illuminate them. Surprisingly, the general visibility was better
in the meanest streets, where the gas-lamps were sparse.
Looking up Morton could see the blurred disc of the moon, its
light diffusing down through the fog. For nine or ten feet
around, the mist was almost luminescent; but beyond was
impenetrable darkness. Suddenly the cab swung down an alley
and, after a short distance, came to a halt. They heard
Beasley's voice enquiring about the fare and flattened themselves against the wall. There came the chink of coins, then the
cab went cautiously on again. In the faint oval of its lamps,
Beasley could be seen inserting a latchkey into a door. He
made some remark and Goulter growled a reply, then the door
slammed shut behind them. Bragg and Morton crept up to the
building. It was a small mews cottage, almost certainly
redundant in this age of the underground train. They waited for
a lamp to be lit, but in vain.

'I don't like this,' said Bragg uneasily. He flattened his face
against the window, but not a gleam of light was visible within.
He gently tried the door, but it was locked.

'We shall be a pair of hardened criminals before this is
finished,' he muttered, as he opened the long blade of his knife
and slipped it between the frames of the sash-window. There
was a slight click, as the catch was forced back, and a moment
later he was easing open the window.

'In you go, lad.'

Morton swung through the aperture, and dropped lightly to the floor . . . The house was empty. There was no furniture, no curtains, nothing. Bragg crept upstairs, while Morton shuffled his way towards the kitchen at the back, hampered by the lack of a lantern. Then he felt a cool draught of air on his face. The back door was open! He edged forward until his foot touched the threshold, then stood listening. Only the distant whistle of a train broke the silence. He took a cautious step into the yard, and his foot rattled a bucket by the wall.

'Who's that?' came a hoarse challenge from the darkness. Morton kept still. There was a click as the shutter of a dark-lantern was slid aside, then the beam flickered on to his face.

'Wot you doin' 'ere?' exclaimed Goulter. 'I thought you was took.'

'I was,' said Morton quietly, 'but I escaped and followed you here.'

He heard a suspicious grunt, then the beam of the lamp wavered as Goulter transferred it to his left hand. In a moment he would be reaching for his knife. Morton stepped sideways out of the light, and hurled himself at Goulter. The impact rocked him back so that he dropped the lantern, yet he was still on his feet. Morton wrapped his arms around Goulter's waist and heaved, but he might just as well have tried to uproot a tree. Now Goulter was fumbling for his knives, but they were under his coat and firmly held by Morton's encircling arms. He began to beat down with his fists, heavy numbing blows on the muscles of the arms and shoulders. Morton tried again to wrestle him to the ground, but he was merely sapping his own strength. He could only hold on and endure the punishing assault for as long as he could—and then . . .

'Hold on, lad!' Bragg came running out of the house, and flung himself at Goulter. The big man half-stumbled, then recovered himself with a snarl; but in that moment Bragg had snapped a derby on his left wrist. Goulter gave a roar of outrage and flailed at Bragg with his arm. The dangling hand-cuff caught the sergeant on the temple and sent him reeling. Now Goulter was pounding Morton's head with the fetter, while trying to get the heel of his right hand under Morton's chin. It could only be moments before the man's prodigious strength prevailed. Shaking his head to clear it, Bragg seized Goulter from behind and got him in a head-lock, his right arm across the bull-like throat, his left hand forcing the head forward. Any ordinary man would submit to this asphyxiating pressure in a few moments. Goulter gave a grunt of anger and, reaching backwards, managed to get a grip on Bragg's left forearm. Bragg could feel his thick fingers tearing at the muscles, as he attempted to drag Bragg's hand from the back of his head. It was a matter of whose strength gave out first. Bragg exerted all his effort to keep the lock in place, but slowly his hand was being forced sideways. Then, with a desperate jerk of the head, Goulter managed to tear Bragg's arm away. They tottered, off-balance, for a moment then all collapsed on the ground.

Goulter was up first, a knife in his hand point upwards—the grip of a practised killer. As he found his feet, Morton lunged forward and seized his wrist. Goulter was momentarily taken by surprise and Morton managed to force the blade upwards, level with his eyes. Goulter gave a hoarse chuckle of triumph and, seizing Morton's wrist, began to drag the knife downwards. He would go for the heart. Morton knew that his life depended on keeping the blade vertical . . . a few more inches, then a sudden twist and it would all be over. He exerted all his force but the handle was level with his waist now . . . He could feel the twist beginning and summoned up every last ounce of strength to counter it . . . but it wasn't enough . . . Then there came a heavy thump; Goulter's pressure eased, he staggered, then slumped against Morton knocking him to the ground. For a moment Morton lost his senses. When he came to, there was a dull pain in his chest and warm fluid was oozing round his neck. He could scarcely breathe for the inert bulk of Goulter on top of him, until Bragg dragged him away.

'Are you all right, lad?' he asked anxiously.

'I seem to be bleeding,' replied Morton dazedly, 'but I cannot find the wound. I thought it was in my chest, but that just seems to be a bruise.'

Bragg felt around in the shadows and, retrieving the lantern, he re-lit it.

'It's Goulter that is bleeding,' he said. 'The knife is stuck in his shoulder.'

Morton laughed shakily. 'That was a near-run thing,' he said. 'What happened?'

'I hit him with that old fencing post. I tripped over it early on, so I knew where I could lay my hand on it . . . Come on, lad, we'd better make sure of this one. We haven't finished yet.'

'They dragged Goulter into the cottage, then hand-cuffed his arms around the newel-post of the staircase. Only then did Bragg stop to pull out the knife.

'Should we not bind his wound?' asked Morton.

'He's got two chances,' said Bragg savagely. 'If he bleeds to death it will only save the hangman a job. Let's get on.'

They crept down a brick path to the remains of a box hedge. There was a gap in it; from beyond came the faint glow of a light. Once through this gap, they seemed to be in a well-tended garden, with trees rearing up out of the fog. They felt their way forward, the light growing ever stronger, till they came to a gravelled pathway encircling a substantial house. Tip-toeing over it, they reached a paved area beneath French doors. Through them they could see Beasley, standing by a table, taking bundles of bank-notes out of his bag and counting them. As they watched, a benign-looking man came into sight and, picking up a pile of notes, took them across to a safe in the mirror.

'Who is he, I wonder,' whispered Morton.

'I don't know,' Bragg growled. 'But we can be damned sure he's your putter-up. Right lad, you take Beasley—and don't forget his gun.'

Morton crept to the door and, bursting through it, launched himself at Beasley's back. They both went sprawling, Morton sliding over the polished wood floor and fetching up against the wall. Beasley got to his knees and began fumbling in his pocket. With a sudden access of rage, Morton lashed out with his fist and Beasley crumpled up in a heap.

The other man seemed stunned by the suddenness of the onslaught. Then he pulled himself together.

'What is the meaning of this intrusion?' he cried in outrage.

'We are police officers,' said Bragg. 'You are under arrest for complicity in the uttering of counterfeit bank-notes.'

'But this is absurd,' exclaimed the man. 'I am Adolphus Merrick, a bond-broker in the City.'

'I don't care if you are the Emperor of Japan,' Bragg cut him short. 'Get your coat on.'

Late the following afternoon, Morton knocked on Lily's door.

'Who's there?' she called.

'Fred.'

He heard the rattle of the lock, then she opened the door and flung her arms around him. 'I thought I was never going to see you again!' she cried tremulously.

'Why is that?'

'Well, you had not come round for ages, so I thought you'd found somebody else. Then yesterday I went up to Rupert Street and you weren't there. Percy said you were in trouble with Beasley, but he wouldn't say why. All he would say, was that you had gone off with the others and you would not come back. I was frightened!'

'Well, I am back, as you can see,' said Morton, gently disengaging her arms.

'Where are the others?' she asked.

'All taken.'

'Taken?'

'All arrested.'

'Where? How?' she asked horrified.

'At Doncaster. They had gone with the counterfeit notes to the races and were uttering them there.'

Lily's head jerked round at the formality of the word 'uttering'. 'What about you, then?' she asked sharply.

'Beasley became suspicious of me and refused to let me have any of the notes . . . He was right to be suspicious, Lily,' he added gravely. 'I am a police officer.'

'What?' Disbelief and alarm chased each other over her face.

'It was necessary. We could not let this counterfeiting succeed.'

She hurled herself at him, pummelling his face with her fists. 'You bastard! You lousy pig!' she screamed.

Morton grasped her wrists. 'We arrested Kemp this morning, busy printing his obscene pictures,' he said lightly.

'What are you sneering at?' cried Lily fiercely. 'He's a king compared to you . . . you Judas!'

'I am truly sorry, Lily,' said Morton, releasing her. 'It was never in my mind to trade on your feelings, and I am genuinely fond of you.'

'You're not! You're a stinking ozzer!'

'Yes, but I shall forget anything you have been involved in.

I can promise you, Lily, that you will not be arrested. That is why I have come.'

'You might as well cop me! There is nothing for me now.' She sat down on the edge of the bed, blinking tears away.

'Of course there is, Lily,' he said persuasively. 'You are young and beautiful, and you know your way in the world. What about that grocery business in Ilford?'

'It was Saffron Waldon,' she sniffed.

'Why don't you go home to Romford?' he cajoled her.

'What? Without you?' she asked bitterly.

'You must have scores of friends there. You could settle down—maybe marry and have children . . .'

'Oh, you rotten sod,' she sobbed. 'I thought I could . . . make a new start . . .' Her voice choked.

Morton put a hand on her shoulder. 'I can only say I am sorry, Lil,' he said softly. 'And to make it easier for you, I have brought you this.' He slipped a note for a thousand pounds into her hand . . . 'It's all right. It's not one of Percy Kemp's.'

'What is this for?' she asked harshly.

'You were helpful to me. If anyone should have it, you should.'

'I don't want your money.'

'It is not my money, Lil. Through you, we were able to arrest the murderer of my predecessor, the blond man. You have earned the reward.'

'You can keep your blood-money!' she screamed in a sudden rage and, screwing up the note, she flung it at the fireplace. 'Get out! Get out!'

Morton backed to the door. She had turned away from him, her shoulders racked with sobs. He opened the door.

'I am sorry, Lily,' he said quietly, and went out. He felt shabby and dishonourable, yet there was no help for it. He would not have wished to hurt her, but it had to be done. He walked miserably along Shoe Lane, trying to justify himself and failing. But she was resilient, she would get over it—and after all, the screwed-up bank-note had lodged on the mantel-piece . . .

CHAPTER _____ _____ NINETEEN

'I cannot decide which one to wear, Mamma!' Catherine was standing before the cheval mirror in her bedroom, pivoting round and staring critically at her reflection.

'Have you no other dresses that would be suitable?' asked her mother patiently.

'Goodness no! The others are all ages old . . . I think it will have to be this one.'

'Do you not think the eau-de-nil gown would be more . . . appropriate?' ventured Mrs Marsden.

'Why, Mamma?'

'To be taken out to dinner at the Savoy is still rather special . . . and I feel the bodice of that one is rather heavy.'

'It is meant to be, Mamma,' Catherine smiled teasingly, 'and I could wear his cameo on the collar.'

'I have never liked duchesse satin, it is so bulky, somehow; and with the bodice buttoning over at the front, and those notches in the collar, it makes you look . . . well, rather prim.'

'Mamma!' exclaimed Catherine in a shocked tone. 'Would you have me thought fast?'

'Of course not, dear . . . but there are occasions when one should look one's best.'

'But this is the latest fashion!'

'I am not sure,' replied Mrs Marsden doggedly, 'that young men are as aware of fashion as we would like to think.'

'Perhaps I will try the other one on again. Would you unbutton me, please?'

With her mother's help, she took off the peach-coloured gown and put on the eau-de-nil. She preened herself before the mirror.

'Do you not think it is a little too décolleté, Mamma? James is only taking me out for a meal.'

'Don't be silly, Catherine,' cried her mother in exasperation. 'It is a compliment to him to look your most attractive.'

Catherine gravely considered her reflection. 'I had not thought of it in those terms,' she said. 'The invitation seemed to me just a routine work-a-day gesture, in recognition of the contribution Ada Smith made towards catching his criminals.'

'I am sure it was no such thing!' said Mrs Marsden firmly. 'And even if it were, there is no reason not to make the most of yourself . . . Surah silk is so soft and fine, and these gored skirts are so flattering. It is much more . . . well, feminine. And you could wear your pearls with it.'

'Perhaps we should let Papa decide,' said Catherine with a smile, 'since it seems to matter more to you than it does to me.'

Her mother looked at her irritably, then went in search of her father. Catherine did a pirouette in front of the mirror, her excitement bubbling inside her. It really was a most beautiful dress. He had never seen her in anything other than a dull tailor-made suit . . . And she could wear her filmy silk wrap.

The door re-opened; her mother came in, still calling over her shoulder: '. . . but she is so obstinate, William.' Her father followed hard on her heels, looking slim and handsome. He stood and gazed at her with a proud smile on his lips.

'The one you are wearing, without a doubt,' he declared. 'You have a fresh skin-tone. You should never wear peach—and, anyway, I like the bows on the shoulder-straps.'

'Very well,' Catherine sighed, as if conceding defeat.

'Come along, William,' said her mother delightedly. 'I want to see that everything is in order, before he arrives—now you only have half an hour, dear!'

Catherine was ready long before James was due and she sat

looking over the park, hugging herself with delight. The last
few days had been breathless with excitement. First, James's
appearance at her office on Thursday morning, tired and
dishevelled, to give her the details of the arrests. Then, the
thrill of getting it on to paper, and the dash to the *Star*'s office.
The editor had read the story in near-disbelief, and it had taken
a cautious telephone call to Sergeant Bragg, before he had been
convinced it was genuine. Then there had been the banishing of
other news items to less important pages, a minor editing of her
copy, the setting of the type—they had even let her watch the
first print-run! And she just an occasional correspondent for the
paper—a mere stringer! Instead of the editorial on Irish Home
Rule, the editor had substituted one praising the bravery and
selfless dedication of the police. It had been wonderful! The
scoop was complete! No other newspaper had even a whisper
of the affair. She had been told that they had sent reporters to
Old Jewry, in the small hours, in a vain attempt to get some
crumbs of news . . . James, of course, had asked her to play
down his role in the matter; but it was much too good a story,
and she had written it up for all it was worth. By Friday
lunch-time he was a national hero—and not just on the cricket
field!

And despite the anonymity of the *Star*'s contributors, it had
soon become known that it was her story—not only amongst
newspaper people, but throughout London society. She had
received a great pile of letters during the day, congratulating
her and wishing her well. It had been an unimaginable triumph.
Mr Tranter, the editor of the *City Press* darkly forecast that she
would be leaving them, and seemed genuinely downcast at the
prospect. She had never dreamed that life could be so satisfying!

She heard the bell and tip-toed to the door. Down in the hall,
Joan was tapping on the sitting-room door, announcing
James's arrival. Her father came out with alacrity and greeted
him. Then their voices faded as they went into the room.
Catherine took a last look at the mirror, patted some eau-
de-cologne on her bosom and, picking up her wrap and
handbag, went downstairs. She stole up to the sitting-room
door and listened.

'So you were Fred?' her father was asking in a jocular voice.
'I am afraid so,' replied Morton ruefully.
'You gave us quite a fright, I don't mind telling you!'

That was quite enough of that! thought Catherine; she pinched her cheeks and pushed open the door. The men stood, James's mouth half-open in astonished admiration. It was delicious! After ten minutes of decorous conversation she manoeuvred him out, away from parental interrogation, and soon they were bowling down Park Lane in the milk-warm air. They chatted inconsequentially and she occasionally caught him taking sidelong glances at her. Then they were on the Embankment, with its glowing balls of light amongst the trees. The cab trotted up to the Savoy entrance and a footman handed her down. She took James's arm, and ascended the staircase feeling like a duchess. Their table was in an alcove, slightly raised above the level of the restaurant floor, and with a view across the river. James insisted that champagne was the only wine for such an occasion, and watching the bubbles rising, she felt it matched her own elation. Looking across the room, she saw several people she knew; soon heads were turning her way, and glasses were raised in salute. James seemed pleased but subdued, as if he were standing back, allowing her to enjoy her triumph. Halfway through the meal, Wardle crossed to their table, his raddled face beaming. He bowed over Catherine's outstretched hand.

'May I congratulate you, Miss Marsden?' he said warmly. 'You are the envy of your profession, this evening. I am sure that the editor of *The Times*, himself, would gladly change places with you . . . And as for you, sir,' he turned towards Morton reprovingly, 'I was not aware that you could bowl such a googly. I shall be watching out for you, next time!' He walked away chuckling.

'What did your parents think of it all, James?' asked Catherine.

'I went down to Kent on Thursday evening,' said Morton, 'so I was able to tell them the story before they saw the newspapers. My father was proud and relieved, my mother indulged in a bout of retrospective anxiety, if such a thing is possible! You were right about their being upset, when I merely wrote to say I was going to Australia. But I dared not face them. They would have wormed the truth out of me in no time, and then what would have happened?'

'I am glad they were spared what I went through,' said Catherine, 'and I am no more than an acquaintance.'

Morton cocked his head at her. 'At any rate, it was fortunate that you happened to have the keys to my rooms in your handbag, on Thursday,' he rallied her. 'I was able to bring Mr and Mrs Chambers back with me. They insisted that I should spend another night in a hotel, but I have great hopes that they will allow me back into my home tomorrow evening.'

'Poor things!' said Catherine. 'They would scarcely have settled into their cottage.'

'Not a bit of it. They felt that they had been put out to grass. They were most aggrieved! They will be as glad to be back in Alderman's Walk as I shall.'

'I really must go over and see Sergeant Bragg,' said Catherine. 'He was most protective and solicitous, when I was acting as your courier. Is he savouring his triumph?'

'Oh yes, indeed! He pretends to be embarrassed by your references to his astute planning and so on, but he is revelling in Inspector Cotton's discomfiture. I popped in to see him, this afternoon. He is conducting the interrogation of the prisoners, and he said I could bring you up to date.'

'Oh dear. This stupid handbag is too small for a note-pad!'

Morton laughed. 'Don't worry, there is not much to tell. The men who stole the paper were duly picked up by the Hampshire police, and have made a full confession. Then, to Sergeant Bragg's intense satisfaction, Goulter has admitted to murdering my predecessor. It appears that he was employed by Merrick, as much to keep an eye on Beasley as to give us protection. Merrick was the real villain. He had planned a coup on these lines three years ago, when he had the original plate engraved by Kemp. Once he had been imprisoned, Merrick had to postpone the scheme. But during the interim, he had refined it to a point where it really deserved to succeed.'

'I do not know how you can begin to say that, James,' exclaimed Catherine.

'But it was extremely clever. By the time Kemp was released, the counterfeiting had become of secondary importance. It seems that his bill-broking business had been in decline for years, because the banks were discounting more and more bills. So he planned his revenge. He teamed up with Beasley and they put some forged notes, cheques and so on into circulation. The intention was to weaken confidence in the City's institutions. It was small wonder that the Governor's attempts to keep the matter secret were of no avail; Merrick was cultivating the rumours and feeding information to the press.'

'But why?' asked Catherine.

'Therein lies the sweetness of his revenge. The reports that forgeries and counterfeit were circulating depressed the value of bank shares. He was able to buy them for a minute fraction of their worth, in the secure knowledge that, once he stopped the forgeries, the value of the shares would rocket upwards. If we had not arrested him on Wednesday night, he would be the owner of a medium-sized bank, by now!'

'It is incomprehensible that a respected member of the financial community could stoop to fraud on such a scale.'

'In his twisted logic, he was daily cheated of his place in society by the depredations of the banks; so he was justified. The amusing part is that Beasley had worked out Merrick's scheme, and was doing the same himself. I think that most of the money I obtained for Beasley, went to purchase bank shares. They must have been bidding against each other on occasion!'

'And what are you going to do now, James? Will you re-join the police?'

'I think so,' Morton said slowly. 'It solves a certain number of problems.'

'Whatever problems have you?'

Morton grinned. 'None, except for deciding whether to change my parting back to the centre!'

Catherine pushed back his hair with a touch of possessiveness. 'Leave it as it is,' she said slyly. 'There were some things I liked about Thorburn!'

Morton laughed. 'There is one unwelcome aspect to re-joining the force. The Prince of Wales was at the St Leger; apparently he was fascinated when he learned of what had been happening under his nose. Now, because of your wholly unmerited encomium, I gather that he has enquired if I might be spared to join his personal group of detectives for six months.'

'Would you like that?' asked Catherine, pulling a wry face.

'No, but a royal request can hardly be refused.'

'Perhaps it would be interesting—and at least it should not be dangerous.'

'And what will you do?' asked Morton.

'For some time I shall concentrate on being a dutiful

daughter,' said Catherine with a smile. 'I think my mother suspected that the phrase on the postcard "Wed on course" was an invitation to elope with you! And as for "sequential love", well! . . .'

'At any rate, Miss Marsden, our relationship is back on the old footing?'

'I think so, James.'

'And am I forgiven for my enforced intrusion on your maidenly seclusion?'

'Perhaps . . . At least, from now on I shall never be able to forget that I am a woman.'